An AGE *of* MADNESS

An AGE *of* MADNESS

a novel

DAVID MAINE

RED HEN PRESS | *Pasadena, CA*

Book design and layout by David Rose

Library of Congress Cataloging-in-Publication Data

Maine, David, 1963 –
  An age of madness : a novel / David Maine.—1st ed.
    p. cm.
  ISBN 978-1-59709-234-0 (alk. paper)
  1. Mothers and daughters—Fiction. 2. Women psychiatrists—Fiction. 3.
Domestic fiction. I. Title.
  PS3613.A3495A7 2012
  813'.6—dc23
                        2012003927

The Los Angeles County Arts Commission, the National Endowment for
the Arts, the Los Angeles Department of Cultural Affairs, the James Irvine
Foundation, and the Ahmanson Foundation partially support Red Hen Press.

First Edition
Published by Red Hen Press
www.redhen.org

Acknowledgments

The author wishes to thank Dr. Jeffrey Nathan, PhD, for his kind assistance in the preparation of this manuscript. His suggestions and common sense made for a better book; any oversights or inaccuracies, of course, remain purely the author's responsibility.

for my students

ONE

LUNACY

1. Freud would say I'm a lousy mother. But then Freud would say lots of things. He'd declare me a textbook case, overbearing but emotionally distant, doomed to produce maladapted children. There's even a name for women like me: schizophrogenic mothers. Of course, Freud invented names for all sorts of things whether they existed or not, and then happily accused anyone nearby of doing, or being, or having, most of them.

Take penis envy. I can honestly say I've never felt it, nor has any woman I've ever known. I prefer to think of Freud as having bosom envy. Big, floppy, bouncing-out-to-the-sides, aching-when-pregnant and never the same afterward, envy of the teat.

Unlikely? I should hope so. About as unlikely as my hankering after some sperm-heavy flashlight hanging between my thighs. Thanks anyway, the oozing uterus is quite enough. Not that mine oozes anymore, but that's another story.

2. This evening the swollen belly of a gibbous moon hangs over the Charles like a misshapen Chinese lantern, not full yet but getting there. I'm driving to work faster than I ought because I'm late, having been on the phone with my daughter. Anna is a freshman at a small private college in Vermont, very exclusive. She's having a difficult time, to the surprise of, I suspect, no one who has ever met her. This is late January. She's been there since August and is still having adjustment troubles and I know I should be more supportive but geez Louise, buck up. There are worse things than living in an expensive, highly regarded private institution. I should know: I put myself through medical school with a newborn at home and a husband whose idea of hard work was splitting a hemlock stump into firewood.

Which will cause some people to think: *This is what Freud meant by lousy mothers.* Well, overbearing I might be (pushing her into college like that), and emotionally distant for sure (leaving her there on her own). So convict me. I probably yelled at her during toilet training too, and told her that puppies don't go to heaven.

And neither do people.

3. Anna: There's so much work!

Me: Well, that's why they call it school. If it was a vacation, you wouldn't have to do as much.

(*Pause.*)

Me: Anyway, you're past the halfway point. Another few months and you'll be home for the summer.

(*Pregnant pause.*)

Me: That'll be nice, won't it?

Anna (*sighing*): Yeah.

She hasn't been home since Thanksgiving, an overnight following too much food at my parents' house. At Christmas she begged off, citing overwhelming work and plans with a classmate in the dorm who "has a shitty home life and really needs some friends around her right now." She did at least call me on the morning to wish me a Merry Christmas.

Anna: You know, Mom, a lot of the kids, their parents send them stuff once in a while. You know?

Me: Send things? Like cookies or something?

Anna: Or they write emails, or—they're just more interested.

Me: Yes, well, I'm a firm believer in—

Anna: And I know you have this thing that I should deal with all this myself? But I can't, it's just too much.

Me: New phases are often difficult, it's nothing unusual.

Anna: Yeah but. Anyway. (*Pause.*) So, I've been seeing a counselor here.

Me: Oh?

Anna: And she's really helping me. I told her my mother was a psychiatrist and I was really depressed, and she said that didn't surprise her one bit.

Me (*biting back a variety of responses*): Lovely.

Anna: And I told her how you have this thing about me being the youngest and how you didn't want to spoil me, and how you think I should just go out and do things myself. And how it got worse since Daddy died and stuff. She's a real good listener.

Me: I hope so.

There are so many things I could have said. Things like, "Anna dear, I managed to get through Organic Chemistry when I was eight months pregnant, so why are you complaining about freshman comp?" I could have said, "You're right, ever since your father died, I *have* expected you to do things on your own. The alternatives for me were, one, quit work and collect food stamps, or two, marry someone else."

I did not say these things to my daughter. I have never said these things to my daughter. So much for Freud.

Anna: She says I'm making good progress.

Me: That's nice. Which medical school did she go to? Oh that's right, counselors don't go to medical school.

Anna: She really understands what it's like for kids these days. She's young, she's hardly older than we are, so she can relate.

Me: Imagine.

Anna: And she doesn't think trying to medicate away our problems is the answer.

Me: Well, there's something we can agree on.

(*Long, pregnant-and-then-some pause.*)

I try to think of more to say. Anna's right, other parents are probably nicer. Other counselors are more insightful. Then again, other children are probably a tad more expressive. If Anna's ever had a secret boyfriend, ambition, aspiration, I've never been privy to it.

As for myself, there's little to talk about except my professional life, which Anna is profoundly uninterested in. And, I suppose, my personal life, which I am profoundly uninterested in sharing with my daughter. On the pad by the phone I scrawl some notes: *Anna – counselor – clingy – summer trip together?* There are also a number of topics that we don't—won't, can't—discuss.

Me: So I guess that's it then.

Anna: I guess. Have you called about the tree yet?

Me: No. I will.

Anna: Right . . .

Me (*growing impatient with this recurring chorus*): So there's nothing special I need to worry about?

Anna: No more than you ever do.

The bait is there, dangling. I try to resist, but I'm weak this evening.

Me: I thought your point was that I don't worry *enough*.

Anna: About some stuff. That's the thing, right? You pick and choose.

Well now! This is unusually forthright coming from my daughter. Maybe this counselor knows a trick or two after all. On the other hand, if this is what counseling leads to, let's hear it for good old-fashioned repression.

It's not till I'm in the car that I think of the correct response: *Yes dear, I pick and choose. But then, so do we all*.

4. Eight p.m., I'm late for work and driving too fast. At a red light on Mass Ave. I tap the steering wheel and mull the conversation. I don't mind that she's seeing a counselor, it's not a bad idea. And the whole taking-down-the-tree business goes back many years. What I do mind is her talk about being "the youngest," when she's the only child I've got. It's never a good idea to lie to one's therapist.

The light turns green. "As long as she doesn't start going to church," I mutter, and put the Saab in gear. Some forms of irrationality are too much even for me to tolerate.

5. The Acute Care Center at Saint Mary's is Boston's holding tank for public-sector mentally ill. Private patients have a choice, depending on insurance and inclinations; but indigent chronics, the homeless and underclass and uninsured laborers get referred to ACC. Nobody I know pronounces it by the letters, "Ay-see-see," instead coughing out the name, "Ack," as though they've just seen something comically disturbing.

There's ACC I and ACC II. ("With a twenty-minute intermission," is a little joke that I keep to myself.) ACC I is where patients are brought for intake: suicide attempts, delusions, manic episodes, a whole slew of profoundly depressed people. Once a month I meet Jesus Christ himself, also Hitler, Mother Teresa, Marilyn Monroe. Lately we've been doing a good trade in Osamas and Omars and Ayatollahs. ACC II is where they go once they've stabilized. Meaning, even if they still think they're the messiah, they've at least quit trying to walk on water. If we locked up everybody with irrational thoughts—*Jesus loves me! Professional sports are meaningful!*—we'd have most of Massachusetts tucked away.

I pass through the bank-vault-style door into ACC I. Inside the unit, two thickset men like football linebackers wait in attitudes of alertness. I faintly recognize them: low-wage help on loan from college psych departments. They get a few dollars and experience for their resumes; we get bodies.

The duty nurse is named Becky. I join her at the counter and say hello and she grunts but is occupied with Tony. Or rather, Tony is trying to occupy her. She's ignoring him, writing notes in the patient logs while keeping an eye on the day room. Tony offers me a half-sneer and leans across the counter to Becky. "Y'know what I'm sayin, though. The reason they're afraid is they know what we represent. People like you and me."

Becky scribbles assiduously. It is unlikely in the extreme that she and Tony would "represent" the same thing in any imaginable incarnation.

"We understand each other," he adds, which is equally tough to credit.

I scan the unit. ACC is shaped like a blocky cross, with the nurse's station occupying the shortest branch. Becky stands at the counter and behind her is the plexiglass-fronted office where records and medication are stored. The rest of this area is a kind of anteroom-cum-waiting room. Patients aren't supposed to linger there, but they do.

Facing the desk is a set of wire-reinforced glass fire doors leading into the day room, the center of the cross. Heavy plastic chairs and tables in bright colors, a TV high up on the wall, bookshelves bolted into the floor. Board games and jigsaws, no potted plants. No lighters, no sharps, no keys, no belts. The wards with patients' rooms make up the other arms of the cross.

In the day room everything is jittery but normal. A three out of ten, which is about as relaxed as it gets. We're supposed to have piles of psych aides around, like those linebacker types who met me at the door and who have now preceded me into the room. The preferred patient/staff ratio is two to one, but this is bureaucratic magical thinking.

It's after dinner and the meds are kicking in, so most of the patients have retired to their beds. Roughly twenty are awake and alert enough to be a concern. A half dozen aides mill around, the males standing in pairs like prison wardens, chests puffed out, while the girls—there are only two—sit with the patients, doing puzzles, playing checkers. It's a pattern.

At the nurse's station I glance over the day's notes. "How are you tonight, Tony?"

He looks at me with his for docs only unfocused stare. "All right." He shuffles off sideways, greasy black bangs veiling his eyes. The satiny pajama robe he's wearing hangs open: no belt. Into the open space droop his breasts, no bigger than they were a week ago but far larger than they have any right to be on a scrawny twenty-six-year-old male. He pushes open the day room door and calls, "You take care, Becky."

"You too, sport." Becky remains unfazed: she could audition for a movie about women bikers. "How's it hanging, Gina?"

"Fine." My eyes linger on Tony as he sashays through the fire doors and joins Edna at the puzzle table. "How's he?"

"Same. Don't know whether the pills are helping, but we're watching the bathrooms and I've got Anton keeping an eye on him."

Anton is one of the linebackers who met me when I arrived. Here he comes now, through the fire doors, up to the nurses' station. Big and blocky with a face the color of meat. He licks his lips like he's tasting them. "Um, Doctor Moss," he says. "That guy, uh, Tony." Then stops, bewildered. Just a kid—where do they get these guys? We're supposed to have licensed techs on the ward, but licensed techs are hard to come by, so we fill the gaps with undergrads, or grad students if we're lucky. Three days' training, and presto—*earn beer money and college credit at the same time!*

He looks so lost I almost feel sorry for him. "I'm sure Becky has filled you in on the patient," I say, to help him along.

The kid's face betrays confusion and disgust. "She said he, uh, he likes—urine."

"He drinks it, yes. Other people's, mostly." Anton's eyes, small and deep-set in a soft rectangular face, flick to where Tony is sitting with his arm around sweet sad Edna, old enough to be his grandma. Together their hands flit across the puzzle pieces. "But he's here because he tied a telephone cord around his neck and jumped off the banister." The girlfriend called the cops, who brought him to us. It was only during intake that we learned about the urine, from the girlfriend, not from Tony.

"And the tits?" Anton stutters. "Becky said they're from the Pill."

"We generally call them 'breasts' in clinical settings, but yes—the estrogen in his girlfriend's urine gave him those, probably the soft skin too." But the sneer, the attitude, the us-versus-them mindset? Can't blame the hormones for that.

Anton's partner joins us now. I've seen him around these past few weeks, a quiet presence, shorter than Anton, sinewy. Not a linebacker, more of a tennis player. He's also not so young, which is good, maybe he's here for more than beer money. Face like a hatchet blade, raven-feather hair past his collar and a nose that could punch holes in leather. But startling eyes, gray-green. Some ethnic percolation going on there, Indian or Spanish with a hell of a tan. Arab maybe, Greek, who knows.

Anyway, he shouldn't be lingering around here: these people are paid to be on the floor. I turn away as he approaches. "Rustle," he says, or something close.

"Mm." I'm leafing through Becky's notes on the shift. Edna spent most of it crying, as usual. Behind me there's a cough and he says, "I'm Russell. We've never properly met, doctor."

"Probably not." I hate being interrupted when I'm reading, a pet peeve that goes back many years. "Shouldn't you be on the ward, instead of chatting with us?"

Softly, Becky says, "Gina."

I look up, she tilts her head. Behind me this Russell has extended his hand and I feel a hot flash of embarrassment. *Wouldn't kill you to be civil, Regina*, I tell myself.

I attempt an apologetic grin but before I can say anything his hand drops, smacking his thigh with a noise like a shot. His face is like a coffin, nailed shut. "Of course, Doctor. Sorry to *trouble* you." As he pushes through the doors into the day room, I dismiss him. There's work to do, and I'm far too old to worry about everybody in the world who's looking for an excuse to feel wronged.

6. Anton sits with me and Tony in one of the tiny evaluation cubicles off the nurse's station. Plastic chairs, humming fluorescent lights, tiled walls: like an interrogation room from a TV cop show.

"You've been here a week. The medication's working for you?" Before me dance the notes scrawled by the shift nurses: *Patient oriented x3, exhibits signs of depression but no suic. ideation since intake*. And my own note from a week ago: *Calmotec 50 mg TID*. The other docs have made no changes.

Tony eyes me warily, glances over his shoulder to sneer at Anton, who sits edgy by the door. Tony's manner is both flirtatious and sullen, like Lauren Bacall in an old movie. Lauren Bacall mixed with James Dean. "I'm in Happy Valley now."

"And you haven't tried to hurt yourself during your time here?"

He leans forward so his robe falls open, a satiny gray kimono with an embroidery dragon. His breasts dangle low in the gulf. The belt was confiscated at intake. He tosses his head. "You can't say I haven't thought about it."

"Does that mean you have?"

"Let's just say," he settles back, legs crossed at the thigh, "the possibility is still on the table." He bounces his foot: if he wore a slipper, it would be dangling from his toe.

I write his words verbatim and add a parenthetical note of my own (*histrionic tendencies?—r/o borderline*), then say, "I hear your urine drinking is under control."

"With this bitch dogging me?" An angry thumb jerks backward. "Not like I have much choice. It's worse than having a *broad* around all the time."

Anton shifts his weight.

I leaf through medical reports, blood work. "All your tests came back negative, which suggests that these secondary sexual characteristics—the changes in your body—come from the hormones in your girlfriend's estrogen pills. You'll start seeing a reduction in symptoms soon, if you haven't already."

"What if I don't want to?"

"That's not in your control, I'm afraid. It's going to happen." I close his file and meet his eyes. And wait. Wait long enough, they always talk. They all want to tell their story.

"Don't you want to know why I do it?" he blurts.

The answer to that, Tony, is: not particularly. No doubt you have an explanation that makes sense to you, but my life is none the poorer without it. Instead of saying this, however, I shrug elaborately. "There are a number of possibilities."

"Yeah? Like what?"

Some patients like these conversations. Maybe they get the feeling that they have some control, if they know a bit of the jargon. "Well, there's something called behaviorism, which argues that people act according to what we learn, so maybe something good happened when you began doing this."

He sneers. "Just a theory."

"Exactly. Or there's psychodynamics, you know what that is?"

"Freud."

"Right. He'd look for some trauma in your early life, something to do with toileting or washing, buried in your subconscious."

"Nobody believes in Freud anymore. Except feminists."

"I'll take your word for it. Of course some people would argue that you're just the helpless victim of a great pharmacological-industrial conspiracy, with me acting as the agent of your repression."

This elicits a grin. "Thomas Szasz, *The Myth of Mental Illness*. You believe that?"

"Not for a second."

The grin vanishes. "Never met a doc that did. So what do you believe?"

"I believe in diagnosing symptoms and relieving them." All the analytical jargon is meaningless as far as I'm concerned. As long as the medication averts the symptoms—and I'll count urine drinking as a symptom—I'm happy to leave the mumbo-jumbo aside. I tell him, quite honestly, "I don't care what got you started, I only care that its consequences seem to have made your life so painful that you tried to end it. If those circumstances have changed, that's enough for me." Ostentatiously I check my watch. "We'll pick this up next time. Stay out of the toilet a little longer and I'll transfer you to ACC II. Keep doing well and you'll be back in the world in no time."

He sits stony-faced and silent. I prod him, "How does that sound?"

"I heard your husband killed himself."

Just that sudden. The meanness of it catches me off guard, and it takes some moments to locate my stock answer: "We're here to talk about you."

"Everybody on the ward knows it. They're saying he took a shotgun or something and blew himself away, along with a bunch of other people. Fucking blood bath."

"That's an entertaining story, Tony. We never owned a gun in our lives." *Why am I explaining myself to this person?* "See him out, Anton."

Tony's voice insinuates itself in my ear. "I guess the marriage wasn't ideal, hey doctor? Maybe he acted according to what he *learned*. Maybe something *good* happened when he did it."

"Anton."

"Or maybe there was *trauma* in his early life."

"*Anton*." The edge in my voice brings him to his feet, and he shepherds Tony through the door. It swings shut and finally I'm left alone, breathing deep.

It's always worse when it's unexpected. The routine dates—birthdays, anniversaries, Thanksgiving—those I can prepare for. As much as anyone can, which isn't much, but at least I know they're coming. But this sudden wrenching up from nowhere, the corpse, the neck at an impossible angle, the stink of shit soaking through clothes—it's like something jumping out from a dark closet.

Maybe he acted according to what he learned.

I squeeze my eyes tight, right there in the eval room, and drive the memories down. Down and away and buried and gone. It's not easy but I can do it, I have plenty of practice. Something I've gotten good at, otherwise it's constantly with me, that night. Ready to rush up, swamp me like a tide, pull me down in its undertow of memory and futility: the night the cold the silence the moon. The trees, motionless and naked, black silhouettes rinsed to gray as I'm running outside, stumbling across the yard, shrieking against the terrible calm. Hysterical at what's out there, waiting for me in the ghastly silver light.

7. There is a letter, upstairs.

8. Some background now. My name is Regina Moss, née Park. I am forty-one years old, in the prime of my life: I jog six miles three times a week and eat right. I've done so ever since the birth of my child, twenty—make that seventeen years ago. I streak my hair, get my nails done, lift weights for muscle tone and take care of my skin. Last year the fibroids growing on my ovaries became large enough to be uncomfortable, and I had a hysterectomy. Besides that, my health is excellent.

For twelve years I have been a psychiatrist licensed to practice in the state of Massachusetts. I earn a good living, but my insurance premiums make my accountant's eyes water. I have a small neat house in Stonebury, a little town forty minutes north of Boston, with more backyard than I need and a thicket of oak and white birch and sugar maples—one of which my daughter presses me to remove—complete with an elaborate, neglected treehouse. A front garden full of tulip bulbs and crocuses. Amaryllis in pots by the front door, a legion of stray cats that I haven't the heart to shoo away. Inside are hardwood floors and a big living room picture window that looks out on the porch. The strays like to lounge out there and glare inside through the screen on hot summer days.

I'd rather have too little furniture than too much, a few pieces nicely upholstered in pale canvas. There are a few glass-topped tables, some low shelves, hanging planters. Prints of Matisse, Monet, Degas, Toulouse-Lautrec. In music my taste runs to Vivaldi, Corelli, Albinoni. Monteverdi for rainy days. Bach will do in a pinch, though he's a bit mathematical. Anything but those overwrought Russians.

It's not a cluttered house. Light and air and space are what I like. Throwing away all that horrid black-leather stuff was one of the first things I did after Walter died.

His name was Walter.

Yes I had a husband. Yes he died. No, he didn't shoot himself or take out a bunch of other people in a "blood bath," as my patient Tony so charmingly put it.

Regina Park went to Tufts for undergrad and stayed on for medical school. At twenty-four I got pregnant by my then-boyfriend Walter Moss. I wanted an abortion; he begged me out of it, citing eternal love and eternal damnation, not necessarily in that order. I don't have much truck with God or damnation, but admit to being a sucker for the love bit. Walter and I had been together for some years already, and although I'd have preferred a more controlled commitment, it was too late for that. Getting an abortion would have finished us. My girlfriends urged me to do it anyway. Instead, for the first and last time in our relationship, I gave in to Walter. Conditionally.

Occasionally a doctor will say that getting through medical school is the hardest thing anyone could ever do. He is lying. (It is men who say this.) I'm here to say that getting through medical school *while pregnant* is the hardest thing anyone could ever hope to do.

The timing was fortuitous in a way. She was a summertime baby, mid-July, which gave me a few weeks to recover before classes resumed. At least I wasn't a resident yet; that truly would have killed me.

It was after Anna was born that I started running regularly. Slowly at first, shuffling along in my New Balances, but building my stamina little by little. Within a year I reached my current standard: six miles a day, three days a week.

9. The condition I laid on Walter was that the child would never, ever interfere with my career. This meant Walter wouldn't have one. He would quit the literature program, stay home with the baby, feed her and change her and take her round the Common on sunny afternoons. We'd get by on student loans and money our parents pressed on us and once I started my residency, we'd pay the cash back. Which we did. I was determined that no one would ever be financially responsible for my child other than myself. I understood this was my duty. Duty is big in my family.

It took a lot of work on both our parts, and I had more gray hair than I expected by twenty-nine. But I also had my degree and a part-time position at a local hospital and a few private clients. There were two kinds of patients, I learned: those who prefer older, experienced doctors, and those who liked young, enthusiastic ones. I worked this to my advantage.

Anna turned five and started kindergarten. Walter became a real hausfrau, worrying about the public schools—we moved out of the city, at his behest, to Stonebury. ("Small, clean, and safe," is how he described it.) He fretted over the merits of brown eggs versus white. We were that rarest of things, a modern couple liberated from the roles laid upon us by history: househusband and working mom. Things seemed all right. Obviously they weren't.

Post-mortem it's easy to second-guess. Walter was a big rangy guy who favored shaggy beards and quilted flannel shirts. Liked to drink beer from the bottle, outside in the winter while splitting logs. Liked fishing and pickup trucks and took pride in maintaining the equipment. Knew how to use power tools; his workshop out back was—still is—full of saws and drills and sanders. Most of the cabinets in the house are his work, ditto the bookshelves, rocking chair, hanging planters. Our lifestyle gave him the free time to hone his skills: I thought he liked it that way.

A couple times every fall he'd run down to Foxborough to catch a Patriots game with his buddies, even though, over time, those buddies drifted away. Maybe that's when the problem started, his friends ribbing him about being a homebody. Maybe the jokes turned serious, then mean. He would have taken that to heart.

Walter saw himself as some kind of man's man, but with an artistic bent. Sensitive and caring, sure, but also tough and capable. Maybe I took that side away somehow. Castrated him, emasculated him, robbed him of his manhood—whatever cliché works. All that inner warrior hogwash: his role as fire-bringer usurped in favor of nanny and caretaker, bed-maker and maid. Which is, of course, exactly what women have been reduced to throughout all of recorded history, and probably a good deal longer than that. But you don't see *us* leaping to our deaths from tall trees.

Which was where I found him, seven years ago. Splayed on the ground and cooling already. Anna was ten; I was thirty-four. The treehouse he'd built for Anna had been his diving platform. Apparently he'd hauled himself onto the roof, then leaped. It was plenty high enough to snap his neck against the hard November ground. Two weeks before Thanksgiving, no less.

There was a full moon that night, shining down on the scene, silvery light turning the white birch to dead things around me, painting black shapes on the dirt.

What an idiot my husband turned out to be. What a God damned idiot.

10. Tony—my truculent patient with the boobs—got the details wrong, but that's to be expected. Walter didn't need a shotgun or a .38 or anything other than plain old gravity. How the rumor started or spread, I don't know, but tales grow in the telling, especially when one's audience is irrational to begin with. No doubt in another few years the story will involve a Wal-Mart and a box of hand grenades.

When I got home from Walter's funeral I changed into sweats and laced up my running shoes. Anna was at my parents' in Brookline, mysteriously—but happily—silent: numbed by the whole ordeal, at least for the time being. I envied her.

I did some stretches and started running, down my tree-lined street, over the bridge into Stonebury's quaint little downtown. People waved to me tentatively—everyone knew what had happened, and many no doubt wondered what I was up to. Husband barely cold in the grave and me carrying on like I hadn't a care. Well the hell with them.

I ran along winding byways fringed by fields gone yellow and brown, cut through the underpass to the highway and back around again in a big loop across the green. There was a long slow hill that I usually avoided: that day I attacked it like the Rough Riders. I ran and ran and ran. I turned myself into a machine, steel and chrome and chemical fluids, pushing on, unstoppable. I didn't stop. Didn't even slow down. And I've maintained the pace ever since.

11. The morning after my ACC shift I call Anna. Last night's conversation has left a sour taste in my mouth and a sense of foreboding in my gut. Unscientific, yes, but there it is.

Anna's cell, however, is turned off, or perhaps has been chucked into a landfill somewhere. The message I leave on her voicemail vanishes into some great pit of unwanted parental phone calls, and I resist the urge to try again in the afternoon. Maybe she's in class, I tell myself. She's a college student. Maybe she's at the library.

"Or her counselor," I tell the spider plant that occupies my picture window, which, happily, has nothing to say in return as I mist its overwrought shagginess. "Maybe she has an appointment with her *counselor*. Of all things."

12. Three nights later I still haven't reached her and I'm back at ACC, where the ward is swathed in 2 a.m. quiet. Strictly speaking, I don't have to be awake; in fact I needn't be here at all. It's standard procedure for on-call docs to stay home and give instructions over the phone. But I like being on the unit, even after all these years, the hands-on grittiness of it, the lull between midnight and dawn. Most of my colleagues would find this incomprehensible—I must be the only psychiatrist in New England who is actually physically present for her on-call shifts. But it suits me, and—to be perfectly honest—since Anna left, there are plenty of nights I'd just as soon not be alone at the house.

I sit at the nurse's station with a patient chart open in front of me, but I'm not reading it. I'm wondering what to do about my daughter and her nagging adjustment problems. Maybe I should go to Vermont for a visit. It's not far and it might cheer her up. Or cheer me up. Then I can't help wondering whether a visit would accomplish any such thing.

A shadow passes through the day room, and through the fire doors I see the aides, Russell and Anton, making their way among the tables, quietly straightening the chairs and neatening up. Anton clunks along as you'd expect, but there is something so domestic about Russell's movements, the way he makes a point of keeping quiet, that is quite touching. As I watch through the wire-mesh windows, I see my lamplit reflection superimposed on him, as if we're some weird alien from one of Walter's sci-fi movies, some mutant being made of disparate body parts that don't quite fit together. Then he pauses as if he's sensed me, and turns to look my way, and the illusion vanishes.

In the morning I talk to Becky about setting up a token economy for Tony, to reward him for staying out of the toilet. I have no great faith in this sort of thing but it's worth a try, it may reinforce what the meds are doing. "Let's find out what he likes," I tell Becky, "and give him a way to earn it."

"He likes urine," Becky deadpans. "He *fahkin* loves it." She's like this in the morning, and most other times.

"Let's find something else. Whatever we do has to carry over to ACC II."

"We'll need the girlfriend on board."

"There's your reward then, time with the girlfriend. Monitored of course."

The girlfriend's critical. Whatever behavior-mod we devise will need to continue out in the world. If she fumbles it, then Tony's back to his old habits.

Outside, the morning cold is sharp and piercing. I pull the Saab out of the parking lot and spot Russell waiting at a bus stop, intent on a newspaper. I lower the passenger window and call to him. "Heading north?"

"South." He scrutinizes the car without expression. "Nice wheels."

"Thanks. Sorry I'm going in the wrong direction."

"It's all right," he says.

For a moment I contemplate going out of my way, taking him wherever he's heading. But I'm exhausted from the shift and need to get breakfast, so I pull away, glancing in the rearview as I go. He squints intently after me as the Saab pulls up the deserted, six-in-the-morning street. If I didn't know better I'd say he was taking note of something. Or maybe I'm just being paranoid.

13. At home I go for a short, glorious run through my neighborhood. The air is cool and fine against my skin, and the woodpeckers and chickadees take no notice of me. On my voicemail is a message from Josh, a married man who saw me four times in a week last month, then stopped. He wants to see me again, his message says. His voice sounds sheepish yet husky, a combination I find difficult to resist.

Josh is part of the personal life I choose not to share with my daughter. I think about him as I slip into a piping-hot shower. Maybe a little Josh-ing is just what I need right about now, notwithstanding his perpetual three-day beard, which I find tiresome.

The shower leaves me flushed and tingling. For a few minutes I nestle onto my front porch love seat—weathered wicker, weatherproof vinyl cushions—with a vanilla soy smoothie and a magazine. It's below freezing but I'm bundled in sweaters and love the feel of the cold biting my flushed cheeks.

My neighbor Mrs. Flynn sets out on her morning power-walk. I wave and she waves back. She is wearing an iPod and I wonder what she's listening to. Mrs. Flynn is one of those unnerving elderly people with more energy than I have and an apparent determination to accomplish everything she never did in her earlier life. Which is, to all appearances, quite a lot.

That afternoon I see clients in my Stonebury office. The Hayeses are my last appointment of the day, a sweet elderly couple, anxious and depressed. Apart from their melancholy, which neither recedes into insignificance nor balloons into anything dire, they're manageable and don't demand much besides an hour of my attention every two weeks.

Back home that evening I'm plenty tired and I still haven't heard back from Anna. I resist leaving another voicemail, opting instead for Vivaldi on the stereo and a cup of chamomile tea. Waves of harpsichord and strings wash over me like a massage. This is good. This is very good. There's something about the symmetry of a piece of music that is immensely soothing when confronting the irrationality of my job, or—I'll admit it—my life.

The chamomile steams in my hand. I pull on my heavy brown sweater and go outside to talk to the cat camped out on my front porch. He's absolutely enormous, a Maine coon with seven toes on each paw and an air of breezy alpha-male contentment. I ask his name, which he refuses to tell me, so I christen him Brutus. Vivaldi drifts thinly through the glass, like someone else's thoughts. The night is frozen and my breath pours from me in ropes of mist.

I rattle around till the CD finishes, then turn on the TV news for distraction. It's enough to make anyone depressed—riots in the Middle East, a baby sitter stabbed on Long Island. Some new virus in Asia. Airplanes bombing people in what we are supposed to believe is a war for freedom. An interviewed soldier bears a striking resemblance to Russell, the tech at ACC, and I find myself wondering what he makes of all this. What are kids thinking these days? About politics, war, whatever? Are they thinking at all, or are they just playing video games and looking at porn on the computer?

I've no idea, and I doubt my pal Josh does either, seeing as he is older than I am. Ditto my friends Steve and Lee and Nick.

Okay, so Russell's not exactly a *kid*. But he's under thirty if I'm any judge of things, while I'm over forty, and that puts a fence between us that cannot be overlooked. Although he's not quite a child and I'm not quite an old lady, we're hardly the same generation. The same goes for linebacker-type Anton. Has anyone ever taught these people to think critically, to be skeptical, to read between the lines?

Or maybe this idea is quaintly dated—from what I can tell these days, nobody reads at all anymore, between the lines or elsewhere.

Walter contrived to miss all this—all the inanity and insanity of the past seven years. The quotidian lunacy that we have somehow, as a species, become accustomed to. There are moments when I almost envy him his ignorance, and many more when I wonder what he would have said about it all.

14. "Hi Dad." I bend to catch his eye but he's not with me. Dad developed Parkinson's some years back, fought it bravely for a while, then succumbed. Partly, anyway; some days he's lucid, more and more often he's not. Today he is bedridden and slurring. "Thlll," he murmurs, and shuts his eyes. Somehow he still has all his hair.

My mother resembles a tree that hasn't been dead too long. She smiles brittlely at me and twists twiglike fingers. "Today's not so good."

"No." I kiss Dad's cheek and follow Mom into the kitchen. The condo is as cluttered and homey as when I was growing up in it, with a ground-floor garden and bay-windowed living room where I'd sit and look out at New England blizzards. Somehow Mom and I always wind up in the cramped kitchen, with its gummy brown linoleum and too-small butcher block table. She pours instant coffee and indicates a plate of organic oatmeal cookies from Star Market. Or as Becky would say: *Stah Mahket.*

I take one. "So how're you doing, Mom?"

She smiles thinly, as if contemplating the many ways she could respond.

1. *Who cares?*

2. *That's not important.*

3. *Oh, fine.*

4. *Don't you fret about me, dear.*

5. *Ironically enough, I feel terrific. It's you I'm worried about.*

She opts for a mute flutter of her fingers which somehow manages to encapsulate all these non-responses, plus a few more. She's cut her hair again, almost as short as Becky's at ACC, two or three inches brushed flat against her head. It's gone pure white and this, along with the bleached-newsprint texture of her skin and the polyps erupting from her knuckles, so disorients me for a moment that I feel as though I'm seeing my grandmother, not my mom. The moment passes, quickly replaced by guilt.

"You're looking nice," is what she finally says. My mother, the question-deflector. Or reflector: ask her anything and she bounces it back at you. "How's things?"

"Oh, fine," I say. That's answer #3. She taught me well.

She sips her coffee. "Anything new?"

What she means is: Any*one* new? To which I answer, "Not really. I go on dates now and then—" How's that for euphemism? "—but nothing serious."

To her credit, Mom avoids looking heartbroken, or even censorious.

Only once has my mother ever shaken off her customary reserve and pressured me to, in essence, settle down, forget about Walter and get myself married already. For the sake of familial stability—not my stability obviously, but Anna's. This was two years ago, when Anna was having problems in school, had started smoking cigarettes, and was generally looking a mess. She'd gone to her grandparents and blubbered about I don't know what but it's easy to imagine who the villain was. I was on-call at BMHA at the time and got home after dinner to find Mom tight-lipped on the porch, not so gaunt and gray as usual. In fact, quite regal: she has this side to her too. "I've come to say a few things," she began, "so let me finish without interrupting."

"All right." We went inside and I rooted around the fridge for something to eat. I was tired, having spent the afternoon with a bipolar Vietnam vet who'd chucked his lithium into a dumpster before flipping out in the Park Street T station. The first thing they teach you in residency is to assess your patient's willingness to understand what you might have to say, and tailor your approach accordingly. In other words, there's a right time for everything, and many many wrong ones. This subtlety however eluded my mother, and I was too tired to point it out. "Fire away."

"You seem to have forgotten your daughter. She's at our house with your father, and she's distraught. Do you know she describes herself as an orphan?" Mom patted her dress and took a steadying breath. "We all loved Walter, but you've got to get over what happened. You can't carry this around forever. It's been five years—you have to think about moving on. Anna needs a father in her life, and if you're not ready to provide that, then she at least needs a mother."

It's as if I was chipped out of an iceberg. "Done?"

"No. It's been difficult, we know that, we all know what you've gone through—"

"You have *no idea* what I've gone through."

"We were all involved, Regina."

"I can't believe this. Last I checked, Dad's still alive. So am I—do you know one single person who's ever done this kind of thing before? And you stand there and tell me to, to, *get over it,* to marry somebody else so my daughter has *structure* in her life. Here's a shocker, Mom—I'm not a day program, all right?"

"Five years, Regina."

"You keep *saying* that. Have we got time limits now? You want me to stoke up on Happivil so I don't worry about it and just marry the first one who'll say 'till death do us part'? I tried that once, and guess what? Death *did* us part—and pretty *fucking* quick."

She barely breathed: if I was ice, she was carved from granite. A single block most likely, from someplace stern like New Hampshire. We're not a family that curses much, so she wasn't happy to hear me spitting like Leif Ericson, but more than that, we are people made uncomfortable by naked displays of emotion. Standing there in the kitchen with the fridge door open, swearing myself hoarse at my mother, qualified as a naked display of emotion.

Her lips were a colorless line, and she'd drawn into herself with that customary reserve that comes to her so easily. The same reserve that allowed the wives of Nantucket whalers to knit sweaters for years while their husbands were at sea. Suddenly my mother was a fisherman's widow, counseling me to be strong and think of the children. The child. But she was done talking. She'd said her bit, and what I chose to do with it was my business. Mom was always big on duty, and now she'd done hers. It had taken her five years to get it out, and barring another crisis, she'd keep it to herself from now on.

15. Today, sitting here in her kitchen, with Dad groggy in the bedroom and Mom looking worn, I wish I had something to tell her. Some good news. But I don't. Anna's seeing a therapist, my patients are gossiping about Walter, some teenager walked into a high school—in Texas? Michigan? Nevada?—and shot a bunch of people. Again. Not exactly a four-star week.

So I do something that I periodically do with my patients, or my parents. I decide to lie. I tell my mother, "Anna's finally settling in. We talked the other night, she's happier now."

Imagine my surprise when she answers with, "Yes, she told me the same thing."

"She did?" I struggled to keep my voice level. There's nothing quite so disconcerting as telling a lie, only to discover it's actually the truth.

"Oh yes." Mom finishes her coffee and pops an organic oatmeal cookie. "She's written once or twice since Christmas. We've gotten the drift that things are improving on the college front. I guess that trip to Atlanta with her friends really cheered her up."

I feel as though I've been taped to a chair and spun around. Training kicks in and I stay noncommittal. "What did she say about it?"

"Oh, just that it was fun, everyone had a good time. Quite a crowd of them went, I gather. Some concert or other."

I sip the coffee, keep my hands occupied, voice steady. But I'm well and truly baffled. Road trip? Atlanta? Crowds of friends at a concert? This is news to me. The conclusion is obvious: she's lying to Mom. But why?

Realization dawns moments later: maybe my daughter isn't lying to my mother, but to me. Or—we're getting out there, but—

maybe the both of them are spinning some conspiracy. Thinking this way makes me feel like one of my own patients, but there it is.

I say, "She told me she'd sent a postcard, but I never got it. Did she send you one?" I feel like a cheap TV detective.

"Nope." Mom stands up with the empty plate. "More?"

"No thanks." As she washes the dishes with a practiced economy of movement, I take my place beside her and dry them, then put them away. Our conversation turns banal: neighbors, aunts and uncles. The flakiness of Dad's doctor, a scandal with the mayor. The on-again-off-again glory days of the Celtics—Dad was a big fan—and the looming disarray of the Red Sox. Nothing else unusual comes up, but when I leave that afternoon I'm still perturbed, and I'm still wondering what it is that's got my mother, my daughter and myself all lying to each other.

16. The next time I arrive at ACC, Becky is looking harried and patients are milling about the day room, yakking excitedly. It feels like midmorning rather than eight at night. The techs keeping watch are mostly new and inexperienced; they flinch at loud noises and look around nervously, like puppies afraid of being hit. There are too few of them and they bunch up uselessly, instead of moving among the patients. I shouldn't blame them—they're supposed to learn from their peers, but their peers rarely stick around long enough to teach.

Russell is a slender, soothing exception, lounging at a card table with Edna and Tony and a couple of our most labile patients. It takes a moment to spot him, but once I do it's hard to stop noticing. Edna's never a problem, but the others could be. As I watch, Russell murmurs something sideways and Tony chuckles—ironically I'm sure, but he chuckles. After a moment the others join him.

I push through the fire doors. The sight of me, a familiar face of authority, has a soothing effect on some of them. Not all, but it helps. Edna stops sobbing and offers a shy smile. Dorothy quits haranguing some helpless sorority girl and trundles off to smoke. Louis swaggers over to the puzzle table with a couple others, grumbling like Popeye. Nobody actually does the puzzle, they break it up and shove the pieces around. But at least they're sitting down.

Russell catches my eye and nods. The only other tech I recognize is skinny, goateed Guy, who's been with the unit for years. "What's going on?"

He brushes away his bangs. "New intake last shift, totally manic. Doctor Sullivan sedated him, not enough I guess. Tore through here, flipping tables, knocking into people. Smashed the TV."

I look up. Sure enough, the picture tube has a big crack running diagonally across it. "What'd he use?"

"His hand."

"His *hand*?"

Guy is elflike and mischievous, but right now he's not joking. "Jumped three feet vertical and smacked it with the heel of his palm." He mimes. "Some kind of judo."

"Lovely." Just what I need, a bipolar karate expert on a night we're short-staffed. "Is he sedated now?"

"Oh yeah, Sullivan gave him a shot of something, Steadivil I think."

"Good idea."

"I suggested two shots but he didn't listen."

"Must've taken a mob to hold him down."

"Four of us, yeah. Russell and Kristy were both great, by the way."

"Could be worse," I acknowledge, glancing around.

"Some of the others were getting pretty wound up."

"I can imagine." Emotion breeds emotion, as the nurses like to say. Around us the excited conversations continue, but there's less agitation than I'd expect. Body language is excited rather than fearful. "When did all this happen?"

"Couple hours ago," Guy says. "They were pretty jazzed for a while, but evening meds went out at seven-thirty and a bunch of people asked for PRNs."

Meaning they should settle down soon. "Are you staying the night?"

"Yeah, me and Kristy and Russell."

"All right then." Over at the puzzle table, Louis's hands twitch as he monologues. Russell lounges in a chair nearby, body relaxed, eyes alert. Tony sits on his stool with his kimono loosely open, eye-balling the staff and smirking. "Get that TV out of here."

Guy says, "I'm on it."

By midnight things are quieter. The new arrival is asleep and most of the other patients are down too. Those who aren't have gathered in the courtyard for the last smoke of the night. The baby techs hover while Guy and Kristy—heavyset, sweet-voiced, no-bull—glide through the twilit ward like shadows, checking rooms.

Becky outlines her new behavior-mod plan for Tony. "Girl-friend's on the same page, so we've got a shot. Right now he can earn time with her, in person or on the phone, by being a good boy. Out in the world, she promises to drop a dime if he starts acting bizarro again. No dinner, no snuggles, no poon."

"It's the best lever we have," I say.

"Two things though. We still don't know why he tried to kill himself in the first place. The meds'll help, but we haven't touched the underlying causes."

"We can live with that."

"Number two, the girlfriend's wicked flaky. You know, judge not and everything, which is fine—"

"Sure."

"—but when your boyfriend starts drinking piss, it's time to throw a few stones."

"You're afraid she'll say, 'Don't change, darling, I love you just the way you are'?"

"Who can understand straight people?" Becky shakes her head and her piercings glitter. More of them than I care to count, six or seven on each side, and that's just the ears.

"Seems to me you'd be in favor of non-judgmentalism. You don't exactly court the mainstream yourself."

"None of my girlfriends drink urine. If they tried it, they'd see just how mainstream I can get."

There's no more we can do for Tony. If he stops taking his medi-cation out in the world, or starts in with some other aberrant be-havior, we're helpless till he puts himself or someone else in danger.

"It's a good thorough plan, Becky. Now if you could write up some-thing for my daughter, I'd be obliged."

"Huh?" She looks startled.

"Kidding. You know, the joy of motherhood."

"Not entirely familiar with that, myself."

Once introduced to my imagination, the idea is hard to shake. *Quick, I need some behavior-mod for my teenage daughter.* It should make me smile but doesn't.

Becky interrupts my flight of ideas. "Couple things you should know about tonight. One, that guy Anton was a no-show. He's not that smart, but he's big, and it would've helped to have another body around."

"I'll call Rod Menzies tomorrow, see what the story is. And?"

"And your new boy Russell—he's a keeper."

"Guy likes him too."

"Do what it takes—give him a raise, whatever. But don't let him get away."

As if he's a gangster or something. What's there to say? Even worldly, ironic Becky, with her multiple piercings and multiple girlfriends, will need to learn it on her own: sometimes we have no control over who sticks around, and who gets away.

17. Sometime after midnight I lurch awake in the staff room: Russell sits curled in one of the chairs opposite the couch where I've stretched out for a nap. It takes me a moment to blink away the dream—a garden, a maze, some kind of statue that I couldn't find—and recognize him, to place myself and remember the time. *Oriented x3*, as we say. What year is this? Who's President? A sin-gle, heavily-shrouded lamp throws murky half-light, reminiscent of the dream.

"Didn't mean to wake you," he says, softly.

"Not sure you did." I check my watch. "Did you?"

"Not really. I've been here fifteen minutes." He uncoils himself, stands briskly. If he's tired from staying up half the night, it doesn't show. "I should check the ward."

"Good idea."

He's nearly at the door when I say, "By the way." He stops. "Whatever you did tonight got rave reviews from Becky and Guy. Guy's easy to please, but Becky's not."

"Oh. Thanks." In the gloomy room it's hard to make out his face. He stands there long enough to make me feel uncomfortable for stopping him. "Anything else?"

Suddenly I feel foolish for patting him on the head like a second-grader. Positive reinforcement, something I was never too good at. But all the books say I'm supposed to do it. "Anyway, good work. Glad to have you around." I wouldn't bother with this, probably, if I was completely awake.

He snorts. "I'm sure you are, now that I'm, ah—doing my job. Right?"

Then he slips out the door. I sit there a minute, my hair in all directions, thinking *Regina, why even try to compliment people if they lack the grace to accept it?* Then I lie down and try to doze off again, but of course that's been spoiled now.

18. It would be unfair to say that when I call Anna I am seething. I have done seething a time or two in my life, and this is not that. I am undoubtedly *annoyed*, perhaps even a little *tetchy* if that's how one is inclined to interpret things. Seething, however, is well off the mark.

She picks up on the fifth ring, as I'm about to resign myself to another voicemail. "Yeah?"

She sounds like she's just woken up. No, in fact she sounds as if she hasn't woken up entirely. I find this unexpected at 8:30 on a Friday night. "Anna?"

Anna: Yeah.

Me: It's me. I've been calling for days.

Anna: Yeah . . .

(*Pause.*)

Anna: Yeah, sorry. Been really . . .

(*Pause. A voice somewhere, but not, apparently, talking to her.*)

Me: Busy?

Anna: Uh huh. That's it.

She doesn't sound busy. She sounds catatonic.

Me: I guess the work is piling up, now the semester's gotten going. (*Nothing.*)

Me: And that Atlanta trip must have been a distraction.

Anna: Mm?

Me: You must have known I'd hear of it from you grandmother. Running around with your friends, having a grand time while whining to me about how much you're struggling.

Anna: Jesus Mom. I hate it when you get like this.

A complete sentence! Subjects and verbs and who knows what else, adjectives probably.

Me: Get like what exactly?

Anna (*struggling, it seems, to link together a series of complete thoughts*): Why's everything such a big deal with you? Except the stuff that really *is* a big deal, that really *should* be talked about, that's the stuff you'll ignore the rest of your life—

Me: Excuse me for thinking this is a big deal. You're either telling stories to your grandmother or to me. Which is it I'd like to know.

Anna: It's always about you, isn't it?

Her audacity leaves me momentarily speechless. Outside in the dark, a cat yowls.

Me: *I'm* not the one running off with my friends while my mother pays the bills. I'd love a nice vacation right about now. Believe me, a vacation would suit me down to my toes.

Anna: Then do it for once.

Me: Maybe I will . . .

Anna: Instead of acting like such a martyr about it.

Me: . . . somewhere in the woods. With, with log cabins and birdhouses—and bird feeders—and nature hikes—

She says something but I don't catch it exactly because I'm still talking and she mumbles. But it could be "I don't have to hear this" or some equally witty riposte and then she's shut off her phone and I'm snapping at the ether. And breathing too hard, the wind whistling out my nose and probably my face gone pink like it does when I'm annoyed.

I breathe deep. I try to *chill out* or whatever it is that high-strung types do these days when they're upset. I give her a few minutes to call back and apologize for shoveling that counselor-fed hogwash into my craw. When she doesn't, I call her instead. And get her voicemail, of course.

I push my way out to my front porch and stand in the cold. The neighborhood hunkers deep into its winter lethargy. A fat moon, full or close to it, hangs over the street like a thumbprint, and a thin orange glare burns up from behind the tree line, the meager light of Stonebury's downtown hurling itself senselessly against the stars. The sound of traffic murmurs against my ear, cars buzzing along the freeway's artery. The cold makes me shiver: it's been a lousy winter and it doesn't look to get any better soon. Where do my cat visitors go at night? Someplace warm, I hope.

Above us all, Luna glowers down, a changeable queen, heavy with all her threats and tides and transformations.

19. The next morning I'm still nagged by my little non-conversation with Anna. And isn't *that* annoying—as if I don't have more to think about than my daughter's irrationalities. I charge through my morning run, my dumbbell workout, my shower and smoothie, while it gnaws in the back of my mind like a retriever with a bone.

Not until afternoon, in the middle of an appointment with a private patient named Dick Smalley—no wonder he's depressed— does it occur to me to wonder why our exchange has bothered me so much. Is it just her ingratitude that's gotten under my skin? If I'm honest, I'll admit there's something more. If I'm entirely forthcoming, I'll admit to some surprise that my own flesh and blood, with whom I've shared so much and gone through so many difficulties, should be so coldhearted and selfish. Probably I shouldn't be surprised, but there it is.

Please understand: I am not someone who's given to putting on a display. Some might call me reserved, okay, sure. I'm a firm believer in letting one's actions speak louder, so I'm not partial to grand speeches or lengthy nagging e-mails. And the crying-on-the-shoulder business has never been my forte, notwithstanding the legion of therapists out there urging us to get in touch with our inner et cetera.

But this doesn't mean that I lack intimacy or passion or even plain kindness. That I have. That I have in plenty. I have it, as my dead husband would've said, *in spades*. What my current lovers might think, I can't vouch for. A wide range of responses might reasonably be expected. But Walter would've stood up for me, that much is certain.

This has gone on for two days when I call Rod Menzies, administrative chief of ACC and the man in charge of the workers on the ward. "Rod? Regina Moss. Have a minute?"

"Sure." His voice drops a notch. "How you been?"

"Fine. Everything okay with you?"

"You bet."

Rod and I had a thing for a while, two or three years ago. A series of, I guess they might be called *workplace trysts*, in his office. But that sounds so seedy. Anyway I put an end to them before they developed into anything serious, and he went back to his wife soon after.

He clears his throat, injects his voice with heartiness. "So then."

"I have a question about one of the techs at ACC, Anton something."

"Anton, Anton . . . hold on." I hear him tapping a keyboard. "Here he is. Anton Murphy. DOB, hm . . . should be about twenty, started maybe two weeks ago?"

"That's him. I've got some ah, concerns about him, was wondering what his references looked like when he came through."

"You're living in the past, doctor. Anton was lost but now he's found, was blind but now he sees."

"Oh. He quit?"

"I have it on good authority that his last words were something like, 'Nevuh fuckin' *again*, maaan.'"

"You've got someone to fill in?"

"For now. There's a guy named, hmm, Guy. Believe it or not. Know him?"

"Yes I do, he's fine. Listen, no one else has quit lately, have they?"

"No." I hear computer keys tap-tapping through. "Looks pretty steady. Anyone in particular you're worrying about?"

"This person named Russell something. He started a few weeks ago I think, he seems reliable and the night nurse Becky likes him."

He snorts. "There's a first."

"He's still around?"

"Russell—hmm—Blanco. Yes, as of this moment he is still gainfully employed with our fine, fine mental health organization."

"Good. You have a date of birth on him?"

"He's, let's see—twenty-nine years old. Turns thirty in October. Planning some cradle-robbing?"

"Thanks for the update."

"Gimme a call sometime, doc." And then he's gone.

20. The phone goes off at 2 a.m. and it's just by chance I'm still awake. "I have to get this," I say.

Anna: Did you ever call anyone about the tree?

Me: Good evening to you too.

Anna: Did you?

Me: Is that why you're calling at this hour?

Anna: Just tell me, yes or no—have you called anyone yet?

My daughter has a certain predictable attitude toward the tree that Walter fell from. Jumped from rather. Tempting to call it an obsession, but I know what a proper obsession is and this isn't one. It's more of a preoccupation, something that comes and goes. She forgets for a while, then it's all she thinks about. She wants it taken down. Cut down and chopped up and carted away. When she remembers it, she calls to remind me.

Me: I'll look into it.

As if this will bring her father back.

Anna: You've been saying that for years.

Her voice has a hollow quality, almost as if it's an echo of itself. I've gotten teary midnight calls before, but tonight she sounds not so much teary or on the verge as well beyond it, in some altogether new realm of emotional turbulence.

Me: I'll do it. Just settle down.

Anna: Don't *tell* me to settle down!

Nathaniel: Is something wrong?

Anna: Who's that?

Me: It's nobody important.

Nathaniel: Hey, thanks a lot.

Anna: Who the fuck is that? You've got somebody in the house at two in the morning?

Me: Forget it. He's not important. He's a colleague.

Anna: Oh right.

Nathaniel: Is that a promotion?

Me: Shut up.

Anna: *What*?

Me: I wasn't speaking to you, dear.

Anna: Yeah what's new.

I take a steadying breath.

Nathaniel: Maybe I should get dressed.

Me: I'll look into having the tree taken down. And I'll call you when I do it. Will that be acceptable?

Anna: Believe it when I see it.

She hangs up and I sigh slowly and listen to the silence and say, "Goodbye."

Nathaniel, half-dressed, says, "I'll see myself out, don't bother getting up."

A few moments later the front door slams.

She really took her father's death very hard.

21. BMHA is a state agency that runs group homes. I do consulting work for them, focused mainly on a home for chronics in Quincy. It's less stressful than ACC, more reliable than my private patients. The house is run by a sedentary earth mama named Muffin, who checks in at something over 250 pounds. The clients—Helen, Ellen, Ak-Ak, and Marshall—love her, more or less, sometimes a lot less.

Today I'm here because of Ak-Ak, alias Andrew Keith, alias Andy the Kid. Andrew got a dose of local notoriety a few years ago when he strode onto a junior-high playground, waving an assault rifle over his head. The chaos was predictable. Turned out the thing wasn't even loaded, but still it was scary and Andrew, nineteen years old at the time, got taken in on charges of reckless endangerment. What they found during questioning was that Andrew was both incredibly foul-mouthed, and that he had no intention of harming anyone bar himself. Enter the shrinks, enter BHMA, enter me. Dx: bipolar disorder, aka manic depression, made more complicated by a secondary diagnosis of Tourette's.

Muffin tells me Andrew has had a rough week, barely getting out of bed, rejecting food, refusing to go to his day program. "We've weathered these episodes before," she tells me, "but this one's pretty bad. Doughnut?"

"No thanks."

The group home is a regular old house, down there in a regular old neighborhood in Quincy. From the outside it looks perfectly normal except that there are always three or four staff cars parked in the driveway. Inside looks pretty normal too, shag carpets, overstuffed furniture, pretty wallpaper in the kitchen. A visitor has to look carefully to spot anything odd: no knives or scissors, no glass in the picture frames. No potted plants. The fridge is locked, windows are plexiglass, et cetera.

Andrew lies in bed with a sheet pulled over his head. I park a chair beside the open door, with a line staff named John sitting nearby. "Andrew? It's Doctor Moss."

From beneath the sheet comes a voice: "Nice tits."

"I hear you're having a tough time lately."

"Old," says the voice. "But I'd fuck her though."

Behind me John clears his throat. Some people never get used to Tourette's no matter how much they're around it.

The room is dim, curtains drawn. Muffin favors soothing blues. The room is small to begin with, made more so by the clutter of dirty laundry and ranks of meticulously arranged toy cars: circles of them, pyramids, X's and O's. Movie posters jostle for position on the walls: movie and rock stars, various glamour girls.

"Andrew. Are you in there?"

"Fuck you." Then a moment later, apologetically: "I'd like to fuck, you."

"Can I see your face?"

The sheet drops away. It's a ferrety face, chinless and long-nosed, milky white with startled eyes. Muffin's right, he hasn't been eating: his cheeks have sunk. He looks like something out of Dickens. I ask him, "You angry about something?"

"Don't want to talk, you just get money for it. You don't give a fuck. Wouldn't mind giving you a fuck."

"What's making you angry? Something at work?"

His gaze darts off to linger on one of the posters. "God she's beautiful." And still watching the poster, he says, "I wish you were my mom."

My teeth chomp down on my tongue, hard, to keep it from saying: *I'm not so sure about that, kiddo.* If I had Tourette's myself, I might set him straight. Andrew's real mom ditched him soon after the gun incident, she's now in California, working as something called a personal trainer. I want to ask, *A trainer of what?* I want to ask, *Are there also impersonal trainers?* A more jovial person might say these things out loud.

After a time I say, "Muffin says you've hardly eaten all week."

"Fat fucking sow eats anything."

I have to bite my tongue again. "She, ah—"

"Should mind her own business, but she can't do that 'cause then she wouldn't have a job."

"Don't you feel hungry?"

"Ain't hungry, ain't angry. Wish you'd go away so I could jerk off."

"How's the greenhouse? How's your day program?"

"It's not a *day* program. It's *work*."

"How's work then?"

"Work sucks."

"Something bad going on over there?"

Silence. Which, for Andrew, reveals extraordinary self-control.

Tourette's has a variety of symptoms, mostly facial tics and bizarre sounds, but manifests itself most memorably through a fortunately rare symptom called coprolalia. A patient with this syndrome is unable to avoid verbalizing his thoughts. In other words, the patient actually *says* what he or she *thinks*. If he thinks someone is lying, he'll say, "You're lying." If he thinks someone is stupid he'll say, "You're stupid" or possibly, "I think you're stupid." We call this a disorder, and have decided that such people are unfit to function in society, because they say what they are thinking. It's worth a moment or two to ponder *that*.

Fortunately for everybody, tics are much more common.

Downstairs I initial his chart and okay an Impulstill 5mg PRN. "Need to find out what's going on," I tell Muffin.

"We're trying," she tells me. "Pretzel?"

"No thanks. How's his family?"

"Same." Muffin reclines behind her desk, looking regal. She's partial to head scarves and flouncy batik-print tent-dresses from places like Java. Her chins jiggle when she chews or talks, which means they jiggle nearly all the time. "Dad's here every Sunday. They go out, the mall, mini golf, whatever. Same routine last weekend. Monday he comes home from the greenhouse, crawls into bed, and goes on strike."

"What's work say about it?"

"They claim to know nothing, but promise to look into it. We'll keep on them." She stifles a burp before reaching behind her for a plastic container. "Deviled egg?"

22. February slides away and March comes slouching in, bad-tempered as usual. Mrs. Flynn stops by to show me the photos from her latest globe-trot, to Egypt this time. A widow with thinning salmon-colored hair and gray, perpetually wide eyes, my neighbor is one of those undiagnosed carriers of a disease that hasn't yet made into the DSM but should: *Unipolar cheeriness syndrome, undifferentiated type.*

But I ought to be nice—it's thanks to Mrs. Flynn, in part, that Anna and I got through the emotional wasteland following Walter's death. Her casseroles and pot pies made it onto our dining table more often than I care to admit, and apart from the odd apple crumble, I've been fairly horrible about reciprocating.

She sits beside me now at the dining table, knobby fingers playing across the enormous digital camera she bought two or three trips ago, Venice I believe it was. (Mrs. Flynn is positively technophiliac, among her other symptoms.) I smile vaguely and nod as the latest images click by: Mrs. Flynn and the pyramids. Mrs. Flynn atop a (sitting) camel. Mrs. Flynn, mouth wide in alarm, atop a (standing) camel. Mrs. Flynn atop the camel whose own mouth stretches wide in alarm. More pyramids. Mrs. Flynn pointing to a brown body of water which is, the flesh-and-blood woman beside me avers, the Nile. More pyramids. More camels. Mrs. Flynn in a carpet shop, surrounded by brown-faced men and boys, the men smiling, the boys trying to look serious. Drinking tea with the men. Drinking tea in a carpet shop alongside an elderly gentleman with sad eyes. Mrs. Flynn standing alongside a much younger man, smiling toothily, eyes hooded in shadow—"Our guide," she tells me. "Abdul. *Won*derful man." Mrs. Flynn with her group, a dozen preternaturally energetic elderly people, armed with identical tote bags and visors bearing the logo of the tour company.

There are, I'm guessing, several hundred images locked into her little digital machine. To her credit, she notices my fading interest somewhere upriver of the Valley of Kings. All those hieroglyphs, or is it glyphics? Walter explained the difference once but I can never remember. Same with stalactites and mites.

"But that's enough for now." Mrs. Flynn shuts off the camera with a *ping*.

"Oh no," I protest, halfheartedly I'm sure. "They're lovely. Must've been a terrific trip."

"It certainly was. Very smooth, no problems at all, and you know, all-inclusive. I like that."

"Sure."

"Frankie would've loved it too, but." She shrugs, her mouth pursed in a rueful little quirk. "Not meant to be. But—he'd've been glad for me to go. Wouldn't have wanted me at home, mooning for him."

"Sure."

"He'd have said, 'Lottie, you get out there and have some fun.' I can just hear it now. He called me Lottie you know, everyone else calls me Loretta."

I smile to show I'm paying attention.

Our own family attempts at international travel, to England when Anna was young, to Toronto before she was born, were both disasters. Maybe I was too high-strung to be a good traveler, or maybe Walter was too uninterested in cultural things. It didn't help that in London we all got food poisoning and in Toronto, Walter lost his wallet the second day. Whatever the reason, both trips were different kinds of wretched. We stuck to the Cape after that, or New York if we were feeling adventurous. Now I admit, "We always meant to get out west, the Grand Canyon and everything, somehow it never happened. Birdwatching, you know, my— Walter was always very interested in that."

Mrs. Flynn nods as if she's the therapist. "Well. I don't know what you'll make of this—but there were nights out there, in the desert, when I was sure I felt he was right there with me. Frankie I mean. Just close enough to be sort of, you could say, watching out for me."

"That's interesting," I say. I'm lying.

After Mrs. Flynn decamps to her own house, I linger on my front porch, where Brutus has set up a permanent squatter's residence on my vinyl-cushioned love seat. "Hey you," I tell him, "don't get too comfortable. I catch you stalking chickadees, you're out on your backside." He squints up at me as if to say, *Talking to animals is one of those early warning signs, Gina.* True enough, but it's not till they start talking back that you really need to worry.

I retreat to the porch swing, an elegant affair built of dark-stained maple. From here I have a nice view of my scrappy lawn and the corner where my crocuses should emerge in a few weeks. The view isn't terribly heartening right now, but somehow they manage to pull off their little resurrection trick every year.

Somewhere a car passes, blaring loud rock and roll which has, I believe, attained the status of "classic." Brutus yawns. I agree with him.

23. Anna answers on the second ring.

"Hi Mom. What's wrong?"

"Hello. Nothing," I say. "Is it really so strange for me to call?"

"Hmm. I guess not." She hesitates. "Who was that guy the other night?"

"I told you, a colleague."

There is a significant pause. "Are you ever going to stop lying to me?"

Well doesn't that knock the air out of me. "I didn't call to have an argument."

"Okay, whatever. I don't want to fight either." She sounds like she means it.

"All right then." There is a pause then as if, in the absence of an argument, we are unsure how to proceed.

"So," she says eventually, "what else? Have you called the tree guy yet?"

"Hmm. Not yet."

"Right."

"How are things with you?" On the love seat, Brutus extends all four legs in a luxurious stretch and then, with admirable aplomb, falls asleep. "Still seeing that counselor?"

"I have been," she says vaguely. "But, not this week yet. Maybe I'll skip it."

"That's fine." Then I wonder, is it really?

The ether crackles. I almost, but don't, then almost again, but don't, push her again about the Atlanta trip. In all likelihood, she deliberately told my mother, knowing it was bound to come up in conversation—thus planting seeds of uncertainty and concern that would sprout into a dense forest of maternal worry, as they obviously have done. Running circles around her long-suffering mother, in other words. Who ever said shrinks were smart? Not me.

Anna: Mom? Are you there? I can hear you breathing, it's like you're a pervert or something.

Me: Yes I'm here. I was thinking about.

(*Pause.*)

Anna: Yeah?

Me: I was wondering about your major. Are you still leaning toward econ?

Anna: Oh God, I don't know. You know, I been thinking about that too. I have this *huge* econ exam coming up. I'm really worried about it. (*World-weary sigh.*) That's one of the things I was talking about with Dolores.

Me: Dolores?

Anna: My counselor.

Me: I see.

Dolores means "sadness." A cruel name to inflict on any child.

Anna: I mean, I know econ's like a good field to go into, very practical and stuff? But I really hate it. It's just so dry and, and, mathy.

Me: Mathy.

Anna: So I was thinking of, I don't know. I was thinking of trying some other classes. You know, there's a lot here, and a lot of things to ... The world is just—there's so much out there, you know what I mean?

Me: That's always been my impression.

Anna: Did you know that the Chinese have a saying, um, "crisis means," wait a minute, I wrote it down. Here it is, "crisis equals opportunity"?

(*Jesus Mary and Joseph. I shut my eyes.*) Me: I bet Dolores told you that.

Anna: Yeah. She's really good.

Me: Maybe the name is appropriate after all.

Anna (*ignoring what she doesn't understand, as is her tendency*): So I was thinking next fall I'd take some different stuff. You know, like sophomore year there's still time, but after that you need to focus on your major? I want to do something, I don't know—something creative. (*Long, lingering pause.*) What do you think?

What do I think? How kind of her to ask.

What I think is that my daughter deserves better than this, even if she isn't alert enough to realize it. What I think is that my tuition dollars are going into the pocket of a counselor (where's *her* degree from?) who tells my daughter to forget her responsibilities and go get a Bachelor's degree in Something Creative. While spouting Chinese clichés to boot, no offense to the Chinese, but there it is.

If you can print it on a bumper sticker, honey, it probably *won't* change your life.

Anna: Mom? You're creeping me out again.

Me: What do you mean, creative?

Anna: I'm not sure, just like, you know, not like so regimented ...

Me: You mean you want to be an artist? Like Trish?

Anna: Not exactly. Maybe. I don't know.

My dear friend Trish makes tile mosaics out of objects she collects: beach glass, cracked thrift-store ceramics, quarry chips. She fashions these items into everything from necklaces to table tops to entire outdoor installations. She can cover a whole wall, interior or exterior, or fashion a nose stud. "No job too big or small," as she likes to say. She can nip together a pair of earrings in twenty minutes; her biggest job to date, tiling the sunken garden of a New Hampshire newspaper maven, required eighteen months of design, planning, material collection and assembly. And the punch line: she nets almost as much as I do, taking into account my insurance premiums and the fact that her cash-only business is a little dodgy in the revenue-declaration department.

Me: The thing you need to remember is that Trish was virtually a pauper for a long time. It's taken her years to get where she is.

Anna: I know. I just, I don't know.

Me: There's a lot of ways to be creative, it isn't just about making jewelry.

Anna: I know that, Mom.

Me: Fixing a car can be creative, or teaching a class full of ten-year-olds. For that matter, raising a child, there's a creative challenge for you.

Anna (*snorts*): You sound like you want me to get pregnant.

Me: That's not funny, dear.

Anna: Hey, I could probably find a guy happy enough to do the—

Me: Don't even *joke* about that.

The iron in my voice subdues her. We say our goodbyes soon afterward, leaving our conversation about her unfulfilled creativity unspoken, as we leave so many things. Sometimes I worry that this isn't right, that it isn't healthy or normal. Then I think of my own mother and our strained silences, and I think, well, it's not exactly *ab*normal, either.

24. Next week at ACC it's uncommonly dull, one of those rare nights when everything converges to conspire for quiet. I retire into the staff room to initial the charts. Guy sits with me for a few minutes, then Kristy. Then some of the new puppies, who seem more scared of me than of the patients. Then finally Russell, who settles into the brown vinyl chair and eyes me warily. "Doctor Moss."

"Mr. . . ." I cast about for his last name. Hadn't Rod Menzies mentioned it? ". . . Blanco."

He smiles a little at this. "Russell. Mr. Blanco was my father."

"All right." Note the past tense. "And call me Regina." I almost say *You can call me Dr. Moss*, but it won't kill me to loosen up.

He nods and I study his face a moment: long and narrow, with cheekbones that cast shadows and that eagle's nose. Hair thick and shiny—oiled?—and brushed back straight. He props a book on his lap, his fingers narrow and veiny. He looks Cherokee or something, or at least Hollywood's version of Cherokee or something. "Quiet night," he says.

"Yes. We get them once in a while."

He hesitates, as if deciding whether to ask a question. Then smiles. "Kristy says it's because of the new moon. Is it true there's a connection?"

I shrug. "People thought so, back in the old days. It was either that or evil spirits. It's where we get the word *lunatic* from."

"Seems kind of weird, doesn't it?"

"So is mental illness."

"Uh—yeah." Out in the ward, techs move through the half-light, shadows on tiptoes. "But the moon? I mean, evil spirits make sense—"

"Maybe to some people."

"—but what's the moon ever done to anyone?"

Becky sits reading a novel at the nurse's station. Times like this, ACC is almost peaceful. So I play along. "You see it hanging up there, but you don't know what it's for. It changes constantly, disappears and comes back again. Not the most reliable thing in the world, so you think, hm, maybe its job is to make people crazy."

"Uh-huh."

"Not like demons and evil spirits and all these invisible bogeymen."

He gently rubs a thumb along the side of his nose. "Why does this feel like I'm learning something vital about you, doctor?"

This annoys. There's nothing I hate more than amateur psychiatrists—of which there are many—except for amateur psychiatrists who practice on me, of which there are mercifully few. He plows on, oblivious, "You believe in things you see rather than things you don't."

"True for most people, in my experience."

"There's more to life than that, though," he says, but quietly, as if he isn't sure.

There is no answer to this that interests me, so I let the conversation flounder and go back to my charts. After a time he takes the hint and leaves.

25. In the morning he accepts my offer of a ride. I hadn't intended to ask, but driving past him as he waited groggily at the bus stop seemed coldhearted, like ignoring a sick puppy. I roll down my window. "South, as in where?"

"Jamaica Plain."

"I can manage that. Hop in."

"Appreciate it."

I pull into traffic. "How long have you lived there?"

"I don't. I'm going to my other job." He stifles a yawn, rubs a hand across his bristly cheek. He's the kind of man who sprouts a thick growth in a single day. I ask him, "You get any sleep last night?"

"Sleep on the job?" He looks exhausted. "How dare you suggest such a thing."

We glide along South Street, past the SPCA and the arboretum, both of us bleary from the overnight. Near the Forest Hills T stop I pull over next to a small whitewashed building with a big ice-cream-cone-shaped sign. Past the plate glass is an array of square red tables topped with upended stools. "You work here?"

"For now." Russell unwinds his lanky frame from the front seat and bends down before slamming the door. A ring of keys has appeared in his hand. "One day I'm going to own this place."

I blink. "Really? Why?"

He exhales noisily and I wonder if that was the wrong response. "It's got potential. Anyway, thanks for the lift."

"Don't fall asleep in there," I say.

He grimaces. "Good advice."

In the rearview I watch him lingering on the sidewalk as I drive off. Flat-orange sunrise glow outlines him, unnaturally sharp and clear against the street's gray asphalt.

26. Dad lies in bed, propped up by pillows, a blanket over his knees. A little more lucid today. Mom clatters in the kitchen.

Stubble clings to Dad's cheek like frost on a window, scratchy when I bend down for a kiss. Breath is sour too but he's my dad so I don't turn away. Pajama buttons are only half done and his skin sags wherever it's visible. Whoever invented aging had a lousy sense of humor.

"Anna?" he says abruptly.

"She's fine," I tell him, settling into a chair. "Almost done with freshman year." It's mid-March already.

"School?" says Dad.

"Yeah, up in Vermont. You remember? It's very small, but good. Supposedly."

Dad starts breathing heavily. Almost gasping. It's unsettling but there's nothing to do but let it pass. The docs insist it's a tic, not a sign of impending suffocation. How they can be so sure is a mystery to me. In time he manages to cough out, "Single then?" and I answer, "Yes, Dad, I'm still single."

"Meant," he gasps a little more. "Anna."

"Oh yes, her too." Mm—as far as I know.

Dad's always been taciturn, rarely expending five words when he could get by with one or two: "Birthday," he'd announce to me as a child, bending to kiss the top of my head, or "Proud," when I did something especially noteworthy. Or rarely, at times of extreme emotional intensity: "Love you."

Now he says, "Heritance."

I lean closer. "Sorry?"

"In . . . heritance. Yours."

"Dad, there's no point going into all that—"

He interrupts me with a jowly glower, yes he can still do that, degenerative illness or no. He lifts a shaky finger to tap at my collarbone. "None for you."

"Dad that's, of course, it goes to Mom, whatever." Why does he think I need money anyway? I make more than he ever did, all those years of poking about his patients' teeth.

"Not her," he whispers, then pauses, collects himself, manages to wheeze, "For . . . church." He's watching me, mouth drooping open, a little thread of saliva. "Pray for my." He pauses to gather himself. "Soul."

He's shaking just perceptibly, but he's not coughing, or shivering, or trembling. He's laughing. My father has just made, surprise surprise, a joke.

If I had Tourette's, I might say something like, "That's not funny, Dad," but I don't. I have many flaws, I'll admit this, but coprolalia isn't one of them. Dishonesty is, so I pretend to chuckle along with my father as he lies there wheezing on the bed.

27. This cemetery has sections, or more properly layers, built up in accretions like sedimentary strata. To one side, graves from the Revolutionary War and earlier, men with names like Ezra and Eli and Caleb, wafer-thin gravestones worn smooth by centuries of rain and decades of acid rain. Modest headstones hardly larger than a cereal box, stained with lichen, blanketed in moss and bird shit. The history of our nation—what little history we have, as a nation—falling to pieces as we watch.

The occasional snatch of legible writing pleads from all those years ago: ". . . now with Go . . ." ". . . ll remem . . ." ". . . as ever so cher . . ." The vets from the Revolution were awarded some kind of plaque, years ago from I don't know whom. Coated in tarnish and gunk after just a few decades, the plaques now look almost as old as the stones.

Further on, the years slip by fast. Here are the Civil War dead, a sobering number of them, and later still, women named Ornetta and Lispeth, whole families decaying under grand obelisks and pyramids, ornately carved cherubic angels and bouquets of red-marble roses. The 1900s make their appearance in the form of headstones firm and square and sensible, with carved scrollwork and handsome lettering: "Caring mother—devoted wife—beloved daughter." This for a woman who died in 1919 at the age of twenty-one. I wonder if the flu took her. I wonder if her husband had died somewhere in France the previous year.

Further on come fresher graves, ranks upon ranks of them, some sporting bouquets of real flowers—wilted, fresh or in between. More memorial plaques too, for the World Wars, Korea, Vietnam, Iraq, Iraq again, Afghanistan. Men and women both, and more than one might expect, if one had gone through life thinking the country lived more or less at peace in the world, with war an occasional aberration. The numbers suggest otherwise.

The newest portion of the graveyard has evolved into a flat grassy expanse, as if someone decided headstones were too impractical. My God, have we run out of *rock* of all things? So now we use simple markers flat on the ground, carved as plainly as possible, flat gray granite or marble or, for all I know, some kind of eternal plastic epoxy. We've gone full circle, our headstones have again become as modest as those from the 1600s. The difference being that you can still read the new ones, for now.

I stand alongside Walter's grave for a time. The wind bites, sharp against the manicured lawn, chasing the clouds and annoying my hair. Some ways off a cluster of mourners surround a fresh grave. In the other direction an old lady stands motionless.

I squat beside Walter. Not beside the marker, but beside where his body rests. I'm carrying a small bundle of crocuses, the first from my garden, and I set them on the ground over the point where his hands lie folded across his stomach.

"Here you go," I say.

Walter always loved the crocuses. He wasn't a man given to noticing things, generally speaking, that didn't call attention to themselves; but he did love to see these pop up out of the thawing ground each spring. So every year I have a little ritual, I know it's irrational but there it is. I bring him the first flowers of the year and set the bundle in his hands.

This year the flowers are yellow and white, with one rusty-red in the mix like a spot of old blood. No purple as yet. Walter's favorites were the purple. This would not surprise anyone who knew him.

After a while I wipe my face and blow my nose but there's no point since I just have to do it again a minute later.

Around me the birds peck at the ground, fly up into the trees, fly back down. Sugar maples mostly, and oaks. Some tall cypress spiking up like a row of columns. The birds flutter, sparrows and finches, chickadees, titmice, the odd cardinal.

The afternoon passes slowly. I've tied the crocuses in a bundle and now attach them to a slender metal rod provided for just this purpose, sinking the shaft into the soft, well-tended grass. The flowers won't blow away, or be carried off by rabbits. They could be stolen, yes it's true, by some casually horrible kind of vandal; but they're unlikely to tumble away by accident.

The next time I come here, the groundskeeper will have removed them.

"I don't know, Walter," I say. "I just don't know."

28. Somehow it's gotten late. Forcing myself back to the present world, this present world, standing up now. Brushing at my stockings and my behind. I look at the nearby graves. The one next to Walter is just a child, a boy, fifteen years old. The despair in that threatens to swallow me up altogether, so I force my legs into motion, move along one step at a time.

I wipe my face again, blow my nose, add another soggy tissue to the mass growing in my purse. The clot of mourners has left but in the distance, the solitary old woman remains, standing like a sentinel.

The sun hovers low in the sky, removed but insistent. Bearing witness, like God, for people who believe in God, or like history, for people who believe in that. I follow the gravel paths toward the parking lot, past the Roaring Twenties and the Reconstruction and the War of 1812 and the colonials. I wonder where the slaves lie buried, where the Indians are. Maybe they have their own graveyards. Or none at all. All the while I never lose sight of the old lady standing wordless beside someone's grave. She's a tiny thing in a big gray coat and knit cap, a gray woman whose face has been stamped for ever and always with lines of indelible sadness. Like stains of ink that make no writing you can understand but still say something anyway. She stands there like she hasn't a friend in the world except for the one moldering beneath the ground.

Mrs. Flynn she's not. I can't help wondering if I'm looking, somehow, at myself. Perhaps that sounds melodramatic, or morbid, but this is what happens when I spend too much time at the cemetery.

29. When I get home I call Lee's number and catch him as he's driving home. I convince him to stop by for a drink, which isn't terribly difficult. When he arrives there are no drinks in evidence and I'm lying on the couch without any clothes on. Lee likes to find me this way, and in certain moods I like it too.

Lee is a once-strong man who is now going soft, but he fights the decay with vigor and enthusiasm, which is why I tolerate his pinky ring and hair gel. Some nights I'm in the mood for desperation and longing and this is one of those nights.

Picture window curtains are wide open but there's no one to see but the cats and the owls.

He finishes quickly and will get home a half hour late. I give him a bottle of wine to present to his wife as an explanation for his delay.

30. The next day I wake up with a faintly sore throat and a head full of mucus. Thanks very much, Lee. If there's one thing I hate, it's being sick, and on Sunday besides. I brew myself some strong sweet tea, glower at the unseasonably sunny morning, and decide that my plans, such as they are, won't be interrupted.

An hour later I'm on the discount floor of Fully Booked in Harvard Square, poking through the cookbooks, trying to figure out why my ceviche never tastes right. I don't have many dinner guests but I still like to cook. I've been told this is surprising, but it has never surprised me. The remainders aisle is one of my favorite weekend haunts, with its gardening manuals stacked atop detective novels, travel guides elbowing against biographies of famous people who've been dead longer than I've been alive.

"Hello, doctor. Um, Regina I mean."

It's that moment that my nose decides to erupt into an already-tired wad of tissues. My eyes open to focus on Russell of the night-time ACC shift, wearing a Patriots sweatshirt and baseball cap, backward. Since the team started winning Super Bowls nobody's immune, it seems, except me.

"Hey," he smiles.

It's disorienting to see him out of context. "Never imagined I'd bump into you here."

He looks bewildered. "In a bookstore? I read things, sometimes. Does that—surprise you?"

Oh geez Louise. I don't need a kid with some chip on his shoulder, not today when I've already got a head full of snot. "All I meant was, Harvard Square isn't exactly close to your house *or* mine, and I'm poking through the cookbooks when who do I meet but a guy who's usually running from one job to another. If you want to get mad about it, go ahead and get mad. But don't pin it on me."

He watches me for a moment with that look people use on dogs when they're afraid they might have rabies but aren't sure. *Maybe she just needs a pat* . . . "I'm not mad. But I look at cookbooks all the time, you know? I work in a restaurant. Anyway—can I take you to lunch?"

Now it's my turn to stare. *Maybe he just needs a pat.*

Twenty minutes later we're sitting in The Hearthstone, my favorite lunch spot in the Square. "Why so eager?" My voice sounds loud and croaky. "I'm just a colleague, not a very nice one at that."

He bursts out laughing. "See? That's why—because you stay stuff like that."

"Mm."

"You're an interesting person. You're like, a legend on the ward. Half the patients are terrified and the other half are in love with you. That's true for the staff too."

Is he really saying this? I can't tell, congestion has my ears half-plugged. I let loose another sneeze and my ears unclog, partially. Really I should just forget all this and go home where I belong. But I had planned on lunch out, after all.

We sit at a little round table near the fireplace so we can take in the merrily crackling flames in case the conversation lags. There seems little enough chance of that: Russell chats amiably—about his restaurant, about the group home where he puts in occasional shifts—while I interject occasional pithy remarks.

The waiter sports a goatee and multiple tattoos, a look I'm not terribly partial to, despite the vogue it enjoyed for a while. He delivers the menus as if we're interfering with his serious work, whatever that might be.

I say, "The soups are good here."

Russell answers, "Thanks for heads-up, Reg." Seeing my look, he asks, "Can I call you Reg?" Pronounced *Rej*.

"I'd rather you didn't."

"Okay." He renews his interest in the menu. "Sorry, did you say soups?"

The conversation lagged a bit then, after all.

31. One Halloween Night more than twenty years ago, a seventeen-year-old named Benjamin Hayes attended a rock concert at the Paradise Theater on Commonwealth Avenue, near BU. Ben lived in Medford and had to take the red line trolley downtown, then switch to the green line. He left home about seven o'clock and reached the club an hour later, where he was due to meet some friends.

"We told him to be home no later than midnight," says his mother.

"It was a school night," his father adds. "We take that very seriously."

"Took," corrects the mother.

"Right," I nod, dabbing at my nose. Several days have passed since my cold flared up in Harvard Square, and it's hanging on stubbornly, though much less explosively.

"So then," the Hayeses say together, then Mr. looks at his wife. "You go ahead."

"No, you tell it," says Mrs. Hayes.

"You sure?"

She nods.

Benjamin attended the concert. According to his friends, he had a fine time. The band was called The Devil's Reaper; the closest they ever had to a hit was a little ditty entitled "Sleep When You're Dead." The parents show me the band's records, *Vacation in Hell* and *Evil Fears No Evil*. They handle them as if bewildered by the cover art and song titles, as if these items are inscribed with hieroglyphics, runes, or the secret language of trolls.

The concert was short. The band didn't have a lot of songs, and they weren't the sort of musicians given to lengthy improvisation. Ben left the club around ten o'clock in the presence of Shelly Wasserman, a friend. "But not his girlfriend," Mrs. Hayes clarifies, as she always does. "He had loads of friends, but never one particular girl."

"He was just a kid," says Mr. Hayes, as if this has some relevance.

Benjamin was typical Boston Irish with a wiry build and mischievous eyes, the kind of teenager who could talk himself out of any situation. Did well enough at school, nothing memorable. Shelly was a nice Jewish girl whose family lived in Arlington, straight A student, "A charmer," Mr. Hayes calls her. "A real charmer."

They had met through the swarm of mutual friends that carried them through all the rituals of adolescence: the concerts and proms and summer holidays and—for all I know—the drug experimentation and sex and near-scrapes with the police. But I know none of this for sure, and if his parents know anything of it, they've never said a word.

32. Anna sounded singularly odd when she called last night. Not hysterical, weepy, high-strung or shrill. These are all familiar. This was new: She sounded almost . . . defeated. Or bewildered. My own mother's word for it would be *dopey*.

I asked her: What's new?

Anna: Oh nothing. I saw my counselor.

Me: And?

Anna: I don't know. I feel like I'm in a rut.

Me: Mm.

Anna: And it's time for some kind of change. Some action.

Me: Such as?

Anna: Some drastic action.

Me: Well let's not, you know, go overboard on this.

Anna: But then I don't know.

(*Pause.*)

Anna: Maybe it's not such a great idea, this whole counselor thing. I just, I don't know. You know? It's bringing up a lot of stuff.

Me: About your father?

Anna: Yeah. Partly.

(*Pause.*)

Me: Well if you're asking my advice, and I realize you may not be, but if you are then my advice is that sometimes it's better to let sleeping dogs lie.

Anna: I know.

Me: You do?

Anna: I mean, I know you think that.

Me: It's better than drastic action anyway.

Anna: That's pretty much your philosophy of life, isn't it?

Me: Well.

Anna: I don't know if I believe you, though. I mean I know you're smart and everything? But I don't know if you're right about this.

Which is more or less where we left it.

33. After the concert, with the music still roaring in their ears, Benjamin Hayes and Shelly Wasserman got on the green line and headed downtown, where they changed at Park Street station. At Porter Square their friends Brad and Richie Donohue got out, waved at them through the train's windows and watched them pull away into the tunnel. Benjamin and Shelly were never seen again, alive or dead, sane or deluded, by anyone who could identify them.

A terrible story, yes. But I've heard it so many times now—every two weeks since the Hayeses first appeared in my office—that I could recite the whole thing verbatim. I try to concentrate, but I'm still fighting that cold, and as Mrs. Hayes's voice maunders on, my mind flips backward like an acrobat, to the night before last.

Russell Blanco asked me out. As in, to dinner or a movie. "Or something." As in, a date.

This was at ACC. This was at three in the morning, and the only conceivable answer was: geez Louise. "I'm a fair bit older than you," I reminded him. "With a kid in college. Maybe you should ask *her* out." I didn't say *I'm a widow, I have fibroids, you're not, you don't*. If I had Tourette's, I might have said exactly that, but then they'd call me crazy. "No don't do that, actually."

I didn't quite know what to do about Russell Blanco. Amours I've had in plenty, but never with a subordinate, and it's not something I've ever wanted to introduce onto the unit. And yet, despite my pre-emption of his advances, the attraction was undeniable. In both directions apparently, against all expectations.

"Um." He licked his lips. "That means, I guess—"

"That means, let's keep it professional, hm?" It was early, but I managed to call up a patient-friendly, mirthless smile. "Respect the boundaries and all that."

"Oh yeah," he nodded, "yeah." A great word, *boundaries*. It can be used anywhere, anytime, under nearly any circumstances to invoke more or less immediate obedience. A handy thing indeed, to keep people from straying, from clambering over lines better left uncrossed. Full moons notwithstanding.

34. Mr. and Mrs. Hayes first appeared in my office three years ago. I got the story of their son's disappearance in the first hour, followed by a variety of complaints: poor sleep, feelings of unease, low appetite. Years ago some quack had diagnosed the husband as depressed and dosed him on Liftovec. Almost as an afterthought, he did the same for the wife, despite her symptoms being significantly different. Not surprisingly, Mrs. Hayes was left feeling groggy and dull, but still anxious and unable to sleep.

When the doctor got married and moved to Florida, the Hayeses shopped around for someone else. "We heard you were very nice," Mrs. Hayes said, smiling at me sadly. I was of course immediately won over. Professional distance only takes one so far. I quickly amended the wife's diagnosis to an anxiety disorder and changed her meds to an anti-anxiety PRN. The improvement was startling, the only downside being that the medication she's on now has to be doled out and monitored, as it loses effectiveness over time.

They're in their late sixties, early seventies, and medicated or no, the world weighs heavy on them. Their son, if still alive, would be close to forty. They await his reappearance the way some people wait for Jesus.

Meanwhile I worry about my daughter. I am, in fact, on my way to becoming scared for my daughter. Not scared *of*; scared *for*. I am scared of *drastic action* and what that might entail. I'm scared, not because she sounded hysterical and needy, but because she didn't; she sounded morose, almost flat. She sounded like she meant what she said, which is troubling indeed.

I wonder what to do. There must be someone to call at the school, a dorm monitor or something. Someone to reassure me that she's eating, going to class, talking to friends. Or am I being precipitous? I know how annoying it can be to have somebody—okay, to have a mother—meddling in one's personal life.

"Every time the phone rings," says Mr. Hayes, "I think, 'Please God, let it be him.'"

The wife nods. I force myself to pay attention.

If the Hayeses were animals, he would be a bear, she a rabbit; but worry has lined their faces and anxiety rounded their shoulders until they both seem to view the world from under an equally intolerable burden. Mr. Hayes's face flops to one side as he talks, like a deflated balloon.

Mrs. Hayes says, "The worst thing isn't that he might be dead."

"No," says her husband, leaking air next to her. "God help us."

"The worst thing is not knowing for sure." She fixes her tired-rabbit eyes on the window that looks out at the parking lot, as if expecting her son to be standing by the Chevy, waving. "Never being certain, is the worst."

Mr. Hayes fiddles with his ring finger. "That's the thing. If we knew, we could just put it behind us."

"People do it," she adds. "It's not easy but they do it."

"Move on," nods Mr. Hayes. "God help them."

I nod in commiseration although I disagree. Each session with the Hayeses concludes like this, their litany of woe culminating in the lack of certainty as the worst thing, the most horrible possible outcome. It is not therapeutically indicated to argue with them, to shoot them down, to use examples from my private life to illustrate how stupid and superficial their own griefs are. So I just nod sadly and bite my tongue and force myself to not say: *Oh no, it gets worse than that, believe me. There are far worse things than not knowing for sure whether or not he's dead.*

35. Dad answers the door when I ring the bell. I'm so startled to see him like that—upright and face to face—that I just stand there staring till he says, "Lazarus." I pull him to me, his face grinning lopsidedly.

"Careful," he murmurs. "Catch something."

Suddenly I'm ten years old, here's my father smiling down at me, the guy with the answers. I have to fight back tears.

"You look great," I tell him, which is either a 75 percent lie or 100 percent truth, depending on which year I'm comparing him to. His hair sticks up in little shocked white tufts and the lines on his face have taken a hard, permanent look. But he still manages a smile and his eyes are focused.

Mom's waiting in the kitchen. "Your father's back to his old self."

"So I see."

Dad makes pancakes while the ladies sit. This was our Sunday morning ritual for, oh, twenty years more or less. Not every week of course, but often enough for it to be burned into my cortex: him standing next to the griddle, beside a big red bowl of eggs and flour and buttermilk. Just like he's standing, right there, right now. "Gigi?"

"Bring 'em on," I manage to say. I can't remember the last time I ate a pancake. Of course, neither can I remember the last time my father was bustling around the kitchen, firing up the griddle, ladling out batter. If it would allow him this resurrection on a permanent basis, I'd eat thirty pancakes a day.

Mom's eyes glitter. She says, "Some days are better than others. Ups and downs, you know."

"Sure." I know all about that.

A plate is set before me. I take a bite that dissolves in a cloud: Parkinson's or no, my father can still make the best damned pancakes on earth. "These are fantastic."

Mom picks at hers, but then, she always did. Dad asks me, "More?"

"Let me work on this a while."

He joins us at the table with his own plate. "Crazy, huh?" He squints a sad smile at me. "Months, nothing. Then . . ."

"Well."

"No sense."

"Mm—I guess Parkinson's is one of those things, it cycles up and down." As I speak, Mom watches me—her doctor daughter—with a degree of neediness that's disconcerting, coming from my own parent. To Dad I say, "The important thing is to, to take advantage of those days when you're feeling stronger."

He shovels down food with little apparent regard for what I'm saying. I swear, this could be thirty years ago.

We sit and eat. It's the coziest time we've had in a while, and part of me feels guilty for not raising the topic of Anna. I had planned to ask Mom about her; lay it all out, all her erratic behavior, the charged strangeness between us. But then Dad happened. I can't bring myself to sabotage the moment.

This, in all likelihood, would confirm Freud's assessment of me as a lousy mother. But there's little I can do about that at this late date, so instead we sit and eat and enjoy our pancakes.

36. I call Anna and a boy answers the phone. "Yeah?" It takes a moment for me to mentally regroup.

Me: I'd like to speak to Anna, please.

Unknown male: Who's this?

Me: Her mother.

Unknown, slightly chastened male: Oh.

(*Muffling at the other end, as if a hand is being held over the phone.*)

Muffled voice of unknown male: It's your mother.

Anna (*muffled, but not muffled enough*): Tell her I'm not here.

Unknown male (*unmuffled, dutiful*): Um, Anna's not here right now.

Me: I heard.

Unknown, not very bright male: Yeah. Wait, what?

Me: Tell her I called.

And I hang up.

37. I pick up a new private patient named Beth Ann Kim. She sits in my office in a neat blue skirt and white blouse, sensible white pumps and matching handbag, tidily coiffed hair. She's groomed and pretty, and she smiles without showing her teeth. I ask her to describe herself and she says she is "50 percent American, 50 percent Korean and 100 percent depressed." Then she smiles tidily and waits, I presume, for me to laugh, or possibly clap. Her fingernails are trimmed right down to the quick, but bitten or cut, I can't tell.

I ask about her family. Which family, the one in American or the one in Korea? America, I say. She's an only child, she says. Parents in Honolulu. Mother has lots of friends, lots of social engagements. Very involved in the "Korean community thing." Dad's retired. I ask if she is close to them. "I guess," she shrugs. "As close as anybody can be to their parents." She pauses and I think she's going to offer more. Instead she asks, "What about your parents? Are you close to them?"

The response is automatic. "We're here to talk about you."

"What about children?" she presses. "Do you have any?"

"Beth. Please." I offer her a conspiratorial smile that says *I know you're a bright young woman who has a lot to offer, but right now we must abide by the rules of our little game.* "Let's stay on the subject."

The Korean family, I gather, is a large conglomeration of aunts and uncles and cousins headquartered in Seoul. She visited years ago. They were cold to her. She pauses. "Resentful. They kept saying, your family left, but we stayed." She frowns. "Does this even matter?"

"Sure it does," I assure her. "It's all grist for the mill." She rolls her eyes as if she's heard this cliché before.

What about friends? Yes, of course she has friends. From work, from college. But they're doing their own things, getting married, having babies. Does she want to have babies? She wouldn't mind, she says.

"You wouldn't mind. But is it something you think you want to do?"

She shrugs.

"Do you have a boyfriend?"

She says, "I have lots of boyfriends." There is a brittleness to her smile now, as if her lips are being stretched in a manner unfamiliar to them. As if she stood at home in front of a mirror and practiced. "I can get a boyfriend any time I want."

"Okay." I search for the way to say it. "Is there a special boyfriend? One in particular who you care about?"

She doesn't shrug. She says: "No."

It goes like this for a while. What's her job? She works for a telemarketing agency, recently and swiftly promoted. Making good money. Is she satisfied with this? Shrug. Does she have any ambition in her work? No, not really. Does she have a dream?

"Dream." She murmurs the word, sucking it between her tongue and the roof of her mouth as if it's a mint. "If I had a dream, then it would be the dream of actually wanting something. You know? Really having a strong feeling of desire for something."

Part of me wants to say: Well honey, take away that job and that paycheck and those sensible shoes, put you out on the street for a few weeks and you'll start wanting things pretty quick. But I'm a doctor, it's my job to help the people who come to me, not to accuse them of whining. So I say, "You said you were 100 percent depressed. Is that something you want—to stop being depressed?"

She gives me her creepy smile. "I call it depressed because I don't know how else to describe it. I'm not sad, I don't feel sad or cry or anything. The thing is I don't really feel *anything.*"

Something in her answer reminds me of hysteria, the old hysteria, the way it was originally understood: a kind of self-induced paralysis. Nowadays we call it conversion disorder and it's rare, but time was, people were constantly coming down with things they couldn't feel: paralyzed limbs, nerveless hands, sightless eyes. It was almost fashionable. These problems had no discernable physiological cause: there was no physical problem with the patients. Tongues just wouldn't speak one day, ears didn't hear. And hearts? Maybe that's what got me thinking of this. Maybe Beth Ann's got a conversion disorder of the heart. And geez Louise, doesn't that sound like a country song.

Victims of hysteria were almost always women. And naturally, men had plenty to say about *that*. Men decided that women demonstrated these symptoms when they didn't get enough sex. Maybe if I were male I could understand the logic: if a woman wasn't getting enough sex, the theory went, her womb would migrate to different parts of her body. There, predictably enough, it got up to no good. What self-respecting womb wouldn't? A womb in the thigh resulted in paralysis. A womb in the eyes, blindness. The very word *hysteria* comes from the Greek word for womb, *hustera*. Ditto *hysterectomy*. So even today, women can address various medical problems by having their hysteria removed.

Beth Ann has stopped talking. She watches me now, intent, with bangs cut flat above her eyes and that sad little smile. "Doctor?"

I force myself to focus. "Sorry, I was just—reflecting."

"I see." She gives me a quick smile then, a real one that flashes for a moment as if she's seen through my dissembling and is tickled by it, then her face closes down again.

It becomes apparent that Beth Ann Kim has come fishing for medication. I give her a little, not as much as she wants, and we make an appointment for next week. When she's gone, I'm left alone in my office. Outside the nuthatches cheep and a dog barks distantly but relentlessly. I wonder if I'll see Beth Ann again. If I don't then someone else will. I don't have to wonder if she'll be any different next time: she's on for the long haul.

38. As the week goes on I find my thoughts turning, at the most unexpected moments, to Russell Blanco. Wondering what he's eating for dinner, what he's watching on TV. Slapstick comedies from the forties? He doesn't seem the wacky-comedy type of guy. (Then again, the same incorrect observation has been made about me.) Maybe he's keeping up with current events, renting lots of documentaries from Netflix. Most likely he's too busy for TV, what with the restaurant and ACC and the group home and who knows what else. Or who else.

I realize with a twinge of amusement that I wouldn't mind sitting with him on my own front porch as the sun sets over the front lawn, burning the grass golden. Then I wonder, what am I turning into, some kind of moony teenager? Get a grip, Regina.

I wonder if I'm losing my mind. It's possible I suppose, after all these years of exposure to my clients. Psychosis through osmosis, as my friend Trish would say. (Walter would never say something like that.) Because that's what these preoccupations signify: little bouts of irrationality. Despite all evidence to the contrary, despite generations and millennia of evidence to the contrary, despite our bickering parents and miserable friends and divorced siblings and bitter co-workers, we go on thinking that the presence of some other person can deliver happiness and restore meaning and fulfillment to our otherwise stultified little lives.

Talk about delusion. Talk about magical thinking. I might be expected to know better, considering certain events in my past.

39. Friday night I pick up the phone, but instead of Russell I call Anna. It rings a long time before she answers. "Anna? It's your mother."

"Oh, hi Mom." Immediately the sound is muffled, as if she's placed her hand over the mouthpiece. When the connection clears I hear laughter in the background. "What's up?"

"Just checking in. You've got company?"

"Some people from my English class. We're doing some um, studying."

More muffled laughter. I say, "It sounds as if you've made some friends these days."

"Oh yeah, yeah . . . I guess I have."

"That's nice to hear."

There is a lull. In the background someone seems to be saying "Where's the blob?" which makes no sense to me. I wrack my brain for something to talk about.

Me: Did you have that econ exam yet?

Anna: Exam?

Me: The one you were so worried about—you mentioned it the other night.

(*Pause.*)

Anna: Oh yeah. Yeah, it was fine.

Me: You think you did well?

The voices rise in the background, while some sort of alleged music throbs in the lower registers.

Anna (*ignoring my question*): So, I was thinking about this summer? My friend Janice has a summer place on the Cape, in P-town. She's invited me, and I was thinking it'd be cool to go there for a while?

This is the first I've heard of Janice.

Me: And what will you be doing out there?

Anna: Oh, you know. She's got some ideas about where we can work. It's tourist season so there's tons to do.

As plans go, I've heard them vaguer, but not by much. I suppose there is something to be said for flexibility, but offhand I couldn't say exactly what.

Me: And her parents are okay with this?

Another lull. More murmuring voices, and then, distinctly, a man's: "—mother."

Anna: Janice's parents? Oh—I'm sure it's okay with them, they seem really cool.

Girl's voice (*rising up from the background*): Yeah right!

Me: I suppose it's okay. What are you thinking, a month or so?

A burst of laughter escapes from the background babble. I think, but I'm not completely certain, that I hear Anna say: More than that, Mom.

This is not a conversation I want to pursue in her present state of apparent dorm-party distraction. "Why don't we talk about this later," I say, and she eagerly agrees.

40. I call Josh and get no answer. I call Steve and leave a voicemail. I call Nick but the number has been disconnected. I call Nathaniel and a woman answers and I hang up. I call Lee's office and the line is busy. I call Rod Menzies but hang up while it's still ringing. I call Steve and leave another voicemail.

My daughter, it would seem, has summer plans that don't involve me. Who or what do they involve? I have no idea. But I can guess. Oh yes, I have an active imagination, not paranoid, just active.

She sounded disoriented tonight, almost drugged. Come to that, she's sounded drugged during our last several calls. And I know that for a certain demographic of college student, nothing is more appealing than spending one's days lounging on some beach a la Provincetown, smoking dope and making patterns in the sand and doing God knows what else. Getting tattoos. Sharing needles. Exploring *spirituality*. Being *creative*.

I stand on my porch and stare at the stars. Not a cloud in the sky, just a sharp smile of moon up there laughing down at me, at Anna, at all of us.

41. Becky gives me the name of Russell's restaurant. I'm at ACC tonight, he's not. I call and he answers on the third ring. "Scoops!" he hollers over the background noise.

"Russell? Is that you?" I've sequestered myself in the staff room but can barely hear him over the kitchen noise and general carrying on. "Is that work or a party?"

"Same thing, man," he hollers back. "Who's this?"

"Regina."

"Who?"

"Regina—Dr Moss. From ACC."

"Oh—*hey* there. Hold on." A moment later the background becomes muffled, as if he's ducked behind a door. "That's better. To what do I owe this honor?"

Is that mischief in his voice, or mockery? I inhale and tell him the simple truth. "I was thinking about what you said the other day. About wanting to go out, and I was feeling bad that I shot down that idea so quickly." I pause, hoping he'll take the bait, but he doesn't. So I press on, "Would you still like that?"

"Sure. Thing is, uh, my schedule. What did you have in mind, exactly?"

"I don't know, actually. Exactly. What are you interested in, besides ice cream and psychosis?"

"Me—um, music I guess?"

Probably not Telemann and Vivaldi. "Keep going."

"Surfing?"

"Try again?"

"Flea markets—no wait." He hesitates. "Maps."

"Sorry?"

"I really like maps. I know it's weird."

I don't contradict him. "Do you collect them or something?"

"Wouldn't mind, but they're expensive, the old ones anyway. The cool ones. With countries that aren't there anymore."

"Mm."

"But unless there's a museum with an exhibit, I don't see us having much luck nurturing this particular hobby."

Something occurs to me then. "You'd be surprised."

"Really?"

From there it's just logistics, date and time, what to wear, what to expect. The Rubicon has been crossed, as they say. I hear Walter's voice in my ear—*Who the hell says that, Ranger?*—but ignore it.

42. My father-in-law doesn't ask questions because he wants to hear my answers. He asks questions so that I can hear *his* answers. The psychological term for this is "crashing bore," but I tolerate him because he's my daughter's grandfather. One of them—the one who talks in complete sentences, as it turns out. Plus, he's a thread of connection to Walter. So Hugh and I go to concerts together, and tonight the Camarata gifts us a transcendent mix of Telemann and Locatelli and Bach, with a little Mozart for the tourists. It's heavenly. No Russians, no Schubert, no godforsaken *Mahler*. Afterward Hugh takes in the view on Comm Ave., the bay-windowed brownstones, the swooshing traffic, as if making sure it's all still the same as before. Which of course it's not.

He asks, "Drink?" and before I can answer he says, "I could sure use one."

We find a sushi place and duck in. Low wood-topped tables and subdued lighting. Hugh's not crazy about sushi but he humors me. Actually he doesn't care about the food, as long as he can get a gin and tonic and flirt with the waitress. Walter's mother Stella died within a year of Walter's death, so Hugh has time on his hands.

He's the only man here past retirement age. The silver sweep of hair, straight back from his forehead and falling nearly to his shoulders, lends a vaguely Egyptian air. Eyes slate-gray and twinkling, miraculously unlined—has he been getting Botox or something? A trim figure despite his age, lean without being scrawny, suavely accoutred in designer jeans, an open-necked shirt and suede jacket of lion-pelt tan that's more stylish than anything in *my* closet.

Mostly what defines him is his mouth, which carries what Walter would call a shit-eating grin on more or less permanent display. As if he and I are sharing an ongoing, private joke. Walter grinned like this, too, but only once in a while.

"So then," Hugh says, tearing into a pile of fish cakes. "How's work treating you?"

"Fine."

"Lemme tell you, retirement's not as easy as it looks." And he's off.

One thing in Hugh's favor, he never hints that I should be getting married again, never moans that Anna needs a father figure. Or that a woman like me is helpless without a man like his son around. I suspect this is because he thinks no man has any business trying to take his son's place.

"How's Anna liking that school she's at, there?"

"Oh, she's adjusting."

"You told me she was a bit," he holds his hand out flat, wags it back and forth, "at first."

"That's been ongoing, I admit I'm a little concerned."

"Ah, she's got a good head on her shoulders."

"You think?"

"Sure." He devours another wad of greasy fish. "Don't you?"

"I'm not sure. Sometimes she seems—flighty."

He opens his mouth and bobs his head: it looks like a laugh, but no sound is coming out. "Flighty, sheesh Regina. She's what, fifteen years old—"

"Seventeen."

"I think a kid's entitled to be a little unsure of herself at that age. Better than being certain about everything."

"I suppose. She wants to change her major, you know."

"What was it again?"

"Economics."

"Can't say I blame her."

"It's steady."

"So's picking trash." He nods for another drink. "What's she want to do instead?"

"She has no idea. She wants to go be *creative*." I allow myself to roll my eyes, hoping he'll roll with me.

No dice. "Depends. Some of these singers these days, they make a good living. Actresses, whatever, *American Idol*."

"Oh come on." I stress-gulp a big mouthful of wine, maybe a mistake but there's another glass coming. "Anna's a wonderful girl and she's my daughter and I love her to death. But she's hardly Britney Spears, or whoever."

"I didn't say she was. But there's more than one way to make a living these days." Fresh drinks appear and he takes a healthy sip. "We just heard a concert by a bunch of people who decided to do something creative. How many of their parents disapproved?"

The sushi arrives, arranged in pieces like a mosaic: deep scarlet and veined marble-white and pale orange. "We don't know anything about their parents," I remind him, "we were talking about Anna."

He holds up his hands in a stop-the-train-there's-one-more-passenger gesture. "Listen, when I was young you took the job you got and you were grateful. When *you* were young, you picked the job you wanted, and when you got it you stuck with it. Nowadays, kids don't even know what jobs will exist in ten years—with all these computers and whatever."

"Some jobs will always be necessary. Psychiatrists are at the top of that list."

"Yeah, up the rebels." We tap glasses and sip. But Hugh's not ready to let it go. "Seems to me that Anna's using her brain, thinking the only guaranteed jobs for human beings in ten or twenty years might be painting pictures or singing songs."

Oh dear. Far from having enlisted her grandfather's sympathy on this issue, I've created an unlikely ally for Anna. Change the subject, Gina—quick. "So, how's the single life?"

It works. He pauses in his sipping long enough to roll his eyes. "Listen. I could tell you stories."

Which, of course, is exactly what he does.

43. Three days later I'm standing in the Mapparium, tucked away inside the Christian Science library. A bewildering oxymoron, "Christian" hybridized with "science," but I'll save that digression for another day.

I'm craning my neck. The Mapparium is a giant stained-glass globe of the world, forty feet wide, circa 1935. A little metal walkway spans it as blue light filters through the oceans and other colors—rust-red, gray, yellow—leak in through all the nations of the world. Or at least the world as it existed back then, so you have Rhodesia and Ceylon and Belgian Congo and French Indo-China. No Israel, no Pakistan, no Bangladesh or Vietnam or Sri Lanka.

Russell stands beside me, drinking it all in. The prerecorded light show is over, so at the moment we've got the place to ourselves, and as usual I find the ambience oddly moving. Russell tells me, "This is great."

"I didn't know if you'd like it."

"You kidding? I love it."

"It's a map."

"Yeah I got that. And it's so—" he gestures at the globe, the world as it used to be. "It really makes you think."

This, I decide, is a good sign.

The air outside has a wet not-quite-spring chill to it, with knots of people striding against the damp as dark comes on. It'll be cold later. A bunch of taxis clog at a streetlight, and some black kids in baggy outfits jog along, their laughter popping in the air like firecrackers. We join the throng making its way toward the T station.

"This was nice," he says.

"I liked it too." Part of me notes with some surprise that this is, in fact, true.

"Maybe we could have another one sometime."

"One what?"

"Sorry?"

"Have another what sometime?"

"Another of these, uh—another date. That's what we're having, isn't it?"

Such a funny word, *date*. Such a teenagery ring to it. "Is it?"

"Well yeah. I mean I think so." His face darkens. "I thought so." His confusion is palpable. Unlike mine, which is just floating out there somewhere, formless, like radio waves.

Then the whole situation strikes me as absurd. I manage a laugh, or something reasonably similar. "Yes. I mean yes, a date is exactly what this is. I've been resisting the thought because it's so alien. I mean I haven't been on a proper hello-let's-get-to-know-each-other date for something like twenty years, so I haven't been able to—" What's that expression my daughter uses? "—*get my head around it* all day."

"Wow."

"Wow indeed. Wow to the nth degree."

He chuckles at this, as if I've just made a joke, but I'm perfectly serious. I tell him, "Which makes it even more surprising that not only have I enjoyed myself, but that you feel the same."

"Yeah, well." He's getting his composure back, and flashes a grin at the sidewalk. "I'll take that as confirmation. About having another one."

We stroll a little further when he says, "And maybe one after that."

"Don't push it," I tell him.

I'm still serious, but he just laughs again.

44. I don't pray. I don't talk to Walter's picture beside my bed. I don't stretch myself sobbing across his grave, or leaf weepily through the photo album—the gray one with the cracked binder on the bottom shelf, separate from the others. I don't talk to him in a dream, asking his forgiveness, or his blessing either. As I think I have established by now, I don't believe any of that crap. A Marxist

I am decidedly not, but truer words were rarely, if ever, spoken than the whole "opiate of the people" idea.

However.

None of the foregoing means that I don't wonder about Walter, about what he would think if he were here, about what he'd tell me if he could. I will, of course, never know. And the various speculations I can come up with are none too satisfying either.

Do what you want, Ranger.

I'll let you take a stand on that one.

The guy seems nice. What's the harm?

Of course, there were times when Walter himself fell a little short in the taking-action department. In fact, one could say that my husband had a habit of abdicating his throne at moments of decision. It was a problem sometimes. On the other hand, it's tough to imagine him actually accepting infidelity. That issue had never come up, in all our years together.

You want to see him, what's the harm? Go ahead, have a date. And screw him while you're at it, if that's what you want. That's what you did with all those other guys and it never bugged me a bit. I'll stay out of your way. I'll be in the workshop. Hell, I'll even make a fookin' fire in the fookin' fireplace so you two can get comfortable.

No. If he were here, Walter would *not* be so sanguine. Laid back he may have been, low-key almost to fault, but even he would've felt compelled to rise up, assert his authority. His ownership. Stamp his brand on the filly, or whatever it is they do in Westerns to tell the horses apart. Something I resist in theory, but would have found reassuring in actual fact. If he were here to do it. But he's not. And that's exactly the problem. Isn't it.

45. Sunday evening I make dinner for Russell. We could have gone out to some restaurant or other, but it's been so long since I've really cooked for someone else, and as he put it, "I see plenty of restaurants." So I bake a nice fish gratin with fresh sole, put together a Greek salad with olives the size of a big man's thumb. Steamed asparagus and brown rice. Blueberry tarts for dessert. Uncork a bottle of pinot noir to let it breathe and then there's nothing to do but wait for the guest to arrive.

And fret about my daughter. Despite my best attempts to maintain a healthy, dispassionate distance from Anna's irrationalities, I have conceded the obvious: she isn't doing well, and I need to do something about it. This pipe dream of running off to P-town for the summer does nothing to alleviate my concern. She needs to be home.

Maybe she needs to be home for more than just the summer. I'll admit this too: maybe I was, in fact, a trifle rash in sending her away to school. Maybe she should take a year to work at Starbucks and find herself, or whatever the equivalent is nowadays.

So I step onto the front porch, and I call her. And the phone is answered on the first ring, to my surprise, which quickly cools to bewilderment when a man's voice answers. "Yeah?"

"Who is this?"

The voice hesitates, then: "Who're *you*?"

"I paid for the phone you're holding. I'd like to speak to Anna, please."

"Ain't no Anna here. Wrong number."

"Hold on!" I take a breath. "This *is* her number, and you're holding her phone. I don't know who you are but you'd better explain yourself."

"The *fuck*?" comes the insightful response. "You threatening me, bitch? My buddy gave me this phone. I don't know where he got it, so fuck off, arright? There ain't no Anna here, and you keep harassing me, hey, I got your number too ... *Mom*."

The connection closes. I'm staring out the picture window as twilight descends over our street, sparrows nagging the lawn, oak trees leafing into their full glory.

I'm numb. I should be furious, or possibly terrified, or at the least very very anxious. Foul-mouthed boys have come into possession of my daughter's phone, so where the hell is my daughter?

A battered sedan pulls up to my driveway, hesitates, swings in. The engine shuts off and out gets Russell. Unfortunate timing, but here he is, taking forever to extricate himself from the car and saunter up the front walk. During this time I tell myself certain things:

1. There's an explanation for all this.

2. Most likely it's some sort of misunderstanding, even a prank.

3. Anna is *not* lying unconscious in an alley.

4. If I don't hear from her tonight, I'll take some sort of drastic action tomorrow.

5. Tomorrow will *not* be too late.

46. Russell has dressed for the occasion: purple turtleneck, khakis, shiny maroon loafers. I slip the phone into my pocket and tell him, "Don't you look dashing."

He eyeballs me, hand extended, and I take it. He says, "I can never tell when you're being sarcastic."

"Sorry, I'm a little preoccupied. But seriously, you look very nice."

"Thanks. Preoccupied with what?"

"Make yourself comfortable." Inside, I head back to the kitchen. "I'll be a minute."

"I love looking at other people's houses," he calls from the living room. "You learn so much about them."

"Mm," I say.

I'm chopping parsley when an eruption of noise bursts from the living room, drums and thudding bass lines and a spitfire, angry voice. My stomach sinks into my shoes: I hate rap music. "What's this?" I ask with forced lightness—he's a guest after all—when Russell appears in the doorway.

"Something I brought."

"How thoughtful."

He approaches the oven. "What's in here?"

"Don't open it. Fish."

He opens it. "Sweet." When he straightens up he's mischievous and twinkly. "I have this theory, when people tell you not to do something, it's because they really want you to do it."

"Great theory. Let's see how it works. Ah—*please* don't take off the kill-whitey music and replace it with some Monteverdi harpsichord concertos."

His look is owlish. "Are you having a bad day, Regina?"

"You could say that."

"Seriously, I had no intention of looking into the oven until you told me not to. And let me say, it's looking great, whatever it is."

"Let's sit down."

"You don't like the theory?"

"It's s lovely theory, Dr. Jung. The porch is nice this time of day." Plus, the hump-yo-ho music—Walter's term—will be harder to hear if we're outside.

> *Cruisin' through the hoods of this po-lice state*
> *People lookin' at each other full of nothin' but hate . . .*

I wonder where the hell my daughter's gotten herself to.

The swing is a relic of Walter's carpentry, six feet wide, hung on what I've always imagined were anchor chains. "Talk about solid. Your husband made this?"

"Yes he did."

"Sure built stuff to last."

I try not to choke on my drink. There are so many snotty responses to this, I don't know which one to pick. "Mm."

He rubs the side of his nose with his thumb. "You've lived in this house a while?"

"Since I finished my residency," I tell him. "Ten years, more or less."

"I've never been in one place more than maybe three years. My family moved around a lot while I was growing up. California mostly."

"I guess the Parks had less imagination. Supposedly I have ancestors who came over on the Mayflower, but we never made it out of New England."

"That's amazing."

"In more ways than one. Anyway, so claims my cousin Alice, the genealogy expert. How she can trace that far back I don't know, and Park is a pretty common name. But she claims it's true." Of course, cousin Alice is also mad as a hatter, in and out of institutions since the '70s and convinced that one day the mothership will descend from the stars to take us all to God, so she may not be the most reliable source of information in the world.

Russell sips his Scotch. "Must be good to feel so tied to a place, like you've really got history here."

I stand up. "I need to check something."

Upstairs I find the number under a pile of papers in my desk. The RA of Anna's dorm is named Heather, which does not sound promising. She answers on the third ring.

Heather: Yeah?

Me: Good evening. My name is Dr. Regina Moss, I'm the mother of Anna Moss.

Heather: Okay.

Me: Anna lives in your dorm, in room, ah—

Heather: I know who Anna is. Her room's right over mine.

Me: Yes, wonderful. Can you tell me if she's doing all right?

Heather: Sure.

Me: She is?

Heather: I mean, you know . . . Far as I know, she's fine. You know. Nobody's like complained about her or anything.

I take a breath and struggle with Heather. Why oh why do people insist on naming their daughters after plants? Heather Daisy Iris Holly Rose. Lovely to look at, not very smart. Well now, maybe that's the answer right there.

Me: I'm not concerned about complaints. I called her this evening and her cell phone was answered by a man who apparently didn't know who she was, much less where. Or for that matter how he came to have her phone.

Heather: Have you tried e-mailing her?

Me: No I haven't. I would like to talk to her in person. Could you please go knock on her door and ask her to talk to me? I'll hold.

Heather: Okay . . . Look, I'll go up and ask. But I won't keep the phone on. I'm like almost out of minutes. I'll call you back, okay?

Me: Thank you. And please, even if she's not there, call me anyway so I know.

Heather: Right.

Downstairs, Russell still sits on the porch swing, smiling as an excited Mrs. Flynn regales him with details of her Egypt trip. He looks genuinely interested, but may just be a good actor.

"Well, I'll leave you two young people now," she says upon my emergence, and trundles off.

When she's gone I say, "You're very polite."

"Quite the character," he shrugs. "She was moseying by, and swerved right on over when she spotted me."

"I don't have much company. And I think the music threw her."

"We can turn it down if you like."

"There's an idea."

When he comes back I tell him, "We've been neighbors a long time. I know her grandchildren, she knows my daughter." I don't bother explaining that she just about kept Anna and me alive for the year after Walter died and I was too much of a wreck to think of minor distractions like food, laundry detergent, car inspections.

Russell nods, as if he understands anyway. "Neighbors like that are a rare breed."

I rattle the ice in my glass. My cell hasn't rung. How long does it take to go upstairs and knock on a door?

Across the street Mrs. Flynn's face appears in her picture window, gazing quizzically for a moment before disappearing again. I'm reminded of a TV show I saw once, about prairie dogs.

47. We're eating. The food is delicious, I think, but I barely notice. Heather has not yet returned my call. What's she doing, plotting a conspiracy or something? A cover-up? Who knows what college students get up to these days. Then again, maybe she just forgot. She is a Heather, after all.

Somehow we've gotten onto genealogy. "Check it out," he says, "I happen to share precisely the same ethnic mix that the United States itself will have by the year 2030."

He seems so pleased by this that I almost feel bad at not understanding the significance. I start for the asparagus but change course and go for another gulp of wine. "Meaning?"

"Meaning," he leans back, "if you take my sixteen great-grandparents, I'm six parts white, three parts Latino, two parts black, one part Japanese, one part Indian—from India I mean—one part Arab, and one part Navajo." He leans back, looking faintly smug. "Not to brag, but I am, *literally*, the future of this country."

"Meaning people like me are . . . ?"

"No offense, but, the past."

I find this conversation annoying, for reasons that elude me at the moment, and anyway the pinot isn't helping me think. I am, however, clear-headed enough to ask, "Those people you mentioned, there are only fifteen of them. Who's the sixteenth?"

He grins wider. "That's good, Regina. Most people miss that. Number sixteen is my father's great-grandfather. He didn't stick around very long, either he died or ran off, and nobody knows the first damn thing about him."

"Mystery man."

"Exactly. He might've turned Mormon for all anybody knows and gone to Utah with a dozen wives. Or maybe he was a Sioux who hung around the trading post, or a Jewish bootmaker who went out west in '49 to try his luck." He pushes back his plate. "I used to be sort of ashamed of him, about not knowing who he was? But I've grown fond of the guy."

"The black sheep."

"Exactly. In a family full of them. But I used to, I don't know." He pours himself more wine and tops off my glass, emptying the bottle. "I was so happy to know all the other pieces of the puzzle that made up Russell Blanco, I used to resent him for spoiling it. I'm over it now."

My cell phone rings. "I'm sorry, I have to take this." I go into the kitchen, leaving him at the table with his ancestors.

Heather: Um, she's not here actually.

Me: Excuse me?

Heather: She's not here. Nobody here has seen her for at least a few days.

Me: I see.

I sit on a chair to keep from toppling over.

Heather: I mean it's probably no big deal. She's probably at the library or something. Or with her boyfriend.

Me: She has a boyfriend?

Heather: I don't know. Do you?

Me: No.

Heather: She was kind of a loner at first, but she'd been seeing more people lately. Since like, Christmas break.

I say nothing.

Heather: I'm not trying to worry you or anything? I'm just saying—at first she was sort of having a hard time. It's not that unusual.

Me: Yes, I understand. But then she made a lot of friends.

Heather: Yeah.

Me: And now she's disappeared.

Heather: Well that's kind of, I mean—

Me: Nobody there knows where she is.

Heather: Not right this second. I think you should send her an e-mail.

(*Pause.*)

Heather: Hello? Are you still there?

Me: Oh yes, I'm here all right.

Russell is where I left him at the table. Maybe he squints at me quizzically, but my head is whirling and I don't pay proper attention. "Coffee?"

"Sure."

"I'll bring it. Let's move into the living room."

I'll give him coffee and send him on his way. I return to the kitchen and hear him call, "Hey, are these photo albums?"

Well doesn't *this* bring me up short. But he's just fingering the two blue ones on the top of the living room bookshelf. "Have a look. They're mostly of me and Anna, some of my husband. Just, ah—leave the gray one alone." The gray album, older, cracked along the edges, sits alone on the bottom shelf, half-buried under a stack of magazines.

His eyes drop down. "Oh—right."

I don't tell him anything more. I don't say: *The things in there are personal, there are things I don't want you to know.* Maybe I should say this, but I don't. It doesn't seem necessary. But maybe I should have remembered the fish gratin baking in the oven, and Dr. Russell's cute theory.

48. In the bathroom I splash water on my face. I need to get rid of my guest. *Hate to be rude, but my daughter's vanished and I really ought to look into it.* I wonder what's happened. I try not to worry, with limited success. She's fine. She's tired, napping at the library. She's stoned on someone's living room couch. She's going to P-town with her stoner friends. None of whom, apparently, live in her dorm, where nobody has seen her. She lost her cell phone and didn't notice. I wonder what else she's lost without noticing.

I stare at myself in the bathroom mirror. My cheeks are flushed and the bags under my eyes are minimal. It's a shame I have to send Russell away, but I do, because I need to spend the night putting things in order before I leave. Anna's college is a five-hour drive; if I leave at sunrise, I can be there by lunchtime.

Too bad. It would have been pleasant to spend the night with Russell Blanco, but family first. I exit the bathroom and pour us coffee and walk back into the living room. Wrap this up in twenty minutes and au revoir. And then throw some things in a suitcase. And then. There's Toby.

Russell smiles up at me from the floor, his smooth brown face and half-lidded eyes and purple turtleneck against the fawn carpet. In his hands he holds a photo album, the old gray one with the cracks along the edges, and my stomach twists. (It's Toby.) Old pictures, me and Walter, Anna as a little girl. She was so tiny. Mom and Dad before Dad got sick. (Toby.) "Time for a tour," he grins. "Who are all these people?"

49. There is a letter upstairs. In my desk drawer, buried under some other papers, birth and death certificates, police reports, photos. A yellow envelope, taped shut across the back, sealed like a tomb.

50. I don't trust myself to speak but a little gurgle slips past my lips anyway, as if my social-skills autopilot is trying to stifle the words that the rest of me is fighting to blurt. A tremor of panic darts up my back, the feeling of missing the last step coming downstairs in the dark and those countless nanoseconds of flailing at emptiness. Falling halfway and then halfway through that and then halfway through what's left and then halfway again and knowing the bottom will never come no matter how long the falling lasts.

"Hey Gina." Russell's smile tightens, then slips off. "You all right?"

(Toby.)

I don't answer. Of course I'm not all right. His face slides away, blurry, off-screen, and it's suddenly impossible to catch my breath. I want to tell him and maybe I do to shut the album, put it back, shove it back where it belongs. It was buried there for a reason, don't you think I have reasons for not digging it all up again? You stupid child. Stupid ignorant child. Stupid *fucking* child. Unlike some people I have reasons, unlike some things that just happen because of nothing at all except that a day can't simply go by without something filling it and there are only so many days of sunshine and puffy clouds and birds chirping in the trees like the ones Toby would draw happy children and birthday parties and neighbor-hood kids in pointy hats. Birthday cakes with candles. Rainbows.

Toby drew pictures and Walter would tape them on the fridge door like any good househusband. They were inseparable the way only a father and son can be, skipper and first mate, hiking and chopping wood and horsing around in the yard, snowball fights and fishing trips and birdhouses and sometimes just pitching a tent out back under the white birch, cooking over the camp stove that stank of butane and I don't know, maybe sharing a beer or two. Roughhousing, building the treehouse, being boys together. Watching stupid movies with zombies and barbarians. Walter liked his beer, partial to Belgian ales and German pilsners and by that time Toby was what, fifteen. Not a baby anymore not in the sense of a little boy but not grown up either, not yet not fully. A person understood better by his father than by me or so I thought. That's what I thought. There were voices out back, muddled, Walter calling up to Toby and then quiet for a time and I thought things were okay and then the urgent voices, louder now. Then the yelp, panicked, abbreviated. It punched a hole in the night and knocked the spoon from my hand where I sat at the kitchen table and my first thought was *Don't hit him!* and then it ended, smack, stopped with a dead thump that sounds like nothing else on earth and the silence afterward was worse than the shout had been. Then an-other flurry, no shouting this time but maybe a quiet moan like wind through the eaves mixed in with the rustling of branches giv-ing way and a strange flurry of sound like a flock of birds beating against the sky and then a second thud against the night like a slap at the back of my head and by then I knew, acid was swelling in my throat as I ran back across the lawn.

Moonlight washing down silvery on everything, gray light like something dead or crippled and Walter lying crumpled in a pile with his head twisted around and his arms pinned beneath and another pile underneath him please no, please don't, it isn't Toby, Toby going cold already his blood sprayed across the dead leaves and his legs trapped awkwardly by Walter's barrel chest and I'm a doctor and *so fucking what*, the crazy unhappy son of a bitch.

He was dead, they were both dead. A keening in my ears, a thin-pitched cat-shriek that ripped through all the dead trees like a siren, echoed from the branches as if the trees themselves were wailing along with me.

An abortion fifteen years late is what I got from Walter. He paid me back for everything I never let him do, every resentment every petty bitterness every stored-up hurt and smear of squashed ego. I thought I was pretty smart but he got the last word all right. Paid all that bitterness back with interest: before dropping forty feet from the treehouse he made sure that Toby my Toby my baby went out first.

Two

HYSTERIA

FABIAN: Why, we shall make him mad indeed.
MARIA: The house will be the quieter.

—*Twelfth Night*, III, iv

1. So.

A person might think: *What else you got, doctor?*

But that person would be wrong. There is no more. No skeletons in the closet, bodies under the basement floorboards. Or hidden treasures for that matter, pots of gold, winning lotto tickets. Just Toby.

2. There is the chronology to consider. Everything I said about my pregnancy with Anna was true. I really was in med school when it happened, et cetera. Except that Walter and I had already had a son, five years earlier, during my freshman year at BU. I dropped out then, stayed weeping with my parents while Walter commuted to class and spent long evenings looking terrified and sheepish.

We were such children.

I lost a year of school having the baby, and raising him those first few months. I'd already figured my dreams were gone, evaporated forever; had settled in for a long, withered life when my mother said: "We'll take care of the child. You get yourself to class." She was not the kind of woman who brooked an argument or relished one, then as now.

Marrying Walter was not a priority for me, but it was for him, and more so for his parents. Hugh and Stella expected their son to make an honest woman of me and so on. Welcome to Boston. So that's me at nineteen, married with a baby, repeating my first year of undergrad. Walter, a year ahead of me, dropped out to stay home with Toby, then we started together again as sophomores. The grandparents chipped in over the years as we finished our degrees and went on to Tufts—me for med school, him for comp lit— where I managed to catch the baby virus once again. A girl this time. We named her Anna.

3. Right now I'm driving too fast because I got a late start this morning, having stayed up half the night juggling my calendar, leaving voicemails, pushing my appointments back. This morning I had to get word to my receptionist Jade, plus Muffin at BMHA and Rod Menzies at ACC. All this took longer than it should have, no surprise. All the while Anna has been a shadowy presence in the background, impossible to get a fix on, just as impossible to ignore. Much as in real life.

I'm driving too fast because something nameless and intuitive is telling me that my daughter is in trouble. And yes I fully recognize the absurdity of that statement, how ridiculous it makes me sound. At the moment, I don't care.

The highway north is crowded but not as bad as the phalanx of traffic rumbling south toward the city. Sunrise flares across rows of windshields as orderly as ranks of armored Romans. I wonder whether the Romans were partial to mental illness—they had Caligula after all—and what they did about it. Ditto the Greeks and Spartans and Persians and so on. I know all about the Middle Ages and the Victorians (summary: things were bad), but the further back I go, the less I know.

These are not new thoughts.

I can just about imagine Anna's perplexed reaction to such meditations: "God, Mom, so what? Maybe they stuffed them into barrels and floated them down the river. Or maybe they baked them pies all day. Does it matter?"

Come to think of it, that sounds more like Toby than Anna. Anna would say—what, exactly?

I grip the steering wheel a little tighter, swerve to pass a tiny woman piloting an enormous SUV. It occurs to me that I don't know what Anna would say. In fact I can barely imagine the sound of her voice. How strange.

4. Toby possessed an uncanny stillness, an ability to be in a room for minutes at a time before I even realized he was there. He could watch something with an intensity I usually associate with cats. I remember his preference for blue shirts over red and purple over blue, and the way he would eat: a bite of burger, then a french fry, then a green bean, then a swallow of milk, then repeat the process, until it was all gone. Somehow he managed to finish everything at the same time.

I'm making him sound disturbed. He wasn't disturbed, he just had his own way of ordering the world and securing his place in it, as we all do with our routines and rituals and patterns of organization. I don't much care for red blouses myself, and I tend to eat my food one item at a time.

Physically he took after Walter: slightly pudgy, sanded smooth at the corners. But skinny arms and slightly bandy legs. A big baby who slept well and rarely fussed. Mentally he was more like me. He didn't like noise and didn't make it, wasn't fond of bluster, could spend hours at a time with only himself for company. And birds. Animals of any sort really, but he especially loved birds. This he got from his father, a bird enthusiast himself. By age five Toby had established himself as feeder of the birds, sprinkling handfuls of seed along the windowsills so he could watch them squabble and feast. At ten, he'd learned to use a saw and hammer well enough to knock together a collective of rudimentary birdhouses. An off-kilter birdbath made lovingly but unevenly of hand-molded concrete took pride of place on our patio for years. This meant of course that our patio was coated in a more-or-less permanent layer of bird shit all summer long, but so be it. As Walter liked to say, "Little bird shit never killed anyone, Ranger."

To which I usually nodded and said, "I believe you're right." And he'd smile at me, apple-cheeked beneath his red-brown beard, and we'd have one of those moments of connection and appreciation. Then he'd go back to whatever it was he was doing that day, varnishing a bookshelf or taking Anna to her riding lesson or making corn chowder.

In college Walter was sweet and bumbling, prone to overstatement and a residual childhood stutter. The Walter I slept with was eager and nervous and solicitous and—obviously—unschooled in the ways of birth control. The Walter who stayed home with Toby and, later, Anna, was devoted and soft-spoken, expanding round the gut, bearded like a suburban, new-age Grizzly Adams. His buddies were leftover high school friends who took him drinking and ribbed him for being a good hausfrau. He'd come home a little shaky those nights, stumbling over the boots in the foyer, cursing his way up the stairs, but was still the Walter who stuck his head in the kids' bedrooms, checked they were sleeping, whispered goodnight before collapsing across my ankles.

And the Walter who was out back with Toby that night? The quiet loving one, or the one who blustered and shouted, who loved a drama, a big show with a loud bang? For Walter was a real boy that way; although he hated guns, his heart was stirred by cars and bowling and fireworks, any source of loud and surprising noise. Movies with dragons, armies, explosions, sudden squalls of orchestrated shock. When those diversions grew tiresome, which didn't take long, I sighed and reminded myself of his good points.

He was not a man who carried a lot of anger with him. So far as I knew. But how much do we ever really know? There was some tension that night at the dinner table. Nothing serious, I didn't think. At least, nothing particularly new. A suggestion that he'd been hitting the bottle a little heavily. A request that he take as much interest in Toby's academic performance as in his hobbies, which happened also to be Walter's hobbies: fly fishing and bird-watching, movies like *Prom Night Zombie* and books with titles like *How to Survive in the Woods*.

I had received a phone call that afternoon from the math teacher, a Mrs. Ouellette, who had some well-intentioned but poorly-articulated concerns about Toby's behavior in class.

This was unusual. "He's misbehaving?"

"He's not making trouble exactly," Mrs. Ouellete explained. I had never met her but I imagined a kindly elderly woman, a career teacher with dyed hair and bifocals. "It's more like he's . . . tuning out. In a world of his own, sometimes."

I was twenty seconds away from my next patient. I asked her to call Toby's father and explain it in more detail.

She inhaled softly. "Well, I—I think you should know this, but—I have spoken with your husband. Several times in fact. He seems to think it's normal, or else that it will pass. I'm not sure what he thinks actually."

I managed to stay calm. "I see." I had received such calls before, from the occasional teacher who admitted that Mr. Moss wasn't terribly concerned. "I'll look into it."

That evening over dinner I suggested to Walter that phone calls from school rated highly enough to merit some response, at least a conversation with me if not a visit to the principal or a consultation with the teacher concerned.

"Shit, Ranger, you're the brains of this outfit," he said. "You concerned about the school, give 'em a call."

I pushed my plate away and bit back my exasperation. "I'm at *work* all day. You need to call the school, and you need to talk to the teachers, and you need to ask what they recommend."

He didn't yell, or get gruff and belligerent. A lot of men would. He looked like the type, but it wasn't his style. His shoulders drooped a little, sitting across from me at the kitchen table. Quilted flannel shirt, red and black checks. I knew he wore no socks despite the cold. *Toenails like tree roots*, I remember thinking. But affectionately. He knew that, didn't he? I was demonstrative enough, wasn't I?

His eyes didn't meet mine, but wandered away somewhere to the edge of the table. "All right then. I'll take care of it Monday." This was Friday. "I'll call the school when you're at *work*. He's outside right now?"

"As far as I know."

"In the treehouse?"

"That would be my guess."

Tuning out, those were Mrs. Ouellette's words. I knew what she meant. Like my son was going away somewhere we couldn't follow. I couldn't shake the fear that one day he wouldn't come back. But that was foolish. We all got moody sometimes. And needed time to ourselves, whether or not we actually got it.

Dinner residue littered the dining table. Toby had skipped the meal again, something he'd started doing lately. He'd taken to spending every free moment alone, either up in his room or in the treehouse. The treehouse had been a project for the boys a couple years ago, a summertime diversion that now felt like a mistake. Attempts to interest him in a movie, a ball game, a pizza, were rebuffed with eyes that were by turns stony, dreamy and distant.

Outside, a cold November night. Walter ran his fingers through his beard, a habit when he was unsettled. Lately a few white shoots had grown in among the russet brown.

He stood up. "I think I'll go check on him."

For a reason I couldn't exactly name, I thought this was the wrong thing to do. "Leave him," I said, but softly.

"Why?"

"I can't explain." This was typical: having been stung by an accusation of inattentiveness, Walter would now make up for it with none-too-subtle bluster. But the moment for confrontation was wrong, and I was inclined to give Toby room. "Let him be."

"He's been weird lately," was Walter's clinical assessment, delivered Boston-style: *wee-yud*. "Fookin' spooky if you ask me."

Walter adopted jokey Irishisms when cursing: everything was *fookin'* and *Jaysus* and *shite*. I said, "That's why we should leave him."

Walter stood there, sipping his beer. I knew he was unsure: when he was certain about something, he guzzled. Sipping beer was his equivalent of fingering the rosary or casting the I Ching. Finally he said, "I'll talk to him. I don't want him falling out of the damn treehouse because he's too spacey to know where he is."

He set down the beer and stepped past me, out the kitchen door into the dark in back of the house. I never saw my husband alive after that. Or my son.

5. I cross the line into Vermont. The Green Mountain State, I am informed by the signs along the highway. The Socialist Republic of, according to certain New Hampshire talk radio hosts that I do not make a habit of listening to.

I look at my watch. I'm nearly halfway there. I wonder what I'll do if I don't find her in her dorm. My plans, to put it generously, are loose. Picking Heather's brain seems a thankless task but one never knows. Or I could ask at the registrar's office for Anna's schedule, try to intercept her at class. Going to the police station to file a missing-person report seems a trifle premature.

Sure it does, Ranger, says Walter's voice in my head. *That's why you're driving north at 70 mph—because you don't want to do anything premature.*

God, I wish he were here right now.

6. There was a service, a double funeral in a leafy green cemetery up in Lowell. Walter's parents had bought a couple plots, for themselves. "Or so we thought," as Hugh put it. Instead they were donated to Walter and Toby. Two plots for the two of them. Nobody talked about where I would go.

The funeral was a standard-issue affair. Bouquets of bright flowers, awkward guests, Father Somebody. Hugh took care of it all, and good thing too. I was numb. I stood silent throughout the funeral, my hand clasped on Anna's shoulder. When it was over I sent her home with my parents, drove myself to Stonebury, pulled on my sneakers and went running.

For a year I self-medicated, washing down Acceptorals and grogging through the day like some ghoul, a zombie from one of the boys' movies. It was unconscionable but I had to get through the day, get Anna to sixth grade—whimpering and spooked, poor thing—and get myself to work. Some people retreat from the world after a death, crying for seven years. Isn't that in a Shakespeare play somewhere? Not me. I immersed myself in activity, zombie or not, designed treatment plans and interviewed patients and did crisis intakes at Boston General. The irony was not lost on me as I jotted notes in patient charts. *31 y.o. white female reports severe depression and thoughts of self-harm. Recommend Happivan 5 mg TID—or more, maybe as much as her Blisstoril-sucking shrink is taking just now to keep from going off her rocker.* More than once, I was tempted to write exactly that.

Work wasn't my only distraction—I used Anna too. Maybe we used each other. Isn't that what families do? At ten, she was old enough to be traumatized by the emergency vehicles and the crazed weeping grandparents, but I flatter myself that I did all right by her in those days. We went out a lot, to the beach, the park, to every birthday party every one of her friends was giving. Threw a few of our own too, not my preferred activity for a Sunday afternoon but there it is. There were those godawful Disney movies and amusement parks and the children's museum on weekends, and quiet evenings after dinner when I wasn't on call. And of course my parents, and Walter's. Dad wasn't sick yet and Anna adored him. Hugh's wife Stella was still alive too, though fading already.

So we got through it. Of course we did. One always does, that's the wonder of it. There are people out there, in Calcutta and Bogota and the West Bank, who've lived with things this bad their whole lives. So maybe it's not such a wonder. Somehow we managed that first awful Christmas with the grandparents—Hugh and Stella in the morning, with elaborate presents and much faux cheer, then Mom and Dad in the afternoon, with an elaborate dinner and much faux cheer—and then a school play that spring and a summer trip up to Trish's rustic cabin on the water, followed in September by Stella's untimely death. But no ambulances this time, thank God, just a quiet hospital room and a bewildered goodbye. Then Anna was in sixth grade and the cycle repeated—Halloween and Thanksgiving and Christmas, school play, spring break—then seventh grade and eighth and she was getting self-conscious around boys and wanting to choose her own clothes and fiddle with make-up. The house still felt empty and the sound of sirens at night made me twitchy, but somehow time kept on going wherever it goes. I'd long since dropped the Blisstoril, and my heart didn't stop beating. There was the occasional stab of despair, sure: sudden and unexpected and wrenching and sharp. But that was to be expected. It was nothing that would kill me.

7. This morning, when I went downstairs at 5 a.m., I found the note that Russell had left on the kitchen table. He must have put it there before he left last night, before I sent him away and stormed up the stairs. This was after I had passed through the worst of whatever it was I went through—I can think of no better word than *fit*, which sounds so quaintly nineteenth-century, like *grippe* or *ague*.

The note was just a scrap of paper, with four words scrawled on it: *I'll be in touch*. But I know he won't. He has seen a side of me that I keep safely tucked away from people, a side that would frighten anyone with any sense. And since he seems to be a young man with plenty of sense, I know with certainty that I won't be seeing him again. Maybe later this will sadden me; right now all I feel is tired. And also anxious about my daughter—impatient to get where I'm driving and find out what hell is going on with her.

8. The college is typical small-town liberal-arts New England: rows of whitewashed A-frames, some bigger granite buildings for admin and classrooms, less ivy than might be expected. An unassuming cluster of bunker-like brick dorms squats within walking distance of the downtown's modest main street.

I find a parking lot, find the registrar's office, find someone who will tell me something. Then I hunt around for the dorm and manage to locate Heather, the RA with whom I spoke last night. She's surprisingly solid, a big-boned five foot ten with russet curls and a thick bloom of freckles across her cheeks.

When I introduce myself, she nods like she's not surprised to see me. "Right, well, I don't think she came in last night but maybe she did? Let's check."

When we knock on her door, we hear a muffled "Just a minute," then the doorknob rattles and there she is, looking bedraggled and worn out—but physically present, in the flesh. "Yeah—*Mom*? Jesus Christ, did somebody fucking *die*?"

I bite my tongue. Heather glances at us both, says, "Okay, I guess this is taken care of," and vanishes before I can shout *No, this isn't taken care of at all*.

I scan the room. It's cramped of course, it's a dorm. The light is dingy and yellow. The room is also filthy, not just in the expected ways—with heaps of moldy clothes and books spilling everywhere—actually I don't see a lot of books, or even notebooks—but with unexpected slovenliness: food wrappers, piles of crumbs, pizza crusts in the corners, empty beer and wine bottles. Candle stubs have dripped wax everywhere. Cracked ceramic ashtrays overflow with little Everests of butts and ashes—geez Louise, has she started smoking now?

The last thing my eye falls upon is my daughter, sitting on her unmade bed in a filthy T-shirt and nothing else. Her toenails are lime green beneath a sheen of grime, her hair's a mess and gray bags have settled under her eyes. At first glance, she looks older than I do.

"Mom?" she croaks finally. "Are you going to say something, or is this just one of your little episodes?"

I wince. It's difficult to see her like this, her skin gone pasty, hair a useless tangle. I cast about for words and settle on the truth. "I was worried about you."

She exhales sharply through her nose—a laugh, or a snort? "I'm doing just fine."

Besides the bed, the only furniture is a small built-in desk and chair, which I sit on now. "I don't think so. Why don't you tell me what's going on?"

She leans back against a muddle of pillows. "What're you talking about now?"

"I'm talking about losing your phone, and nobody knowing where you are for days at a time. And these vague plans to go to the Cape." I take a breath. I've always been a good student. "I went to the registrar's office. You've withdrawn from half your classes and you're on the verge of being kicked out of another one for poor attendance." The only one she's managing to hang on to convincingly is art history, and she's on thin ice with freshman comp. "*That's* what I'm talking about."

She stares at me with flat fish eyes until she manages to croak out, "Jesus, I don't believe this."

To which there's really not much to say, except maybe: sometimes there's an advantage to doing your homework.

9. An hour later I'm sipping cappuccino at a noisy café near the school. A sign tacked to the wall advertises "House—Dubstep—

Breakbeats—Dancehall" and I have not the slightest idea what this means.

Anna asked me to wait here while she made herself presentable. I agreed readily, and prepared for round two of our conversation.

Round one had gone like this:

Me: I think you should come home.

Anna: No thanks.

Me: You can re-enroll in the fall. Take the time to . . .

Anna: To what?

Me: To pull yourself together.

Anna: It's not like I'm falling apart.

There were a variety of responses to this, none of which seemed especially constructive. When she suggested meeting an hour later at the café, I'll admit to a certain relief.

The cappuccino finishes and I order another. Allow myself a half packet of sugar, a small indulgence. Stir for several minutes, longer than I need really, then sip it slowly till it's gone. Frown and check my watch: she's thirty minutes late.

My cell rings, Heather's number but Anna's voice. "I think you should just go," she says by way of greeting.

"I think you should come home."

"No."

"And stay the summer."

She says nothing but sighs again, mightily, through the cell and into my ear.

I deliver the speech I've been rehearsing for forty minutes. "Here's what I will do. I'll continue paying tuition as long as you stay in those two classes. But if you drop them, or get dropped for not attending, that's it. You'll come home and we'll figure out the next step, but this particular gravy train will be over and done."

"*Jesus*, Mom."

"Get a new cell phone, too. And call me with the number."

"Have a nice fucking day to you too."

She hangs up, sounding furious. Maybe she is, I don't know. What I do know, for certain, is that I am *seething*.

10. On Monday I see Andrew, my twenty-two-year-old with Tourette's. "I hear you're having trouble at work," I tell him. This is what Muffin told me Friday, over the phone. Andrew works at a greenhouse/landscaping program that hires MI in exchange for state funding. "Something about your supervisor?"

"Bitch."

Muffin or the supervisor? "And the supervisor's name is . . . ?"

"Hank."

"I see." Score another one for Tourette's.

"He's going out with Jane. All the boys want to fuck her but I don't. I want to fuck Alanna."

I digest this. "And Alanna is . . ."

"Accounting. Black girl, no tits. Nice ass though. Mike fucks her I think, he's in charge of work crews. He has a truck, so, you know."

"Mike's a nice guy then?"

"Mike's a fucking *dick*."

"Right." I rub the itchy spot behind my ear, wondering what life would be like if we *all* had bad cases of coprolalia, if we all said what we were thinking, all the time. Would life be any better, for all that honesty bouncing around? More likely, a whole lot worse. "Have you spoken to anyone about this?"

"Course not, I ain't stupid." I see his face struggle to keep the words inside, where they belong, tucked beneath his tongue and teeth. He loses. "Bitch thinks I'm a fucking *re*tard or something." A *ree-tahd*. A *fahk*in' ree-tahd, no less.

The thing about Andrew, aka Ak-Ak, aka Andy the Kid, is that he can be very sweet. The next time he sees me he'll be weepy and sniffling like a little child, moaning about how much he misses me when I'm not around and how he wants me to visit him as his *friend*, not just his *doctor*. And he'll mean it, just like he means it when he calls me a fucking stupid cunt who should mind my own business. With Andrew, I know where I stand. It may not always be comfortable, but I can count on its being true. And what a relief that is, in a way—me knowing he's not lying, and him knowing he doesn't have to.

11. Mr. Hayes looks at me, smiling helplessly. I have never seen a smile with so little joy in it. "The thing is," he says, "if only knew for sure that Benny wasn't coming home, we could, we could . . ."

"Let it go," his rabbity wife suggests.

"Exactly," he sighs, shifting his bulk in his chair. "But the way it is now, we just." He shakes his head. "We just, we replay it. It's like a song you can't get out of your head."

"How long do you think you'll need to wait," I ask them gently, "before deciding that he's not coming home?"

They shift in their chairs, looking bewildered. He looks at her but she stares at the floor between her feet. "If only we'd paid a little more attention," she offers. "Then things might've been different."

"That's a common reaction," I tell her. "But I'm sure you realize that whatever Benjamin did, it was outside your control."

She nods hopelessly. "Obviously. But we can't help thinking that way. Even if it doesn't do any good."

"But knowing *that* doesn't do any good, either," says Mr. Hayes.

"Exactly."

"I can see that," I say.

"You can't just throw a switch," she says.

"Of course not."

"Be easier if we could." He smiles without mirth.

"It's like we're paralyzed."

"That's it."

"I understand."

We all sit there. After a time I ask them about their medication.

12. Dad's asleep in the other room.

"Something on your mind?" Mom asks. She's always had that radar. She drinks from a mug that says *#1 Grandma*, a long-ago gift from Anna. My own mug says *You Don't Have to be Crazy to Work Here . . . But It Helps!* I have no idea where this artifact came from.

"It's nothing." I fiddle with my mug handle. "Lot of work these days."

This is such a lame excuse that I feel crummy even offering it up, but my mother lets it go. Maybe she's relieved at not being made a confidante for her grown daughter's traumas. Or maybe she's just given up on ever being brought into the loop.

Well, doesn't that make me feel lousy. So just when I'm about to say, "Actually there's something spooky going on with Anna," she stands abruptly and starts washing her cup in the sink. Her back is to me and the water's gushing, with *#1 Grandma* getting a good thrashing under the tap, and that's just too much of a barrier for me to hurdle myself over.

13. "So how are you doing these days?"

Beth Ann Kim shrugs. "Fine, I guess."

"Feeling any better?"

"Hm—not that I notice, especially."

"Feeling any worse?"

She almost smiles. "No."

"Well then. How about that therapy, you've had, what, five or six sessions now. How's it going for you?"

She considers. "Well, it's something to do, isn't it?" Her smile is brittle. I write her another prescription.

14. I get a call from Anna on her new phone. Our pauses are strained.

Me: Are you getting to class?

Ana: I haven't missed once, since you were here.

Me: That's great.

Anna: Glad you think so. I've got finals in two weeks, so.

(*Pause.*)

Anna: What about you? Called anyone about the tree yet?

Me: The—not yet, no. Maybe I'll do that this week.

(*Pause.*)

Anna: Yeah Mom. Maybe you will.

(*Long pause.*)

15. Overnight at ACC. Becky talks awhile on the phone and hangs up. "Russell," she says to me. "Calling in sick. *Again*."

I make a vague *mm* sound and scan the ward. "Edna's discharged?"

"She'll be back."

Edna's sweet, elderly and depressed. "Probably. Have we got enough staff?"

"Barely."

ACC is sleepy and has been for a couple weeks now. Just as well. Russell has been missing his shifts, and I haven't seen him since— *that* night.

16. Next weekend, Dad's in an in-between phase. No pancakes but no drool either, he makes a couple cracks and Mom and I laugh like he's Groucho reincarnate. We watch *Sink the Bismarck* and Mom asks, "Any excitement lately?" and I shake my head and she looks disappointed and I pretend not to notice.

Later Mrs. Flynn stops by my house with a casserole and we discuss the weather for twenty minutes. No kidding, twenty whole minutes. There shouldn't be that much to say about it, should there? It's either hot or cold, wet or dry. But no, once we got going on the unseasonable cold snap, the April snow that melted the same day, past snows in past years, moving to the blizzard of '78 when her pipes froze, then various floods, hurricanes, droughts, forecasts for the summer, remembrances of last year, global warming, the melting ice caps—well, just look at the time. Twenty minutes fled, like prisoners off a chain gang. Never to be seen again.

But with Mrs. Flynn out the door, it's just me and the shepherd's pie, alone in my sweet little house that keeps having people *leave* it.

17. A week slips by, stealthy like a secret agent. Still no Russell at ACC. Becky tells me he's quit the unit. "He phoned in while you were asleep," she explains, one morning after I've done an overnight.

Still groggy, still stupid, I ask her, "Did he ask for me?"

"No." She gives me a piercing, pierced Becky look. "Why?"

"Nothing," I mumble. "Is there coffee?"

Sitting there with the styrofoam cup in my hand, I wonder what to do with this information. I've been thinking about Russell Blanco quite a lot these past few weeks, in a casual sort of way, or a casually helpless one. The last time we saw each other, things fell apart rather dramatically, and if he's smart, he ran away from all that and didn't stop till Canada.

"Later," says Becky. The shift has switched over and I didn't even notice.

"Oh—bye."

I drive home and sit on the porch swing sipping hibiscus. It's eight o'clock Saturday morning, April hurling itself toward May, puffy cumulus clouds hovering like airborne whales. Trees coming into leaf, green shoots so bright they seem startled. My crocuses are long gone.

I have three options.

1. Forget about him. He's another generation, and what was I playing at anyway?

2. Give him a call, feel him out, see what happens.

3. Wait for him to come to me. Or call. Or e-mail or send a text message or smoke signals or whatever it is people do these days.

I understand that 3 is essentially the same as 1. He's not the one who got hysterical; he's not the one who needs to make a decision. The ball, as they say, is in my court. It's just a question of deciding: do I want to hit it back to him? Do I want to keep playing whatever match we're playing?

My tea cools as the sun rises higher, spilling a silver-gold smear on the underbellies of those whales. Walter's porch swing shunts back and forth, back and forth, like breakers at the beach, like a tennis ball mid-match, like someone trying to make up her mind about something.

18. "Hello," I say.

"Hi," he says back, sounding tentative. "Been thinking about you."

Oh I bet. "That's nice to hear," I murmur, striving for casual confidence. But in light of my last encounter with him, confidence is in short supply. I'm not helped any by the fact that I'm standing in the bathroom, examining my receding gums.

He says, "I've quit the unit."

"Becky told me. I'm sorry if that had anything to do with me."

"No no. It's just, I'm crazy busy. You know."

"Sure." Being crazy will keep you busy, ha ha. There is a silence between us that stretches for a time, building up in little layers into something hard, like sedimentary rock. Finally he says, "I'd like to see you."

My stomach tweaks a little. "I don't know that it's such a good idea. Anyway I thought you were busy."

"I can make time."

I stand gazing at my reflection, which stares back at me. A pale yellow singlet shows off my biceps to good advantage. I've upped my dumbbell routine recently, I've increased the weight, changed the angles. I like the way the veins on my arms bulge out slightly.

"You there?" comes his voice.

"I'm here."

"What are you thinking?"

I lean forward till I'm almost touching the mirror. My lips against my lips. I exhale quickly, and my hot breath condenses into a Rorschach blot. *Vhat might thees be?* I draw a smiley face in the mist, then wipe it away. I exhale out again, form another cloud, draw a frowny-face, wipe it away. "I'm thinking that I need to think about it."

He laughs as if I've just made a joke. I tell him, "Let me call you back sometime."

"Sure, Regina."

After we hang up I survey myself in the mirror. Forty-two years ago, I didn't exist; forty-two years from now, in all statistical probability, I won't, again. I'll be a rapidly decomposing cluster of chemical, acids and fibers. And all the dumbbells in the world won't do a thing to prevent that.

Despite this fatalism, I buy another pair of dumbbells, five pounders. I use tens for my biceps and triceps, but need lighter weight for fly exercises, which are meant to strengthen the quads and pectorals, and (ahem) help prevent my breasts from sagging. I modify my running regimen slightly, adding a new long slow hill to my route early on, then allowing myself more time to cool down. It's necessary to do this sort of thing every few months—vary the route, vary the intensity—or I'd lose my mind. At least it's nicer outside, now that May is warming up and the sun comes out for whole hours at a time.

The exercises are simple enough. Three sets of ten, rest a minute between sets. Drink some water. Breathe deep and remember to exhale while my arms are closing inward. Pay attention. Maybe this is what meditation is like, or praying. And then, in the middle of it all, I start thinking about Ondine's curse. Why? I haven't the faintest.

19. Anna calls after her exams are finished. More than a week after.

Me: How were finals?

Anna: All done. I did fine too, I'm sure I passed.

She sounds as if she's doing me a favor.

Me: Congratulations. (*Pause.*) Listen, this Provincetown business, I'm not sure it's such a good idea.

Anna (*immediately frosty*): I'm sure it is.

Me: Yes, well—

Anna: It's all set up and you can't stop me. (*Pause.*) All right?

Me: That sounds like a threat.

Anna (*suddenly deflated*): It's not a threat. Why all this drama? It's just something I'm doing, it's all arranged, I'm not backing out on them now.

Yes, just imagine how heartbroken Janice's parents would be at Anna's "backing out."

Me: You're going directly there from school? You're not coming here?

Anna: Don't see why I would. (*Pause.*) The tree's still there, right?

(*Pause.*)

Me: Well.

Anna: There you go then.

Me: I see. (*Pause.*) So you won't be here for your birthday.

Anna: It's not a huge deal, Mom. I mean I'll be turning eighteen finally, so I can go get drunk and stuff but ah—there's no big novelty to *that*.

Me: I'm thinking of Grandpa Hugh, you know, he likes to make a fuss. He'd probably take you out.

Anna: Yeah—*he'd* probably take me drinking, actually.

I manage a laugh, short and awkward. None of this is the least bit funny.

Me: I bet he would. Might leave you to pick up the check, though.

Anna: Totally.

We stay on the line a while, both of us, talking from time to time but saying very little.

20. The apartment was quiet. Beyond quiet: silent. Not just our apartment either but the whole building had gone dead. Strange enough that Walter had no TV going or noisy game with Toby in the living room, but odder still that the whole building, the whole block, lay hushed under its blanket of midsummer heat, its imminent-thunderstorm heaviness. Dogs too hot to bark, that I could understand; but horns too tired to honk, radios too sweaty to blare? That was new.

This was Allston, not Stonebury. Our old apartment on the third floor, with the chronically noisy neighbors downstairs and the spooky old lady on the first floor (who actually turned out to be perfectly nice, but that's another story). The whole place was calm as a mausoleum, like the pyramids or the Taj Mahal, one of those famous places I'd given up hope of ever seeing.

I felt exhausted, having just gotten home from the hospital the previous day, Anna on my lap like a prize. Walter had tucked me into bed and promised to take care of everything and I was happy enough to believe him. Slept like the dead through the afternoon and night and woke to this, whatever this was. A calm as supernatural as the afterlife.

Something drew me out of bed, an awareness that there was an odd vibration in the atmosphere. Not necessarily alarming, but not necessarily *not* alarming either. My feet carried me through the living room, past Walter's welter of magazines on the coffee table (*Craftsman*, *Fangoria*), past the kitchenette with Toby's drawings magneted to the fridge (rainbows, houses, smiling families), down the carpeted hall. That awful vomit-green carpeting from who knows when, the '50s probably, worn thin in the middle and ratty at the edges. Straight ahead was the bathroom, to the right, Toby's room. Soon to be Toby and Anna's room. In a few years that could be a problem, but—we knew this even then—in a few years we'd have moved to someplace bigger.

I paused outside Toby's door, probably holding my breath without knowing it. Gently pushed the door open.

The tableau that greets me is thus. Toby cross-legged on the floor, a look of transcendent calm on his face. Anna in his arms. She was a chubby baby—I guess most babies are—and prone to wriggling and fuss. But in Toby's arms she exuded a kind of restfulness that belied her later fidgety nature.

Watching all this from Toby's bed was Walter, wearing a teary what-have-I-wrought type expression. I caught the briefest moment of that look, utterly unguarded, before he caught me eye, wiped his face, pasted on a grin. "You're up," he said.

"Yeah."

"Hungry?"

"No thanks."

"I can make you some eggs or something."

I didn't answer. I wanted him to be quiet, to not spoil the moment. Toby seemed to understand. He glanced up at me, at his father, then back at Anna, but said nothing. He held his arms utterly still and his sister utterly still within them. He watched her face with absolute attention. For her part, Anna dozed through it all, oblivious.

21. Ondine's curse is a very rare and very unfortunate physiological condition. The patient's brain lacks the mechanism that detects the presence of oxygen, or its absence, so that for example, someone sitting in a crowded movie theater won't experience that sensation of stuffy air. As the relative density of O2 drops, she continues merrily enjoying the movie. Which sounds convenient enough— it's not like a crowded room can kill you—except that sometimes it does. Asleep in bed, for example, when a fire breaks out in the other room, the person won't be aware of the decreasing air supply. Or if she piles a pillow on her head to help her sleep, she lacks the mechanism to wake herself up: there are cases of people literally smothering themselves. Other times, breathing stops altogether, usually during sleep; the body doesn't realize it, doesn't have the proper response of gasping and choking and sucking in huge lungfuls of air. *Game over*, as the kids say these days.

Lately I find myself haunted by the idea of Ondine's curse, the weirdness of it. The fact that it *is* a fact seems, somehow, particularly bizarre. It sounds like something out of a movie but it's not. What must it be like, to be unable to detect the lack of something so critical? Oxygen or food or whatever else, a person is incomplete without even realizing it. I wonder what it must feel like, to walk around with a vital piece of oneself missing. A curse indeed.

22. I call Russell. "Hello."

"Hi," he says. He sounds surprised. There is no background noise and I ask him, "You're not at the restaurant?"

"I'm home."

"Oh." I'm at the market, buying vegetables. The impulse to call had just swept over me, right there in the produce aisle, and I gave in to it before I could scrutinize my motivations too closely. "Guess where I am."

"Mm—talking to your therapist?"

"I'm buying eggplant."

"Eggplant, yeah. You know, I never really knew what eggplant was *for*."

"And you work in a restaurant."

"Not a lot of eggplant in ice cream."

Without warning I blurt, "I've missed you, somewhat."

Now why did I say that? He seems to be thinking the same thing, as the silence on the other end of the line grows heavy. Finally he says, "Me too," very softly, as if trying out the words to see whether he means them. "Somewhat."

"I'd like to see you," I tell him. "But not yet."

"Oh . . . kay."

"I'm not trying to be erratic, it just—I don't want to never go out again, if that makes any sense. But I also don't want to go out right away." I'm holding a cabbage in one hand, staring at it as if I don't understand what it's for or how it works. "I need some time." Of course, that's what I've been having, for the last, oh, month or so. "I realize I told you that weeks ago."

"Yup."

"But I just wanted to, I didn't want you to, think I wasn't going to call."

"Regina." He takes some time to either a) collect his thoughts, or b) silently write a note to himself to *Keep away from that person before she breaks something.* "You told me you needed time to think, right? And I've given you that, right?"

"Yes."

"Okay then. So take whatever time you want, do whatever you need to, then call me. I'm not going anywhere."

"All right." It sounds simple when he puts it like that. "Bye then."

"Bye." But I stay on the line to hear him hang up, which he does, but not before a high-pitched voice, distinctively shrill like a teenager's or a young woman's, says quite clearly in the background: "Who was *that*?"

Then just silence. I look at my cell and the little words tell me *call ended.* I stuff the phone into my purse and stand there, bewildered.

23. I ask Becky, "Have you ever been in a situation where you were faced with different options and neither of them seemed exactly right? When choosing one over the other just brought a different set of complications?"

She sets down her pen and squints at me. "You okay, Gina?"

"I'm not sure."

Two a.m. at ACC, all quiet, and for once we have plenty of techs. Becky steers me into the staff room. "Take a nap."

"I don't need one."

"Not to be argumentative or judgmental, but I think you do."

I start to argue but she holds a set of silver-ringed Becky fingers against my lips. "Doctor. *Gina*. Please, whatever it is, sleep on it. It'll make more sense in the morning."

And it does.

The next day I realize I need a break, some sort of distraction. I consider a night with Steve or Lee or Josh—Lee has been calling lately, leaving not-very-subtle voicemails, and I admit I'm tempted to spend a couple hours in his company, notwithstanding his tedious insistence on *role play*. But it's all rather pointless—I know the person whose company I really want.

Besides Walter of course. It goes without saying, doesn't it, that the person I *really* want to be with is the person I can't have.

24. We meet at my favorite restaurant, a fish place on the Harbor, and small-talk over salad. I drink my shiraz too fast and it goes straight to my head, which is no bad thing. I've decided this will be the night I come clean and tell everything about Toby. When I had my meltdown, Russell had gotten the gist, not the details. At this point I figure I owe him the details.

"I need to tell you something," I begin.

"There's something I need to tell you, too." His face and shoulders carry the air of someone gearing up for a confession.

I scan my responses. Part of me feels undercut, but partly I'm relieved that I won't be rehashing my dead son and his murderous father just yet. My professional instincts are on orange alert, so to speak, but apart from that I'm calm enough. "Is it something horrible?"

"Not at all. Just the opposite." The Grin flashes briefly, illuminating the room.

I sip my lovely shiraz and wonder if his happy news is related to the woman's voice I heard on the phone—"Who was *that*?" But instead I say: "Let me guess. You wake up every morning not knowing who you are, and have to read the notes you left yourself the night before."

"I saw that movie too. Can that really happen?"

"Rarely."

He makes a steeple of his forefingers. "Try again."

"Mm—you always say what you think."

Confusion clouds his face. "Well, I try to. But that's not crazy, is it?"

"You'd be surprised." I polish off the shiraz and signal the waiter for a fresh glass. I feel strangely giddy, even reckless. As if I'm crossing some personal Rubicon. Anna went to P-town yesterday in the company of her mystery friend Janice. "So what's the secret?"

He licks his lips, hesitates. "It's no big deal. It's just—I'm saved, is all."

Maybe the wine has dulled me, or maybe I'm just operating within different parameters. In any case, I don't get it. "That's good. Safe from what?"

"Saved. Redeemed. From, you know, sin and stuff."

Finally the penny drops. "Oh Jesus—"

"Exactly."

"—oh Jesus *Christ*, sorry, that's probably rude."

"Not—well sort of, but it's no big deal." He essays another grin. "I forgive you."

"Oh come *on*. It's the twenty-first century, at least for some of us." Probably I should be a little more understanding, we all have our foibles, our little crutches that get us through the day.

"If you don't want to hear this . . ."

"Oh no, let's get it out in the open."

I should make more of an effort to stay calm, distant even. Professional. But here's the second glass of wine, and if there's one thing I can't stand it's some smug so-and-so banging on about being saved from sin by the glory of Jesus H. et cetera. All of which is a bit much to blurt out in a room filled with two dozen good-natured diners, so I settle for gagging out, "Jesus Mary and Joseph," an expression I picked up from lapsed Catholic Walter, who I presume learned it from his not-quite-so-lapsed dad. Like them, I only use it ironically, and only when things are dire.

Russell sits there looking pained. I eat a couple calamari, crunching grimly against my fillings, I've got to be careful about fried food but the alternative is to drink even faster. I swallow a mouthful of wine anyway and demand, too loud, "Where's our food?"

Russell says, "I know you have some issues with religion."

"Issues?"

"Well I mean—"

"Issues." I hate that word. My god, I hate that word. You might say I have *issues* with that word. "Actually, no I don't. Do you have *issues* with Red Riding Hood and Cinderella?"

"Maybe this was the wrong night to bring it up."

"Too late now." Those Australians know a thing or two about making wine. "I understand religion for precisely what it is—irrational behavior on a global scale."

Russell continues to sit there looking pained. For some reason he doesn't jump up and storm out of the room, which suggests that I haven't insulted him beyond all hope of, pardon the term, redemption.

The waitress chooses that moment to bustle up, all false bonhomie and turbocharged cheer. "And here's your grilled snapper, sir—oh, *sorry* ma'am, it's yours? And for you, sir, the shrimp! Careful with the plates now, they're *hot*! Can I get you anything else right now? Okay then—enjoy your meal!" Finally she's gone, leaving me to grind my teeth. Why do we need people to tell us to enjoy our meal? Why do we need people to tell us the plates are hot? Why do we need people to tell us that Jesus will make everything better when we die? Why does this upset me so much?

I attack the food as if it's offended me. Snapper, leeks, ginger, a pile of garlic and some herbs I can't name, streaming with juice and grilled just to the point where charred black bits cling to the corners. I devour them first and they hit the wine in my stomach and fumes cascade upward. Everything gets better.

Russell pokes at his shrimp. They're covered in marinara sauce and gruyere and will probably take six years off his life, but he's too glum to enjoy them. "What is it?" I ask.

"Nothing."

I sigh, not loud enough for him to hear, just enough to know I've done it. The problem with dating a psychiatrist, I want to tell him, is that it's difficult to lie. "I'm sorry I made fun of religion. It was, ah—" *An honest, unguarded reaction.* "—just a surprise to hear you say it, that's all. I should've thought before I vented. I apologize."

I avoid saying, "I was wrong," or words remotely close to that effect.

Seconds tick by. He keeps his eyes on his food—not a good sign—as his fork twirls one of the shrimps, tearing the cheese into long tomato-stained strings and making a mess. Finally he shrugs and glances at me briefly. Lifts his fork, gulps the shrimp down. Stabs at another one. I exhale. He swigs his beer as I slice into the snapper. He believes Jesus loves him. I mean, *personally.*

"So," he says. Clears his throat and presses on. "So, can I talk about it?"

"By all means." I'll listen to anything: it's what I get paid for. But of course I don't say as much. I'd have to be a *real* bitch to be that mean.

25. I have a patient named Charles, early fifties, white, corpulent. No insurance, pays by check, but the checks haven't bounced yet. A fairly unspectacular specimen. He's losing his hair and uses large amounts of grease or gel or pomade, whatever it's called, to hold what's left in little scraggly strings across his scalp. The effect is odd: he has stripes. But nothing unduly alarming.

Diagnosis is schizophrenia, mild, late onset. He believes certain unlikely things, that angels communicate with him and so on, but his hallucinations aren't frightening and his behavior has never been violent; symptoms are, in fact, manageable with the medicines currently available. One of the lucky few, in other words.

The first time he told me about his church, his congregation—he referred to them as his flock and himself as their shepherd—I thought these were more delusions. I became less certain as the details grew more specific and verifiable. Finally I asked, "Where's this church again?"

A north shore address. The next Sunday I drove out, in disguise (long coat, knit cap, Jackie O sunglasses), hunted around and found it. "Church" was a bit grandiose. A converted storefront abutting a vacant lot, one of those small freestanding brick rectangles on the outskirts of town that are always selling porn or guns. But the sign outside was freshly painted: "Northeastern Church of Christ. Services 10 a.m. All welcome."

Parked outside, maybe thirty cars. Inside, at least a hundred people. Folding chairs ten across, fifteen rows. Plenty of empty seats but more full ones: families, couples. Very few old people— maybe they stuck with the Catholics and Lutherans, the established brands. But guess who was going full force at the front of the room, strands dangling from his scalp, Bible firmly in hand?

I crouched in the doorway, hiding in my sunglasses and fisherman's gear. I prayed—for one of the few times in my life—that he wouldn't notice me.

"And I know Jesus," Charles proclaimed, not in a loud, televangelist voice, but in something softer, more urgent, more profound, his gaze hovering somewhere above the heads of the crowd (cross bolted to the front wall, American flag in the corner). "I *know* Jesus is here, and I know that he knows we're here, and that he loves us. Because—because I've heard his voice." Eyes descend, rifling the congregation. The flock. I huddled lower in the doorway.

Charles tapped his temple. "I've heard his voice, in the night. When he talks to me."

I slipped out the door and hurried to my car. I practically sprinted. Driving home, I wondered how many of the congregation would think twice about their religious affiliation if they knew their shepherd was a) certifiable, and b) on medication.

By the time I got home I'd decided, not many. Maybe none at all. Half those people could've been on meds themselves, for all I knew. Or to look at it another way, maybe that church was the only thing keeping them *off* the pills.

26. Russell polishes off the shrimp and sets the fork down. Goodness, that was fast. I still have half my snapper left. "Look," he says, "I don't expect you to understand any of this, or even believe it." Which is nonsense, of course: one doesn't need a psych degree to know that whenever people say they don't expect you to believe something, that's *exactly* what they expect.

But I keep my snide comments to myself. "I'm listening."

He takes a moment as if deciding how to begin. "It happened when I was nineteen. Ten years ago already—anyway. It was right after my mom died. I told you she died, right? It was cancer. Of the liver, but it got into the lymph system and then—" His hands mimic an explosion. "It was pretty fast. From diagnosis to her passing was something like a month. I'm sure she felt something wrong for a long time before that, but she wasn't, you know, she didn't like to complain."

"Sure." I know the type.

"So, you know, there I was. Halfway through my sophomore year, Dad's out of the picture since I was like, five, and now my mom's gone. Helen, that's my sister, she was off in Miami, married for about a year and getting into the whole newlywed routine, husband, baby, mortgage. All my friends at school suddenly seem stupid, you know? Just dumb party boys drinking beer and chasing pussy. Pardon my saying so, but—well, you know what it's like in college."

"I can imagine." Actually I never had a lot of college fun, but hey, we're not here to talk about me. The waitress clears my plate, and I take advantage of the moment to meaningfully display my empty glass.

Russell plods on, "So where's this leave me? No parents, I was never close to my sister, no romantic relationships, no interest in my academic career. I mean I was pre-law, for God's sake. I had zero interest in becoming a lawyer, it was something my mom wanted. My so-called friends were a waste of time. I'm sure you can see where this is headed."

"Sure. You became a psychiatrist." He looks at me with genuine hurt until I mumble, "Sorry. Little drunk."

"Regina. I tried to *kill* myself."

That sobers me, some. He's right: I should've seen where this was headed. Ordinarily I would have, but those clever Australians make such good shiraz. "I'm sorry to hear that. You must've been very upset. What happened? Obviously you didn't succeed."

"No, I didn't. But I came this close." He holds up a thumb and forefinger. "There was a railroad bridge a little ways outside of town, it runs over this gorge must be a hundred yards deep. The trains hardly run anymore, and high school kids dare each other to run across it and every so often someone falls off and dies. That's how I got the idea."

He pauses to drain his beer. The waitress delivers a fresh glass that I'm not even sure I want now. "I was standing there and it was, like, midnight. I'd gone out late and didn't want anyone to see me. I thought, you know." He coughs. "No point traumatizing anyone else."

Except the high school kids who'd discover the body. I sip the wine, but slowly. My stomach is starting to ask questions of the *What do you think I'm made of?* variety.

"So I'm standing there on the edge of the tracks. Feet on separate ties, facing the drop. I shut off my flashlight and then there's only a little moonlight spilling up behind one of the hills. I can see the lights of the town reflected in the sky. Anyway that's above me. Below it's just black, it's like, I don't know, a cave or something. It could be three feet to the bottom, or three thousand. And it's gone totally still. I remember noticing that. It had been breezy all day, this was March, it's always unsettled weather, windy and stormy and stuff. But this stillness, it wasn't even natural, it was like . . ." He gropes for a comparison.

"*Super*natural," I suggest.

"Yeah." He leans elbows on the table, palms pressed together, face leaning on them. He looks sincere and wide-eyed and lean and dark. Shocks of hair frame his forehead, straggle past his collar. He looks, as the saying goes, *good enough to eat*. All the words that describe his complexion refer to food: coffee, caramel, milk chocolate, chocolate milk. I can't remember the last time I've been this attracted to someone. I'm no stranger to sexual allure, but this is something new.

This awareness sweeps over me like—like I don't know what. Like something overwhelming, undeniable yet indefinable. Like religion I guess. But it's more bluntly physical than religion: there's a throbbing in my groin, as if an electrical cable is connecting us and Russell is a turbine.

"And then, right in the middle of all this calmness, I'm working up the guts to fling myself off—it's not an easy thing to do, so, I'm rehearsing all the problems I've had, you know, my Mom, no dad, my loser friends and school I hated—I'm trying to remind myself why there's no reason to go on. And I think I would've got there too, when suddenly I felt this thing. This pressure." He rubs his forehead. "Up here."

"Pressure."

"Yeah. Like a, I know this sounds crazy, like someone was in there, sharing the space. I got dizzy and shut my eyes."

"Hm." Dangerous, considering.

"Then I felt this voice, I can't really say I heard it, because it wasn't like—" He flaps his fingers beside his ear, "—yap-yap-yap. It was like, I was hearing thoughts, but it wasn't like hearing my own thoughts. It was like, my consciousness was being shared with something else, okay? Another organism."

"And this organism spoke to you."

He nods, again reluctant to look me in the eye. I ask, "What did it say?"

"It said," he clears his throat, "it said, 'I am here.'"

God's as pithy as ever, it seems. "That's all?"

"That's all. Except—two things. One, I understood exactly who the 'I' was who was addressing me. And it wasn't me, Russell Blanco. And two, remember how my eyes had closed during all this?"

"You were dizzy."

"Right. So when I opened them, I wasn't standing on the bridge anymore. I'd gotten off somehow and was back on solid ground." He pauses to gauge my non-reaction. "I was safe, in other words."

I tried to look open-minded even as I parsed his symptoms. Auditory hallucination, maybe a tactile one—rare, but they occurred—followed by a brief fugue state. Remarkable more for its brevity than anything else. And it's timing of course. Well, whatever gets you through the pain, honey. "And that was it?"

He nods.

"No more voices since then? No more blackouts, or—this is the important bit—ideas of killing yourself? No voices whispering, 'Hey, we got it wrong last time, and there's a lovely bridge over there'?"

He's shaking his head with steady determination. "You're vicious. But the answer is *no*. Never heard—never *felt* the voice again, though I wouldn't mind if I did. Never blacked out again either. As for killing myself, well I'd just gotten pretty clear instructions not to."

"Mm." *I am here* equals *Don't jump off the bridge*? "So you just, went back to your dorm?"

"Went to the dorm, stared at my books and wondered why I was studying law when I hated it so much. No good answer to that, so I thought about what I wanted to do and ended up taking a bunch of lit and psych courses."

I drained off the rest of the wine. "It sounds like everything worked out for the best."

"Hope so."

"You found those new classes more to your liking."

"Yep."

"And you destroyed your note, I presume."

His face grows still. "What?"

"Your note. You must've left a note."

"How do you know that?"

"Everybody does it."

"That's—I never knew that. I thought it was . . ." He gropes. "Optional, sort of."

He's so sweet in his naïveté: *I thought I was unique!* As gently as I can I tell him, "Everybody wants to tell their story."

He frowns into his empty glass. Then: "And Walter?"

It's like I've been cuffed. My head spins and my stomach roils. "What?"

"Did he leave a note?" Then his face softens but it's too late to take the words back. "Sorry."

"Well," I manage to choke out. "*Almost* everybody."

If he says anything in answer to this, the rushing sound in my ears blocks it out. Damn wine.

27. The newspaper is full of things that make a person wonder: the kid who walks into school and murders a bunch of his fellows. (Never, you notice, *her* fellows.) The boy who poisons his parents. Black-marketeers in human organs. The abortion-clinic gunman who kills the doctor to show he's pro-life. The government that bombs the village to show it's pro-life. The mob that tears apart someone innocent. The policemen who fire into a peaceful crowd. It goes on and on.

Sometimes it seems a miracle that a) anybody's left alive anymore, or b) that people still trust in the stability of the world enough to keep bringing children into it, or c) that we're still falling for those same delusions—freedom, happiness, charity, love— that had our parents so bamboozled.

But we do. And the sobering thing—I don't know if it's a scary sign or a hopeful one—is that no matter how many school shootings and carjackings and arson-set forest fires we live through, we'll keep on falling for those delusions.

Me: So, how's Provincetown?

Anna: It's . . . fine. Whatever.

(*Pause.*)

It doesn't sound terribly fine.

Me: If you need to come home, you know, you always can. If you need a break or something.

Anna: Yeah.

Me: So what is it that, ah . . .

Anna: It's just really hard, okay? I thought it wouldn't be, but it is. Things aren't like I thought. . . . (*starts crying*) I don't want to talk about it.

Me: Anna. Sweetheart.

Anna: Wherever I go, it's always the same.

Well. There's not much to say to that, except, *Yes that's how it works*. Whatever her particular problems are, and I don't pretend to understand them, I could have told her: *Running away doesn't take you away from them. You just bring them along for the ride.*

I don't get more from her. At least she's with friends, parents, adults. I ask her for Janice's parents' phone number, and surprisingly she gives it with no argument. After we hang up, I call the tree surgeon.

28. It's a terrible feeling to look back at someone long gone and say: "He was lacking in this particular regard." Could there be a deeper betrayal? "Now that Aunt Hilda's passed on, can we finally all admit that we hated her Jell-O salad?" Or, "Of course I'll miss Dad, but I won't miss his drunken rants." To dwell on the negatives, it's an unkindness at least, if not something worse. Besides, you're practically inviting people to do the same to you, once you've *cashed in your chips*, as Walter used to say.

What would Mr. and Mrs. Hayes think? My clients with the long-disappeared son. "It's a shame Benjamin never came home, but at least we don't have to listen to that awful music anymore." No, they think nothing of the sort, I'm sure. Their grief is too demanding, too pervasive, to allow such sedition.

So then. Walter was a good man and a lousy lover. Can I admit that now? I don't mean "lover" in terms of affection, attention, doting, the little daily gestures of devotion. In those departments he excelled. I mean "lover" in terms of raw carnality, of erection and dilation, of physical expressiveness and attention to detail—the detail in question being, specifically, me, and what made (or didn't make) me writhe and moan and breathe hard in ever-accelerating gulps.

Early on of course we were equally maladroit. If he fumbled, so did I; and if his fumbling came from eagerness mixed with embarrassment—both at what we were doing, and at the fact that he wasn't doing it better—well, I was inclined to find this sweet rather than irritating. That wouldn't come until later.

Walter had broad shoulders, big hands, plenty of stamina. This was all fine. Okay his legs were a little bandy, but I found that cute. And everything else was in the right place and worked according to spec. No, Walter's body wasn't lacking. It was his application, and—this may surprise—I found it a difficult subject to discuss with him.

I tried. "Maybe you could wait for me to finish first."

"Oh—sure, all right, of course." Then his face took on a familiar furrowed-brow look, like the horse in *Animal Farm*, whose answer to every problem is *I will work harder!* He lurched over me with eyes fixed, basset-hound style, on my face, his expression silently asking, *Are you finished yet?* Or if not finished, at least finish*ing*? It was, perversely, the kind of awkwardness that I imagine would come from having sex in front of someone else, an audience, except that the person I was in front *of* was the same person I was sleeping *with*. Porn stars must feel this way, or prostitutes. Feeling comfortable in neither role, I soon gave up asking Walter to wait for me. Some favors are worse when granted.

Not being dull, Walter sometimes did what I needed without being asked, and at those times I would forget he was watching, or I'd look the other way.

Like many couples, I suppose, we settled into a routine. Walter did his thing for me and I did my thing for him and then we went to sleep. There were spicy interludes: a week at the Cape that resulted in a string of breathless sunset trysts on the beach ("Where's Toby?" "In the hotel." "Are you sure?" "*Trust* me!") or a sudden burst of let's-try-it-this-way that flamed for a while, then faded. These episodes passed, and it was back to our usual routine.

If I sound jaded, I'm not. I like routine. Routine is the glue that binds human behavior. Routine has gotten me through the past several years. Has in fact gotten me to where I am now.

29. It's morning. A week has passed since the dinner with Russell at which he confessed his suicidal tendencies and religiosity. Since then there have been other dinners, other conversations, none quite so dramatic. I'm adjusting to this new idea of him. Trying it on like a coat, getting used to it. Seeing how if fits, if it fits at all.

Morning sunshine spills gauzily through my bedroom curtain. Sparrows and finches outside, the occasional cry of *chipita-dee-dee-dee*. It's Sunday. The *Globe* will be on my front porch, Brutus and the other strays slovenly and entitled on the steps. I'm due for my run, my smoothie, my decaf, my shower. Overdue in fact.

Beside me Russell stirs, blearily lifts himself onto one elbow, looks me up and down. "Hm," he says, or grunts rather.

"Mm," I answer.

Further words, or semi-words, seem redundant. He levers himself up, leans over me, and nibbles. I shiver. He moves slowly, sniffing, poking, tasting, then prising open my thighs. I allow this willingly, and he moves with deliberation, eyes fixed somewhere else, as I start to breathe hard in ever-accelerating gulps.

The night before, we had come home from the restaurant—same restaurant, same wine, even the same waitress, but different conversation. Something about movies we watched over and over and vacations never taken. At my front door I fumbled with the key then led him inside up to the bedroom and unbuttoned his shirt. He started to say something but I was *so tired* of listening. So I laid my fingers on his lips and he hushed. I wondered if he could taste the fish oil on my fingers. Then I pulled his head toward mine and tasted coffee and scallops and wine.

I lay on the bed, pulled up my skirt, let him feast. "You sure God doesn't mind this?" I was being serious, not snide.

"God doesn't want us to do hurtful things," he said. "There's no way this is hurtful."

I couldn't follow this religious logic—what's new?—so I let it go while he touched me. I closed my eyes and remembered the story of his being saved. Like Russell on the railroad bridge, I got dizzy, and like him, when I opened my eyes later, I was momentarily confused as to where I was and how I'd gotten there.

30. He calls me an hour after he's left the house, while I'm getting ready to run. "I can't stop thinking about you," he says.

"That's sweet." I'm stretching, leaning against the front porch railing: left ankle, right ankle. "I think about you too."

"Are you at ACC tonight?"

"No."

Pause. "I thought you were. They called me to fill in, remember? I told you last night."

So he did, during the small talk warm-up. Left calf, right calf, then both together. "Schedule change." I don't tell him, I changed it myself ten minutes ago with a quick call to Rod Menzies.

"Well then—can I see you before I go in tonight?"

Hoist my foot to the top of the railing, lean forward. Left thigh, right thigh. "I don't think so. I need some time."

"Okay. Sure, I understand."

I bend down, palms flat on the porch, and loosen my vertebrae. Not easy doing this and talking on the cell at the same time. The phone drops from my ear, I catch it just before it hits the ground.

"—ow much time?" he's saying.

Straighten up, aligning the spine. People think of foot and ankle injuries, but it's my back that's always given me trouble. "I don't know. Listen, I'll call you when I'm ready. Okay?" I try to keep impatience out of my voice. "This is all new to me. I mean, I'm out of practice."

"Sure," he says dubiously. He's probably thinking: married woman, kids, widowed, casual partners on speed dial—which part of this is *new*, exactly? I say goodbye and hang up.

The phone rings. I tell him, "I'm serious, I need to think about this. Don't call back."

He calls back anyway. "Sorry. Do you mean, you have to think about what we've been doing these past few weeks, or you need to think specifically about what we did last night?"

"The former. Don't call back."

I hang up and the phone rings again and I'm getting fairly annoyed. It's cute to be a nuisance in the movies but not in real life. "Listen, I need time to work this out, all right? There's no changing what happened last night but I need to decide whether I want to take it further."

No answer but an intake of breath. I say, "Russell? Are you there?" I check the cell to make sure he hasn't hung up. Oh shit.

Anna's voice in my ear. "Mom? Who's Russell? And what happened last night?"

Geez Louise.

31. Early June, and the trees are in full leaf, the air is thick with humidity and downpours. I put in my shifts at ACC. Becky gets a haircut she does not even begin to need—I can see the scalp above her ears. Patients get released and come back, some sooner, some later. Almost everyone shows up again eventually. Tony, my patient with the breasts who drank his girlfriend's urine and tried to hang himself, doesn't come back. Maybe the plan is working. I say as much to Becky, who says, "Maybe he decided he likes his boobs."

I don't see Russell. I play for time. He's different from my casual lovers, my Joshes and Steves and Lees. I need to think about what I'm doing with this, let it settle into my bones until I can decide whether it's a good idea or an awful mistake. I've made some awful mistakes in my life, and had some good ideas too. I might be expected to know the difference by now.

There's me, eighteen years old, thin and awkward, pale, lank-haired. Not a beauty, too uncertain in my own body for that. Sitting on the dorm toilet, pants down, feeling sick and enraged in equal measure. A new sensation for me, rage: fists bracketing my head, demanding, urging, willing the fetus inside me to abort, to die, to flush itself from my body, *demanding* that it not ruin my life, forever and ever, amen.

Walter on the other side of the door, jolly at first, then concerned, then gruff, then wheedling. Finally just small and tentative: "Gigi? What is it, what's going on in there?" His voice more plaintive with each word. "Come on, let me in, okay? Let me *in*."

"No," I told him. I meant it too: as much as I had ever meant anything, *ever*. Maybe he could sense that, even through the closed door. He stayed there a while, silent, then finally went away, leaving me to do whatever it was I was doing. Cursing, praying. Same thing.

32. I see the Hayeses. I see Beth Ann Kim, to no apparent effect, but she attends her appointments faithfully, so maybe something is percolating in there. I see Ak-Ak and Reverend Charles and Mrs. Flynn and Hugh and my folks, my whole usual crew. And life goes on, the way it does. Except that for some people, it doesn't.

Sooner or later of course we all wind up on *that* list. But not yet. For now, we can still engage in the magical thinking that says *Not me, not now, not today. Maybe not ever.*

Nights expand into endlessness. The past comes hurtling back and there's nowhere to run or hide, cower or crouch. Lots of people have nightmares of being chased but at times I get that feeling even while lying in bed wide awake.

There's Walter, eyes teary—that didn't happen often—telling me the story of Toby's first steps. (I'd been at work.) Years later, repeating the story of Anna's. I contrived to miss their first words as well. And of course there were the events I did see: birthday parties, trips to the beach. School plays. Him with the kids, or making me omelets when I was sick. The four of us playing badminton in the back yard of the old house, me hopeless at it, Walter surprisingly good. Full-body dives into the mud to save the point and so on.

Who would have expected such things? But then again, why not? Walter was full of surprises.

33. Now that she's got her teeth into a mystery, Anna displays a familiar persistence, something that would be admirable in someone else's daughter, or even in Anna if it were directed toward, let us say, a career. "Hi Mom. Who's Russell?"

"Hello." I'm on the front porch, settling into the wicker settee alongside Brutus. He allows me to stroke his shaggy neck while he closes his eyes and purrs, it's quite grand of him. I shift the phone to my other ear. "How's Provincetown?"

"Great." Displaying typical lability, Anna has decided after two weeks that P-town is thoroughly enjoyable. We'll see how long this lasts.

"It didn't seem so great, when you called before—"

"It's *great*, Mom. Who's Russell?"

"We'll get to that, but let's catch up first. You're staying with your friend Janice, right? Are you comfortable? Are you eating all right?" Anna tends toward junk meals when feeling uncertain or transitional, not that I would ever make this observation within her hearing. "And your grades arrived. Two A's, I'm pleased." Actually an A-minus in English comp.

She sighs profoundly to let me know that my petty delaying tactics are transparent—trans-*parent*—in her sight. "Glad you're happy about it. It's really nice up here, Janice's parents are really cool, they say I can stay as long as I want. So everything's copasetic."

I nearly cry out. Copa*set*ic? Do people actually still say such things? I think of it as a word Burt Reynolds would have used in the '70s, or William Shatner, along with "anyhoo" and "marvy."

But Anna would be uninterested in my linguistic anthropology. "You still haven't told me what you're doing out there," I remind her. "You could be up to anything with your mysterious friend Janice and her copasetic parents." This is true. It's now the middle of June, and apart from some vague notion of "having to work," I haven't a clue as to what fills her days. Drug dealing? Performance art? Lesbian encounter groups? Knowing P-town, maybe a combination of all three.

Now she sighs again. Where did this habit come from? Not me certainly, nor my mother for that matter. Walter was never big on sighs. "Yes Mom, I have secrets. Just like you do. If you want to know mine, you have to spill some of yours, right?"

"Hm," I say. Interesting theory.

"So are you sleeping with this guy or what?"

"Anna, really." This is what a year of college has done to my daughter. Transformed her into this bullying secretive young woman, who—when not a tearful addled wreck—brims with confidence and irreverence. If I were her therapist, I'd be thrilled with her progress, but alas I'm her mother. "That's hardly an appropriate question."

"I'll take that as a yes. Because 'No, I'm not sleeping with him' would be a perfectly appropriate answer. When do I see him? I can't wait to meet this guy."

It occurs to me to wonder what Russell would think of my daughter. Anna has many attractive qualities, as I know better than anyone, and don't men have some fantasy of sleeping with mothers and daughters at the same time? Some men anyway. Some mothers and daughters.

This train of thought has turned distinctly unpleasant. My fingers are knotted in Brutus's ruff. He blinks at me quizzically, no longer purring. Perhaps the fur across his neck is pinched uncomfortably tight. Deliberately I loosen my fingers and begin stroking his back. Vigorously but calmly, with long even strokes. He closes his eyes again: balance has been restored to his world. Lucky him.

I've been careless and caught off guard, and I need to shift attention away from myself. So instead of the logical response— "You can't very well meet him when you refuse to come home, can you?"—I bounce her confrontation right back: "So who are *you* sleeping with, then?"

Several moments of startled silence, then, "Mom, geez."

I let her chew on it a moment. "I'm serious, Anna. To put it your way, I'd like to meet the man who seduced my daughter. Is he out there in P-town? Is that what you're not telling me, why you're so eager to stay the summer?"

Another, longer pause. Followed by a doleful sigh and, "No. There's nobody out here, I mean, nobody like that. I'm working with this whole, like group, okay? But there's no romance and definitely no sex."

I am, unaccountably perhaps, relieved. Yes it's hypocritical. Yes I know I was having sex at her age. Actually, I wasn't anymore—I was already pregnant. This is why I'm relieved that she is not. Is that so hard to understand?

"Well," I say.

"Yeah," she answers.

In a way, my daughter and I have just talked about something. In a way, it's a more substantive conversation than we've had in years. Maybe that's why it's left us feeling so awkward and unfinished.

"I should go," she says.

"Wait. You will tell me what you're doing out there, won't you? Sooner or later."

"Yeah I will." There's no sighing exaggeration in her voice now. "But I want to finish before I tell you about it, okay? It's sort of a, it's like a project. It's nothing illegal, don't worry. But I don't want to talk about it till it's over with. It's not just you, I'm not telling anybody. I don't want to jinx it."

How touchingly rational. "All right," is what I tell her. I guess it will have to do.

Not till I've hung up, and sat stroking Brutus's long-haired spine for another ten minutes, that I realize I never asked Anna whether what she's doing out there in P-town could be described as being, in any way, *creative*.

34. There is a letter, upstairs in my bedroom dresser. It's tucked into the back of the drawer, buried under odds and ends of papers and things. The envelope has aged and there's a strip of tape running across the back of it.

I go upstairs and hold it in my hand. Something I haven't done in years. Put it back after a while, inter it under a pile of papers and close the drawer with a jolt.

35. In college Walter had no beard, he was just a big good-natured slightly fleshy guy, the kind with an expanding gutline-in-waiting even as an adolescent. Faintly orange cast to his hair and pale complexion, a possibly Scottish look to him. He wore Brut cologne, a perpetual smile and a T-shirt that said *BEER: It's Not Just for Breakfast Anymore*. I was reminded of a golden retriever.

We had a class together and one day he shuffled up to me in the hallway. He didn't seem to know what to do with his hands. "Hey," he said, then waited, smiling. The hands worked from his front pockets to the back ones and then the front again. "I'm Walter. I'm in your Humanities class."

"Oh. So am I." Yes, I actually said what is probably the stupidest sentence in history: *I am in my class also*. But I was seventeen, skinny, bookish, a trifle snooty, and I lacked experience chatting with good-natured almost-hippies in funny shirts.

"So, how you like it?"

"The class? It's okay. It's good actually, I like it quite a lot."

"Yeah." He nodded vigorously. I've often thought that he would've nodded vigorously no matter what I said: "The teacher deserves a Nobel Prize," or, "I think the teacher worships Satan." But it was true that I liked the class.

"I was wondering if you wanted to go to the movies this weekend," he blurted. Before I could even grasp what he saying he added, "You know, it's cool if you can't, I totally understand if you're busy."

"Well—yes, I should be studying."

His face clouded and he said, "Studying?" as if that weren't the kind of *busy* he'd had in mind. He looked so lost I rallied and—didn't exactly take pity on him, but threw him a lifeline of sorts. "What movie is it?"

"There's this film festival starting Thursday, they're showing three movies a night or something."

"Sounds interesting. What are they, foreign films?"

"Um, not exactly. Though actually one is Mexican I think . . ." He dug in his pocket, extracted an oft-folded blue flier. "It's actually, um, a bad movie festival. I thought it would, I thought it'd be funny."

Words failed me at this juncture, so when he held the paper to me, I took it in silence. I had many fine qualities as a teenager, but I was nobody's first choice as a date to the Bad Film Festival. At least not until that moment. I looked at the paper. "Which night were you thinking?"

"Um, whichever," he said. "They're all cool for me. Different movies each night though."

"I see." Thursday's offerings were *Invasion of the Bee Girls*, followed by *The Thing with Two Heads*, followed by *Women in Prison*. "I think I'm busy on Thursday."

"Friday then?" The droop in his voice was unmistakable.

Friday kicked off with *Zombies of Mora Tau*, followed by *Wrestling Women Versus the Aztec Mummy*, concluding with what was touted as "the most notorious bad movie ever made," *Plan 9 from Outer Space*. I had at least heard of that one. "Okay, Friday then. Do we have to see them all?"

He looked as confused as if I had said, "Do we have to wear clothes when we go outside?" And he gave what would probably be the same answer to both questions: "No, um—not if you don't want to."

But the prospect of missing *Wrestling Women Versus the Aztec Mummy* seemed to really shake him, so I said, "Why don't I meet you at the theater after the first two. That way I can get some work done beforehand."

His face cleared. "Great."

When Saturday came I experienced the curious mix of apprehension and excitement that most girls probably go through at age thirteen but which I'd somehow missed out on. That night, I wandered to the theater to meet him. He wore a T-shirt that said *Nobody's Perfect—But Parts of Me Are Amazing*. When he saw me he hollered, "Yo Ray-gee-*nuh*!" I hesitated, unsure whether he was addressing me or someone else. Turned out it was me.

There was a lull after we took our seats. Not an uncomfortable lull exactly, but a distinct, measurable absence of conversation between us. To fill it I asked, "How were the other movies?"

"The ones last night, or tonight?"

"Ah—tonight I meant."

"Wicked," he answered with relish. "*Zombies of Mora Tau* just sucked." He said this with a certain undeniable appreciation. I found myself intrigued by this response.

Then the lights dimmed, and surprisingly, I wasn't bored into catatonia or even listlessness. The unintentional hilarity of the movie caught me off guard: the stilted dialogue, cardboard sets, ridiculous plot, foofy narrator. Walter laughed alongside me in the packed theater full of whistling, catcalling wiseguys. How much fun did I have? Well, I attended Sunday night's showings in full (*Teenagers From Outer Space*, *Flight of Terror* and *Horror of Party Beach*), so that should indicate something.

There was joy between us at first, I won't deny it. I'd never dated much—all right, I never dated at all—and I found the attention gratifying. Walter was largely uninterested in things that interested me, but he was warm-hearted and inquisitive enough to take to some of my passions (gardening, cooking) even while he brought some things into my life, such as an appreciation for a finely-turned piece of woodwork. I even grew to share—if not entirely embrace—his love of pop kitsch, of zombie movies and tacky postcards and old paperbacks with lurid covers and titles like *I Was a Gangster's Girlfriend*.

The manner of my pregnancy was predictable enough, something that had happened to countless girls before and since. But even then, after we entered that new phase of our courtship, the joy wasn't entirely gone. There were still surprises, there was life. After the baby was born, we rented a small apartment in Allston and got on with it.

Things got harder as we became better off. Studies have been done, the results suggesting this was in no way abnormal. In our old, cramped, cluttered, never-enough-room apartment in Allston, we fought less than in our comfortable, plenty-of-elbow-room house (with yard, attic, workshop, maple trees) in Stonebury. When the kids were tiny and I was up all night studying or doing my residency and Walter was still trying to figure out where he fit in my life, in all our lives, we managed. Bumping heads, surely, I'm not claiming there was no stress. There was *plenty* of stress. But there was also something swimming just out of reach, an idea, a dream of what we were striving for and what it would look like when we got there. Then we got there, and it didn't look the same at all, somehow.

Are all human beings malcontents? This is what I think at times, what I walk around thinking most of the day. It would explain a lot of things. It would explain why, when one is young and struggling, nothing seems better than that imaginary future of fulfillment and why, once it's attained, we look back on those decades of struggle as a golden age.

Or maybe people aren't malcontents; maybe they just get tired. Whatever it is, I've seen this happen over and over, enough to believe it's universal or close enough. Show me a contented human being, and I'll show his medication. Or her religion. Same thing.

Walter had a passion for birds, the way other men have a passion for cars or sports. Or hunting, and maybe that sums up best what made him different from so many other men. He didn't love killing things, he loved keeping them alive. In high school he'd built a half dozen feeders at his parents' house, and still kept them stocked. It was all new to me; I knew a few of the local birds—chickadees, titmice, the c*ah*dinal, everybody knows that one—but Walter introduced me to a whole world of overlooked specimens: juncos and finches and towhees and whatnot. He was partial to sunrise walks at the Arboretum or weekend drives out to Walden to creep about, binoculars in hand, trying to glimpse a scarlet tanager or some migrant warbler. The day he spotted a bald eagle soaring over Concord—this was years ago, before they started coming back in serious numbers—his face glowed like he'd set eyes on the Madonna.

He took care to pass on this knowledge to his son. (Not his daughter, and not for lack of trying; Anna was simply less interested in the wild world, preferring to help her father in his workshop, amid his power tools and varnishes, rather than accompanying him on his hikes in the woods. She did go through a brief, predictable horse phase, which ended after two months when she got thrown by a gray monster named Tonka.) Toby leeched it up like a sponge, and once he was past toddling, Walter bought him his own feeder to maintain. Once we moved to Stonebury, Toby kept the birdbath clean and put up dozens of birdhouses in the trees closest to his bedroom windows, so he could sit and watch the finches and crows collect dried grass and feathers and strips of plastic garbage.

It was Anna who took the feeders down after Toby died. I didn't even see her do it. One day as I was staring out the windows,

I noticed something indefinable and strange. This was spring, six months after the—incident. It took me a while to realize what had changed.

Anna sat on her bed with an array of coloring books featuring winged horses and fairies and so on. Her concentration was absolute. She didn't even notice me in the doorway, and this was so much like Toby had been I let out a little strangled cough.

She looked up. "Hi."

"Hi. Coloring?"

"Yeah." She showed me. At age eleven she was still meticulous in her work. Not a scrap of color strayed outside the lines.

"That's wonderful," I said.

"You can put it on the fridgerator when I'm done."

"Okay." I went to the bathroom for a tissue and came back after several minutes. "Did you . . . do you know what happened to all the bird feeders?"

She didn't answer for a time. Snow White's dress glowed an unearthly magenta. "Anna?"

"Took 'em down," she said quietly.

I mulled this over but before I could say anything further, she pinned me with her wise-little-girl look. "Threw them away so we wouldn't have to look at them."

"Oh . . ." I tried to keep the sadness from my voice. What's done is done, but—I would have much preferred that those things hadn't been thrown away.

Anna, maybe sensing my reaction, drew further into herself. "Did it a long time ago."

"You did?"

She nodded. "Right after Christmas. I was looking at them and they were making me sad." Her voice was tiny. "I thought you saw."

At Christmas I'd still been hopped up on meds. I wondered fleetingly what else I hadn't been noticing.

And then I realized my little girl was exactly right to do what she did—to pull down those little memorials and drop them in the dumpster at the end of the driveway. The sight of them, abandoned and weathering, would've been too much to bear. "Thank you for doing that," I told her, and she nodded dumbly.

We stayed like that a while, her drawing and me watching and neither of us saying very much.

36. All of which brings me—I'm not sure how, but here I am—to this man Russell, whom I know so little about. What he thinks about art, or war, or politics, or love. Or anything really, apart from a particular incident on a railroad bridge. But there is so much more—what the best day of his life was, whether he wants kids, whether he wants anything at all, besides an ice cream parlor. What bores him. I don't even know if he likes birds, or hunting. I don't know if seeing a bald eagle would put a shine on his face. I do know, however, that he just *loves* Jesus, and he believes the inverse is true.

I close my eyes. Who would have ever thought it would come to this?

There are some things I take pride in. I'm a firm believer in, among other things, standing on one's own feet and staring reality in the eye as unflinchingly as possible. Not to put too fine a point on it, but that's probably one of the impulses that led me to my profession in the first place: the desire to confront irrationality head-on. I've never had a great deal of sympathy for people too weak to withstand the universe as it is—heroin addicts, Scientologists—people who try with all their might to make the rough edges of cold hard life into something soft and fuzzy and welcoming. Sometimes I'm tempted to throw the whole pile of them into ACC and say: *Here. Deal with it.*

Now, against all odds, I find myself involved with a young man who tolerates (more than that, who pursues) this impulse. What on earth am I doing? The honest answer is: I have no idea. There must be a reason for it. If I step back from myself, look as coldly and dispassionately at myself as at my patients, a whole constellation of reasons would doubtless come into view. Physician, know thyself, et cetera.

The time has come, I decide, for a little field research.

37. I find a place to park under an amber streetlight on South Street, not far from the Forest Hills T stop. Keys jingle on my fingertips as I walk to the whitewashed storefront with the big ice cream cone sign. Jamaica Plain has undergone gentrification in recent years, but this stretch still looks tired. Storefronts are dingy, the curb is tacky with gum. Plastic bags roll like tumbleweeds. It's no slum by any stretch, but Cambridge it ain't, either.

The restaurant glows like a beacon, pushing back the gathering twilight with almost physical force. Inside it's standard-issue ice cream parlor: black-and-white linoleum, square tables with wrought-iron chairs, a long counter running the length of the back displaying multicolored tubs. It's crowded too, everyone gulping down cones and sundaes with that intensity peculiar to consumers of ice cream: the focus of the eyes, the spoon gliding into position, the satisfied roll of the tongue.

Behind the counter stands Russell in a white apron. The man actually glows with animation as customers smile at him and he gives back, everybody happy. I've seen this in stand-up comics or ballet dancers or tennis players: the feedback loop of audience response. It is not a sensation to which psychiatrists are prone.

I make my way to the counter. He sees me and double-takes, then does it again for exaggerated effect. "Of all the ice cream joints in the world, she's gotta walk into mine."

"If I'd known it was so much fun, I'd have come sooner."

"Yeah well." He ducks his head, leans both arms on the counter glass. "You're here now."

My eyes flicker across the colored tubs. "I came to apologize. I've been fairly unforgivable in my behavior."

"Nothing's unforgivable," he says quickly.

I don't know what to make of that. An article of faith, maybe? "We've had some, how can I put it, some emotionally heightened times together."

"You mean, *intense*? That's true." He raps on the glass countertop with his ice cream scoop. "Sometimes it feels like we go straight for the peak experiences, good and bad, and skip the in-between stuff."

"Yes. So I needed to step back, and—take stock."

He nods. "Okay."

I catch his eye. "Maybe you need to step back awhile too."

"Sure."

"You do?"

He stops nodding. "Actually, no. I just felt like I should be agreeable."

"Oh. Well, for me it's not so simple."

"Didn't say it was simple, just said I didn't need to step back." When I don't answer he hoists an empty cone. "What's your poison?"

"Nothing for me, thanks."

"On the house. Doctor's orders."

I stay till midnight. The cone leaves me bloated and lethargic: I'll need a double-length run in the morning, before visiting my parents. The thought helps fight the nausea every time I burp up chocolate and mint.

At midnight Russell chases out the stragglers, including a willowy redhead with a nineteen-inch waist. She giggles and calls out, "See you tomorrow, Russell." He smiles back at her—sheepishly? Conspiratorially?—and locks the door behind her. The voice is nasal and distinctive. It might have been the voice I heard on the phone, a month ago, when I called him at home: "Who was *that*?"

Midnight or no, it's too awkward to leave now, so I sit in my corner leafing through an old *Cosmo* ("Your Orgasm Face: What Does *He* See?") while Russell goes through the till with his co-workers. Lawrence is a six-foot-four white guy, ghostly pale and gray-haired, all gangly angles and elbows. Big Mack is black, with a bouncer's robust build; I match him for height but he weighs in somewhere over three hundred pounds. He's got the kind of neck that has layers. I've seen men like him on TV—boxer's bodyguards, professional wrestlers—but never in real life.

When they finish, the table is littered with little stacks of receipts. "Not bad," says Russell. "Could be better."

"Could be a lot worse," says Big Mack.

"Could be better," insists Russell.

Big Mack smiles thinly while Lawrence rolls his eyes. They zip the cash into a bank deposit bag and divide the tip money. Lawrence and Big Mack vanish into the night as Russell tells me, "Best night for a long time. Getting warm now, people coming out."

"It's not like this every night?" We step outside, onto the sidewalk.

"Hardly. Weekends are best, and summers of course. Otherwise it gets real slow. That's why I want to branch out, do sandwiches and stuff, real food. With the right menu, this place could be a hot spot." A ring of keys appears in his hand and he locks up behind us. "One night in January, I think it was a Wednesday? We grossed something like thirty bucks. Wasn't even a blizzard or anything, just too cold for ice cream."

My Saab waits forlornly down the street and we make our way toward it. I tell him, "You enjoy yourself in there?"

"Sure, why not? It's good atmosphere. And you—there's—" He searches for the word. "There's honor in feeding people. Even if it's just dessert."

"Mm." I wonder if this is true. I wonder if Russell is one of those men who falls back on that old standby, *honor*, to justify every bad decision he's ever made. *There's honor in getting into this senseless fight. In not paying the traffic fine. In not listening to the woman. In hitting the girlfriend . . .*

He glances at me sideways. "You don't sound convinced."

My car is approaching fast. We slow our pace. I want to ask about the giggly redhead and who the girl was on the phone, but at the same time I don't want to be one of those pathetic middle-aged women with a grudge against college girls. I waver between asking and not asking; neither choice satisfies. "Can you really see yourself doing this, years from now?"

He frowns. "You make it sound like a chore. But I love my work, how many people can say that?"

I don't answer.

38. Russell and I do things together. We snatch time for lunch, a movie, a stroll round Walden Pond. We avoid drama, opting for distraction instead. It sneaks up on me before I realize what it is: real, actual dating. We trade my favorite sushi place for his favorite Thai place. We go to a bar in Allston and drink draft pints and listen to a blues band called Jack Hammer and the Power Tools. The movie we see is an indifferent romantic comedy called *Alan's Got it Now!* which, I can't help noticing, keeps Russell in stitches throughout.

Afterward, while we're standing in the lobby, I ask him, "What was so funny about that? The whole thing with the swordfish was just sick."

"I know, but—oh God," is his answer. "That bit with the monkey—and the Norwegian guy—" He starts giggling again.

Okay, I will acknowledge that the bit with the monkey and the Norwegian guy was kind of funny, in a droll, one-sided smile kind of way. I glance around the lobby, which is filling up with people going to the next show. Most of these people look about fourteen years old. "Coffee?"

He checks his watch. "I've gotta roll—"

"Please. Ten minutes."

"Sorry Gina. Mack's there on his own, he'll be swamped."

Through it all, something unexpected develops. I grow to enjoy watching Russell laugh, head thrown back, mouth gulping air. Without restraint. So it's a pleasure to hear him tell me, one afternoon when we steal an hour at a café: "I love it when you laugh."

That gives me a tingle. I take a moment to sip my cappuccino and savor everything—the coffee, the compliment, the big serious dark eyes looming out of that good-natured hatchet blade face. "Because it's so rare, I suppose?"

"Don't be like that." He rubs the side of his nose with his thumb. "Your laugh is different from anybody's I've ever known."

"Get out of here." I deliver the line in heavy Bostonian: *Ged ahdda hee-ah.*

"No, I mean it. When something catches you off guard and you're really laughing, you're like this." And he mimes a kind of head-thrust-forward, eyes closed, mouth-half-open shudder.

"You look like you're having an orgasm."

"Yeah well." He opens his eyes. "I guess you're a woman who really enjoys a joke." A glance at his watch. "Gotta go."

It's all a far cry from me and Walter, this dating business. I got pregnant fast and Fun took a vacation while tight-lipped Duty took over. After Toby was born, Walter and I went out only rarely, usually staying home with the TV or a rented movie. Walter's choice as a rule: *The Walking Dead* or *Zombie U.* or *Insectoroid.* Some of these I sat through, some I didn't. Sometimes I worked up the enthusiasm for his kitsch but more and more, as time went on, I couldn't be bothered. Walter was a wonderful man and a loving, devoted father but geez Louise, his taste in movies was shit. Shite. Pathetic, rather. And he never told me that he loved to watch me laugh.

39. My client Charles, aka Reverend Charles of the Northeastern Church of Christ, arrives agitated for his appointment and tells me that he is having doubt.

"Doubts about therapy?"

"*Doubt,*" he stresses gesturing vaguely with his hands. "About everything, the big picture, the whole ball of wax." He eyeballs me. "You know?"

"Are you talking about God, Charles?"

"Bingo."

Oh my. Was there ever a psychiatrist less qualified than I to address this particular anxiety? "What are you doubting—the existence of God? Whether he's benign, whether he loves you or forgives you? Whether you've got him figured out after all?"

He nods mournfully, his normally steely eyes collapsed into sunken puddles. "All of the above."

I manage to prevent myself from hooting *Congratulations, you're cured!*

As if reading my mind he asks, "What are your thoughts on the subject, Doctor?"

My smile is professional. "We're here to talk about you."

40. I get a call late one night at ACC.

Girl's voice: Hi—Mrs. Moss? This is Janice. Um, Anna's friend?

Me: Oh yes. How—is everything all right?

Janice: Oh sure, yeah. I just thought I'd call and say, you know, hi. Introduce myself?

Me: Okay.

It is half past midnight, not that it matters when I'm at work, but still.

Janice: So, how's everything at your end?

Me: Just fine, thanks.

Janice: Great. So, nothing unusual going on, that's good.

Me: Not at all. I trust my daughter isn't giving your parents a hard time? Sometimes she can be, how should I say this.

Janice: Oh she's fine.

Me: A handful.

Janice: No no. Nothing like that.

(*Pause. Becky passes by.*)

Me: Well. I should be moving along. Thanks for taking the time to call.

Janice: Sure, yeah, so keep in touch. All right?

When I hang up I think *What an extraordinarily strange thing.* But then some cops show up with a new intake and I have to go deal with that.

41. The next day I phone Russell and tell him, "I should explain a few things."

"About . . ."

"About what happened, that night with the photo albums."

He hesitates. "That was months ago."

"Exactly my point."

"Water under the bridge, Gina."

"Not for me it isn't."

He makes a sound like *Mm-hmm*. I tell him, "An explanation is overdue."

"If you want."

"I do. If *you* want to hear it."

"I do."

I rub my forehead. "We sound like we're getting married."

"I know a club we can talk," he says. "Mellow jazz kind of place."

"Sounds nice. Sure you've got time?"

I don't mean to sound bitchy but it comes out that way. His voice is a little tentative when he says, "Yeah I have time. Lawrence and Mack can close without me, so I'm free until—"

"That club sounds perfect then."

We meet that night at The Red Lantern, tucked into some unlikely side street in Somerville, murmuring with an almost-full house of young professionals. The waitress brings us sweet drinks, a black Russian for me, mudslide for him. He clinks his glass against mine and says, "Up the rebels."

"As long as they're the right rebels."

Onstage the sax player is lean and tan, outfitted in a red tuxedo that Walter would describe as a pimp outfit. He caresses the gleaming horn as though he's seducing it, coaxing moans and grunts from the brass. I'd never before noticed just how sexual musicians could be.

I sip my drink and say, "I'd never noticed just how sexual musicians could be."

"Oh yeah." He sips his mudslide. "Horns especially, the whole blow-into-it-with-your-mouth thing."

I cock an eyebrow at him. "I think this is something men notice more than women."

"Hard to miss," he shrugs. "You ever look at a guitar? It's shaped like a woman's body. If that's not sexy, what is?"

"Especially when you blow into it." I'm not entirely comfortable with flirtatious double entendres, but it could be worse. We haven't slept together since that one night, and Russell isn't acting as if he's entitled to more sex, which is a plus.

I take a breath and tell him, "I should explain those photos you came across that time at my house. When I sort of went off my head."

His face turns instantly serious. "First off, I shouldn't've looked. You told me not to and I went ahead anyway. I'm sorry, please believe that. Second, if you want to talk, I'm ready. But it's not really my business, I know."

"Okay. Thanks." And I go ahead and tell him. It's just an overview but it covers the major topics: Walter, Toby, Anna, my unexpected pregnancies and unorthodox marriage. And that's just for starters. Russell is quiet during this recitation, unobtrusively ordering a second drink for himself—I barely touch mine. By the time I'm finished with Walter's incomprehensible murder-suicide, the red-suited sax player has taken a set break, is being crowded at the bar by well-wishers.

Russell is quiet for a while. Then he says, "That's some serious shit."

"Yup." My ice has melted into a little clear layer atop my drink. "Serious shit is exactly what it is." I manage a smile for him. "Now you have some idea of how messed up your friend Regina is. Couldn't even keep her husband from killing her son. Some psychiatrist, hey?"

"Don't be like that."

I shrug. "Horrible things happen. This is one of them. I try not to dwell on it because it would just overwhelm me. When I saw Toby's pictures that night, I just, I don't know."

"Lost it."

"Something like that."

"It's all right."

"Maybe."

"Gina. I said it's *all right*." His hand snakes across the table, rests on mine. "I mean it. Serious shit makes people do other serious shit. Strap on bombs and go blow themselves up, or whatever."

I sniffle. "I'm not quite there yet."

"I didn't mean that you were. I'm just saying—look, let's put it behind us."

"I'd like that. Boy oh boy, would I ever like that." I look at him and he doesn't really understand, he's putting it behind him already with his hand on mine and his palm is dry and surprisingly smooth and I don't try to force a smile and I'm forty-one years old and utterly naked. "Which brings up a question."

"What's that?"

"What are we doing?"

For several moments he looks positively scared. Then he grins, and the tension breaks, or at least warps into something less threatening. "We're having a drink. And listening to him." I follow his glance to see the sax player taking the stage amid applause from the crowd. He's a real showman, striding around the stage, barking commands to his band before flashing a neon smile at the club. Then in an instant he is seriousness itself, he takes the horn into his mouth, bends it to his crotch, and fingers it till it wails.

The spell doesn't last though: Russell checks his watch and says, apologetically, "Gotta run."

It takes some moments to sink in. "You're—*leaving*?"

"Yeah, sorry." His eyes are pained. "Believe me, I'd cancel if I could."

"You said they were closing without you."

"They are. But I'm working an overnight at the group home."

"You neglected to mention that."

"I tried."

"You didn't try too hard." Something crumbles in me a little. I spill my guts about my murdered son and dead spouse and he responds by trotting off to work. He must see my mouth tighten because he says earnestly, "I'd like to, stay, really I would, but."

"Go ahead. We're just finishing up anyway." And when he signals for the bill I tell him, "I'll cover it."

"No, this is my—"

"I said I'll *cover* it." I rarely raise my voice but I do so now. Heads turn. "I'll pay for the drinks, you obviously need to save up for your—investment." I gulp the black Russian, its sweet burn slides down my throat like a communion wafer. "To buy your business, make your dreams come true, et cetera. Go."

He's staring at me.

"Just *go*."

He goes.

42. I'm in a rotten mood when I get home. When the phone rings it's well past 11:00 and I have no interest in hearing Russell's rationalizations. Then it occurs to me that it might be my mother, or my daughter. I had shut off my cell phone at the club. "Yes?"

"It's me."

I was right—it's Mom. A sudden unseen hand grips my windpipe. "Has something happened with Dad?"

"Nothing like that. But I, you need to get over here. Can you?"

"I, well, yes." Anxiety has worked its way into my spine, I'm standing very straight, like a ballerina. "What's wrong, Mom?"

"It'll be much easier to explain in person."

43. Anna sits at Mom's kitchen table. She's filthy, not just unkempt like at school, but actually caked in dirt. The only clean spots on her face are the runnels of dried tear-tracks streaking her cheeks.

I am speechless for a time. We all are.

"Hey," she says.

"Anna, what on earth?" I move toward her but something brings me up short, maybe the tilt of Mom's chin in my peripheral vision. So I hesitate, frozen by my own uncertainty as she sits, staring at me, then turns away. If only she would cry or shout or something, but she doesn't. She gazes into nothingness while I watch her and my own mother watches me and my husband and son lie dead in the ground, miles away.

44. We decide she should stay with me for a while. "But only a few days," Anna tells me defiantly. "The others are waiting for me in Provincetown. They need me."

"Need you for what?"

She says nothing.

I remember the midnight phone call from Janice. Of course, she was checking to see if Anna had shown up, trying not to seem obvious about it. "Maybe you should call Janice, tell her where you are." I don't bother asking where Janice's phantom parents are. Not in P-town, obviously, or they would have been in touch themselves.

In the car I try to get some idea out of her as to what's going on, why she has come, why she looks so unraveled, but she remains tight-lipped. No surprise there. It runs in the family.

45. I watch her carefully the next couple days. She looks un-healthy, her face pale despite her stint at a beach town, and she seems softer, pudgier. She's also picked up some bug that leaves her vomiting for two days and strung out in bed. "Got rained on, com-ing here," is her explanation.

On the third morning she's feeling better and we sit on the front porch with our breakfast. I'm coming off an overnight at ACC and she's droopy in the morning as usual. But rest and hot showers have got her looking better. Except when she turns that heavy-lidded, accusatory glare on me, the one she's using now.

"Tree's still there," she says.

"Yes it is," I tell her. "The tree man said he couldn't get down before August, so he'll do it when he can." I sip my coffee.

She keeps staring. "Are you telling me the truth?"

"Anna!"

She shrugs. "Mom, I gave it up a long time ago, trying to figure out the system to when you were lying." I am speechless—justifi-ably so—so she goes on. "Whatever, if he does it he does it. But don't expect me to believe it till it's gone."

Then Mrs. Flynn canters by, waving frantically, and the three of us have a nice little reunion, as if everything is normal.

Later, while she showers again, I look through her things. They are few enough. One skirt, pale pink (stained almost brown with road grit); one ratty black T-shirt that I realize with a start that is one of Walter's that she must have rummaged from the attic as she was packing for college. Also one pair very worn flip-flops; one charm bracelet I've never seen before; one silver wrist watch that Grampa Hugh gave her for Christmas; one pair underwear; one bra. That's all she arrived with. No purse no billfold no money no water no food no hat.

I'm sitting on her bed when she reappears. She sees me and says, "I guess some things never change."

"How did you get all the way here?" I ask her.

"I had a ride from a friend partway."

I say nothing.

"After that, I hitched."

I inhale involuntarily. "At night?"

"It was more like sunset when the guy stopped. He took me as far as 128, then I hung out at a Denny's until I found someone going north." She catches my eye as she pulls on a pair of shorts. "It's not a huge deal, Mom. It's like a hundred miles door to door."

"You could've been raped, you could've been *killed*." I press my hands against my eyes but the pictures won't go away: Anna lying on the ground, arms skewed, head twisted back at an unnatural angle. Blood and shit on the leaves under the moonlight.

"Mom, lose the drama, it's not like you give a shit."

I have to replay the sentence to make sure I've heard right. "*What*."

She extracts a salmon-pink T-shirt from her closet, pulls it on and leans toward the mirror to inspect herself. "You never got over Dad and Toby, fine, I can deal with that. I'm still trying to, myself. But save the Anna angst for someone gullible enough to believe it."

It's as if I'm watching someone else. I stand up, grasp her shoulder, wheel her to face me, slap her across the face. Not as hard as I could—as hard as I'd like—but enough that she knows I've done it. Enough to redden her cheek and startle those complacent heavy-lidded eyes.

I have rendered her as speechless as she left me.

"I'll be downstairs," I tell her, "when you're ready to apologize."

46. I'm at ACC that evening, lost in thought while—apparently—gazing at Becky. Eventually she straightens and pins me with a look. "I told you, I already *got* a girlfriend."

"Sorry. Just—thinking about something."

I had planned on asking Becky about dating these days, the etiquette, the expectations. For example, if one's date is constantly running off, claiming other commitments—work, et cetera—at what point am I justified in being annoyed? It's something I've been wondering for a while. Modern times and so on.

But now that Anna's showed up, such concerns suddenly seem less important than before. They seem, frankly, juvenile.

47. I half-expect Anna to leave after I hit her, but instead she stays. Neither is any apology forthcoming as she mopes around the house, "fighting this bug," as she puts it. She eats little and I hear her vomiting in the bathroom.

At some point I really ought to come clean with my daughter. About Russell I mean. She already knows his name, and they're bound to meet sooner or later now that she's home. Who knows, they might get along just fine; after all, Russell is as close to my daughter's age as to mine. But that line of thinking leaves me nauseated, so I push it away. There may come a day when my daughter and I discuss our respective love affairs, but today is most certainly not that day.

48. I'm getting gas when I hear a voice behind me: "I can *pump* it for you if you'd like. I'm always ready to *fill her up.*"

Oh dear. I turn to see Nick, one of my less fortunate choices for casual carnality over the past few years, leaning rakishly against his SUV. Nick tried to sell me insurance one afternoon, failed in that endeavor but succeeded in another, more immediately invigorating one. He has grown more corpulent since then, is squinty-eyed as ever and, saddest of all, remains prone to double-entendres that would entertain a slow sixth grader. I'd never have looked at him a second time were it not for his penis, which is the size of a large flashlight. "Hello, Nick."

He squints a smile my way. "Been ages."

"Has it?"

"Keeping busy?"

"Yes."

"You look fantastic." He licks his lips. "Good enough to eat, or at least lick."

"You too." I'm lying and, to his credit, he knows it. "Got to run."

"We should get together sometime, old times' sake, all that?"

By way of answer I point to the sign over the pumps, the one that says *Self Service*. "No time," I call cheerily, and get out pronto.

49. I wake in the middle of the night to a presence in my room. A silhouette sitting at the foot of the bed, limned by reflected moonlight and the orange street lamp on the corner.

Me: Anna?

Anna: I didn't mean to wake you.

Me: Hm . . . It's not so late.

The clock by my bed reads 3:11.

Anna: I just thought I should tell you, I'm heading back to the Cape pretty soon.

Me: You just got here.

Anna: I know. I think it was a mistake. I mean, being there was hard, you know? A lot of pressure. But I think it was kind of helping too.

Me: Helping you how?

Anna: Oh, you know . . .

Me: Actually I don't.

Anna: You know, with like getting confidence.

Me: Oh *that*.

The archness slides into my voice involuntarily, probably because I'm still groggy. Did she really just say she's about to leave again? I wonder, not for the first time, what on earth is going on with my daughter. I know I should be supportive of her so she can work through her difficulties, but come on—exactly how much support am I expected to give?

Then I wonder why I find it so difficult to do this for my daughter, when all day long I give it to clients who barely know me? *Ah, Herr Doktorr, your answer ees een your question . . .*

Anna has gone silent, sulking probably.

Me: Help me out here. I knew school was stressful and you'd been seeing a counselor, but I thought you were trying to leave that behind in Provincetown.

Anna: Leave it behind? That's a joke. What happened to Toby wasn't something you can just sweep under the rug. Though God knows you try.

(*Pause.*)

Me: I see. This is about Toby then.

Anna: And Daddy.

Me: Of course. (*Pause.*) They go together, after all.

Anna: Do you still dream about it? You used to wake me up with all your screaming.

Me: Well I—but they're, ah. They don't happen anymore now.

Anna: Really?

(*Pause.*)

Me: Not so much.

Anna: I mean, I still get them sometimes.

She is barely whispering now.

(*Pause.*)

Me: So do I, baby. So do I.

(*Pause. She is crying, I think.*)

Me: Not very often though, not anymore. Mostly I'm fine.

Anna: Why did he do it?

There is no good answer to that. I think about saying *Maybe we can ask him someday* or some nonsense but I refuse to give in to cheap One-day-we'll-all-stand-in-the-shadow-of-the-Lord sentiment.

Me: I don't think we'll ever know. He might've been upset about something. He was calm most of the time but you know, he didn't let his temper show. He kept things bottled up. Sometimes it's healthier to be honest.

(*Pause.*)

Anna: Yeah.

(*Pause.*)

Anna: Do you really believe that, or is it just something you tell your patients?

Me: Of course I believe it.

(*Pause.*)

Me: Anyway you said Provincetown wasn't helping much.

Anna: It wasn't, that's why I came here, but . . . I don't know. Now it feels like I might as well have stayed. I was talking about it—about what happened?—with the others a little bit, and they're really cool about it. You know, I never said a word before. All through high school and everything. It was like this horrible family secret.

I wonder about "the others." She's mentioned some mysterious group project, but the only name I have is Janice.

Me: It's understandable, keeping it private. Not that you had any reason to be ashamed but it's not the kind of thing to go around broadcasting.

Anna: I used to think that. But now I *am* talking and it's like, I'm letting it go by facing it.

Me: I see. (*Pause.*) Well, that's one way to try it.

She snuffle-snorts quietly. I consider asking about her other friends but decide to let it pass. If I want her to stick around, I'm probably better off not reminding her of her crew of pals on the beach.

Me: His birthday's tomorrow.

Anna: I know. I think that's really why I came back.

Me: We can go up together.

Anna: I'd like to.

She has stopped crying now. So have I, I suppose. She just sits and I watch the darkness and occasionally a car drives past. After a while it's 4:00 and the birds start up. They sound chipper from the get-go and I wonder if birds ever wake sleepy or dopey or in a bad mood, the ways cats do, if they're ever just *not into it*.

Anna stands up and says, "Guess I'll try to sleep," and I say, "Sweet dreams," and she says, "You too," and it's as if we're a normal mother and daughter, just regular people who could be anywhere instead of this crippled and scarred duo who have to tiptoe around each other wondering who's really saying what and whether the awful secrets we're standing guard over will uncoil and spring out into our lives like zombies rising from their graves, like serpents in the garden.

Her silhouette moves slowly, with a heaviness in her that I recognize. Of course I know why she came home, and why she's afraid to stay. I wonder who got her pregnant and when, or whether, she plans to tell me about it.

50. Wednesday, July 2. Toby's birthday. We drive up to Lowell to visit the graves, put flowers on them, anchor them into the ground with the bent wires. And then, as usual, I stand there a while. If I were the praying type, I might do that.

Russell calls while I'm there but I don't answer, and Mom, and Hugh. Even Rod Menzies, who knows me a bit better than some of my other occasional visitors. I answer none of them. The afternoon darkens down to twilight as I stand there, or sit, or after a while lie outstretched between them both.

Toby would have turned twenty-three today. He'd have graduated college already, maybe started work, maybe gone on to grad school. He'd have a girlfriend no doubt. Or a boyfriend, whatever—I'm not judgmental. He'd have dreams, infatuations, hobbies, biases that made no sense to anyone but him. Little idiosyncrasies, irrationalities. Musical tastes, guilty pleasures, favorite jokes he told over and over. Peeves. Secrets. Skills only recently discovered. Pets he doted on. And he'd have a mother who loved him, probably a father too. And other things of course that I can't even imagine.

I lie there for the longest time. Someone approaches, hovers, tiptoes away. Groundskeeper? Who knows.

After a time I get up, wipe off my face. It's gotten dark and my arms are peppered with mosquito bites and flakes of grass. I wish I had some water to rinse the gummy taste from my mouth, but I don't, so instead I go search for my cell, lying somewhere in the grass in the dark, wherever I flung it.

51. In the car she says, "I think I miss Daddy more and you miss Toby more. That's one of the differences between us."

I grip the steering wheel and try not to howl.

"Dolores and I talked about that for a long time."

It is unclear whether this is simple thoughtlessness, or if she is actively trying to wound me. Either way doesn't matter really. "I can*not* have this conversation right now."

She studies me for a moment before turning to stare straight ahead, through the windshield. I gun the engine and we leave.

52. Fourth of July: Anna and Hugh and I catch the fireworks downtown, over the Harbor. Afterward we go slumming in a wretched Mexican place called Mama Chiquita's: sombreros on the walls, tricolored tablecloths, that kind of thing. Olé-olé music blaring over the sound system, a waitress about as Latina as I am: a goth white girl with black lipstick and studs in her eyebrows. She and Anna exchange bored glares. Hugh doesn't even bother trying to flirt with her.

Anna is wearing another black T-shirt, one of hers this time, not Walter's: *Rehab Is For Quitters.* Now she tells her grandfather, "Mom's all about the *honesty* these days."

Hugh makes a little parting-of-the-hands gesture, as if to say *Well now, that's not such a bad thing.*

"That's why she has a boyfriend half her age who she sleeps with but doesn't introduce to any of us."

Hugh looks around. "Anybody seen that waitress?"

I stop grinding my teeth long enough to say, "How about those fireworks?"

She smirks. "Nothing like *yours* lately."

"Chips?" Hugh calls out to our goth friend, who looks through us, then away with no acknowledgment.

"I think I want a beer," Anna announces. "I'm turning eighteen in a couple weeks, Grampa, don't you think I'm entitled?"

"What's the drinking age these days?" he asks her.

"Fourteen."

"When did they raise it?"

She shouldn't drink while she's pregnant. Should I say anything?

"Chips please," Hugh says to the waitress, who rolls her eyes and slouches off.

"Jesus, who died and left her a bitch?" says Anna. Hugh tells her, "Glad you're finally over that bug."

"Oh yeah. It was bad for a while, I was throwing up everything. But I haven't puked for days now."

"Mm," I say.

We receive chips and salsa and order enchiladas (Hugh), fajitas (Anna) and a salad (me). Hugh treats himself to a Cape Codder while Anna orders a beer. The waitress considers asking for ID—the thought flickers across her face before disappearing into the vast closet of things she can't be bothered about. Then she's gone and Anna says to Hugh, "Mom hit me the other night."

"Did you deserve it?"

This takes her by surprise. Sometimes I adore my father-in-law. "No," she says, but too late; we all know she spent too long thinking about it.

Surprisingly, the food isn't bad. Anna inhales hers as usual, leaving Hugh and I to eat in a companionable silence. At length he pushes away his empty plate. "Enough," he says, and it's just me and my salad, thirty chews per mouthful.

"Let's go out on your birthday," Hugh says to Anna. "Just us two, leave your mother to her own devices."

"I might not be here, but if I am, okay."

"We can go bar hopping. Or something. We can go to the Rathskellar." He looks at me. "Is that place still open?"

"I've no idea."

Anna is frowning. "Never heard of it."

Hugh's fingers flutter in an ah-it-doesn't-matter gesture. "We'll find some places. There's plenty to do. How's that sound? Assuming you aren't with your friends."

"My friends have all left—and anyway it sounds fun. Thanks, Grampa Hugh." She says this with no trace of irony or spite. "If I'm still here, let's definitely do it."

I say nothing, but heartily approve.

53. Lately I walk around feeling an edginess, an unsettledness of heart. A kind of internal bedlam. Thoughts and feelings jostle against each other, trying to find their usual places and failing. Nothing settles where it's supposed to. Partly this is related to Anna's presence in the house, partly it's other things. One of those other things is the letter, upstairs, in my bedroom dresser, that I have never opened.

My patients seem to feel restless too: the Hayeses and Reverend Charles and Ak-Ak and Beth Ann Kim and the rogues' gallery at ACC and all the rest. More bedlam. Nobody seems comfortable in their lives, everyone is restless and dissatisfied. Normal enough, one might say, but it's more than usual lately. And it seems to be catching.

Interesting word, bedlam. Bethlehem Hospital for Men opened in London in the 1500s, Henry VIII's gift to his people. This particular hospital was specifically meant for mental patients, and it lasted for hundreds of years, quickly gaining notoriety for its raucous mayhem. Imagine hundreds of chronically mentally ill cooped up in a stone prison with no treatment besides fetters, chains, beatings. Visitors shuffled through to gawk at the loonies, copping a vicarious thrill from someone else's misery. Not so different from a night at the movies nowadays, *Cheerleader Bloodbath* and so forth.

The hospital charged a penny per visit, with close to a hundred thousand tourists per year. Something to think about. And as Bethlehem Hospital deteriorated from treatment center to jail to tourist attraction, its name crumbled as well. From Bethlehem to Bedlehem to Bedlam. Until there was no distinction between the place and the situation, between Bedlam and bedlam.

"Crazy times," Walter had said, when I told him about it. This was early on, during my undergrad years. Toby a toddler and Anna not even an idea on the horizon. I'd learned about Bedlam in some psych class or other, and thought the story would appeal to Walter's well-honed appreciation of the absurd. But instead he'd looked startled, even annoyed. "Those people were living in crazy times, Ranger. Treating people that way. I'm glad we're better than that now."

To which I found that I had no answer, or more properly, such a multitude of answers that no single one stood out.

54. For a time I give up on sleep, at least, regular nighttime sleep that refreshes and rejuvenates. Instead I spend long hours out on the porch, staring late into the night, sipping chamomile tea and listening to the crickets. Other times I wander into the yard, the woods in back, linger beside the towering sugar maple with its long-abandoned treehouse. In the night I can't see it, can't hear it, can't touch it but I know it's there. This is what some people say about God.

Anna takes to locking herself in her bedroom and talking to herself. I can hear her voice, muffled through the door. She seems to be having whole conversations. Maybe she's talking to the baby. When she comes out of the room she acts perfectly normal.

55. Insomniac, I slip into the car and zip down the highway, past Cambridge, over the Charles and into the city. The John Hancock building heaves against the sky, straight-edged and sinister, like a gravestone. The Pru tower is still the ugliest skyscraper ever built—supposedly it drove one poor fellow to suicide back in the '50s. (Walter used to say: "Only one?") Sometimes I worm the car through the narrow lanes of the North End, eyeball the cannoli in the bakery windows, enjoying the sensation of not giving in.

I don't know what to do about my daughter. This is probably obvious. I don't know what to do about Russell Blanco. Maybe this is obvious too. They both want more from me, or maybe less, or maybe just something different, than I am prepared to give.

The lack of sleep is unhealthy but I don't realize how much it's affecting me till I nod off in a session with the Hayeses. When I jerk my head up, they're no longer in their seats, but looking at me from the door.

I am mortified. "I'm so sorry, I—"

"It's all right dear," says Mrs. Hayes. "You look exhausted, are you feeling okay?"

"I'm fine, it's just, I'm just—" I grope for words. This is unconscionable, it's the kind of thing that should be reported.

"You need some sleep," says the husband.

I take a breath. "Yes. But that's not the point."

He winces at my tone. "Get some rest."

"We'll see you next time," says Mrs. Hayes.

I see them out the door, still woozy but energized now by embarrassment and shame. "I can't apologize enough, it's really been a strange week."

"No need to apologize," says Mrs. Hayes, patting my hand with her own rabbity paw. "I'll never forget, you're the one who got me off those other medicines."

Mr. Hayes smiles agreeably, a wry, worn expression. "And we know all about strange weeks, don't we dear?"

Which just makes me feel worse than ever, though I know he means well.

56. Did I ever talk to my children before they were born? Honestly, I can't remember doing it. There was some theory, for a time, that doing so would make the child smarter. Teach them their numbers or the Japanese alphabet or some such, and they pop out as little proto-Asian mathematical geniuses. The theory, as I recall, didn't last.

It's something I can imagine Walter doing, but strictly for laughs. Bending close to my swollen belly, leering like Groucho Marx: "What d'you think of that, buddy?" Or, "Any comments from the inside?" It's the sort of thing he would have done. But really, I might just be making it up. I don't know who to ask. My mother? The idea is mortifying.

Anna is in her room, talking.

I tap on her door and I say, "I think I'm cracking up. Can I come in? I'll try to be nicer than I have been."

A brief pause, then the door swings open. I step inside and perch on her bed. She sits at her desk holding a slender book. Maybe she is reading stories to her baby. "What's going on, Mom? Why are you like this?"

"Nothing's going on."

"*Mom*. Is it me, am I bothering you, should I go?"

"Of course not." I take a breath. "Some things aren't great, I'll admit."

"I'm leaving after my birthday, if that helps."

"You know that's not what I want."

She shrugs. "That's what I'm doing though. I—have to." When I say nothing, she peers at me. "It's that guy, isn't it? That Russell guy."

"We don't need to talk about him."

"That's exactly who you need to talk about. Seriously, get a counselor. Or a shrink."

I manage a lighthearted, fluttery laugh that sounds something like a chicken being thrown beneath a train. "I can't imagine where you get this stuff."

"I get it from *you*, Mom."

I wish I had a glass of wine. "I'm sure you're having a ball with your friends, but that's no reason to fall into some *Endless Summer* reenactment. July's half over already."

"That's sort of the point, I don't have time to—I just can't stay, okay? I got, geez, I have responsibilities out there. You know?"

"Actually, I don't."

"You're always going on about how I need to face up to things, well, here I am doing it." Her tone is midway between pleading and defiant. The defiance is new and theoretically healthy but, I admit, not entirely welcome at this juncture. *Patient resistant to treatment* . . . I ask as calmly as possible, "What exactly are you doing that requires such fortitude?"

"I don't want to go into all that."

Something in her tone brings it home and I stay as calm as possible—which is, all things considered, pretty calm indeed. "It'd be better for—well." She continues staring at me owlishly. One eyebrow arched. If she won't bring it up, then I need to. "Better for the baby."

The silence lasts a beat too long. "What did you just say?"

"It's nothing to be ashamed of—" Well yes it is, I know that better than most, but we're not here to talk about me, "—and you must have known I'd figure it out. You're twenty pounds heavier, you throw up every morning, you obviously haven't been out lounging on the beach . . ." I break off. My daughter is staring with a look poised midway between fury and hysterical laughter. And a fair amount of relief no doubt. I pull myself together: "For goodness' sake Anna, I can't believe you wouldn't tell me a thing like this." My hands are trembling and my own breath whistles in my ears.

Some time trickles by. I sit at the edge of her bed with my head propped up in my hands. Do we parents forever doom our offspring to repeat our own mistakes? The answer would appear to be yes. Anna says nothing for so long I start to wonder if she's still there.

She is. I know this because after some minutes she says, "Mom." Her voice tight and cautious, the tone you adopt when talking to a cat that might, or might not, decide to use its claws on you. "Listen to me. I'm not pregnant, okay? None of my friends are pregnant. I'm in P-town because I'm in a play, all right? I wasn't going to tell you but you're acting so *fucking* weird. It's Shakespeare, okay? So it should meet even your high standards."

This takes some time to settle. "A play?"

"I guess that's why I'm pale—I didn't think I looked so horrible but hey, I guess my mother does. I'm inside all day rehearsing, see? She waves the little book in front of me. "Learning lines. As for those twenty pounds, it's more like ten, but yeah I gained some weight at school last year. Thanks for reminding me to feel like shit."

"Anna . . ."

"And the puking? I had the flu, remember? Or maybe you never believed me, maybe you thought I was just making up some cover story." She throws the book on her desk and storms out the door. "Who knows *what* the fuck you think anymore."

"Anna wait. Come back."

Her voice floats up from the stairs. "Why? So you can hit me again?"

The front door slams.

57. I call Russell. "Can we go somewhere?"

"Sure."

"If you want to. Are you sure you want to?" I'm still in Anna's room, scanning the photos adorning her dresser, desk, walls. Little-girl frames with seahorses and rainbows, older-girl frames of sleek blue plastic and stained wood. Anna with her high school friends, or by herself. Older ones with her father and brother. I notice there are multiple photos of Walter and Toby, only one of me. Smiling weakly, standing next to the Saab, which was brand new. I look eager to drive away.

He says, "Of course I want to."

Maybe she took the rest of my pictures to hang in her dorm room. Yes that must be it, ha ha.

"You're not too busy?"

He sighs whistlingly through his nose. "Sure I'm busy, but I want to see you."

The photos create a recognizable chronology: little girl with daddy and big brother; school kid at a birthday party (hers? I'm not sure); high school girl, angular and reedy; high school grad, suddenly slender and even, to some degree, poised. Mischievous smile and a dimple on the left side. Was I ever that graceful? I'm pretty sure I wasn't. Certainly not then, probably not now. "Why?"

"Sorry?"

"*Why* do you want to see me?" I ask him.

That's a stumper, apparently. After a time he says, "I don't follow you."

"What's the big appeal? I'm older than you. I'm in the second half of my life, statistically speaking. You aren't. There's any number of lithe college cuties in your restaurant who'd love to hang on your arm. Or elsewhere."

"Godalmighty, Gina." He pauses a moment while I gaze at a picture of a bikinied Anna hamming it up for the camera alongside some other girls. I wonder who took the picture, what day it was, what year it was. Russell says, "I guess you're fishing for compliments, so here goes. You're beautiful, you're smart, you have a wicked sense of humor. I'm never bored when I'm with you, which is more than I can say about most women. You're . . . intense. You don't talk about pointless shit, I like that."

Mm—according to some people, I don't even talk about important shit, but we'll let that go for now. "Plus I have a steady income. More than those college cuties, most of them anyway."

"Right. And a nice car, which is really really important to me. And a big house." He pauses for breath. "And you're good in bed."

"Okay that's enough." I refrain from saying, *And your mommy died years ago.*

He says, "So what do you want to do?"

His turn to stump me. It's quite some time before I can formulate an answer.

58. "This summer rep company is doing *Othello* and my friend Janice, she's done stuff with them before and convinced me to audition." We're on the front porch as twilight settles like a shroud over the neighborhood. Anna sprawls on the love seat, bonding with a contented Brutus, while I swing moodily on Walter's handiwork. "So I tried out and they picked me and now I'm Desdemona, that's the female lead."

"I know."

"You know?"

"I mean I know Desdemona is the female lead, I didn't know you were playing her." Desdemona, as I recall, dies. Tragically young and at the hands of her lover, a man old enough to be her father. I decide not to point this out, lest it dampen my daughter's newfound enthusiasm for thespian pursuits, and/or give her another reason to exit stage right. But really, consider the unfairness of it all, the girls always getting smothered while the boys stand around soliloquizing.

It could be worse I suppose, she could be playing Hamlet's kid sister Ophelia, psychobabbling her way to the bottom of a river.

"Anyway, the director got sick suddenly, so rehearsals were put on hold. We all went off to learn our lines and get together at the end of the summer. So, I'm going back after my birthday."

"I see. Well, congratulations. I'm proud of you." I resist the mean-spirited impulse to make comments about *doing something creative*. "When is it?"

"We pushed it back to the end of August."

"I'm sure you'll be wonderful."

"Glad one of us is."

"Hush. I can't wait to see it."

Another pause, and I know what's coming. "I'd rather you didn't go."

This hurts more than I expect. "I see."

A good deal more in fact.

"It's just, this is my first play, and I'm pretty nervous about it, and knowing you're out there, you know, you're always so critical about everything."

"I won't be critical."

"Honest, I'd rather you just didn't. Okay?" When I don't answer she repeats herself. "Okay?"

I wish I had more wine. "I feel like I hardly know my daughter anymore, it's as if you had some, a hidden life of some sort."

"Funny, that's just how I feel, when you won't like tell me a thing about this Russell guy who's freaking you out so much." She sniffs. "You can't expect me to do things for you that you won't do for me. But listen, if you like him? Then go ahead and see him. There's nothing wrong with it, you're not letting anybody down if you do something you want to do."

"I don't—I'm not worried about—"

"It's not some betrayal, is what I mean. Of Dad or Toby or whatever."

"My daughter, the therapist." I mean it to come out light, but it sounds bitchy.

"Mom, whatever."

We sit there a while and then she goes inside and I stay there on the swing, crying. But quietly, not so as anyone would notice.

Brutus looks at me and squints.

Desdemona is the only one of Shakespeare's heroines who dies in view of the audience. I wonder if Anna knows that. (I wonder why *I* know it—Walter, probably.) Ophelia is safely out of sight when she throws herself in the river, Cordelia and Lady Mac are run through offstage. As far as I can remember there are no women in *Julius Caesar* at all, certainly not one who gets smothered while we sit and eagerly soak up every shudder and shriek of the performance.

Oh Anna. Why does it have to be *this* play?

59. My daughter celebrates her birthday by going out with her grandfather as planned. I meet Russell at his favorite jazz club. The band is between sets when we arrive. In the spirit of openness and an honest exchange of information, I talk again about Walter, our brief courtship, our married life. I go into more detail than last time. As the evening wears on, I come to the night that everything changed. Is this such a good idea, to go over this sorry ground one more time? I find myself unable to judge. "Anyway, that's what happened and I'll never know why."

Russell frowns. "And there was no note?"

"No note," I say, and leave it at that.

He frowns. "That's unusual, isn't it?"

"Not necessarily. Usually there's a note, but not always. It depends."

"On the individual."

"Exactly."

He nods, eyeballing me peripherally but intently. "I don't mean to push, Gina—"

"It's all right. I think I—we need to talk about this. Push all you want."

"Okay. I appreciate that, I really do. It's just."

I wait, raise an eyebrow.

"I mean, I don't know what was going on in Walter's head."

"Neither did I. Obviously."

"But one time you said there was always a note, and you said it was very rare when there wasn't. Remember?"

"Actually I don't. This was when exactly?"

"I was telling you about my—about the time I almost, you know." He lowers his voice and leans close. "Jumped." He sits back. "But didn't. Got saved, whatever, you don't believe me anyway. Remember? You said I must've written a note before I left the dorm—and you were right."

I sip my wine. "I remember now. I told you then that Walter didn't. It's unusual, yes, but not unheard of."

He grins, sort of. "Okay. I'm not trying to, like, trip you up or anything."

"I know."

"I just, you know. It would make things easier to understand, maybe."

"Maybe."

He inhales deeply. "I like you a lot."

"I know."

He lets it drop. We talk about other things. His buddy who's moved to Hawaii, we joke about moving there too. I get going on Anna, realize how typical I sound, change the subject. He picks up with his sister in Miami and their recent tentative attempts to reconnect. I tell a few high-school war stories, from back when I was wild: wailing down Storrow Drive with Trish and some other girls, happy from blackberry brandy, my parents at home thinking we were on a school trip. Which in a sense we were.

"Just goes to show," he smiles. "You can't trust anybody. You never know."

But the whole time we're talking, Walter is on a low simmer in the background. Like he was in reality, I suppose. And Toby too: my changeable son, mercury leaked from a thermometer. Given to long sulks and sudden uncalled-for bouts of affection. Friend to all creatures, cuddly and otherwise, birds in particular. But other things too. He went through the phase when he wanted a puppy we never got around to buying. (Walter was, against all expectations, a dog-hating cat lover.) Maybe we should've gotten Toby a puppy.

Maybe not. Just another corpse, half grown, covered with golden fur and a twisted neck. Another sharp cry in the dark. Oh Christ. Toby's not on a low simmer for long—he's there, rising up, covered in mud and blood and dead leaves.

"Gina, you listening to me?"

But no note.

"Hey, Earth to Gina. You all right?"

That's unusual, isn't it?

"I hope I didn't just tell the entire story of Lenny's Camaro for nothing."

I don't mean to push.

"Excuse me—miss? Can we have our bill? The sooner the better."

I'm not trying to trip you up or anything.

"Here's a tissue. Come on, blow your nose, you're leaking all over the place. Shh, it's gonna be okay."

You don't believe me anyway.

"Keep the change, thanks a lot. Come on, Gina, here's your jacket. One arm at a time. First left then right, you got it."

Depends on the individual.

"She'll be all right, man. We had a little more than we needed is all, but thanks."

Why did he do it, Mom?

"Let's get you home now."

I still get dreams sometimes.

I try to say something but it comes out a wheeze. Outside the warm summer air washes over me and I crawl into it like a quilt. Everything seems distant: traffic sounds, neon flashing red against the pavement, Russell's hand on my elbow.

why

The air is heavy with the promise of a midsummer cloudburst.

But no note. That's unusual, isn't it?

Oh Christ, Russell. Just let it *go.*

60. The envelope is business sized, plain white gone a little yellow now with age, bent at one corner. It's been stashed at the back of my chest of drawers for years, like a tumor, like a boil gone septic, growing more painful the longer I wait. Sealed across the back with a ribbon of Scotch tape as yellow as piss.

Nearly featureless but not quite. On the front is a single word, handwritten in spidery faded pencil, stuck in the corner where it stains the white like a squashed bug:

why

I have never unsealed the envelope to read what is inside. The very idea terrifies me. If I knew less about what such notes could contain, I might've done it long ago. But I know plenty. A page-long rant of recriminations, guilt, pain, despair and self-pity is not what I need to come to terms with my husband's death, or my son's for that matter. So I've never looked. I stuck it in the drawer and proceeded to not forget about it.

Funny things, suicide notes. Written when the person is alive, delivered when he's dead. (Or she, but statistically speaking, it's usually he.) Hard to imagine sitting down to write a letter, knowing I'll have murdered myself by the time someone reads it. I try to put myself in that position, imagine that state of mind, but fail. I fail again and again and again.

61. Russell drives me home in his car. When he gets me to the house I pull him inside and hold him to me and begin tugging at his clothes.

"Really?" he says. "Are you sure?"

"Yes. More than anything."

Still he hesitates. "You seem upset, I don't want to take advantage of—"

"Just lay me on my back and fuck me."

That dispels his hesitation. Spare a thought for the poor guy, he barely has a free hour these days and here he's hitched his wagon to some moody career broad with *issues*. Well, that's the price of chasing older women: they have secrets. Not that I have many left, at this point.

Later, I loll on the bed with a glass of wine. My dress is still hiked up and the bedcover is rumpled, but since we never bothered with actually getting under the blankets, the disorder is minimal. I stare at the ceiling while he pulls on his underwear—modest boy, the white glows luminescent against that all-over tan—and finds a place to sit in the rocking chair by the bay window. After a time he asks, "You all right?"

"Better now, much." I'm not lying. I sip my wine then raise my glass in invitation. "Go ahead get yourself something."

"I'm okay."

My postorgasmic glow is fading and he looks disconcerted. I decide it's time for some music and hit the play button on the console next to my pillow. Locatelli bubbles from the speakers, filling the room like potpourri.

Russell folds into the rocker, almost laughably awkward. Walter made that chair, one of his last projects before his—before he died. I've always loved it, but Russell doesn't know where to put his feet: on the floor, on top of the runner, pulled up under himself. He tries all three positions, and others, with varying degrees of success. It occurs to me that he knows how to sit up straight and how to walk at a brisk clip, and under duress he can even lie down and relax. But this lounging, this dreamy-eyed gazing out the window while rocking back and forth, is something alien to him.

He'd be lousy at the beach. Great in the water, great playing volleyball or throwing a Frisbee or riding a Jet Ski, but crummy at reclining on a big towel and staring into the surf.

"Really," I say after a time. "Pour yourself something. You hardly touched your drink at the bar, and I'm much better now. Just a bit of temporary madness."

Legs shift in the rocker. "I'm arright, really, and anyway." He hesitates. "I should have a clear head for the road."

His words have the unfortunate effect of a poke in the eye: my newfound calm disperses instantly. Or as Anna would say, *That really pisses me off.* "You're leaving?"

"Can't help it, Gina, gotta be at work to close up." He checks his watch. "In fact I should've left by now, but you were feeling, you know."

"Oh was I."

"Thought I should stick around."

"Thanks." There's a hornet buzzing somewhere just behind my eyes. My God, his words infuriate me. "Trust me, you needn't do any charity on my account, you don't need to be the—what do you call it?—the Good Samaritan."

"Come on, don't be like that.'

It's unfortunate that one of my pet peeves is people telling me *Don't be like that.* "Just clear out now and take your, your good deeds with you." I sound awful I know, some grade-A bitch from hell or Texas, but it's as if something irresistible has slipped under my skin and taken control of the levers and toggles. I fumble for a tissue, can't find one. Russell gets to his feet to hand me one from the box on my dresser, my hands twitch like an old boxer's who's been k.o.'d too many times. Maybe this is what I get for letting my guard down: a sharp jab to the chin. "My God, is that why you slept with me, Russell? Do you—look at me while I'm talking to you—do you fuck me out of charity?"

He's back in the rocker. "Gina, what's with you tonight—"

"Get your—just get out of here. *Go.* Go to the restaurant and dish up ice cream for the girlies and leave me alone, which is, ironically, just what the restaurant is good for, isn't it? Leaving me alone, so you get to keep your distance from the woman who doesn't always look so great in the morning—"

He lets out a sound unlike anything I've heard before, an inarticulate grunt of anger, angst, fury, I don't know what. When I look at him I'm shocked: his face has gone such a deep cinnamon I'm sure he's ready for apoplexy, and his fists—fists!—are actually trembling with what I assume is rage. For a moment I'm genuinely afraid.

"Don't hit me," I say.

He snorts out a little laugh.

"I mean it, I'll press charges." Plus I have pepper spray but I'm not about to tell him that. How well do we know anyone, really?

"What the *fuck* is going on in here?"

I jolt upright. Anna slouches in the doorway, scanning us like we're lunatics behind plate glass. She's wearing a T-shirt and panties. I demand, "When did you get back?"

"Before you did." She rolls a sardonic eye toward Russell. "Don't beat up my mom. I know she can be frustrating, but she's still my mom."

His mouth flaps like a fish's. "I'm Russell."

"Figured. I'm Anna, nice to meet you, except, not really." She swivels toward me. "How was your *date*?"

I gather up the remaining shreds of my dignity. "Anna."

She takes in the crumpled bedclothes, my disheveled hair. "Seems like it went okay."

"Maybe I should get going," says Russell.

"Don't let me interrupt, I was just trying to sleep." Anna strives for a kind of airy bitchiness and succeeds rather well. "By the way my birthday was great, thanks for asking."

"Happy birthday," says Russell.

"Good night," I say.

"Oh *that's* subtle." Something seems to cross her mind, and she turns a frown toward Russell. "If you plan on getting involved with this family, good luck with all our secrets. Consider yourself warned."

"I'm already involved," he says, tightening his belt and flashing The Grin.

"Mm. But are you ready?"

"Anna," I say.

"Ready for what?" He frowns. "You mean there's more?"

"*Anna*."

"What's she told you? About my father I suppose—and my brother?"

"Yup." To his credit he meets her eye squarely, and doesn't seem put off by her intense witch-woman-speaking-the-Oracle routine. "In fact we were discussing them tonight, which is what got your mom so mad at me. She thinks I shouldn't have to go to work. Apparently your father didn't, so nobody else should, either."

My hot anger flares up again, then quickly cools to icy fury. "Don't you dare compare yourself to my husband."

Anna says, "Yeah, actually." Stop the presses: my daughter is agreeing with me.

He's on his feet now, pulls on a sweatshirt. "You brought this on, Gina."

"Don't talk about Walter."

"Suit yourself. Me, I have a life, I have dreams. You may think they're stupid, but listen, what I do is as important as what you do. You don't believe that, do you?"

I say nothing, but the fact is, no, I don't believe ice cream is as important as mental health. Silly me.

"I feed people, I give them someplace to go. A lot of them, I know their names. There are homeless guys who come and nurse one cup of coffee all night. Old ladies chat me up and forget to be lonely. I do a good thing, I give families something to do. It's a fun place for a neighborhood that doesn't have many of them. Get it?"

I set my empty wineglass aside. "Don't ever mention Walter's name again. Ever. Get it?"

He looks away at nothing. The dust hovering suspended in the air. "This may be the last thing I ever say to you, ever, but here goes.

Maybe if your husband had been happier chasing his own dream, he wouldn't have done what he did. Have you ever considered that?"

"Stop."

Anna gasps, "*What*?"

Russell stands in the doorway, dressed now. "Maybe if he'd had more of a life, he wouldn't have taken it out on your son."

"Stop. Right now. Please, just, stop." I'm not angry anymore, surprisingly, though I ought to be incensed enraged livid et cetera. How often does one get accused of causing a spouse's death? And a child's in the bargain. But instead of being furious I'm just so tired, and sad right down to my ankles.

Anna is staring at me. "What have you *told* him?"

"I know all about your father and your brother," Russell snaps. "I'm sorry about what happened, I really am. It must've been—very hard for you."

"What do you know about it?"

"Listen, I'm late already."

"*What* do you *know*?"

I sit on the bed feeling as if I'm in the theater. My emotions are pricked, certainly, but they also tucked safely behind several thick layers of canvas or wool, out of reach of these two actors reciting their lines before me.

I watch the spray of emotions sprinkling across Russell's face as he struggles to decide whether to explain himself or just cut his losses and bolt. To his credit, he decides to explain.

"I know your father and brother were in the treehouse that night. There was some sort of argument, maybe your dad lost his temper. Maybe he'd been drinking, or anyway something must've happened, and Toby was in the line of fire . . ." He breaks off.

Anna ignores him, stares at me, her face crimson. "You told him that?"

"I, tried to explain but it, I could never—"

"You said *that*?"

I can barely see her face, or his. I try to speak but can't. I cough up phlegm, find the tissue I dropped earlier and spit into it. Wipe my hand across my nose and it comes away slick with snot. I manage to croak, "Walter."

"Exactly." Which of them says it?

I breathe deep and look at Russell. "It wasn't Walter."

His face is rinsed of all expression. "What wasn't Walter?"

"Walter didn't kill Toby."

"Oh. You mean—there was someone else." His face hardens.

"Jesus *Christ*," mutters Anna. "Connect the fucking *dots*."

"Please understand. That time when I got angry with you, with the photo albums. It was, it's a very difficult thing to talk about."

His expression waffles between *Honey you are truly screwed up* and *I wonder what she'll come up with this time*. I'm pretty well past caring. I don't make it a habit to go into those woods in back of the house but the contours of the scene are familiar enough, acid-burnt into memory: the white birch trunks like ribs from something dead, the moonlight like stale milk. I had no flashlight and it's probably just as well, there was no need to see more than I did. The silence was a threat, and the darkness. I called and called, Walter's name, then vague inarticulate shriekings because I just knew something had gone horribly wrong. No one answered. Dry leaves crunched underfoot like old fingers and somewhere, far off, the celebratory yowl of sirens. I remember wondering how they knew about this already, but they weren't coming to me, not yet. I never called them. It was Mrs. Flynn who would do so, much later, after bustling over to see what had happened.

The first body I tripped over was Walter's. Such a big man, somehow even larger in death. His body huge and humped up on the ground, I stumbled into his legs and put my hand down to steady myself and his flannel shirt met my flesh, his thick unresponsive torso. A weird sensation. Then the reek hit me, blood and shit, mud, dead leaves, mulch. The perfume of futility and death. It's surprising how distinctly a freshly dead body smells, breaking into its component fluids and tissues. It takes no time at all, we're all just minutes away.

No doubt I was shrieking or moaning by then, God knows. I don't remember.

I reeled back and was tripped up a second time, something snatching my ankle like a cold hand, I looked down and my eyes were adjusting to the dark and I realized it *was* a cold hand, twisted backward like the claw of something that shouldn't have ever been. Not Walter's, no, it was too small. Toby's arms were splayed at an angle never intended by nature, his legs too—one trapped beneath him, the other draped across his father's unmoving figure. On top of his father. That's why Walter looked so unnaturally large in the shadowy night, because it was more than just Walter.

Sounds came out of my throat that I had never heard before. They seemed to bounce through the naked branches overhead, the majestic maple shivering in a light breeze, the treehouse glowering like a skull, its windows vacant as dead black eyes peering down at the scene. The keening woman, the broken man, the lifeless boy who had used the treehouse as a birdhouse a retreat a hideaway a launching platform from which to chop off his own life at the knees, first making sure to send his father tumbling out before him.

Three

BEDLAM

"They called me mad, and I called them mad, and damn them, they outvoted me."

—Nathaniel Lee (1649 – 1692),
Restoration playwright and
inmate of Bethlehem Hospital,
1684 – 1689

1. I have not been entirely honest.

And honesty's important. Isn't it? I always say so. It's what I tell Anna anyway, and my patients. So then. I'll try to do better from now on.

For example.

Toby died. Walter, apparently, died first. There are several possible conclusions one might draw from that.

I became a mess for a while, and so, perhaps, did Anna. But we pulled through, one way or another, the way people do. Time heals all wounds as the saying goes, along with, I don't know, love and distraction and a little wine and a little medication.

Some years later I meet Russell Blanco, we get to know each other a little. We become tentative friends, we have a fight, we make up and make love and I get mightily confused and shut things off for a while. Anna's there too, in and out of the picture, not helping things much. Not that I blame her but there it is. I don't know if it's all worth it, this tension and argument, this endless dancing between her and me and me and him. It feels easier to just let it all go.

But I don't know if I want that, and I don't know what to do. And that's where I am, if I'm being entirely honest. And also: there is an envelope. In my dresser, upstairs, in the bedroom. Top drawer. I've mentioned this already, I know.

2. Sea gulls hover like squawking kites on the updrafts. Noisiest birds on the planet, but I like them. Hard to imagine a seagull with a secret. They shine whiter than the piles of cumulus that rear up into a sky as blue as lapis. Surf murmuring below it, gunmetal gray. No beach no palm trees no surfers. Nothing pretty, just harsh rocky Maine shoreline, waves knocking patiently, knowing time is on their side. Thirty thousand years from now, there will be sand. Till then, stunted pines crowd thick along the edge. Inshore they grow taller. The birds harangue one another, the sun silvers the edges of the clouds as they meander south on the jet stream.

I'm sitting on Trish's porch. It's a little past eight in the morning.

Around the cabin, white birch and hemlocks shoulder against each other, oaks loom overhead, a tangle of branches hosting convocations of jays and titmice, goldfinches and chickadees. Nuthatches hop upside-down, peeping. I learned about these birds from my husband, and then again from my son. Trish tells me a colony of puffins roosts on the rocky islands a mile offshore, but I haven't seen any yet. Toby never saw them either, maybe it's something we could've done, or should have. Somehow there never seemed to be time.

Years ago, Trish retreated from Boston and settled about as far north as she could get without a passport. Sitting now on her ragged rattan loveseat, with the salt breeze weathering my face, I feel like I've gone to the end of the world and I'm looking over the edge. It's just where I want to be.

The *ass* end of the world is how Walter described it, loudly, more than once.

The screen door creaks open and Trish appears, carrying a tray. Two steaming mugs and a terra cotta decanter, chunky and green-glazed, her own work. She settles beside me on the love seat and sets the tray between our feet.

She hands me a mug. I say, "Up the rebels," and she says, "Fuckin' right." We tap mugs and sip. The coffee is milky, sweet and heavenly.

She presses into me. Trish is my age but bigger, softer. Her backside is generous, always has been, and she's top-heavy as well. Still she exudes a kind of radiant health, with long auburn hair only starting to streak, her eyes burning with a raccoon's steady brown intensity, and her cheeks—must be all that fresh Maine air—positively rosy.

We watch the clouds awhile. The gulls yap at each other like politicians. I ask, "Brandon up?"

"He's with Jennifer. They needed some privacy."

This is Trish's way of saying they're having sex. Much as I love my friend, there are some things I'll never get used to, and one of them is the casual way she contemplates her teenage child's sex life. But it's Trish's nature to withhold judgment. For her, the only sin is cowardice, both the kind that prevents one from making a decision and that which tries to avoid the repercussions. Apart from this quirk, she's completely nonjudgmental. Isn't that why I came here in the first place?

The morning after the meltdown with Russell, Anna asked me for money. "For the bus to P-town," she told me. I gave it to her and she left. The house rang loud with her absence.

I moved fast. Told Rod Menzies at St. Mary's that I'd been called away, did the same with Muffin at the group home and my private clients. Nobody's on suicide watch; they'll manage. The one person I didn't call was Russell. I left my cell on the kitchen table and gassed up the Saab; by noon yesterday I was well north of 128, and pulling into Trish's long gravel driveway by dinnertime.

"You mind if I stay here a few days?" I stood in her doorway like a waif.

"Long as you don't mind sharing a bed," she answered. "The kids've got the futon, it's lumpy anyway. Why don't you go jump in the water? It'll do you good, you look like hell."

3. There is an envelope and in it is a letter. Or a note, some people might say.

There's an envelope containing a note in my dresser in my bedroom. Top drawer, right hand side. Tucked away beneath a pile of old ticket stubs and insurance statements and earrings I never wear anymore because Walter gave them to me, and his death certificate. And birth certificate. And Toby's too, both of them.

There's a letter in my

There's a letter in my dresser and the envelope has gone yellow and the tape across the back a darker yellow like urine on a hot day. That deep almost-orange that's the body's way of shouting *Slow down, drink some water, get out of the sun before your electrolytes get seriously compromised*. There's a letter. Or more likely a note. Most people would call it a note, given the circumstances. Toby wrote it.

When I told Russell *There's always a note* I wasn't lying. Not at that moment anyway. There have been other times however when I was not so forthcoming. There is a letter Toby wrote me or a note in my dresser upstairs where I put it after I found it on his desk in his room.

On top of my dresser there's a photo in a frame from Cape Cod that we got one summer years ago with little starfish painted on it: the three of us standing in front of the ocean, a beach scene but not a beach day because, typical New England, the wind was whipping down from Labrador or somewhere and we're hunched against it, Toby and me, in our windbreakers, squinting against the glare and wind and grit flying in off the beach. Only Walter is completely upright, grinning hugely, beard and wayward hair framing a hail-fellow-well-met Paul Bunyan look-alike face. Toby is four years old and Anna is not in the picture because she did not yet exist, wasn't even conceived. She was not yet, so to speak, in the picture.

I forget who took the photograph. Some other bewildered tourist most likely, some poor soul from Europe or Japan who was trying to remember why he had chosen the Massachusetts coast as a tourist destination.

In the drawer beneath the picture in the starfish frame sits the yellow envelope that holds the letter or note if one prefers that my son Toby wrote shortly before going outside into the night and subsequently killing himself and his father, whether by accident or design is not entirely clear.

In the corner of the envelope Toby scrawled two spidery words. Not one but two. The pencil is so faded now that's it's nearly impossible to read them. It doesn't matter, they're easy to remember. The first one is

Mom

and the second is

why

4. Perhaps I should clarify what happened with Toby and Walter. What happened exactly. The problem is, no one knows what happened, exactly.

Here's what really happened:

I don't know.

That's it. That's all I can say. Except to add: I'll never know, will I? Not for sure. Nothing is for sure. Not history not the past not the future not God not life. Only death. Okay maybe death is for sure.

5. I've given a bad impression of Walter and for this I apologize. First he's a suicide, then a murderer. The truth, as ever, is more complicated than that. He was a bit baffled at the direction his life had taken, but really, he was a good guy. A big, strong, bearded, Viking-warrior look-alike who stayed home and did the dishes and tinkered with the car even when there was nothing wrong with it. With a wife who was set to make plenty of cash and so didn't need him for that traditional-provider reason, and a son who seemed odder, more withdrawn, more sullen, by the day.

A good guy, Walter, who died the same night his boy died, who seems—we think—sometimes we think he maybe got killed by his own boy. Maybe. But we don't really know, we'll never really know, although that's the explanation that best fits the evidence. Except that maybe it was an accident.

But that wouldn't explain the note.

Something went wrong out there, and it's somehow easier to lay the blame at Walter's feet than Toby's. Toby was just a child, for one thing. Just my child, for another. Even if Walter did nothing wrong, it's so much easier to think *He's the adult, he should have known better.* Not fair to him, though. Not fair at all, especially because he died first.

Of course I second-guess myself. I lie awake and play the If Only game. If only I'd been out there that night. If only I'd gotten back from work earlier, or—hell, in for a penny—had been around more when Toby was a toddler. If only I'd seen him take his first step. If only I hadn't thrown myself into school, into my residency, into Walter's bed yet again, getting pregnant that second time with Anna . . . It's all nonsense of course but one can't help doing it. I listen to patients say these things all the time, I know just how futile it is. *If only I'd known something was wrong.* It's like watching an old, familiar movie that makes you cry anyhow. It's a lot like that.

Toby was never a problematic child. Born big, healthy appetite, heavy sleeper. Not colicky like Anna was later on, or like I was too, if my mother is to be believed. Admittedly he was prone to somberness even as an infant, and his speech was a few months delayed. But he never gave any indication of being unstable. There were never any symptoms. Obviously—if there had been symptoms, I would have seen them.

The chronology is unthreatening enough: first grade, first communion (Walter's insistence), school pageants, model airplanes, comic books. Somewhere around age ten or eleven I noticed that Toby wasn't smiling much, but then he had never been exactly carefree. He spent more time in his room, in his make-believe worlds with imaginary talking birds, rather than with any flesh and blood friends from school. So what? If every kid with an active imagination is at risk, then all children on earth are symptomatic.

He wheedled us for a video game player, got good grades to earn it, and spent summers glued to the screen, thumbs punching little red buttons. What does that prove? As Trish once said to me, "If you hadn't got him that thing and then he'd gone and done what he did, you'd be blaming yourself for *not* buying it."

Good old Yankee common sense. I swear, it's Trish who should've been the doctor.

6. The screen door squeaks open and Brandon tumbles out, a gangly sixteen-year-old collection of elbows and too-long legs and too-narrow chest. He looks like a cartoon character, like a little clay figurine that's been stretched. Corn-silk bangs fall past his eyes, but when he smiles, the dimples and canines—pointed, like a wolf's—are dazzling.

"Morning," Trish greets him.

"Yo," he answers. "Hey Gina. How you sleep?"

"Like a baby," I smile.

"Sweet."

The door squeaks again and Jennifer joins us, or him—she barely looks our way. She's as lanky as Brandon, a little heavier around the hips, and there's very little of her left unrevealed by the clinging brown two-piece. Like scraps of seaweed round a twig of driftwood. Nice hair though, black ringlets, thick, and a deep tan. Some Italian blood in there, or African.

"Time for a swim," Brandon says.

"Don't go too far," nods Trish.

Brandon flashes those dimples again and the kids make their way to the rocky shore, him bouncy like a hound on the trail, her tentative, stepping carefully in bare feet, wary of sharp stones. His feet plop down, unconcerned, wherever they may; hers sniff the ground, then reach a little further than their normal stride. When Brandon reaches the water he glances back but doesn't wait for Jennifer before diving into the water.

"Was I ever that skinny?" I sigh.

Trish snorts. "You're still that skinny."

"Hardly." But secretly I'm pleased.

"So." Trish sets her empty mug down, lifts the decanter, pours refills for us both. "Tell me how you wound up here. I'm thinking A, Anna, or B, this Russell character."

"C."

She cocks her head. "Both?"

"Mm."

"So what's happening?"

And that's the point, isn't it. Trouble is, I'm not exactly sure what's happening. "I'm not exactly sure what's happening."

"Good news first. How's the sex?"

I can't help laughing: with Trish, sex is always the first thing. "It's fine."

"There's a ringing endorsement."

"It's good, Trish. No complaints. He gets me to the train on time."

"Does he make you laugh? Not during sex, but other times."

"Mm. Sometimes."

"An accomplishment in itself."

"Hag."

She sips. "Let's talk about Anna."

I stare at the water. "Erratic." She says nothing as I gather my thoughts. "She's in Provincetown, I thought it was just for fun but turns out she's doing theater. This is after almost flunking out of school."

"Theater's a pretty organized, strenuous activity, Gigi."

"That's what concerns me." I sip my coffee. Trish makes the best coffee in the world. "She shows up at my doorstep a month ago looking like something you'd rescue from the pound, giggling one moment, sulky the next. Making little sniping comments, usually about me, to everyone from Walter's father to—Russell."

"So they met?"

"Oh yes. Anyway it turns out she came home for Toby's birthday, so she says." I struggle to swallow. "Then she ambushes me one night when I'm with Russell, and dumps the whole story on him about what happened." I take a breath. "Poor guy looked shell-shocked."

"You hadn't told him?"

"Bits of it. Not the whole thing, I was, I didn't want to overwhelm him."

"Hm. What *did* he know?"

"About Walter and Toby. That they died, you know."

She's watching me like a raccoon district attorney. "And?"

"And I sort of made it—seem like Walter's fault."

She chokes on her coffee. "Jesus *Christ*, Gigi."

"I know."

"Why?"

"I just." In the water the kids are horsing around, having fun. "I just, I don't know why I said it."

"Yes you do."

Only Trish can talk to me like this. She talked to me like this in the ninth grade. "Listen," she says now, "you like the guy, fine. You don't want to scare him off, I get it."

"It's not—"

"And having a loose-cannon spouse do something crazy is a lot less scary than having a child, a son who—" Here she falters. "Who maybe did something awful."

Trish knows almost everything. She knows who died first, but she doesn't know about the note. I tell her, "Nobody knows what happened that night."

"Of course." She takes my hand. "But some things we do know, right? For example, it wasn't Walter who, you know—started the problems."

"Killed Toby you mean. Walter didn't kill Toby, is what you want to say. But it's what I suggested to Russell."

"Listen, you want to protect Toby, fine. All I'm saying is, in the long run—maybe not such a great idea." She gulps her coffee, cold now, and her fleshy upper arm rubs against my shoulder. "Maybe Anna did you a favor. Got it out in the open and all that."

"I've heard that theory," I mutter, and she chortles.

We sit a while. The gulls have moved off. Brandon and Jennifer are stretched out on a big flat rock by the water. Jennifer has taken off her top. Trish says, "Speaking of which, and I don't means to stir up bad memories . . ."

"They're stirred, believe me."

"I never did know where Anna was during all this."

"In bed. Or in her room anyway." I shut my eyes. Walter and I at the kitchen table, Toby outside, Walter standing up, my telling him, *I don't think that's such a good idea.* Racing outside later, stumbling over the bodies, my own voice shrill in my ears. "I didn't see her until the paramedics showed up. She climbed into the arms of one of them, she was practically paralyzed by shock." A big burly fellow with a beard, no extra credit for guessing *that* significance. "She spent the night with my parents."

Trish's hand on mine. "I was just wondering. You know, we've talked about that night, but you never mentioned Anna."

"There were a few other things going on."

She gives my hand a squeeze. "Sure."

7. Later the kids go inside, for either lunch or sex, so Trish and I claim the big flat boulder by the water. She dives in, graceful as a porpoise, shooting underwater before surfacing in to a purposeful breast stroke. She weaves back and forth as she talks. "Let's review. He's young, good-looking, knows his way around the bedroom, is interesting and funny and apparently thinks the world of you. Remind me again of the downside?"

"Downsides are several. He's young, for starters."

"*Down*sides, darling."

"I'm serious. He's not even thirty. He works part-time jobs, doesn't have health insurance, has some pipe dream of buying a restaurant. When he hits middle age I'll be in my fifties. Then what?"

"Then we see what happens. Christ, we'll all be dead by then anyway, the way things are going." She dives under, leaving me to contemplate her bubbles. Given my friend's propensity for gleefully apocalyptic pronouncements, I let this pass. When she surfaces I say, "There's something else. He's a Jesus freak."

Trish frowns as if envisioning a variation of the apocalypse. "What flavor?"

"I'm not sure. He seems pretty benign, but I think it runs deep. He talks about being saved, as in, Jesus saved him."

"Does he think I'll go to hell for my dissolute sinful ways?"

"Who doesn't? But he'd never say so. In fact he'd probably charm the pants off you."

"That's *my* kind of Jesus freak. Quick question. How does he reconcile the Jesus thing with the humping-Gigi-with-gusto thing?"

"Yeah, that confuses me too. He claims there's no contradiction. Says God is all about love, and if we love each other then the sex is fine."

She shakes her head. "Christians, man. In Doubletalk We Trust." She dives again, and stays under for a long time.

8. Sleep disturbances, short attention span, fire-setting, hyperactivity, cruelty to animals: Toby displayed none of this. There was a bit of a perfectionist streak, even early on—at age four or five he could spend an hour coloring in some farmhouse picture, getting the sky and the rainbow and the meadow and the barn just right. If his colors went too far outside the lines, he'd exhale mightily, blowing out his cheeks like Dizzy Gillespie, and start over. Nothing wrong with that, is there? A healthy case of wanting to do the job properly. If that's a disease, I wish more people had it.

And lest one starts in with obsessive-compulsive: I've seen OCD and this wasn't it. No locking and unlocking the door a dozen times or washing his hands every ten minutes or lining up his Matchbox cars around the perimeter of his desk. He just took a little extra care with things, his drawings, his bird feeders (would the birds really notice whether the roof was sanded, the stain freshly applied? No, but he would). And his clothes.

He liked clean clothes, had an almost unboyish aversion to dirt and smelly things, liked his shirts and socks freshly ironed. He liked to put them on still warm, and I started wondering if he felt cold, if he had some kind of circulatory problem.

So I asked him and he said, "I like the way they smell."

"Oh."

He was maybe six years old at this point and doing some of his own ironing, with supervision. I said, "You like the smell of detergent?"

He puckered his face, didn't answer as he went through his little pile of laundry. First sock, second sock, T-shirt. First sock, second sock, flannel shirt, jeans. First sock, second sock. I wondered if he had heard my question, or understood it.

"They smell like a sunny day."

He spoke suddenly, then grinned at me. I melted. Who wouldn't?

A boy who irons his socks because they smelled like a sunny day might not be expected to have a lot of friends, but Toby had plenty. Lenny and Charlie and Timmy and Dougie, those are the ones I remember most. They were his Allston buddies, the kids who played Battleship in the living room or built snow forts in our cramped, postage-stamp backyard, twenty-four feet from sidewalk to stoop. Charlie had a lisp and Timmy was handsome even at age six and Lenny's father was in jail for some reason and Dougie was so pale as to be almost an albino. They ran around with Boston accents and Red Sox caps and everything was "wicked ah-some" or "wicked cool." Of course they all absolutely adored Walter, who towered over them like Bigfoot, who carried on like a huge kid himself, another in their gang, built on a larger scale.

"Oh my God, Ranger," he would say, collapsing into a kitchen chair after the crew had left for the day. "They're killing me. They are absolutely wringing me dry."

"So leave them alone next time. They'll find a game of their own."

"Maybe I will, hey. Maybe I will."

He never did. The next time they converged on our house it was business as usual, surrounding him with shouts of "Play the game, Mr. Moss! C'mon, let's play the game."

Walter would scratch his head, wearing a fuddled expression. "Which one, guys? You know so many . . ."

"You know which one!" The cries were equal parts exasperation and anticipation. "The one where you walk across the yard!"

"Oh-h-h." Walter's eyes opened wide. "*That* one."

"Yaay!"

"I don't know." A rueful shake of the head.

 Five little faces drooped. "Why not?"

"It's so boring, guys." Walter put his hands on his hips, stared down at his charges with an air of resigned severity. "You know? It's boring because—you *never win* and you *never will.*"

The answering roar—five little boys howling defiance—could be quite alarming. (Or endearing, under the right circumstances.) By the time they were all downstairs, leaving me alone to watch Anna toddle around, I was happy for the peace and quiet. I could sit by the kitchen window and gaze down at the mayhem at a slight remove. A little Bach or Telemann dulled it further.

Walter's game was called, more or less, "I Will Walk Across the Yard and You Will Try to Stop Me." Sometimes he made funny faces and sounds, and then it was called "I Am a Zombie Walking Across the Yard and You Will Try to Stop Me." In any case the rules were identical. Walter, a large burly man over six feet tall and on the far side of two hundred pounds, would walk, slowly and deliberately, from the back stoop, across our yard to the sidewalk gate. The distance was—he measured once—twenty-three feet, nine and a half inches. The boys had to prevent him from reaching the gate: if they knocked him down they were instant winners and also Masters of Creation for All Time, but they could also win if they prevented him from taking a forward step for ten loudly counted seconds, in which case they were Partial Masters of Creation for the Time Being.

Walter liked to keep things simple, so there were only five rules, which the boys had to shout out at the commencement of every match:

1. No punching.
2. No kicking.
3. No eye-poking.
4. No hair- or beard-pulling.
5. The groin was strictly *off-limits.*

Everything else was allowed, which consisted mainly of the boys piling on, trying to shove him over, sumo-style. The need for cooperative action was understood in a distant, purely theoretical way. For his part, Walter couldn't fight back. He was allowed only to walk from the stoop to the gate, the immovable object to the boys' irresistible force.

They never won. If I had to guess, I'd say they never even came close, though I did hear them start counting a few times. But they all sure did love playing that silly game.

The games stopped when we moved to Stonebury. That was the summer after Toby's sixth grade, so he was going into junior high—a tough time by any standards, and maybe we made it tougher by moving. But we thought we were making it easier with a bigger house, more room outside, a nicer neighborhood, peace and quiet. Less traffic, more fresh air, flowers, trees, birds. Of all these, Toby noticed the birds most, the trees somewhat, and everything else hardly at all.

Anna meanwhile, still at dolls and horsies, traded one set of friends for another with barely a blink and took it from there. To this day, she hardly remembers the Allston apartment.

Toby had a tougher time. There were no new friends, no expanded version of "I Will Walk Across This Much Larger Suburban Backyard and You Will Try to Stop Me." Lenny and Charlie and Timmy and Dougie were left to the mercies of the Boston public school system; apart from that first Christmas when they stood around gawking at our snow-covered yard, I don't think Toby ever saw them again. (Thank God for Walter that day, cooking up an impromptu snowball fight to break through the awkwardness of the afternoon.) I fretted a bit over whether Toby would settle into his new life, but as I was also trying to make my own way in private practice, it fell upon Walter to monitor Toby's socialization at school.

"He's fine," was Walter's assessment, shifting to pull me a little closer to him. "His teachers say he's quiet but doing great. No problems, they say he's a terrific kid."

I slid up against him. We often spoke like this, in bed, going over the day. Was this normal behavior? I couldn't say. Maybe other couples did the same. Or maybe they did other things in bed, like sleep and make love.

"I know he's a good boy," I said. "I'm just a little concerned that he doesn't seem to have many friends." Or *any* friends. "Never mind bringing them home, he doesn't even talk about anyone."

"There's that Miss Adams he's always going on about."

"She's a teacher."

"Listen, there's nothing wrong with our kid. He'll make plenty of friends, just give him a little time. Meanwhile he's hot for teacher, nothing more normal than that."

"Mm."

"Anyway he's only been there, what, three months or something."

"Almost six." Walter's sense of time could be a little loose. This was mid-February, I remember because Valentine's had just come and gone and I wondered if it was still a cause for anxiety, as it had been for me. The only Valentines I'd ever gotten were from Trish, jokey ones with messages like "Let's get married if we're still single at 25!!!" Fat chance—Trish got so much male attention, even in junior high, she needed a spare backpack to carry home her love notes.

Walter shifted against me. "Anyway, he'll be fine. Seventh grade is, like, the bottom pit of Hell no matter who you are, but we made it through okay. And it's almost over, a couple more months and bam, he's done."

I resisted the urge to say, "Four more months actually." Walter didn't have a detail-oriented personality, except when it came to carpentry projects. But maybe he sensed my skepticism, because he squeezed my shoulders in his thick arm the way he knew I liked. "Things'll get better from here on out. Wait and see."

I wondered. He was still somewhat perfectionist—Toby, not Walter—still ate his food a certain way and still ironed his clothes before putting them on. But when I had asked recently why he liked them that way, he answered, "I just do."

I remembered what he'd said about this, years before, his sweet answer. "Do you like them to be warm?"

He shook his head and kept at it, the iron swooping down one pants leg, then the other.

"Why then?"

"I just do, okay?" He exhaled through his nose. "They feel better and they fit better. Why does everybody have to make such a big deal out of it?"

"Who makes a big deal out of it?"

A stormy look sweeping across that seventh-grade face.

"Toby?"

"Forget it."

"Who makes a big deal out of it?"

"Nobody. I don't feel like talking about it. Okay?"

There are times to push, and there are times not to push. As in therapy, so too in motherhood, and vice versa. "Okay."

He switched off the iron and draped his pants carefully across a forearm, tidying the edges, then the T-shirt on top of them, then the socks. (He wasn't ironing his underwear, I noted—I'll admit this—with some relief.) But before he left I said, "What about a sunny day?"

"Huh?"

He was wearing a T-shirt that said *Shit Happens*. Walter had bought it for him, thought it was hilarious. Now I asked, "Don't you think that after you iron your clothes, they smell like a sunny day?"

He stared at me like I was mad. No—actually, he stared at me like I was an asshole, for so long that I eventually shrugged and looked away. After a time he left the room. I sat gazing through the window at Anna and Walter, playing in the backyard, and I kept a little ah-what-the-heck smile on my face the whole time. It's good for kids to rebel a little, it's how they form their sense of self. Erikson's fifth stage and all that. All perfectly normal, and anyway nobody wants a Pollyanna for a kid, or for a sibling for that matter. Or a spouse.

But geez Louise, I had sure felt like an idiot under my son's withering twelve-year-old stare.

9. "Maybe you should give her a call," Trish says. She means Anna.

"You think?"

Trish is my dearest friend in the world and would never presume to criticize my handling of my daughter—but I know there are things she disapproves of. How I handled the incident years ago, for example, the time my mother barked at me: *Do you know she describes herself as an orphan?* I took steps to remedy that situation pronto, and Trish, for her part, has always been reticent about it.

But that's in the past. She says, "From what you tell me, she'd probably appreciate it."

10. Anna: Yeah?

Me: Hello.

Anna: Hey! Can you believe I just got back from rehearsal this very *minute* and now you're calling? What number is this anyway?

Me: I'm at Trish's.

Anna: Really? That's so cool the way you guys are still friends even so long.

Not really so long, is it? But— Me: Yes, it's been fun catching up.

Anna: You must be *stoked*.

Me: Mm. How's the play coming?

Anna: All right, not bad, you know.

Me: Actually I don't.

Anna: Well—Olivier, he's the director? He was sick for a while but now he's back? And he seems perfectly okay, so maybe we'll actually pull this off after all.

Me: That's great. You know, I.

(*Pause.*)

Anna: What.

Me: You know.

Anna (*with sarcasm*): No, actually I don't.

Me: I was hoping—that I could come see it.

(*Pause.*)

11. The treehouse. Jesus Mary and Joseph.

We'd been in Stonebury since the fall and our first full summer was coming up. Trips to the Cape and to Maine had been discussed, but we needed more than that to occupy the long months. Walter decided he needed a project and Toby should help. I agreed with him. I still do: Walter's intuition was perfect, I just wished they'd settled on a vegetable garden, or a bird blind for the edge of the woods, or a basketball court. Anything really, so long as it wasn't forty feet above the ground. It doesn't sound that high but it is. Go outside and look, find a tree that's as tall as a four-story building and still hefty enough to build something up there.

"It's pretty tall, isn't it?" I asked, as diplomatically as I could manage. We were all standing in the yard, craning our necks at likely trees. The boys seemed disposed toward the maple, whose thick, robust trunk shot upward forty feet before splitting into a fountain of heavy boughs. It was, I could see, ideal for this kind of thing. But—"I mean, wouldn't twenty feet be high enough?"

Walter bridled a bit at that. Toby said nothing.

"It's taller than the house."

Walter struggled to keep silent, but I knew what was burning to come out: *When have I told you how to do your job?* The answer was never, of course.

So why are you telling me how to do this?

I backed off. Was that a mistake? Obviously. But it gets so tiresome, being always the one who says no, no, no.

I don't remember whose idea it was. Somehow the idea of "treehouse" had simmered in the background for months. One night they were watching some movie on TV, a barbarians-in-the-jungle thing with some benign race of tree people living in hexagonal cabins amid the branches. Thatched roofs and so on. The boys were rapt and Toby paused the movie to declare, "Like that!"

"You think so?" said Walter.

"Just like that!"

"All right then."

I couldn't resist. "Thatch roof and everything?"

Walter threw me an irritated glance.

The debate quickly shifted to which of our trees would be best. The oak had a thicker trunk to bear the weight but the hickory's V-cleft would make an ideal foundation. The elm had good height but swayed alarmingly in strong breezes. The maple was tall, strong, had a thick cluster of limbs and was nicely set at the edge of the yard. The only problem was that that cluster was on the high side, and it would take some doing to get the lumber up there.

"We'll rig a pulley," said Walter. "Bundle up the boards and haul them up."

Toby nodded. "Okay."

"First thing's the ladder. We'll drill in handholds up the side, eighteen inches apart, and maybe," he measured with his hands, "a couple feet across."

Toby nodded. In his eyes the thing was taking shape already. The joy in my guts at seeing him so animated was tempered with profound doubt. Maybe this was what mothers used to feel when their sons spoke of running away to sea. Of course I was happy he'd found something to capture his imagination. Yes. But.

"We'll lay down some framing timbers," Walter went on. "After that we'll design whatever we want, no limits."

"Except the tree," chirped Toby.

Walter looked momentarily caught off guard. "Well yeah, the tree."

Sketches and measurements and discussions followed. Walter sanded down a batch of two-by-fours and bolted the ladder into the side of that poor tree. I didn't see all the cutting and measuring and drilling taking place over the course of several afternoons. One evening I was home from BMHA and there was our lovely maple at the edge of the yard with a tidy ladder running up its side like the ribs of some strange, spindly creature.

"Like it?" he grinned.

I ran my hand over one step: smooth, beveled inward slightly, with a groove along the inside edge to help the grip. Stained so dark that really, you could barely see it against the trunk. "You're a craftsman," I told him, as I often had before, and I meant it.

"Shucks."

"Will it hurt the tree, being bolted like this?"

"Tree's fine," he assured me. "These little nicks are like mosquito bites."

Work went ahead. I saw little but got daily reports. The floor was roughly trapezoidal, wedged between a four-way split of vertical trunk and horizontal boughs, with another split overhead supporting the roof. There would be no walls as such, just guardrails running from post to post. The slightly pitched roof would channel rainwater, while the ladder would run up through an opening in the floor so Toby could climb right into the room, scooting back to sit. The platform itself would be no more than six or seven feet across. More a perch than anything else.

"But it'll have a heck of a view."

Toby grinned and nodded vigorously.

"*Heck* of a view," Walter said again.

"I can't wait," Toby said. He looked so small. He *was* small, even at age twelve-going-on-thirteen. Despite carrying Walter's broad hips and even a bit of his belly, his arms were spindles and his shoulders narrow. (As a child, Walter had been what they'd euphemistically called "husky.")

And I'll admit this: I had reservations about this project, whole boatloads of them, but when I saw my little boy smiling like that, those reservations wavered. They didn't vanish but they weakened: I hadn't seen that look on his face in a long time, I realized, and realized also that that wasn't right.

Now Toby began bouncing his knee. "I can't *wait*."

"You'll need to wait, Tobe-man," said Walter. "Your safety rigging isn't quite ready."

At my urging, Walter had agreed to staple chicken wire across the lower half of the enclosure—where the walls would be, if the thing had walls. A modest precaution, doubtless, but better than nothing.

Walter had seen the sense immediately. "Might keep somebody from falling out," he nodded.

I closed my eyes. "Mm."

Another requirement of mine met more resistance: a kind of net sheath that housed the ladder running up the tree—a vertical tunnel of sorts to provide a degree of safety in case someone slipped on the ladder, or one of the rungs snapped.

Walter's reservations were mainly aesthetic. "It'll look like hell."

"I want it. It might save someone a broken leg." Or neck, but I didn't say that.

He squinted at the tree, trying to visualize it. "It's like a net then."

"Sure. A net, a cylinder of screen or chicken wire—just something to catch you if you lose your balance. Something to slow the fall so you have time to grab the ladder."

He didn't like it but he did it. Soon there was a gray wire-mesh tube running up the trunk like an extraordinarily odd, gray caterpillar. Weird indeed but it set my heart somewhat at rest.

"You okay with that?" he asked.

"Much better, thank you."

"Still looks like shit." He sounded doleful, but seeing my expression, he rallied. "But you're right, safety first. And let me tell you, there's no way anybody's falling out of that now. The only way to get down in a hurry is to jump."

"Glad to hear it," I told him.

Soon afterward I came home to discover the two of them up there, side by side, radio blaring, elbows perched on the guardrail, shit-eating grins affixed to their faces. They looked like a couple of hatchlings in a nest. I shielded my eyes and squinted up at them. "Wow. Is that really it?"

"Stick a fork in us," Walter shouted. "We're done."

"Hi Mom."

"Hello, dear. That's great, congratulations, both of you." They were *so* high up.

Inside, Anna was playing with a couple of friends. Dolls had been laid out in a row, bandages and a thermometer laid conspicuously nearby. "What'cha playing, girls?"

"Hospital," came the gleeful chorus.

"This one's really sick," added Kitty.

"Great. Are you all doctors?"

"Uh huh." Kitty nodded her pigtails with vigor. "I'm a brain doctor, and this one's brain is in really bad shape."

"I'm a baby doctor," said Ellen, who actually did look something like an Ob/Gyn I knew as a resident.

"Terrific." I smiled at my daughter. "And are you a doctor too?"

She shook her head no.

"Why not? Your friends are."

"Don't want to be a doctor because they work all the time while the boys get to play in the treehouse," she said. And while I was still getting my breath back she added, "When're we going to Cape Cod?"

"Oh, soon," I told her. Actually our plans had been on hold but I resolved at that second to finalize them pronto. "We're all going away very soon."

12. Trish says, "This Russell of yours."

"He's not exactly mine."

She waves me off. "Does he have any vices besides Jesus and his mommy complex?"

"Oh please. He doesn't have a mommy complex. He doesn't even have a *mommy*."

She stares at me so long I finally tell her, "Hush," and she bursts out laughing.

13. Years ago I had a patient named Eduardo, late twenties, Puerto Rican, schizoaffective Axis II, no Axis I. Some borderline DD, that's "retarded" to the rest of the world. A heavyset guy, sweet-tempered most of the time but prone to rages. Pick-up-the-chair-and-hurl-it kind of fits, storm-out-of-the-house-and-catch-me-if-you-can episodes.

Eduardo lived in a group home in Medford run by a woman named Lisa. The staff was stumped by Eduardo's fits but dutifully went through the restraints needed to contain him: a swift crisscross hug from behind, one foot planted across the base of his heel, a strong heave backward. Even a petite woman had enough body weight to overbalance him and drop him onto his backside. Lean forward across his back and Eduardo wound up on the floor, pinned from behind him by the staff's weight bearing down. It wasn't comfortable, but it immobilized him without damage.

I had witnessed the maneuver twice, once in the living room following a furniture-rearranging episode. Earl was a gangly and dreadlocked black guy who failed to break a sweat in the nine seconds it took him to complete the move. "Smooth," I said, and meant it.

"Piece of cake," he grinned.

Eduardo laughed and laughed. When Earl let him up, he got busy putting the chairs back where they belonged.

The second takedown was done by Lisa herself, a tiny thing barely five feet tall, who needed only a few seconds more than Earl had to immobilize Eduardo in the driveway. "What concerns me," she told me later, "is how often we're having to do it."

"Which is?"

"Several times a day."

"Geez Louise, that's a lot."

Lisa nodded. She was small-featured and elfish, with a pointy nose and chin and watery black eyes. I half expected her to have pointy ears too and was always mildly surprised to see she didn't. "I wish I knew what we were doing wrong."

I watched Eduardo sitting at the dining table, chuckling over a fistful of art supplies, watercolors and whatnot. "He's happy enough now."

"That's the pattern. He has a tantrum, then a takedown, then he's fine again."

"One way to look at it is that the restraints keep him from getting worse."

She looked like a profoundly unconvinced elf. "And the other way is that they're failing to do anything at all. The behavior's contained, but it's not being changed."

I nod. From the table Eduardo calls, "Painting a pickchah for the *dahc*tah."

"Thanks Eddie."

"Sooner or later someone'll get sloppy and twist an ankle," Lisa fretted, "or set him down on a piece of glass or something. We *really* shouldn't be doing this six times a day."

"Let me think about it."

That evening I hung Eddie's painting on the fridge: childish, but recognizable as a happy family scene, Mom and Dad and child in front of a house. Blue sky, yellow sun, green grass, big smiles, mother and child safe in the embrace of Dad's outstretched arms.

Toby came slouching into the kitchen then, all fourteen years two months nine days of him, rooted around the fridge, found the orange juice and drank what was left from the carton. I couldn't help remembering the years when it was his drawings I would tape to the fridge. Those days seemed as remote now as the Cold War or the building of the Great Wall.

He pivoted toward me. "What's the matter?"

"Nothing. What do you mean?"

"You're sitting there, like—" And he heaves out a huge, gusty sigh. Before I can respond, he squints at the fridge. "What's *that*?"

"It's a, one of my patients made it for me."

He squinted as if the painting contained a secret meaning. "He's a kid?"

"No, he's—grown up."

"What's he then, a retard?"

"That's not very kind. We don't call people 'retarded' anymore, we call them developmentally delayed."

He wasn't listening. "How old's he?"

"He's in his twenties. Almost thirty."

"And he did that? Definitely a retard."

I was left alone with the painting and the fridge. Outside I heard Walter calling, "Time for a little treehouse action, Tobe-Man?"

My son didn't answer. On the fridge, Mom and child stood safe in Dad's embrace.

14. After three days of staring the answer in the face—literally, it was hanging on my fridge—I figured it out and called Lisa. "Eduardo wants hugs."

"Hugs?"

"Human contact. Hugs, squeezes, whatever. Maybe it's sexual, maybe not, maybe both. That's why he's acting out—he's learned your staff will give him what he wants."

"Oh." I could just about hear her brain whirring along. "That's why he ends up in such a good mood?"

"Yup. So you and your staff need to figure out another way to give him that."

"We're not allowed to hug the patients."

"Be creative. His brothers still in the picture?"

"They take turns visiting."

"Get them to swing by more often. Thirty seconds on the way home from work. If they're married, ask the wives to stop in. As for staff, well—not on duty. But technically, if your guy Earl were to come to work thirty seconds early, he wouldn't be on the clock yet."

"Or thirty seconds after his shift ends. Sneaky."

"The alternative is to keep on with these wrestling matches. And try to get it through to Eduardo, that acting out will no longer get him restrained. That'll be tough because he's learned otherwise, but you have to do it."

"Let me put together some kind of plan."

Over dinner I told Walter about it. "So this guy was just acting crazy to get someone to touch him? That *is* crazy."

"Mm—perfectly logical, if you look at it from his side."

Walter rolled his eyes. "If you say so."

Toby snickered. "Good thing nobody ever made *you* a psychiatrist, Dad."

Walter looked puzzled at that, but I admit, I was inclined to agree.

15. After a week Trish gives me a hug and says, "Go get 'em, Gigi." Whether "them" refers to Anna, Russell, or the world in general is not entirely clear. But she's right, it's time to vacate her porch and get on with things. I drive back to the city, to my patients, my life.

16. "Hey," says Russell.

"Hello." How did he know I was back in town? It's enough to make you believe in some kind of psychic connection. Or else just dumb luck. I stand there in the market, my cell phone in one hand, an artichoke in the other, like justice holding her scales. All I need is the blindfold. He says, "I was wondering if I should call."

I wonder what the right answer is, and hear myself saying, "I'm glad you did."

"Listen, I've got some big news."

"Let me guess, you're engaged." I mean it as a joke but it comes out sounding snippy.

"No. What? I—oh hell. I bought the restaurant."

"You *bought* it?"

"From Howard, that's the owner."

It takes a moment to process this information. "That's, wow. That's a big thing."

"Yeah, we worked out a pretty good deal. Actually he's like a consulting partner for the next few years, but I'm going to buy out his share incrementally. Basically he wants to sell but has no other buyers besides me, so this is a compromise."

"Gosh."

"Yeah I agree." Over the line his voice sounds almost giddy. "Guess I'm locked into this for the next couple decades, if not longer."

"That's really something. Congratulations."

"Thanks."

"We should celebrate."

"Ah—"

"Sometime."

"I'm really busy right now."

"Sometime."

"Yeah."

17. A few days later it's August 10. An innocuous enough date, apart from being my birthday. I am forty-two years old today. Long ago I told Russell the date, but no doubt he's misplaced that information what with all the other excitement.

I remember when I turned thirty. Walter coordinated a jaunt to the New England Aquarium—me, him, Toby and Anna. "How romantic," I joked weakly. "Just the four of us."

"You deserve a break," he nodded. Walter was immune to irony, being the kind of American that Europeans make fun of.

We bundled into the car and went. This was the year we moved from Allston to Stonebury, from the city to the suburbs. August 10 was a Sunday that year. (Yes, I'm a Leo. According to Trish, this means something.) Anna was six, Toby just twelve, Walter was thirty-one and driving. If I could have lifted the lid of his cranium and peeked into his brain, I believe his train of thought would've gone something like this: take the kids someplace they liked so they wouldn't be a handful, then cross the street to Legal Seafoods and tuck into a lovely dinner so I wouldn't be a handful. Glaze me with white wine and gorge the kids on crab cakes, then roll us all home, tuck us into bed and pat yourself on the back for another potentially maudlin hurdle successfully negotiated. Alas, Walter had failed to count on Toby's budding oddness.

To be fair, so had I. And to be even fairer, I sometimes think the oddness had never really manifested itself earlier. That day at the aquarium marked the first incident that I would look back on, later, and think: *I wonder if . . .*

The day started well enough, muggy but the thunderstorms holding off. We lingered outside by the seals in their glassy enclosures. Anna was a cheap date: she could've happily stayed out there all morning. But Walter had a floor plan and an abiding urge to see every display. "And Toby, he's crazy about the penguins."

Well, he *had* been, when he was five—but Toby didn't appear crazy about the penguins that day. From where I stood he appeared dull-eyed and distracted, minimally interested in anything at all. On the drive down he'd barely spoken a word. Now I poked him and said, "Ready for some penguins?"

"What*ever*."

His new favorite word. He'd shot up three or four inches in the past year, his hair had darkened from flaxen to dirty wheat, and his voice had cracked a few times already. No pimples yet—that would come later, I assumed—but my sweet little boy was on the verge of becoming a sulky teenager. Didn't that sound like a joy.

"Come on." Anna, suddenly aware of the looming promise of the building before her, tugged my hand with vigor.

We slipped through the entryway, into the darkness beyond, as if diving underwater. Before us, a church-sized glass cylinder rose three stories tall, surrounded by a spiraling walkway: inside circled sharks, sea turtles, barracuda, rays. Eels hunkered in the rocks, skates lingered on the sandy bottom. Around the perimeter of the building, bright schools of fish darted through baroque displays of coral and kelp.

To one side, a guardrail overlooked the penguin enclosure. Toby peered intently as the birds zipped through the water or stood awkwardly atop stones, waiting for something to happen.

"What do you say, Tobe? Sharks or fishies?" Walter's eyes were as bright as Anna's.

Toby, on the other hand, just seemed tired. "Sharks I guess."

"Meet us in an hour," Walter instructed me. "Right here, and don't be late, okay? I got tickets for the Imax show."

"Oh." My husband was never so organized as when he was playing.

Anna and I strolled, oohing and ahhing at butterflyfish and parrotfish and yellow tang and Moorish idols and the petting pool where we could touch real crabs and starfish urchins (she wouldn't do it till I did it first) and then outside for a quick look at the harbor. We were back inside near the invertebrate display when a breathless Walter clenched my shoulder and said, "You haven't ah—seen Toby have you?"

Geez Louise. "No. He was with you."

"No. I mean yeah we were, together. We were looking at some sharks and I turned around to show him something, and—bam."

I breathed deeply. Toby was twelve, not three—the chances were small that he'd been snatched by slavers or fallen into the piranha tank. Most likely he'd wandered off in search of something more interesting than his father. "How did he seem?"

"Fine."

"I mean was he spacey, or talking back, or sarcastic—"

"He was *fine*, Gina."

We found him on the ground floor by the penguins, leaning against the railing, scowling down at the birds. Surrounded by a quartet of security guards in yellow shirts and navy trousers. "What on earth? Are you all right?" I gripped him close and lightened up when he squirmed.

"I'm okay."

One of the guards, a squat black woman with deep eyes and a name tag that read *Sheila*, turned her attention to me. "You're the parents?"

Walter and I said yes simultaneously. Sheila said with gravity, "We have a slight problem with your son. Some people reported they saw him throwing things into the penguin enclosure."

"Throwing things?"

"Dropping, more like." She demonstrated. "Like this, just sort of flipping them casually."

"I didn't do that."

"We can't allow it, obviously."

I faced Toby. "What on earth?"

"Easy Gina."

"I didn't *do* anything."

"We have several people who say they saw it," Sheila went on. Not strident, but I could see she'd made up her mind. "None of the staff saw anything, and maybe all those people are lying and making up stories about your son—"

"They are," protested Toby.

"—but I don't know why they would do something like that."

Walter had his hand on Toby's shoulder. It was, I noticed, a tight grip. Toby slumped beneath the weight. Anna had sidled up next to me, looking bewildered. The other guards had drifted off but stayed within earshot. "Okay," I said to Sheila. "We'll stick with him from now on. There won't be any more problems. Will that do?"

"That'll do," she nodded. "But I'm obliged to warn you, in the event of further complaints, you will all be asked to leave."

"I'm sure that won't be necessary," I told her.

She gave me a look that suggested I was a fool to be sure about any such thing. "Have a nice visit," she said, and moseyed off.

Walter looked at me and said, "Well."

I looked at Toby and said, "Well."

Toby looked at nothing and said, "Leafy seadragon."

Anna clapped and said, "Yay!"

"What?" I said.

"Leafy seadragon." Suddenly my son was twelve years old again, not a moody pre-teen delinquent-in-waiting. He looked up at me and Walter and his face positively alive with anticipation. "I want to see the leafy seadragons. Please?"

I had no idea what he was talking about. A glance at Walter confirmed that I was not alone in this.

Anna said brightly, "I want to see the leafy seadragons too."

"Show us," I said to Toby—needlessly, as he was already scurrying up the ramp to the display in question.

18. At ACC Becky pulls me aside and says, "Guess who's back?"

"Leonardo da Vinci. Amelia Earhart."

"Those too. Also Edna."

"Mm. What's it been, two months?"

"Four and a half, actually. That's a record for her I think."

"Time flies."

Becky squints at me. "You okay?"

In the day room Edna sits hunched at a table full of magazines, copies of *People* and *Newsweek* from three years ago. Her hair is frizzy white cotton wool jutting out at all angles, and her face is wrinkled like a potato gone brown, collapsing in on itself. I say her name, softly, and she lifts her eyes to mine. And smiles. It happens slowly, as if she's out of practice. It wrenches me, to see how much joy I can bring to another person while simultaneously feeling so little, myself.

I do a quick eval of Edna in one of the intake rooms. Her chart hasn't changed in ten years—feelings of hopelessness and despair, culminating in self-harm threats and a voluntary admission to the unit, facilitated by her daughter. No cops this time, which is good, but no contact from the daughter since admission, not so good.

The waterworks start within minutes, and I gather that the long-suffering Levonna, Edna's daughter, had been maintaining some kind of regular contact but had grown distracted and busy with her own life—imagine that!—over the past few weeks. Edna had grown careless about her medications, which left her feeling depressed, resulting in her getting more careless, which left her feeling worse yet. Try to see where this is heading, it's not hard.

"But that's kids for you," she sighs tearily. Blows her nose, wipes her eyes, if she had the strength to rend her garments I've no doubt she would do so. The word *maudlin* was invented for people like Edna. "You give them everything, and what do they do? Cut you loose."

"That's a little harsh, don't you think?"

"You don't know the half of it, honey. You know a lot, but believe me, you don't know about this."

"Levonna does her best I'm sure, but she has her own concerns."

Wet nose-honking interrupts me. "My daughter is too *concerned* with her man-chasing and her money-making to be *concerned* about her own mother. It's enough to, I tell you honey, it'd make anyone sick." Tears struggle to creep sideways out her eyes.

"We can discuss your daughter, but I have to say, I don't think she's the key to your treatment."

"I suppose them pills are."

"They seem to help when you take them. That's all I know, Edna—when you take the pills I don't see you here in the hospital. When you stop, here you are. What the connection is, I don't know." I'm lying through my teeth, but this bit is true enough: "I just want to do what works."

"Put me out to pasture, she did. Like an old cow—like a horse who cain't work no more." She leans back, lips pursed. "You do what you can, they go ahead and break your heart anyway."

"Children need to find their own way, Edna, and sometimes that means their parents do too."

"They teach you to say this nonsense in school?" She flutters her fingers. "I know you don't even believe what you're sayin' even a little."

I say nothing.

"No way round it I suppose. She'll find out soon enough how the world works. Be singin' a different tune then."

I clear my throat. "Well."

"When they're little, you think they're so easy to understand. You think you know just what's going on in their heads. Don't you? They seem so simple. But they never are, not really. They're a mystery, just like the Holy Ghost himself. And about as reliable, come to that." She breaks off to squint at me. "You all right?"

"I'm fine, Edna."

"What you crying for?"

"It's noth—we're here to talk about you."

She sits back. "You go ahead. Ain't nothing wrong with crying, I found that out a long time ago. Doesn't accomplish a great deal, but ain't nothing wrong with it."

19. The leafy seadragon is an animal that looks like a plant. Or like part of a plant—a twig, dangling spindly yellow leaves, twirling through the shallows. It's only after gazing dreamily at it for some time that one realizes *Oh, there's a snout, here's an eyeball, those leaves are really fins, that twig has a backbone.* And the plant transmogrifies into an animal, swimming under its own motive power, anchoring itself with a tail wrapped around a bit of kelp. A creature that—like any of us—eats and sleeps, expels waste and reproduces itself sexually. And possibly also dreams, hopes, remembers, fears, regrets.

Toby stared through the thick aquarium glass at this yellowy daydream drifting to and fro. Plenty of other exotica shared the spotlight, seahorses and starfish and something called the weedy seadragon, which kept the sticklike core but dispensed with the showy fronds. But Toby had eyes only for this baroque phenomenon.

"It's beautiful," I said. He didn't answer. Around us people jostled for a look into the too-small tank.

"They come from Australia," I said. "Maybe we can go there someday."

He didn't answer. I gave up.

Anna was enthralled too, for—I counted—sixteen seconds. Walter was bored sooner than that, being more of a hammerheads 'n' great whites kind of guy. The two of them wandered off. Toby kept staring, entranced. As if, and I admit this unnerves me now, as if receiving psychic messages from the animal.

"Is it your favorite?" I asked him.

He shrugged. Then said quietly, "Maybe."

I bent down to sniff his hair, which smelled of strawberry shampoo and his scalp. "How come? Because it's beautiful?"

"Lots of things are beautiful," he said in a way that made me feel silly for asking. "I just, I like it."

We kept staring. People came and went around us but we didn't move. Someone took a flash photo, something they weren't supposed to do, and Toby flinched. Could this be the same child who'd been throwing things at the penguins? Allegedly.

The seadragon dipped behind a patch of seaweed, then ascended effortlessly. Toby said, "Wish I was in there with it."

Maybe that should have worried me, that comment, but at that moment his words made perfect sense.

People came and went.

Toby said, "I wish I was like that, just like that. Living in there and doing that." The seadragon rose to the surface of the tank, met its own reflection, kissed it briefly and descended once more. For a rare moment, there on my thirtieth birthday, I felt I understood my son perfectly.

Around us, like waves at the beach, people came and went.

20. I found her curled on her bed in shorts and a halter top, far too skimpy for mid-November. Reeking of cigarettes. She was fifteen. A week earlier, my mother and I had fought—*Do you know she describes herself as an orphan?*—and I told her to shut the hell up, more or less.

I'd been at my office when the school called to tell me that Anna was absent for the third time in a week. I felt a brief, selfish flicker of gratitude that they had gotten through to me instead of having to call my mother.

She didn't look up when I sat on the edge of her bed. Her dressing table and the mirror above it were festooned with chipper little-girl decorations—rainbow stickers and unicorns, stuffed animals, funny fridge magnets, snow-globes and cheap plastic ornaments—that felt markedly at odds with the icy mournfulness filling the room. There were any number of photos there too, of her father and her brother.

I looked into the mirror and it stared back at me, tight-lipped. I'd just had my hair trimmed and frosted but there was no hiding the bags under my eyes. "What's all this about?" I asked her, as gently as I could manage.

No answer.

"Is it Toby?"

Stupid question. The wordless pause answered for her. Then, "I miss Daddy," another pause. "I wish he was here. And Toby."

Well, if there was any remedy for that, it required a better doctor than I.

But I tried. Of course I did. "That's perfectly normal."

She jerked upright as if electroshocked. "You keep *saying* that! It doesn't help anything, why do you keep *saying* it?"

Because it was true, of course. "I'm sorry, dear. There's nothing else to say."

"*Think* of something. You're a doctor, you're supposed to be *smart*."

The symptoms had been building for a year. Her friends coming to the house less and less. Inviting her over less and less. A variety of somatic ailments—upset stomach, headaches—with no discernible causes. That fall she began skipping school. Phone calls from the admin followed; things were cycling downward.

She spent the better part of most weekends in bed; at odd hours I heard her sobbing behind her hand. The symptoms weren't a mystery.

I reached under her pillow and extracted a crumpled half-carton of Kools. Menthols of all things. *If you must smoke, couldn't you at least pick the kind without extra chemicals?* "What's this?"

"Cigarettes." Her face slack, like a fashion model's. She didn't seem to be joking.

"Why do you have them?"

"I like them." She looks at the pack in my hand, then at me, then away. "I like the way they taste. They make me feel better, like you and your wine."

Which is how I came to the decision to do what was best for my daughter. Perhaps overdue, I'll admit; but better late than never. And while it wasn't the easiest decision to make, it's one I've never regretted. After all, what kind of mother doesn't want what is best for her child?

21. "Want to do something?" he asks. "Unless you think you'd rather . . ."

"Yes I do. Let's do something nice."

"Saturday?"

"I'm free. You sure you have time?"

"Yep. And an idea of where to go. And—no arguments, okay?"

"Absolutely."

"See you then."

22. Some days I step out of the house and see patients everywhere. The woman at the drugstore is having an elaborate conversation with someone only she can see, the hairdresser is delusional, the traffic cops all look depressed—no surprise there—and the guy at the post office has gender identity issues too complex to easily sort through. What causes days like this, I couldn't say. Weeks will go by, months even, with everybody within normal parameters. And then, *boom*—a crazy bomb goes off, and we're all caught in the fallout.

It's a day like this that Russell and I take in a street fair in Jamaica Plain not far from the ice cream shop, a formerly dodgy neighborhood currently undergoing the long uphill slog toward respectability. Part of this reinvention is their annual *Wake Up the Summer!* festival or some such. A cute enough idea, and I'm the first to admit that strolling in the August sunshine is delightful. But such street fairs inevitably involve great heaps of cheap Indian jewelry and woven bracelets, panpipe tootling and patchouli essence, dreadlocks on white people and all the rest of it.

We're tentative at first, speaking little and overly concerned with the other's wishes—our last encounter was far from pleasant, after all. But the day is lovely and it's hard not to relax. Russell, strolling beside me, inhales the whole scene with a wry smile and says, "God, it smells like a sunny day."

My stomach lurches and I nearly stumble, assailed by visions of Toby, age six, ironing his clothes, age nine, fussing with his cuffs, age eleven, picking a shirt off a rack. But I push the images away, hard—is that what I should be doing, rejecting my son's innocent face, holding it at arm's length?—and force myself to say: "Does it?"

Russell squints at me so intently I feel compelled to say, "I'm fine."

"This is supposed to be fun, you know."

"I know. It is fun, isn't it? Look around." I gesture at the throng clogging the street, try to ignore the fact that they all look like mental patients today—the slovenly white kids, scowling black kids, terminally anxious elderly people, middle-aged guys wearing their baseball caps backward in some delusion of collegiate vitality. "Look at all these people enjoying themselves." I take his elbow, something I know he likes even though it makes me feel like some fading starlet. "I appreciate your bringing me here."

"I figured the timing was perfect, with your birthday and everything."

He remembered after all. And I'll admit this means a lot to me. A little late, but he remembered. So I stroll along now, a few days into my forty-second year of life, while beside me Russell remains twenty-nine. Anna is a freshly minted eighteen, Walter would be forty-three, Toby would be twenty-three and doing something, working somewhere. Doing what?

Driving a car?

Making a meal?

Going to work?

Falling in love?

Making love?

I *really* need to stop thinking this way.

Or maybe not—maybe I need to keep right on thinking this way, to hold these truths close and never let them go. I don't know. I'll never know. Sometimes I get so tired of not knowing.

Fortunately for my mental health, the situation does not allow me to fixate on this train of thought for long. We meet up with a young painter named Lee Lin, a small androgynous man of uncertain ethnicity and the relentless energy of a bipolar on the edge. But today is one of those days. He pumps Russell's hand before taking mine. "How you been, man?" asks Lee, or is it Lin, to which Russell responds, "Not bad, bro. Working hard. You?"

"Hardly working." Suggesting otherwise, he flutters a hand at the paintings hanging all around him in the little stall. Everybody chuckles, me included, notwithstanding the fact that my mind is reeling: I seem to be dating a man who calls other men "bro." Excuse me, I just need a little time with this idea.

They chat a while as I look over the work, oversized paintings on silk that are, I realize with some surprise, exquisite. On one six-foot panel, a gnarled tree branch hosts the silhouettes of a dozen roosting birds, crows perhaps. It's all very simple, a few deft strokes for the branch, each bird delineated in a stroke or two, everything gray and black against a creamy background. A layer of gauzy orange across the bottom indicates—sunrise? Dusk? I gaze at it before turning my attention to other landscapes equally simple and severe, waterfalls, bamboo forests, ferns.

Their conversation dwindles. Russell watches me while the artist chats up another potential buyer. I catch him saying, "Those have all been bought, sorry," as Russell wanders over. I ask, "What's he want for these?"

He names a figure. "That's not bad. Can't you picture this in my living room?"

"Totally. Above the couch, right? Catch the sun through your bay window."

"Just what I was thinking." There's been a framed Monet print there for years, waterlilies. Time for a change. "Does he take credit cards?"

"Happy birthday." His eyes sparkle from beneath heavy half-lids.

"Oh no—really you can't, it's too expensive."

"You just said it wasn't bad."

"Well no, for art it's not bad, but I mean." I swipe a hand through my hair. "Don't get offended, but I do make more money than you do."

"At the moment."

"Fine, at the moment. And you just bought this business, don't you think that's where your money should go?"

"Yeah I do, actually. So long, Lin." Handshakes all around, then Russell steers me into the human tide. "I'll drop it by your house later."

"Okay. But."

"I just bought six of his paintings."

"Six?"

"For the restaurant. It's a business expense, I'll write it off. He gave me a deal on them, and threw in yours—I shouldn't say this, but you're so concerned—threw in yours as a bonus."

"Oh. You mean, it's free."

"That makes me sound cheap. It's not free, it's discounted." He puckers his lips. "In business we call it a concession."

"Do you." We soldier on for a time. Around me the mob jostles and pushes and one woman, I swear, says to the empty sky above her, "I need that like I need a hole in the head." It's the most elaborate birthday present I've gotten in years. "How did you know which one I liked?"

"I picked the one you were staring at with your mouth hanging open."

"Oh hush."

I decide to accept the gift and let it go at that, without questioning his decoration skills—ice cream he may be good at, but do the patrons of Jamaica Scoops really want to stare at sunsets and waterfalls and orange koi while slurping down butter pecan with hot fudge? To which I can readily imagine his answer: *Why not? Why shouldn't ordinary people in a restaurant appreciate a nice picture as much as somebody in a museum?* It's a question that there's no real answer for, of course, not when it's put like that.

23. Muffin says, "Andrew wants to move out."

This is news to me. Muffin indicates the only chair in her office not covered with boxes of files. "Put those bags on the floor. Bagel?"

"No thanks."

"You sure? They're low fat and high fiber at the same time."

"I'm fine. What's the story with Andrew?"

"I think we're paying the price for our own success."

"Meaning?"

She settles back. "You know he was having a rocky time a while back. Something bugging him at work. Whatever it was blew over, but coincidentally or not, this girl who was part of the program was leaving right around then."

"Girl? You mean client or staff?"

"Staff. Black gal named Alice or Alicia or Elaine, something like that."

I cast back. "Alanna."

"That's it—so either he didn't like her, or else he did, and Andrew being Andrew, made his feelings known, then got embarrassed about it."

I recall our earlier conversation. "I'd go with the second option, myself."

"So that blows over, and for a while everything's hunky dory. You'd think summer would be a hot time to work at a greenhouse, but Andy's fine. Then about two weeks ago they throw some kind of party to celebrate him being there a whole year."

"Already? Seems like he just started."

"Maybe to you it does. We're the ones chasing him out of bed every morning."

"Right, sorry ma'am."

She winks at me and goes for the cream cheese. "So, they give him a party and people are going on about what a great guy he is, how reliable blah blah, how he works so hard and all this. This is secondhand info, I wasn't actually there. So, he comes home with a bad case of how terrific he is, and next thing you know it's all, 'I'm too grown up for this,' and 'I don't need a baby sitter' and my absolute favorite, 'I'm ready to take it to the next level.' Like he's Tiger Woods or something."

I experience a brief, disorientating image of Tiger Woods charging onto a junior high school playground waving a machine gun overhead, but chase it away by asking, "How are the meds? I've been making changes."

"They're helping, definitely. There's less of that—" Fingers flutter. "You know."

"Swearing at everybody he sees."

"That's it."

"Can I see him?"

"Be my guest."

He's waiting for me in the living room. Muffin stays in her office. "I hear you want to move out. What's going on?"

His mouth twists. "Nothing's going on. I just want to leave."

"You must have reasons."

"I just—you think—what, do *you* want to live like this?"

"Let's just talk about what *you* want."

His eyes slide sideways, scanning the room: pink overstuffed furniture, big TV, low plastic coffee table with rounded corners. Everything in soothing pastel shades, nothing with any real personality. I can see why someone would hate it. I hate it. Andrew says, "I want my own place. Everybody here, they treat you like you're a little kid."

"That sounds frustrating."

"It fucking *sucks*. That fatass Muffin—"

"Let's stay focused on you, Andrew. Forget Muffin, forget about the staff."

His face tightens its grip. "Yeah, that'd be great. I'd love to forget them."

"What do you have in mind, an apartment in the city? Something around here?"

He inhales slowly. "I don't know. Someplace close by. Not in fucking Boston, that's too much, that'd be . . . Shit. Yeah." He pauses to think for a time. I let him. The meds are definitely helping. "There's this guy at work, he has his own place in the, it's one bedroom in this apartment block, the red sun, the red tower, something like that."

"Red Stone Towers." A little complex of two-story brick units built in the fifties. Utilitarian, sure, but I'm heartened by Andrew's realism. This is a plan, not a fantasy. "Behind the shopping center."

"Yeah. And he does okay. He just lives there and his case worker comes by to make sure he takes his meds and gets to work. And he's fucked *up*, paranoid schizophrenic, he's been in jail and stuff. He's way worse than me and they let him do it and he's a fucking nut job."

"Andrew, you know you were court ordered to treatment."

"Well *duh*."

"And this was chosen as the best place for you."

"Yeah but it's been like two *years*. You could have a meeting and change stuff, I've outgrown this place." He adjusts his rump against the sofa and just like that, suddenly he's more adult than I've ever seen him: no longer a whiny little boy. He's sitting up straight, looking me in the eye. He crosses his legs, for Pete's sake. Give him a haircut, he could pass for a Mormon. For the moment, his face is miraculously still. "Meds are working good too."

"Seem to be."

"I feel like this is my moment, you know? And I'm ready to, to—"

"Take it to the next level?"

"Yeah, totally. *Fuck* yeah."

From the other room comes a heavy thud, as if something bulky has dropped to the floor. It is unlikely, though not impossible, that Muffin has fallen off her chair. Andrew ignores this, instead fixing me with his intent stare. His eyes are a lovely icy blue, with a pair of light freckles marking the left pupil. He says, "Haven't you ever felt that way?"

"Ready for something new?"

"Yeah."

"Of course. That's perfectly natural."

"So I'm *normal*."

"Your desire is perfectly normal. The question isn't do we want things, but rather, how can we make sure the things we want are also the right things for us?"

His stare has lost none of its intensity. "I'm sure. I'm ready for it."

"We need to take this a step at a time."

"I said I'm ready for it." For a moment despair washes over his face again. "Fuck it—nobody fucking *listens* to me."

24. That weekend the city cowers under a lashing thunderstorm. Humidity has built up for days and now the sky cracks open with such ferocity that a person is hard-pressed not to consider questions of heavenly judgment, if one were so inclined, which it seems plenty of people are these days.

Dad shifts restlessly in his sleep as thunder crumbles across the skyline. Mom and I occupy our favorite kitchen positions. My coffee mug has a picture of a kitten in a tree and the caption *Hang in there!* Mom's features a cartoon secretary laboring beneath a sign that reads *Department of Redundancy Department.* Anna gave her these, for birthdays or Christmases, I forget.

"So she's in a play, I gather," I say. "In Provincetown."

"Anna? Mm." Mom sips again, makes a face. "She told me."

"Is there anything she doesn't tell you?" My god—I hope so.

"I should say rather, she mentioned she was thinking of something like this. Back in the spring. I didn't know she'd gone ahead with it. Some classic or other?"

"Shakespeare. *Othello.*"

"Oh dear." She sets the cup down. "Not much for the girls in that one, is there. It's been a while, but I seem to recall—mm, Desdemona?"

"Right. She gets to simper, and then die."

"That's Shakespeare for you."

"Actually that's everything for you, more or less."

She sighs. "At least it's not *Hamlet.*"

We sit for a time, listening to the rain. Then Mom says, "Your cousin Alice turns sixty next month."

"That's amazing." In more ways than one—cousin Alice is the family genealogist who traced the Parks back to the Mayflower but who also believes the Arabs are spying on her through the TV. "Is she as spunky as ever?"

"Apparently. Ron still visits every day."

Ron is my other cousin, Alice's little brother. They both live in upstate New York somewhere—some town named after a foreign country, like Lebanon or Hungary. Ron has an apartment and four parrots, Alice lives in a cozy inpatient facility, bankrolled by the family. "Who'd have thought she'd merrily chug away so long."

Mom grimaces. "She'll outlive us all."

The thunder has receded, steady curtains of rain are sweeping down. In the bedroom Dad coughs and murmurs and Mom goes to check on him. Dad's been going through a rough patch lately. I wait, wondering if my mother will soon join me in widowhood.

"He's fine," she says when she returns. "When's the play?"

"End of the month."

"That's only a week away. You're going." It's not a question.

A distant flutter of lightning: how cinematically appropriate. "I want to of course. I'd love to. But she's asked me to stay away."

"Whatever for?"

"She says I'll be judgmental and make her nervous and all this."

"That's ridiculous. I'll call her."

"Don't call her, I can—Mom. *Mom*, put the phone down. Thank you." Outside, rain pelts against the sidewalk. A fuzzy patch of bright silver suggests that the sun might still exist, despite indications to the contrary. "She doesn't want me to go, okay, I'll respect that."

"Why? Children say things all the time that they don't mean."

There's plenty I could say to that, but I let it go.

"You're her mother, Regina, you need to be there."

"She said not to."

"What she meant was that the play is important to her, she's working hard and she's nervous about it. So please don't come and harp on how silly her hair looks or how marginal her role is or how her inexperience let her down in that critical scene where—oh, I don't remember any critical scenes with Desdemona."

"The one where she dies is about all she gets."

"Well then. Don't tell her she blew the death scene. Whatever she does, you tell her she died very well."

It just comes out wrong, I know that. But she must see the look on my face because she reaches across the table to clasp my hand with unexpected ferocity. "I didn't mean it like that."

"I know you didn't."

"I would never say something like that."

"I know."

"Really, I wouldn't—that was just—"

"Mom, it's okay."

She nods so I know she hears me. But she seems unwilling to let go, and keeps holding on, clenching really, well past the point where it becomes awkward for both of us.

25. I call Anna that night and get no answer. Call again later, no answer, give up for the night. I'm getting ready for bed when the cell rings and she greets me with a chirpy: "Hi there."

"Hello. I hope I wasn't disturbing you."

"No, I had my phone off, I was at rehearsal."

"That went late."

"Yeah well, there's not much time left? I'm tired though."

She sounds it. "Are you going to be ready in time?"

"I think so. Man, I hope so."

Anna used to be a real morning person, popping out of bed at six or seven o'clock, collapsing before midnight even on weekends. Is she still this way? I have no idea. This sudden knowledge of how little I actually know her jars me, like I've hit a pothole in the road. "Let me ask you something. Two things actually, just humor me. Are you enjoying yourself? Are you having fun with all this?"

"Yeah. A lot, actually."

"Even though it's work."

"Sure. There *is* such a thing as work you enjoy."

"Yes, I'm aware. So, what in particular do you find so enjoyable?"

A pause. "God, do you have to psychiatrize everything?"

"I'm not psychiatrizing." I'm fairly certain that's not a real word. "I'm curious is all. Don't answer if you don't want to, but here's my daughter doing something I've never seen her do before, and she says she loves it, and that interests me. I'd like to get to know my daughter better, by understanding this more." I struggle to soften my tone, and fail. "And if that's 'psychiatrizing,' then I apologize. I'll never do it again, I'll just shut up and move along."

"Mom, you don't have to shout, Jesus."

"Get in line with all the other cattle. Sit down, stand up, fall on your knees . . ."

"Okay okay—stop! Let me think a minute, I never really thought about it. Olivier, he's the director, he has this thing that if you analyze stuff too much, you lose the inspiration, you know?"

"I've heard that." Suddenly I'm exhausted. "But it never made sense to me."

She's kind enough not to say, *That's because you never felt inspired, Mom*. Instead she says, "So let me think," and then takes several moments to do just that. "It's funny, 'cause I always used to think that actors were constantly craving attention, they always wanted the spotlight?"

"That seems accurate."

"But the thing is, when I'm doing this and it's going really well?—and I'm like, lost in the moment, which is what Olivier says we should be striving for, I feel like I'm not me anymore. I'm actually someone else."

"You're Desdemona."

"Well sort of, but not really. I mean yeah, because that's the name of the girl in the play but the thing is, I don't walk around thinking 'I'm Desdemona now, I'm Desdemona.' I'm not really thinking at all, I just *am* someone else, and all the attention that person gets, it doesn't really have anything to do with me." Another pause. "But it feels really good."

"What does?"

"Being someone else."

"You enjoy that."

"Yeah, it's just, it's like getting lost in another person? Yeah. I love it. It's like I forget all my own stuff, and just walk around as this blissful other person."

Outside the night is completely still except for the buzz of a faraway siren. "You know, if I was the obsessive psychiatrist you accuse me of being, I'd ask you 'why' about that too. About why you feel so happy being someone else."

"I'd rather you didn't."

"I won't."

"Because, that's one question I don't think I could ever answer."

Oh, but I could take a stab at it, dear.

26. After the blood and police and ambulances and the morgue and the statement in the kitchen—the cops were good, they really were, some of them are halfway to being shrinks themselves—I left Anna with my parents and drove back home. It was three in the morning and I should have been exhausted, but no, I was utterly awake, hyper-aware. Every detail registered: the news magazine open on the coffee table, photos of an angry mob in South America. Wilted irises on the end table by the sofa. Dirty dishes in the kitchen like an art installation, crusted tomato sauce, flecks of parmesan and basil. Walter's down vest on a peg by the back door. Upstairs, Toby's room, dirty clothes in a pile and an unmade bed, a scatter of video games and comics. A car drove past, pumping out some rap headache. His desk, unusually clean. I was drawn to it like a junkie. There it was, framed in an expanse of brown desktop, the envelope. Two words scrawled in shaky pencil.

Mom
why

I looked at it sitting there until I started shaking.

I am not a terribly expressive person, I know this. Call it Yankee reserve, call it frigidity or repression or uptight white chick or whatever is most convincing; I'm not someone who likes to put on a show, thanks. But up there in Toby's room, seeing that envelope and the promise that went with it, I well and truly lost my shit. Screamed as if I'd been kicked—well, I *had* been. Up till that moment, it could have all been an accident, a stupid meaningless example of dumb animal existence at its most futile. *Shit happens.* But not now. Not if there was a note.

I pounded pillows, overturned the desk lamp, disemboweled his stupid comics, swung the baseball bat into the windows. A good heavy aluminum bat: three windowpanes shattered in quick succession. Mrs. Flynn's lights went on and I saw her poking her busybody little ferret-face past the curtains. *Fuck you, bitch!* I shrieked. Or something similar. *I don't give a fuck!* And I wheeled around, the baseball bat a sledgehammer in my fist, punishing the furniture.

It's a good thing nobody smoked in that house. If a lighter had found its way into my hand at that moment, I'd have torched the place. As it was, the bat proved destructive enough.

Fifteen minutes later I dropped it. My breath came in jagged little rasps.

The letter was still there. I snatched it up, staggered into the bedroom, slammed it into my chest of drawers. And left it. Left it. Some kind of sound was coming out of me, out of my throat. I couldn't see very well but somehow made my way back downstairs, away from Toby's room, away from the bed where Walter and I lay every night—where we *used to* lie—stood there in the darkened living room listening to my own gasps settle into fast, shallow, steady breathing.

And left it. Up there, in the dresser, in the drawer.

Sat there a long time, staring at the night through the big picture window. Maybe I dozed off but I don't think so. After a while it occurred to me to go upstairs and survey the damage. It was impressive, in a hopeless sort of way. For a small woman I can make a mess when I set my mind to it.

By the time I turned out Toby's bedroom light, Mrs. Flynn's house had gone dark too.

27. Wednesday afternoon Russell shows up with the painting. "Congratulations," he says. "You are now a collector of original artworks. Next stop, Warhol."

"Hiroshige, more likely. I've always adored his stuff."

He smiles in a way that tells me he doesn't know who Hiroshige is, then gets busy. I let him take down the Monet waterlilies and hang the crows-on-silk above the couch. It's larger than the print it replaces, its severe tone dominating the room. "What do you think?" he asks.

"I'm not sure." This is the truth. "It's kind of . . . stark."

"Regina, you invented stark. And all that white space, it really opens up the room."

"Yeah? You might be right. Give it a day or two and let's see what Brutus thinks."

"Who's Brutus?"

"Secret admirer."

We sit on the couch, beneath the painting—after going to the trouble of hanging the thing, we don't even sit where we can see it. But this feels good. He leans close, radiating warmth, his thigh along mine, and that feels even better. "Wine?"

"Can't. I got work." He ducks his head. "Sorry."

"Don't be. It's an amazing thing, what you're doing."

He smiles a little but doesn't answer. I say, "Shouldn't you be there now?"

"Mm—it's slow on weekdays from three to five." He checks his watch. "Mack can handle it for now."

He bends close to kiss me. I let him. Afternoon sun spills through the picture window and the crows stare down from above the couch.

Time passes. Not as much as I'd like, but there it is. He pulls away. "Gotta go. Hope you're not mad?"

"I'm furious."

"I'll make it up to you."

At the door he stops and looks back. "Beautiful!"

I glance over my shoulder. "You were right, it's the perfect spot."

His hand rests on my hip and he brushes my ear with his lips. "Didn't mean the painting."

28. "Say it again?" says Mom.

"I said I met somebody. Met, as in, I'm dating him."

We're on the phone so I can't gauge her expression. I had expected relief, joy even, heavy exhalations of, "Oh thank goodness," or words to that effect. Instead, this empty etheric hiss. "Mom? Did you hear me?"

"I heard."

"I thought you'd be happy."

"Of course. I mean, if you are, I am." Mom's voice trails off, bewildered, a reaction I hadn't anticipated.

"We'll talk about it in person. I'm going to P-town this weekend, I decided to take your advice." Still no response. "But I'll be over next Sunday, all right?"

"Mm."

I bite back annoyance. Whatever I do, I never manage to please my mother. Memo to fourteen-year-olds: this never changes.

Mom says, "Tell her hello from us."

"I'll do that." Provided of course she isn't livid that I've ignored her injunction to stay away from Desdemona. Hey, I have the perfect excuse: *I'm just doing what my mother told me to.* "How's Dad?"

"Fine. He had visitors this morning, the Cohens. Remember them?"

"Sure." She'd always pinch my cheek, he gave me gum. "How are they?"

"The same. They never seem to age. Your father was lively when they were here, but right after lunch he conked out. Regina, about this boy you're seeing."

"Man. He's full grown, he's almost seventeen, ha ha."

She clears her throat. "I'm happy for you—"

"You're sure?"

"—I'm just saying, just, try not to do anything precipitous."

Precipitous? "Unless I've grown new ovaries, I won't be getting pregnant again."

"Of course. But you know what I mean."

Actually I don't. AIDS? Stepchildren? Background checks? I've no idea, and Mom seems unable or unwilling to clear it up. We talk a bit more and hang up, both of us unsatisfied. It occurs to me that, no matter how baffling one's parents are in childhood, they become even more mysterious as one grows older. And then it occurs to me—no small shock, this—that Anna and I might see eye on eye on this one.

29. "Tony's back," Becky tells me.

"As in, urine-drinking Tony?"

"The one and so far only."

"And the girlfriend?"

"Nada."

"Some treatment plans are doomed from the start."

In the eval room I barely recognize him. Tony's lost upward of twenty pounds on an already-scrawny frame. His face sinks in like an old man's, and two weeks' growth of beard is shot through with white. He sits quietly in a blue plastic chair, hands folded in his lap, something the old muckraking Tony would never have allowed himself to do, and he appears to be compulsively talking to himself. "Hi Tony," I say.

He pauses in his internal/external monologue to peer at me, then drops away. He says something that might be "never will again" or "never well again" or even "never willing then" or who the hell knows. He does not look at me when he says this.

"Tony, do you know who I am? Do you know where you are?" I feel like a cop, reading him his Miranda rights. It's obvious that he's not oriented at all but I have to check. "Tony. Do you know what year this is?"

"Hehm?" He's at least looking at me now. I repeat the question.

"Nineteen forty-seven," he answers with conviction. "Fucking Hitler. Fucking ragheads."

Well that's something, we're getting somewhere, even if it isn't anywhere I want to go. "That's not quite right. Try again?" He doesn't answer so I shift gears. "What country is this? What country are we living in?"

He looks at me like I'm a child. "'Merica."

"That's right, very good. Do you know who the President is right now?"

"Nick, nah . . . Nixon. Fucking Nixon. Fucking nigger Nixon."

"What's your favorite baseball team, Tony?"

"Keep'm away from me. Fucking niggers always looking at me. And the ragheads."

"Baseball, Tony. What's your favorite team?"

He blinks his way to lucidity. "Red Sox." And inevitably, a moment later: "Fucking Yankees."

God help me, I laugh out loud. After a second, Tony joins me.

Later, when the ward has dimmed and the patients are more or less asleep, Becky offers her succinct diagnosis. "He seems really *fahked ahp.*"

"Yes he is. Let me write that in the chart. Patient admitted disoriented x3 and delusional, exhibiting paranoid ideation and observable characteristics of being really fahked ahp."

Becky smiles in the dark. "So what do we do with Tony Baloney? Stabilize on meds, blah blah?"

"The blah blah's the tricky bit. We'll start him on a low dose of Clearazine and titrate up if we need to. It's a shame, he never was on anything before, from what I can see." Late in life for a first psychotic episode, but there it is.

"Nobody ever said anything was easy," Becky muttered.

"Sounds like a line from a movie."

"Yeah, a movie called *The Life of Becky*."

"You need a vacation, don't you?"

"Or something." She yawns. "You got plans this weekend?"

"In fact I do, I'm going to P-town."

"*Ex*cellent. You coming out, finally?"

"I'm *going* out, with a guy."

Her brow furrows. "What's in P-town for straight people? Besides ceramics."

"My daughter. She's in a play."

"I always forget you got a kid."

That stings a bit—*a kid*—but Becky means nothing by it. "A community theater thing."

Becky looks like she's struggling not to make some crack about my daughter finally coming out even if her mom is afraid to. I wouldn't mind—Becky is Becky, she jokes about everything. But apparently my children are off-limits, so she just asks politely, "What play?"

"Shakespeare. *Othello*."

"I don't know that one. Everybody gets married at the end? Or everybody dies?"

"Everybody dies except the girl, she dies in the middle. I'm a little nervous, it's her first time onstage and she could've picked something easy. But that's my daughter for you."

Becky laughs. "Sounds like her mom."

30. The theater is small, maybe three hundred seats, sturdy in a we-may-be-amateurs-but-we-take-this-seriously sort of way. Russell studies his program thoroughly—two pages stapled together, with a "please support our sponsors" banner across the bottom—but I'm too unsettled to concentrate. I keep glancing around, watching the trickle of people enter the theater, and borrow a page from Trish's positive-energy book: I try to will the arrival of a large, boisterous, appreciative crowd, by visualizing the seats filling up. It doesn't happen, but neither does the trickle choke off entirely. Lots of older folks, lots of same-sex couples and obvious New Yawkers out to see the provincials on holiday. With luck the seats will be half full.

"You never told me she studied drama," Russell says suddenly.

"She doesn't."

He points at the cast biographies on the back page, and next to a postage-stamp photo of Anna's face I discover this bewildering entry:

> Annamarie Moss (*Desdemona*) studies Theater and Dramatic
> Arts at Upton College in Vermont. She has appeared
> in numerous college productions, and this is her first role
> for The Provincetown Summer Repertory Company. Her
> favorite playwrights are Beckett and Pirandello.

Theater of the absurd, indeed. *Six Parents in Search of Recognizable Offspring.* Anna*marie*? Where does that come from, I wonder. Marie Curie? Marie Osmond? I fan myself with the program and say to Russell, "Must be something she made up for the program. It sounds better than 'Anna Moss studies economics and asked her mother not to attend this evening.'"

An elderly woman two rows ahead swivels around and shoots me her best toxic old-lady look. Honey, the play hasn't even started yet. Amateur Shakespeare? I sigh, and settle in for a long night.

Against all odds, I'm wrong. The play proceeds smoothly enough, with nary a wardrobe malfunction or embarrassingly flubbed line. I'm no Shakespeare expert, but it sounds as though all the *thees* and *thous* are in the right place. Iago is suitably spiky and evil, sporting a sleeveless vest and copious reptilian tattoos; Othello himself slightly tubby, vaguely foreign looking—Indian maybe?—and as for Desdemona, well.

I'm not ashamed to say that when Anna first appears onstage, I don't recognize her for five or six seconds. That's saying something, as any mother will attest.

Part of my confusion stems from my not knowing the play, so she arrives sooner than expected. Partly I'm thrown by her gown, a sumptuous golden affair that sets off her frosted-highlight coiffure and blood-red nails. (When did Anna start painting her nails? Oh wait, it isn't Anna.) But mostly I'm deceived by the fact that Anna's not there, it's just someone else bearing an uncanny resemblance to her who's swanning around. Someone rather ditzy, more than a little vain, doting and dutiful to a fault, not the brightest kid in class but struggling to compensate with all the powers of decency, modesty, loyalty and goodwill she can muster. Is it any wonder she gets killed? Shakespeare was no dummy. Darwin was centuries away, but the laws of the jungle had been established long since, and wolves like Iago had been dining on scampering furry Desdemonas for eons.

When Othello smothers her, it's traumatic. More than that: it's like watching my own child being killed. If Russell wonders at my silent weeping throughout the rest of the play, he doesn't say anything about it.

But the show must go on, as they say, and go on it does. This being Provincetown, the homoerotic subtext between Othello and Iago is made explicit—in fact, it's downright campy—to the delight of the audience. A glance at Russell reveals his confusion: apparently he didn't know the chief baddie in the play was hot for the title character, and vice versa, and that everybody wore codpieces back in the day. Live and learn.

And, this being not only Provincetown but also Shakespeare, and therefore similar in some ways to life, most everybody with any redeeming qualities dies. But it's far enough removed from life that there is some suggestion of cosmic justice—the bad boy gets dragged away in chains, after all, to a presumably grisly fate. I find that despite this, and despite all the highfalutin *thees* and *thous*, there is no justice, cosmic or otherwise, that can rinse my mouth of the sour taste of Desdemona's brutal demise.

The applause from our half-full theater is respectable, with the men getting the lion's share. That's typical I suppose. But when Russell lets out an ear-splitting whistle at Anna's curtain call, she looks our way, her stage smile morphing to a look of perplexity, a mild frown, before the glazed semi-pro smile makes its way back onstage. And beneath it, I glimpse something else: fury.

31. The wind whips in off the bay, scattering sand into my eyes, destroying my hair. The Cape can be harsh even at the best of times, which is what late August is. A few intrepid bathers dare the water or lie stretched on towels, baiting cancer. The rest stroll along the foamy tide, solitary or in pairs or small family gaggles. Some gesticulate wildly, others hold hands.

Anna and I are not holding hands.

"I cannot fucking *believe* you showed up even when I asked you not to," she snaps, for the fifth time, or perhaps the tenth, or thirtieth. "I just don't believe it. I mean I know you're self-centered but *Christ*."

There is little to say besides *My mother told me to*, which seemed funnier in the car when I was driving here. Now it's just an unsatisfying answer on too many levels to count. So I hold my head erect and say, "I'm sorry. I apologize, again. I shouldn't have done it."

"Yeah, but you did, so—oh screw it."

We shuffle along, past a group of kids splashing in the chilly surf. They seem to be having fun.

Ahead of us stretches a mile or so of beach that terminates in a squat little lighthouse. To the left, across a narrow stripe of sea, lies P-town. We're inside a long twist of land—Cape Cod—that stretches out from Massachusetts and coils in on itself like a snake, or a memory. Or an elbow, followed by another one, and another. Directly in front of us, across more water, lie a series of little towns like Wellfleet, while to our right, too distant to make out over the horizon, lies the upper arm of the Cape. Somewhere behind us squats Boston, Vermont and other places I've only heard of, like Kansas and Montana. Let those prissy Californians have their beaches where they can stand and look past the waves to the distant horizon, wondering what lies on the other side. Here in New England we prefer the kind of beach that looks backward, across the swell and waves, to where we've already been.

"Where's Russell?" she demands later, after much stamping-heavily-across-the-beach sulking.

"At the B&B." Most likely wondering—again—what he'd gotten himself into. "He was impressed by you."

"Yeah thanks." She spits the words and tosses her head like a colt, so I don't say *I was too*.

The wind picks up and flings some more grit at us. Another fine family day at the beach. Anna stops to plant her feet in the sand, but still won't look at me. "Why'd you do it, Mom?"

"I wanted to see you act, obviously—"

"Not that. The other thing." She swipes hair from her eyes, a strand drops to her mouth. She leaves it. "I mean, why'd you put me on the fucking *pills*."

32. She seems to be squinting out tears, but this may just be the wind. "Jesus Christ, of *course* I was depressed. I'd've been crazy not to be—my brother had just fucking killed my *dad*."

The fact is, nobody knows just what happened in the treehouse, but now isn't the time to point that out. "That was years earlier—four years in fact, and the symptoms were getting worse. Even your grandmother noticed, I bet you didn't know she talked to me about it. She was worried."

"Great, Grams was worried so you put me on dope for two years."

"It's not dope, it's Uplifterol, it's perfectly safe—"

"And who knows how much longer I'd have stayed on it? Another two years? Another twenty?"

"It worked," I remind her. "You were much better after that."

"I was *stoned* after that. Too fucking wasted for my problems to register." She starts walking again and I hurry to catch up. She carries her sandals in one hand and lets the tide swamp her ankles.

We struggle along, side by side, like tired soldiers. "It was Dolores, wasn't it? Who encouraged you to stop." I wonder if it was cold turkey—bad idea—or if she weaned herself gradually. "When was this?"

"January."

We're approaching the lighthouse. A small swarm of tourists and kids hovers around it like wasps. She stops. "I don't need to see this."

"You used to like lighthouses."

She looks like she wants to retch. "Toby liked lighthouses, Mom."

So he did—but she did too. We turn around and head back. The beach stretches ahead, then a stone jetty makes a hard right back to P-town. Across the bay lies Boston, Missouri, North America, and so on. No matter what the direction, I end up facing where I've come from.

"It's really hard," she says now. "I get totally depressed for like a week, and then really edgy, then I can't stop laughing and I want people around all the time, then I obsess about one thing for days, then I can't concentrate, then I just space out and stare at the wall." She stops and faces me. "Then I'm fine for a couple days, you know? I study and go to class and everything." She sets off again before I can answer.

I fall in beside her. I wish I had a tissue, the wind is driving my eyes berserk too. "I'm sure you'll be fine."

She snorts.

"I mean it. Seeing you last night, what you were doing, it was something really special."

"I told you, I like it when I'm somebody else."

That hangs between us for a while.

Gulls squawk. We come across a piece of driftwood, a length of planking with rusty bolts running through, so thick with corrosion as to be barely discernible. An old piece of shipwreck. Sobering, to see it like that and wonder about the men who sank with it. There are a lot of them off this coast, bones buried in silt. Further on we discover a half-exposed scallop shell as big as my hand, pearly purple inside. Anna picks it up and carries it away without a word. "I'm sorry," I say.

"You said that already."

"Not about the play. About the antidepressants. I don't think it was wrong to start them, but—maybe I should have cut them down sooner. Maybe they should've just been a short-term thing."

She says nothing for a while. The scallop shell catches the sun from time to time, flashing against my eyes.

We've walked another hundred yards when Anna says, "Maybe you should've gotten a second fucking opinion."

33. Russell and I drive back from P-town and settle into the comforting rhythms of work. The newspaper tells me that one-fifth of the world's coral reefs are dead, frogs are disappearing and SUVs are more popular than ever among mothers of preschoolers, who claim that they buy the vehicles "for the sake of the children." I'm trying to eat breakfast when I read this: the coffee is acrid on my tongue but I know there's nothing wrong with it because the orange juice tastes just as bad.

Outside, the morning is sunny and benign but I'm as aware as anyone of how false that innocuous surface can be. I sit and mull it over as the morning lengthens and the sun heaves itself higher and the paper regales me with all the absurdities, tragedies and occasional joys of the age.

Anna will be fine, I tell myself. It was probably a good idea to take her off those meds anyway. She'll be *fine*.

I spend the afternoon restlessly shuffling through my workouts, my shopping, the daily minutiae of ordinary life. I get a voicemail from Nick, who I saw at the gas station. His voice is small but still hopeful as he asks about a drink, a "quick visit" on his way home tonight. He says he wanted to "feel me out" about it, clever man, and hopes I have time "to fit him in." His unfortunate propensity for childish double entendre has always caused mild irritation, but today it makes me want to yank out my hair, or better yet his, by the roots.

I call his office and get his secretary, leave a message that his client Regina Moss has left town on business and will be unavailable until further notice.

Ten minutes later I call back and tell his secretary that Dr. Moss, the widow he occasionally fucks instead of fucking his wife, has found a younger, unmarried man to fuck, so she won't be requiring Nick's services anymore, and could she pass the message on? The secretary, caught midway between shock and delight, manages a breathy, "I'll be sure to let him know."

I switch on the TV and find a tennis match. Back and forth, back and forth. Love thirty, love forty. Game.

I can't concentrate: something haunts me. Another thing, one of many.

The note—the one lying upstairs in my bedroom, that I've never opened, that will, presumably, explain it all, or at least explain the tiny little fraction of it, whatever fraction that is that can be explained—is addressed to me. To *Mom*. Not *Mom and Dad*. Just *Mom*. I've thought about this and thought about this, and reached no satisfactory conclusion. Maybe Toby wasn't interested in explaining himself to his father. Maybe Walter didn't matter enough to acknowledge, he was just some peripheral figure in Toby's field of vision.

Long ago I decided it had to be something like this. Because the alternative is that Toby knew his father would die at the same time he did. That Toby premeditated his father's death. That it wasn't an accident, or even a suicide attempt that got out of hand, or a confused delusional spasm. That it was murder. And that is something I cannot countenance.

34. Here is what the police decided.

Walter and Toby were outside, in the maple, in the treehouse. Footprints on the roof—two sets—indicated that they had both climbed on top. The police had no idea why anyone would do something as foolish as that, in the dark, in the night. With the roof at a slant no less, to drain rainwater. The police have, in my experience, severely limited interest in such things.

Walter fell out of the tree, or was pushed. Damage to the vertebrae in his neck indicate that the impact killed him. His death wasn't "instant"—death is never instant, it takes time for a body to shut down. But he was well along his way when I stumbled across him.

Toby jumped, or fell, soon after his father. A large bruised indentation at the base of Walter's back matched similar damage to the upper left side of Toby's cranium. Also, although Toby was lying next to Walter, Toby's left ankle was resting on his father's leg.

It is unlikely that this could have occurred had Toby jumped—or been pushed—first. He also died quickly, without regaining consciousness.

Walter lay face down, arms beneath his torso. Maybe he was reaching out, trying to break the impact of the fall. Toby lay on his back, arms and legs spiraled open like a pinwheel or a starfish.

The facts of the police report stop here. Conjecture steps up.

1. This was a bizarre accident. (Unlikely, but impossible to rule out.)

2. Foul play was involved, involving a third party (read: me). But this possibility was swiftly dismissed for lack of evidence and "the subject's state of near-hysteria," not to mention my purported "physical slightness and inability to physically carry out the tasks required." Meaning, apparently, that I was judged too frail to even climb a tree, much less push someone—two someones—out of it.

3. Foul play was involved between the victims, either:

    a. Walter killed Toby but accidentally killed himself too, or

    b. Toby killed Walter but accidentally killed himself too, or

    c. One of them killed the other, then took his own life in remorse.

4. It was a suicide pact.

What astonishes me most, perhaps, is that the police *don't care*. The case is closed, as far as they're concerned. This is because the principals are all dead. Forget about me—I was just the "near-hysterical" spouse who couldn't climb a tree to save her life or, presumably, end someone else's. Whether Toby killed Walter or vice versa, whether suicide or accident or murder, is irrelevant because there is no presumed criminal at large wandering the streets or lurking in other people's maples. Next case, please.

Where does this leave me exactly? Where I started, more or less. So then. What's a person to do in such a situation?

Here's what. She invents. She fills in the gaps, speculates, creates logic where there is none. After a time, this can become almost as useful as stiff unyielding fact.

So then. Here is what I think happened.

35. Walter looked at me and frowned. "Toby's outside?"

"As far as I know."

"In the treehouse?"

"That would be my guess."

We sat at the kitchen table, dinner plates littering the table between us. Toby had skipped dinner again, as was his habit lately. I had gotten a call from his math teacher that day, Mrs. Ouellette. She was concerned about Toby's inattentiveness in class. She had spoken to Walter, who seemed uninterested. I had brought it up over dinner and now there was tension between us.

Outside was a cold dark November. Walter ran his fingers through his beard, as he did when unsettled. I couldn't help noticing that even at thirty-one, his beard was whitening at an alarming rate. Still reddish-brown on his cheeks, but from jawline downward it was heavily shot through with white streaks. Absently I wondered how long before the red was gone for good. Santa Claus in a flannel shirt. Kris Kringle with a router.

He stood up. "I'll go check on him."

For a reason I couldn't exactly name—women's intuition? Analytical expertise? Common sense?—I thought this was the wrong thing to do. "Leave it," I murmured.

"Why?"

"I don't—I can't explain." Walter and I had argued about this too, in low urgent tones so Toby wouldn't hear. Walter veered between an insouciant unconcern for Toby's erratic behavior, and sudden urgent hankerings to confront it. Right now, with dinner over and the day winding down, seemed like the wrong moment to go charging in. "He's been, I don't know, a little withdrawn, I don't think it would be useful to . . ."

"He's been weird lately," was Walter's clinical assessment, delivered in a thick accent: *wee-yud*. "Fookin' spooky if you ask me. In his own little fantasy world."

"Yes he has," I agreed, ignoring his jokey Irishisms. "That's why I think we should leave him be." I made a point of saying *We should leave him be* instead of *You should leave him be, you overbearing meddler*.

Walter stood there sipping his beer, a habit when he felt uncertain about something. Maybe it helped him to meditate on his course of action, or maybe it just occupied his hands. Finally he said, "I'll talk to him. I don't want him falling out of the treehouse because he's too damn spacey to know where he is."

It wasn't till after he left, tromping with vigor across the backyard, that I said, "I have no reason to believe our son doesn't know exactly where he is."

36. That was memory. Difficult, yes, but bearable. What follows is speculation, and much, much harder.

Walter crossed the lawn, approached the woods that edged up against the grass. That grass was trampled down and gone by, the earth frozen hard under frost. No snow yet that year, but the trees leafless, only the evergreens—hemlocks, pines, blue spruce—shouldering their perpetual shrouds.

Walter didn't notice the cold. Or more likely he noticed but didn't care, if anything he enjoyed the blood flushing his skin, exhilarating him, liked the dragon-smoke of his breath dissipating into the chill. He wore dungarees, boots, flannel shirt.

Toby watched from the treehouse as his father crossed the lawn. Kitchen lights threw Dad's long shadow lurching across the grass. Toby hated the cold but being out here was less unbearable than staying inside. Sometimes he tried to think about why that was but he never got very far. He blew on his fingers and stuffed them into his coat pockets, hopped from foot to foot, and wished his father would go away.

"Tobe? You up there, guy?"

It wasn't that he hated his father. That was stupid. He loved him, as much as any kid could love his dad. But when these moods took him, there was nobody whose company he enjoyed, not even his own, and nobody who got under his skin worse than his old man. Other times were different, they did stuff like build this treehouse or strip the coffee table and stain it or build new shelves for Mom. Thinking about times like that, sometimes it was the only way to hold off the emptiness of these moments.

Not that a lot of people understood the difference.

"Hey fella, I'm coming up, all right?"

Toby didn't answer. There was no point, his dad would do what he wanted. Then carry on like it was some idea they'd both had, something they'd planned out, when what Toby wanted more than anything was to be alone with the silence and the dark and the treehouse and. But his dad would never let that happen. It was like he was afraid of it or something. Of course he was afraid of it.

On some level, Toby knew what his father feared. The same thing that his mom feared, and Miss Davis and Mrs. Ouellette at school, and even his grandmother sometimes (when he caught her watching him, lips pursed, jaw set). That one day he would go away into the dark and the silence for good, make himself comfortable there, never come back. If he were completely honest, he would admit to sometimes fearing that too.

Not that it was ever comfortable there. That was something else people didn't understand, that the whistling empty dark was really no better than the house sometimes, or school or the car. It was just that . . . wherever he was, sometimes it was easier to stay than to come back. Coming back took such *effort*.

"Make room up there, big guy, I'm coming through."

Toby ignored his father and listened to the cold dark silence that wasn't really silent, it was populated with noise and movement, a dense array of feelings and whispers and thoughts and promises. Sometimes these were just feelings with nothing attached, other times a wad of anxieties about homework and projects and assholes in gym class and bitchy girls who laughed at him and his big hearty dad and distracted mom.

A scrap of a song unwound through his brain: *Well I went to the mountains, but they wouldn't tell me what they knew . . .*

His cheeks itched and he rubbed them ferociously.

Dad was almost there, climbing up the ladder. Toby leaned over the square-framed hole in the door and squinted down. His father's shadowy figure was just a few yards below. It occurred to Toby that he could drop straight down and catch his father completely unawares, knock him off the ladder and into the soft net mesh that surrounded him. Would it be strong enough to hold, or would it give way to let them both crash all the way down to the frozen ground below? The thought brought him up short, terrified him with its icy appeal.

So I ran to the ocean, but it wouldn't tell me why it's blue . . .

Instead he stepped onto the guardrail and reached overhead, grabbing the bough that anchored the roof of the treehouse, and levered himself up. It was a maneuver he'd performed many times but never after dark, and the swirling shadowiness around him was disorienting and thrilling in equal measure. Like swimming underwater at night, no telling where *up* was except by feeling the earth's pull and listening to his body float toward the sky. He landed on the roof silent as a cat, then scuttled back till his spine nestled against the bole of the maple. Thick and solid, even way up here, but getting thinner. Getting thinner. He could feel the tangle of branches flexing beneath him, as if the tree were shrugging its shoulders, shifting his weight from one branch to another. Everything swayed and he swayed with it. The air was cold—it was *fookin' freezin'*, his dad would say—but he was alone again, so that was good. He shivered.

"Tobe? Hey, Tobe-man, what's the story?" His father's bewildered voice echoed from below. Toby imagined him standing inside the treehouse now, waving the flashlight around—his dad would never leave the house at night without a flashlight, any more than his mom would ever remember to check the tire pressure before a road trip—with a look on his face of—what was the word? Fuddy something. Befuddlement, that was it. A look of *befuddlement* on his face. Some words were just perfect, the way they sounded like just what they meant.

"Tobe, I'm serious, buddy. This isn't funny at all, quit playing around."

Toby thought, *What the fuck?* He knew this wasn't playing. Just like he knew this wasn't funny, any more than it was sad, or hopeful, or heroic or inspiring or scary. Or anything else. There was no word for it, really, because it wasn't anything.

He said nothing out loud. His father's voice had receded to an insectoid buzzing, nearly drowned out by the louder buzzing of the tree, the night, the stars, the dark. Still he wished his father would leave. More than anything he wanted to be left alone. Like an owl in a tree, or a seadragon in a tank. It wasn't the first time he'd thought this. But here was his father anyway, still trying to play Knock-Me-Down like a five-year-old.

Toby looked up through the branches, naked now, leafless against the sky. In the watery moonlight they looked like so many sticks . . . well *duh*, they were sticks. The moon tossed handfuls of light that shattered into little droplets on its way through the branches to the ground. Behind it all the stars buzzed, light dark bright ghostly, some spinning in place others standing still. Toby looked down and saw degrees of blackness, the thick shadow of the treehouse against the paler shadow of the earth far below. A jerky finger of light too, his dad's flashlight probing, yellow against the slate gray night, branches jittering in crazy shadows. He'd forgotten his dad and now here he was. Mothers jerked toward the light like suicidal epileptics.

I crept to the forest and I waited there a year for you . . .

Moths rather. *Moths* jerked toward the light like suicidal epileptics.

"Toby." His father's voice, serious now, wrapped around Toby's neck and squeezed. Gently, like people do when they say *It's for your own good*. Toby knelt at the edge of the roof and peered over. Dad's head stuck out of the treehouse, haloed in holy flashlight, staring into the darkness below. "You get down while I was coming up? How'd you get past me?" And then a new thought entered Dad's head: Toby could hear it sliding into place like a deadbolt. The flashlight swiveled up, into Toby's eyes. He held up his hands, squinted, twisted away, heard: "Jesus Mary and Joseph."

The tree buzzed louder, protesting the light. "Not my eyes, huh?"

"Jesus Christ, Toby, what do you think you're doing?"

"Turn it off! Stop shining the *light* in my *eyes*!"

The shrillness got through. The light dropped away by a quarter turn—90 degrees, Mrs. Oullette would say. It pointed neither up nor down, but flatways into a thick tangle of nothing much. Toby could see his father's silhouette as he leaned, head and shoulders over the railing. Dad was thickset and grizzled, beard and hair limned with gold even though he wasn't blond at all. For a second Toby wrestled with the oddness of that. Then he was distracted by the ringing of the stars and he forgot about his father again. Also there was that smell. Something heavy and meaty and sweet, what was the word? *Fecund*. Another word that sounded like what it meant, like a

Then his father was right there. How had he hauled his bulky frame onto the rooftop without Toby noticing? Dad's shadow was reaching for him and he bolted or tried to. He wanted to fly away, like a fish. He wanted to swim away like a sparrow.

He wanted to be the one nobody could knock over no matter how hard they tried.

He wanted to be too big to hold and too small to see. *Well I went to the mountains*

Dad's idea had been to slope the roof so rainwater would run off. A 10 percent grade or was it 5, he didn't remem

"Tobe, settle down, just settle the hell down—"

The flashlight went careering into the night and this transfixed them both, the way it bounced at the edge of the roof and cartwheeled over, the bright strobe of the beam curling as it fell, illumining the branches, flinging twirling spastic shadows across the night and landing with a smack and going dead and the moon was the only light and it wasn't moving or at least not fast enough to notice and

The sudden dark seemed to galvanize his father into stillness. "Okay then. Okay. Just hold on a second." For a time they stood there in the silence and dark. Then Dad started talking again. "Okay—we've got to be really careful. First thing, let's get back in the treehouse. Then we'll find the ladder and get right back down. Nice and easy. We can do that, right? You've done it lots of times I bet, haven't you, Tobe?"

It occurred to Toby that his father masked his fear with talk. It wasn't the first time he'd had this thought. His mother, he suspected, did the opposite. "I'll stay."

"Don't be a fookin' eedjit. One slip up here and there's nothing between you and the ground." His father's voice was a hiss and here came his hand again, heavy on the shoulder, clenching fingers that sent electric shockwaves sparking through his body like an eel would do. Toby jigged sideways and Dad clenched tighter, above the elbow this time. It hurt it hurt a lot

Dad took a step, for just a second one foot was raised and dangling in the air, he was balanced on the other one and that was the moment that Toby bulled his head at his father's chest but misjudged in the poor light, knocked him in the side, sent him staggering—away from the bole of the tree, the safety of the maple's solidity. Suddenly Dad was spinning on one foot, lurching for balance, dancing at the edge of the

Except that Dad never danced and it showed, and he fought now for balance with a gracelessness that was almost artistic in its totality. His arms flailed like leafless branches in a hurricane. They weren't sticks but they looked like sticks, like dead things already that maybe had been alive once not so long ago

It was happening very fast all together at once

Walter's last words were, "Jesus Christ, son," but Toby didn't hear because the rushing in his ears was so loud it smeared his father's words, even his father's short-lived yelp as he fell. Toby remembered swimming underwater at the Cape, the watery pounding of surf against his ears, and combined with the lightheadedness he felt now—the disorienting murk all around him—he couldn't remember whether he was far underwater or high in the air. One or the other, that was for sure, probably, maybe. That's what Dad had been trying to tell him.

Toby's thoughts settled as he calmed down a little and looked around. Dad wasn't here now, he'd swum away, or soared off on the currents. He was alone now, Toby was, and now that he finally had what he'd wanted, he wasn't sure he wanted it. Was that a joke or what?

Toby took a step toward where his father had disappeared into the water. Maybe it wasn't too late to dive in and catch him. "Dad, wait for me," is what he said, and then he followed.

37. "You look like shit," says Tony. We're back in an ACC eval room. He's been here a week and still looks shaky. But better. Better but still shaky: it could be a phrase out of the DSM, I use it so much: *Patient BBSS after 6 days Mellorone 30mg TID . . .* He's freshly shaved, so his face is gaunt but not grizzled, and he wears jeans and a faded gray T-shirt with a picture of Che Guevara on it. If he has any breasts left from his estrogen-drinking days, they don't show.

"Let's talk about you. How are you feeling?"

He scratches his head, leaving a swatch of unkempt hair tilting up like a patch of uncut wheat at harvest time. "What are my choices?"

"Whatever you want."

"The fact that I'm not locked up in Gitmo with electrodes taped to my balls, that's great. The fact that I'm here, that Amber fucking broke my heart and pissed on it, hey. Not so good."

I wonder if the piss reference is coincidence. "When you came in, you didn't seem to know where you were—"

"Or who the President was, no shit, I been getting an earful of that every day." His eyes flash, the old Tony, and I'm happy enough to see it. "I know who the President is now, okay?"

I can't resist. "And that would be . . ."

"The same joker it is every year. Mickey fucking Mouse. Been running the country since 1963, you know what I mean?"

"Sure."

He glares at me. "November 22, 1963. Get it?"

"Sure I get it, Tony." I jot a few notes. *Patient oriented – mood labile – some hostility – no psychotic ideation apparent.* "You said some other unusual things the other day."

"Oh yeah? Well I'm crazy, right?"

"You talked about 'the fucking ragheads' and 'the fucking niggers.'"

He blinks. "I don't think so." He looks past me, at Nancy sitting by the door. "I would never say something like that, Nance, unless I was off my rocker. I mean, that would just show how far gone I really was, to say something like that."

Nancy's a newish tech, been around a few weeks, black. She gives Tony a reassuring smile and says, "I know that, Tony." I don't know her well enough to tell whether she means it, but professionally it's the right thing to say.

"I like you a lot, Nance. You're probably one of the best staff here."

"I thank you for that."

To me he says, "What'd I say about—them?"

"Not a great deal. You just sort of . . . I'd ask a question, and you say blah, blah, fucking ragheads. Or whatever." He's frowning at me. "It didn't make a lot of sense, but, it's not the kind of thing I ever heard you say before."

"It's not a smart thing to say."

"But I was wondering whether, if there was something that concerned you about those people. Those groups of people. You know, if they're conniving against you, or trying to take advantage of you, or something." I leave it out there. Remain silent long enough, they'll always say something. They all want to tell their story.

He sits for a time, lip trembling; I don't know if it's just twitching or if he's engaged in a conversation with himself. The old Tony would have seen through my charade in a moment, known I was trying to discern any lingering paranoid ideation bubbling below the veneer. But old Tony hasn't quite returned, and I'm trying to rule something out before he gets too clever to let me do so.

He looks up then, very deliberately, and says, "I heard your husband killed himself."

Behind me Nancy shifts in her chair. She's tall and slender with pencil-thin dreads and plastic-rimmed glasses, and speaks with the sweetest Tennessee accent I've ever heard. Now she says in her gentle lilt, "Would you like me to escort the patient to the day room, doctor?"

"It's all right." I take a slow deep breath and say to Tony, "He died, yes. But nobody really knows what happened."

He is surprised at this: we're here to talk about *him*, and I've gone and broken the rules. He sends quick glances left and right as if seeking a punch line, or maybe his next smart comment. I cut him short: "It was years ago, but it's still very painful."

"Huh . . . Sure."

"I think about it all the time. It's the worst thing I've ever lived through."

"Yeah." He shifts against the hard plastic. "I guess so."

"Have you ever experienced something like that, Tony? A death, so close?"

"Me, huh, no." He recovers now and the crafty glint returns to his eye. "I hear he wasn't the only one. He took about, what, ten—"

"My son was with him."

"Your son?"

"Yes. He died too, he was fifteen years old. They died together. They were in a treehouse together and they fell out. The police decided they didn't have enough evidence, whether it was a murder or suicide or just an accident. So I guess I'll never know."

Behind me Nancy has gone completely still. Tony's glance has slid off my face and now lingers in the corner behind me. "That's some fucked up shit."

"I agree with you."

He nods slowly, still not looking. "So, how you get over something like that?"

He seems genuinely curious, so I give him an honest answer. "With great difficulty."

"Uh, yeah."

The fluorescent lights hum. Behind me Nancy doesn't so much as breathe. Slouched in his orange plastic chair, Tony shifts left and right, furtively, as if measuring angles of escape. But I occupy the center of his world at this moment, and there's no way for him to get out except through me.

38. It is, honestly, a lovely day at the cemetery. Mid-70s, breezy, puffball clouds in a sky as blue as paint. Robins and chickadees and all the rest of it. The smell of cut grass against my nose. A child laughing somewhere—laughing at the cemetery, too young to know better. Even the insects are benign: butterflies and ladybugs and a solitary praying mantis perched atop an especially florid pink tombstone.

Russell clears his throat. "It's nice here, in a weird way. Restful, you know?"

Anna snorts. "That's 'cause everybody's *dead*, Rusty."

This is what happens when my daughter visits these days. But I can't blame her for being on edge: it's the first time we've come out here with anyone else. These little pilgrimages have always been something private, shared by the two of us. I realize this with a little jolt—now that they no longer are.

She squints at me. "What?"

"Nothing."

To my surprise, she arrived home from the Cape yesterday, announcing her intention to stay a week before going back to Vermont. She delivered this news with an owlish glare, as if daring me to be happy about it. So I just said, "All right," and she went upstairs.

Later, during dinner, she said, "You had the tree taken down."

"Yes I did."

A pause. "Thanks."

"Certainly."

We sat a while. After a time I said, "You know, for the rest of my life, time spent apart from you will be much greater than time spent with you."

"Don't get all maudlin on me."

"I'm just saying."

"Mom. You never *just say* anything."

Well didn't that shut me up.

Now, today, Russell stoops to read the headstones. There's not much on them—names, dates, the words "Father and Husband" and "Beloved Son"—but he takes his time. I wonder if he's wondering what to say.

Anna settles onto the grass a little ways off. Russell squats next to me, where I'm sitting between the two graves. "Thanks for coming out," I tell him. "I know you're busy."

"It's no trouble."

This, I know, is nonsense. Russell is in the middle of a two-week closure-slash-renovation-slash-reinvention of Jamaica Scoops, soon to be renamed Jamaica Scoops, Chowder and Nosh. New floors are going in, the walls are getting a makeover, Lee Lin's paintings will hang prominently. Large potted plants to guard the door while latticework separates the booths. An overall face-lift with a revamped menu to match, and he'd love nothing more than supervise every moment. Instead he's here, because I asked him to be. For this, I feel a gratitude so profound it startles me.

He shifts his backside against the grass. "How long do you usually stay?"

"Depends. Half an hour, sometimes. Or the whole afternoon." I offer up a wan smile. "Depends how we're doing that day."

He nods. Anna looks at us, expressionless as a cat, then looks away.

I don't say: "Walter, meet Russell. Russell, meet Walter." I'm not a big fan of channeling or spirit guides or *I know he's here with me today*. Such assertions leave me bewildered no matter how often I hear them—which is more and more frequently the older I get. No, the reason I asked Russell here today is that it seems likely I'll be spending more time with him in the future, and if that's the case, he should know about this side of me. About where I disappear to several times a year.

He should also know this won't ever change. I might grow to love someone else, but I'll never stop loving Toby and Walter. I may even get married some day—theoretically, it could happen—but I'll always remain married to Walter.

So I tell him this. And I tell him more. I tell him about Toby's birdhouses and ironing and Walter's belief that a 1944 movie called *I Walked with a Zombie* was one of the greatest films ever made, as in, "Capital G, great!" I talk to him about their hikes and occasional fishing trips and the tea cabinet that Walter labored over for a year before donating it to a raffle for the volunteer fire department. I mention Toby's favorite comic book, one where all the humans have disappeared and different animals have become intelligent and formed their own nations. I tell him about Toby's imaginary worlds, the pictures he drew for hours on end, the birds he talked to by name, how he would sit motionless as if listening to their answers.

Russell watches me talk. Anna stares at the grass but I know she's listening too. The only time she visibly reacts is when I mention Toby's note.

39. It hangs in the air a while. A gaggle of sparrows are squabbling in a spruce over at the edge of the lawn. For such tiny little things, they sure do make a racket. What was Walter's word for them? *Feisty*. Finally Russell says, "He left a note, huh?"

Anna is staring at me now, her eyes as gray as clouds. I nod. "He did. Yes he did."

"Because that other time, you said . . ."

"I know."

We sit a while, till Russell finally asks, "What did it say?"

Up in the sky there's a tiny jet, barely visible, contrails stretched across the sky like they're stitching the two pieces together. Or slicing them apart I suppose, depending on one's inclination. "I've always been scared to read it."

He frowns as if this makes no sense, but Anna, to my relief, nods.

After a time Russell says, "That's some really—there's not much to say."

"I know."

"But I just, I've got nothing but respect for the way you got through it. You know, working and raising Anna and—and everything."

"Not much alternative, is there? Apart from, I don't know, becoming an alcoholic or something." Or a Euphorazine junkie, but I don't say that. Anna seems to have read my mind, though: she stares at Walter's tombstone beneath a sardonically raised eyebrow.

Russell rubs the side of his nose with his thumb. A sign he's deep in thought—and then I feel the startlement of recognition, that I know this person well enough to recognize mannerisms and what they indicate. But before I can take that thought any further, he clears his throat and says, "You may not agree with me on this one, but ah—I have no doubt in my mind that Walter and Toby feel the same way I do."

My mind glazes over. "Walter and Toby?"

"I know what you're thinking." He holds up his hands, as if in self-defense. "And I know, they're gone. But I also think—more than that, I *know*—that they're here with us, with you, right now. They've been with you all along."

For a few moments the bewilderment lingers. Okay, whatever. I imagine Trish's voice in my ear: *Let him believe what he wants. If he's good company and doesn't break your heart, what's the harm?*

But Anna's not buying it. "Been with us? You mean, like—watching *over* us?"

"Yeah. That's pretty much exactly what I mean."

He speaks with such sincerity that I actually feel bad about the laughter I'm holding back. Watching me all along? My husband, my fifteen-year-old son (or do they get older up there in Heaven?) angelically drinking in every moment of the past seven years, nine months and two days?

"Christ," Anna grumbles. "Jesus *Christ*. I sure fucking *hope* not."

I can't help it, I'm overtaken by giggles. Right there in the cemetery, as if I'm too young to know better. Russell stares, lips pursed in disapproval, but after a moment, Anna lets herself join me.

40. Driving home, Anna tells me, "I'm not mad."

"That's good."

"But you never told me there was a note."

"No, I never did."

She waits. She's learning her mother's silence games. Russell is dashing to the restaurant in his own car, so we're alone.

"I was afraid of it. And I didn't want you to be hurt, any more than me."

She considers this. When she says, "Okay," I experience a little gust of relief, which lasts a couple of moments, until she adds, "So when do we read it?" and I feel deflated again.

"We have time," I tell her.

"Not much," she counters. "I'm leaving next week."

41. Mrs. Hayes says, "Sometimes I wonder," and then stops.

"Mm?" I prompt.

"It's just foolishness."

Her husband frowns at her. "You got something to say, say it."

She collects herself. "I just—sometimes I wonder if we should just, move on with things."

The husband looks alarmed. "Move on?"

"How would you do that?" I ask.

"I can't really say." She looks about to collapse into tears. "But you know, it's been so long already, maybe we should admit he's gone, have a little memorial service, pay the church for a Mass—"

"What are you *saying*?" hisses Mr. Hayes.

I sit very still, trying not to spook the horse.

"—and then, I don't know, we could be done with it somehow. Put it behind us."

She breaks off then, looking confused behind her thick glasses, as if she'd just read the words off of cue cards without understanding what they meant. Mr. Hayes hunches in his chair in a kind of compressed fury, a catapult fully cranked, ready to lurch up and swing at something. Very carefully I say, "Is that what you want?"

She looks at her husband, who says nothing. "I . . . don't know. I—no, I don't think so." A few moments pass. "I never thought it was what I wanted, before."

"Of course you don't," he rasps in the general direction of his shoes. "Of course it isn't what you want, that's why you never thought of it."

I say, "I think this is something you should both think about more," and wait for their response, which does not come. After a time I write them both prescriptions.

42. A few days later I find myself upstairs. Early-evening sun splashes through my bedroom window, incongruously cheery. Outside is yellow and warm and filled with gnats, birdsong, a distant radio, a lawn mower, a child's voice. Life, in other words.

"I don't mean to push or anything," Anna says, with a disingenuousness that I find oddly endearing. "But I leave tomorrow, so."

"It's all right," I tell her. "It's about time I did this. Overdue really."

We're sitting on the edge of my bed. I'm holding Toby's envelope in my lap, speculating. Then I force myself to stop. Speculation has gone on long enough. Or more properly, a lack of it, a stifling of thought. I open the envelope. It's so old and desiccated it unpeels smoothly with a whisper of long-dried glue, like an ancient stamp peeling up from its postmark. Wine-yellow tape peels off a layer of paper and a little shower of dust scatters, powder from a moth. The paper inside is delicate as a dragonfly's wing.

"Careful," says Anna. "You're ripping it. Do you want me to do it?"

I ignore her. Inside the envelope is a single sheet of typing paper, unlined, folded into thirds, brittle like old skin. I take a breath and unfold the page and we sit for a long time, looking at it. I look at one side first, turn it over, turn it again. Anna takes it from me for a time before handing it back.

43. Twilight comes on, stealthily, so as not to be noticed.

"That's it?" says Anna.

"That's it," I tell her. "Evidently."

She shifts on the bed, wiping her nose. "I was expecting a little more, I guess."

"You never know, with these things." Part of me feels relief, but I say nothing of this.

The blank page sits in my lap as evening sun turns it from orange to gray, as shadows slide across us, as evening thickens and collects in the corners of my room. I trail my fingers across the paper as if, by some miracle or magic, an explanation will spring to life beneath them. Invisible ink will coalesce as I watch. I know this won't happen, but nothing keeps me from staring anyway. The faithful are capable of great patience while waiting for miracles.

Mom

why

Meaning what, exactly? *Why*, as in, "This is *why* I'm acting this way," and a blank page to show he had no explanation. Or, *why* as in *"Why* am I feeling this way?" and an empty space for someone— for me?—to write the answer. Or something else I can't even imagine. Or none of this, or all of it. I don't know. I will never know. Toby, if he ever knew, never told me and never will.

Outside a radio plays, a child shrieks, a dog barks. Mrs. Flynn doesn't own a dog, none of my neighbors do. It barks again, annoying, a high-pitched yapping, one of those little rodent things. A terrier maybe.

"I wish someone would shut that dog up," says Anna. Then: "I wish someone would run it over."

I agree with her but don't speak. There are plenty of things I'm wishing for, too. More than anything, I wish that Walter were here to step outside and chase it away.

"So," she says at length. "Do you have an answer for him?"

I watch her from my peripheral vision. "What do you mean?"

She runs a hand through her hair. "He's asking you something, isn't he? I mean, 'Why?'—it's pretty clear. Why did you do it—

whatever it was. Or why didn't you do it, I guess. He even left you an empty page to answer him."

I feel a great pressure on my head and neck, as if I'm being smothered by an invisible pillow. It's suddenly very hard to draw a breath.

"Mom?" Anna is squinting at me. "You okay?"

I manage to shudder in some air. Sweat prickles along my scalp line; the room is suddenly stifling. I tell her, "That's not what he means. It's a confession, not a question."

Her eyes rest on me for a time before swiveling away. "You're the expert."

It's some time before I can inhale comfortably again. Meanwhile dusk hurries on. Streetlights flicker on and the barking dog has fallen silent. Anna and I are still sitting on the bed.

"I guess that's it then. We'll never really know what happened that night."

The box spring creaks as she shifts her weight.

"Are you hungry?" I ask her. "Do you want anything?"

"Mom. Do you still not get it? After all this time?"

A flutter of anxiety ripples through my stomach. I try to think of something to say that doesn't invite more unwelcome revelations, and fail.

"'Cause I used to think, okay, you just didn't want to deal with it. Then for a while I thought, okay, she knows but she's just sweeping it under the rug, which pissed me off, but whatever, right? But I've started thinking you actually *don't* know, or at least convinced yourself you don't."

"Know *what*?" Impatience sweeps over me. "Nobody was inside Toby's head that night."

"Right."

"And nobody was with him in the treehouse, so—"

"I was."

"—even the police said there was—nothing." Her words sink into my pores, tightening my throat. The flutter in my stomach settles into a thick ache and the invisible pillow comes back. "What did you say?"

"I was in the treehouse."

"Don't be ridiculous. You were in bed."

She looks bewildered rather than enraged. "Bed? It was dinner-time. I'd just finished eating and gone outside, you and Dad were still at the table."

Well yes, the timing doesn't quite add up— "Don't you think I'd have noticed if you were hiding up there?"

"Hiding? I was *howling*. I was shrieking as loud as I could and you didn't even notice. Okay so you were yelling too, maybe you didn't hear me, but still, come on Mom, one kid was dead, but you did have another one."

Dizziness cuffs the back of my head, I'm finding it difficult to hold still, or for that matter breathe. The shrieks in the night when I found them—they'd been *mine*. "The paramedic. He was carry-ing you, I remember that, thinking how sad that was. He had a beard, and in dim light he could've been taken for your father." She keeps silent. "I always thought he found you, and you climbed into his arms."

"He did," she answers. Her voice is dull, rinsed of anger and hys-teria and whatever else. Only exhaustion remains, and a profound sadness, which might be the same thing. "He climbed the tree-house and got me. I was so terrified, I wrestled him halfway down till I realized what I was doing, then I just curled up and cried."

"And where was I during all this?"

"I've spent years wondering that." The bitterness in her voice is un-derstated but undeniable, like an old stain. "Probably you were hys-terical, or talking to the cops or Gramma Stella. Or all of the above."

I remain tongue-tied until she stands up. "The paramedic brought me to you and we both just stood there bawling. The next thing I remember is waking up at Grampa Hugh's. He must have driven me home and whatever, but I don't remember any of it. It's like I passed out or something." She moves toward the door. "Any-way, if you say you never knew, then I guess I believe you. Though Dolores thinks you've just repressed everything from that night."

"Does she."

"The same way I did, you know?—which is why I never talked about it."

I find myself staring out the window. There is little enough to see out there.

"Anyway, I should eat something and get to bed. Janice is coming early, and I still have to pack."

I sit alone in the dark, staring at the ghostly-lit outlines of my bedroom furniture. The empty paper rests on the bed beside me like the glimmer left burning on one's retinas, after staring at something bright, then looking away.

There is, I realize with leaden melancholy, one thing more I must ask my daughter.

44. "What're you doing here?"

"Playing."

"They know you're here?"

Of course not. It was after dinner and I wasn't allowed in the treehouse then, they thought it was dangerous. I'd get in trouble if they found out but I knew Toby wouldn't tell. "Let's play something," I said. I could always get him to play a game with me, he liked that, even if he took them to strange places sometimes. "I'll be the queen and you can be my servant."

He didn't answer. This was how he'd been lately, talking normal for a minute and then tuning me out. He knelt on the floor and looked out over the railing. It was twilight now and shadows were starting to get heavy in the trees. The only sound was crickets and far off, a little traffic noise.

"I should get down if you don't want to play," I said.

He didn't answer but I could see his lips moving like he was talking to somebody. Suddenly I felt nervous, and pretty soon I was scared. It was one thing when your brother acted kind of weird in his bedroom at lunchtime but something else when it was in a treehouse way high up and almost dark. I moved toward the ladder and he stopped me by saying, "There's something I'm gonna do."

"Okay." I hesitated. "But I should go."

"I gotta do and I want you to watch."

I didn't know what to do.

"So you can tell *them*."

"What is it?"

The crickets were getting loud. Instead of answering, Toby laughed, a short creepy cackle. Then he was quiet again. The light was fading but from what I could see his face was completely blank. Then he held his hand out to me. I stood up to get a better look and it was one of Dad's cheap plastic razors. A blue handle I could hardly see with a silver strip that caught some light from somewhere and shined a little.

I was mystified. Toby was fifteen and if he was shaving yet it was maybe once a week. "What's that for?"

"No one for the six," he said.

"Huh?"

"Not one four six," he said. His voice was high-pitched and singsongy like he was making fun of someone, but there was nobody else but me. "No one *won* for six. Not the one for the *sick*."

I shrank back. "What're you gonna do with that?" I asked him, meaning the razor.

He didn't act like he'd heard me. "Not the one for the six. Not the one. For. The. *Six*." His arms swung around like he was caught in a net. "Not the one for the six not the one one for for the six six. Not the—"

"Toby!"

Dad's voice, from the house, rolling across the yard. Toby froze abruptly and the razor slipped from his fingers, bounced off the railing and disappeared into the lawn far below. Toby said, "Pringles," which is what he said when he was mad.

"Toby!"

"*Pringles*."

Dad was coming now. I could just make out his silhouette as he moved across the grass. It was the end of day when the lights come on looking yellow in people's houses but the sky is still dark violet and the ground has turned dark but you can still see shapes of things like looking through frosted glass.

Toby's mumbling was too fast for me to make out whether it was about Pringles or sixes or anything else. My eyes were on Dad striding across the lawn, I was feeling both fear of getting in trouble and relief that he would take me out of this— "Toby? You up there? Hold on, kiddo, I'm coming up."

I looked over my shoulder and Toby was standing on the railing, his upper half invisible, blocked by the treehouse roof. I almost screamed to see him like that and I suddenly understood what he meant to do—*I gotta do and I want you to watch so you can tell them*. But instead of jumping he hauled himself up, legs wriggling out of sight, and the roof above me creaked under his weight.

I slid my ass backward until the tree was grinding into my spine and I kept pressing even then. I wanted nothing more than to be down from that treehouse that second and I promised that if I ever managed it I'd never go up there again. I don't know who I was making this promise to, but I meant it.

The roof creaked, then fell silent, then creaked. Toby was trying to keep still, to play possum, but was too wound up.

I heard Dad's breathing drawing closer as he climbed the ladder, then his head popped through the opening in the floor right next to me. I could just make out his face in the gloom as he blinked into the darkness. "Toby? That you?"

I shook my head before realizing he couldn't see. "It's me."

"Anna? What're you doing here?"

I didn't answer. Dad pulled himself into the treehouse and squatted on the floor. "Where the hell's your brother?"

His voice was so loud I flinched. "Up," I whispered.

"What?"

I was still whispering. "He climbed onto the roof."

This quieted Dad right down. I couldn't see his face but his body changed, it shifted a little then grew still. I didn't understand it at the time but looking back on it since then, I've come to realize: he was scared.

"Jesus Mary and Joseph," he whispered.

We sat there a minute in the dark and the time stretched so long that I started to allow myself the thought that nobody was going to do anything, that we were just going to stay up there all night and sort it out in the morning. That was a phrase Mom liked to use: *sort it out*. Things sounded so manageable when she said it, like whatever problem you had could be solved by just putting things into the right boxes. The idea was comforting, something to snuggle into like a sleeping bag.

Then Dad whispered, "How'd he get up there?"

I told him and he turned away from me and stared at the railing for a long time. I don't think he had any problem with pulling himself up on the roof so maybe he was gauging whether the timber would support his weight or maybe he had some deeper concern that wasn't so easy to work out.

Anyway he stood abruptly and stepped to the guardrail and spoke clearly: "Toby. I'm coming up, all right?"

In response came a weird *hew-hew-hew* I'd never heard Toby make before, or anyone else either, something halfway between a moan and a giggle and it worked its way down into my stomach. Dad was turned away and it was dark anyway but I would have given a lot to see his face when Toby made that sound.

"Toby," he said softly. An owl tooted from close by. I think it was an owl.

The sound stopped. Dad didn't know what to do. I didn't understand a lot of what was going on but I understood that much.

"Toby," he said again.

Hew-hew-hew

"*Toby*."

He seemed to pull himself together and put one foot on the rail and tested its weight and then stood and twisted and gripped the roof just like Toby had. His legs were thick shadows in the dark and the roof creaked again as he hauled himself up and the *hew-hew-hew* stopped. "Toby." Dad was trying to keep calm, I could hear that, but he wasn't good at this sort of thing. "We need to get down but it's dark so we gotta be careful, all right?"

Silence for a few seconds, then, "Not the one but the six."

"We need to take it really slow, okay? Because if we slip up here, it's lights out."

"I hate you."

The words fell through the air. A flat, emotionless voice that hit like something blunt. There was no anger in it but it made my stomach hurt to hear him say that, like someone had punched me.

Creaks overhead as Dad shifted his weight. "Come on, Tobeman, we'll talk about that downstairs. Right now we need to—"

"Go away Pringles."

"Just take my hand."

"*Pringles.*"

"This isn't something to play around with, here."

"Go away not one for the six not the one for the six—"

"Jesus fucking Christ, cut that bullshit *out*."

Dad must've grabbed him then. A mistake: Toby hated being grabbed or hit and he hollered like a calf and must have wrenched away, maybe this threw Dad off balance, maybe Toby pushed him or smacked him with both arms. I couldn't see any of it, but the roof overhead was a mess of creaking and footsteps, going back and forth like an argument.

Then it all paused again, like the argument had stopped. Like people were dancing and then took a break. I heard voices whispering, Dad hissing something like he was trying not to shout. Sometimes he tried to do that when he was getting really mad, he tried to talk extra quiet.

Then Toby said, "I hate you go away."

Another pause. I wondered if Dad was going to come back and leave him up there. I started getting used to this idea when there was a loud creak like someone shifted his weight suddenly. It must've been Dad because Toby let out a shout and then there was the scuffle of footsteps across the ceiling. I sat there with my back against the tree, looking up, scared to move. Scared to do anything.

I wondered where you were.

A sudden patter of footfalls reeled to the edge of the ceiling and my eyes followed the sound as if pulled by a string. From where I sat the space below the roof and above the rail was a perfect window looking out on the backyard, the house, the streetlights, the empty sky: it was a view I'd seen a hundred times before, in daylight, with things being normal. But now when the silhouette flashed across, a shadow blotting out the world for a second, it passed too fast for me to make out the features. Just before he hit, he let out a thick gurgling holler that sounded more like Dad than Toby and I remember thinking: *My father just died. But my brother's still alive.* I wasn't sure how I felt about that. I mean of course I was shocked that Dad was dead—I knew he was dead, I didn't need to go look, he'd just pitched headfirst forty feet—but what I mean is, I didn't know whether to feel relief that Toby was still alive, or to be mad at him for causing this, or what.

More creaking then, and I knew he was standing at the edge of the roof. "Annie?"

Too scared to talk. Was he going to throw me off too?

"Annie, you there? That was a, I didn't mean to do that, not exactly." There was a pause. "But I'd do it again I think."

I'd started crying by now, the shock receding, I tried not to make noise. Pretty sure I was though. Pretty sure my brother was going to come and kill me now.

"I'm not sorry about it."

I wanted Dad to come back, okay? *Just come back, the ladder's right there, I'll be waiting up here, I won't go away, I'll be good.*

"I don't hate you, okay? And not Mom that much either. But I'm doing this so you can tell them."

I tried not to listen, not to understand. A lot of it I didn't understand of course. Still don't.

My eyes were closed and I was hiccupping out wet gushy sobs. I didn't see him fall, didn't hear the impact, didn't see you come charging across the lawn. What I finally did hear was your screaming, and I screamed then too, to you, to them, to whoever could hear. But nobody heard for a long time. Especially not you. Your own howling was loud enough, I guess, to drown out mine.

45. Freud would say I'm a lousy mother. He'd be right. I guess I'm a pretty shitty doctor too. I wonder what he'd have had to say about that.

46. I spend most of the fall in an Uplifterall-induced haze, 20 mg. BID. It gets me through the day. I stop taking new patients, then I stop seeing my old ones. I take a leave from ACC, quit consulting for BMHA, lose touch with Ak-Ak and Muffin. I refer Beth Ann Kim and the Hayeses and Reverend Charles to other docs who aren't addled emotional wrecks too stoked on pills to think clearly.

Doctor, we understand your son was psychotic.

Well, he seemed to be headed that way.

We trust everything worked out?

Sure! After he murdered his father and killed himself, all his symptoms went into remission.

Wonderful—it's nice to know that psychiatric care is making such advances these days.

I quit exercising. There seems little point, and it requires such effort, and one of the effects of the medication is that effort is more difficult to scrape together. But in just three weeks I gain ten pounds, which leaves me even more self-despising so slowly I force myself back into the habit. It's not like I don't have the time. I shuffle along at odd hours, jog-walk-jog-sprint-stagger. Two weeks later, I have managed to lose exactly one of the ten new pounds. If I believed in God, I would think: *what an asshole*.

Russell drops by and I tell him, "Not now." Anna calls and I tell her, "I'm fine." Becky even calls—Becky!—for the first time in all the years I've known her, and I tell her, "I can't talk." Trish shows up, and it breaks my heart to tell her, "I can't talk." My own mother arrives at my door and I mumble, "God no."

"Your father's going to die soon," she announces. "Go visit him."

So I do, and the scene is hopeless, with him unconscious and me staring at the clock in a gauze-wrapped-head kind of daze. Mom cooks dinner, I forget what, and rattles on about things, I forget what, and I go home.

On my bedside table lies Toby's note, or non-note. His blankness, his—if Anna is to be believed—his expectation of an answer. I leave it there so it can accuse me every time I try to rest. This may not be particularly constructive, but I'm not interested in being constructive anymore. I tried that for a long time and it didn't work. Now I just want to do penance.

47. The weather turns cold early, the sky blue and crisp like some exotic fruit. In just a few days the leaves turn, oaks and maples erupting into fiery pillars of yellow and orange. The sugar maple is gone, I had it taken down and so miss its breathtaking display of crimson. In its place is an empty cavity of woods through which I glimpse patchy hemlocks and my neighbor's stone-walled yard. Detritus litters the grass, kids' toys, something inflatable.

September elides into October, a time for Halloween candy and geese winging south in huge glorious Vs and fresh apple cider and chin-high stacks of butternut squash stacked like cords of wood along the road. These are things I've known my whole life, things that have given me joy. This year I barely notice them. Thanksgiving hurtles toward me with the inevitability of war or old age.

I avoid people, stay home and live off my savings, feed Brutus and the strays, force myself to exercise a little. I dodge Mrs. Flynn as best I can, which is surprisingly easy, almost as if she's dodging me too. At night I lie in bed staring at the ceiling and wondering what else I missed. What other symptoms Toby displayed that I didn't, or couldn't, or wouldn't allow myself to notice.

The cold settles in for good. When I'm jogging, my breath gusts ahead of me in clouds.

Two weeks before Thanksgiving is the anniversary of their deaths. I call Anna. "Hi," she says carefully.

"How are things?"

"All right, you know, considering."

"Sure."

For a time that seems to be all there is to say. Then she tells me, "I'm doing better in my classes."

"That's good, that's great."

Another pause before we both speak at once. I tell her, "Go ahead."

"No big deal, just—I'm in another play."

"Wonderful. What is it?"

"Something I've never heard of actually. *Betrayed* or something, by this guy Harold Painter?"

"Never saw that one."

"Me neither, but the cool thing is, it starts at the ending, then goes backward so that you find out what happened before."

"How about that." I don't know what to say, besides *Is that really such a good idea?* But she seems so tickled by this, so I force myself to agree. "It sounds very . . . creative."

"Listen Mom, the other thing? I was thinking I'd come home for Christmas break. You know, to like see you and stuff."

I don't realize I haven't answered until she says, "Mom?"

"Sorry—yes, that would be nice." I crumple the wet tissue into a tight little wad and force my voice to remain steady. I thought Uplifterall was supposed to prevent labile episodes like this. "I'd like that very much. So would your grandparents. My father is very sick."

"Yeah. But I'd like to see you too, you know."

"Of course."

"Because, you know," she says.

"Of course you do," I tell her. "I do too."

48. A week later I'm in the attic. This is where I keep the old boxes crammed with all the things I've never thrown away but can't bear to keep too close. Walter's birthday cards, to me and from me. His clothes, his copies of *Outdoor Life*, his fishing gear and old VHS tapes. Toby's strange collections, bottle caps of all things, hundreds of them in a huge mayonnaise jar. Coupons clipped from Sunday's paper—why did he save coupons? Was it a symptom? It didn't seem like a symptom at the time, but maybe—stacks of them in shoeboxes. Seashells from the Cape, dusty now and faded. Comic books. Old toys, ones he'd outgrown even when he, while he was still alive. Little metal cars and action figures and so on, playing cards with fantastic creatures on them, elves and ogres and wizards, multisided dice. Legos. Lincoln Logs. Childish things he had put aside on his way to becoming an adult. Not that he ever made it there, no.

And of course his clothes. Some of them still carry his smell.

I've been up here all night. Off the medication for five days now, and clearer-headed than I've been in weeks. Half the new pounds have been worked off too, for whatever that's worth.

An unshaded bulb blares down from the apex of the roof, getting competition now from the eastern horizon. Any moment the sun will hoist itself up and throw flat bright light through the little east-facing window, filling the attic with yellow and illuminating all the dust hanging in the air: little particles I've roused from their rest with my night of shuffling and sorting and unpacking.

According to Anna, Toby told Walter, "I hate you." She was quite certain when I pressed her on this point. But did he mean it? She didn't know. And neither do I. "He sounded like he meant it," is all she could say.

He also, apparently, said he didn't hate me "that much." Should I be glad about that, or devastated? I think again about Toby's note, the blank paper that Anna thinks was meant for me to write my explanation. Just thinking about it gives me tremors. But I wonder, at times like these, alone, whether she might be right.

According to her, Toby took a razor to the treehouse, presumably for the purpose of killing himself. It is unlikely in the extreme that he could have succeeded with one of Walter's ancient, pre-beard plastic disposables. Does that mean he would still be alive if Walter had left him alone that night? And that Walter would be? I will never know that, either. There are so many things I'll never know, and the more I learn, the more those mysteries seem to thicken and codify. *Not the one but the six.* A clang association? Or just nonsense—the kind of jabberwocky silliness that any teenager might fall into?

Maybe I'm up here looking for clues, but they're in short supply. Besides the birthday cards, I've found a few letters. Not many; Walter wasn't much for letter writing, nor Toby. But some college buddies of Walter's stayed in touch for a time, and skimming their letters now I wonder that they were written to the same man I knew. Or thought I knew. But then how well do we ever know anyone, anyway?

> The thing to remember about Proust is that he's a product of his time just as much as Pynchon or Joyce or any of the rest of them. Or Beckett—try reading Waiting for Godot and not thinking about WW2 or the Holocaust, and you'll see what I mean.

This from someone named Mark. I'm drawing a blank: if I ever met this Mark, he's long since faded. I stare at the letter for the longest time. It's not just that I don't understand what's being said—I have no expectations on that score—it's that Walter would have, or at least would've been expected to, by someone else. *Waiting for Godot*, okay, but Proust? Pynchon? I'd never seen him so much as open any such book, but apparently, at some point, he had. I'm having trouble reconciling this with the man who could watch *Zombie Night Massacre* four nights running because, as he put it, "There's so much in it, you see more every time."

There are boxes of notebooks and journals, college stuff, that I've set aside out of simple cowardice. I admit it: I'm not ready to go trolling through Walter's college-age consciousness, not yet anyway. Maybe someday. Maybe never. Maybe those facets of him that lie waiting to be revealed are better left unearthed.

Instead I sit back against the insulation-lined attic wall, sloping to a point overhead, and rummage through a box of Toby's old clothes, T-shirts and shorts and a heavy winter coat hardly used before he outgrew it. Later handed down to Anna who, as I recall, outgrew it more slowly, almost deliberately. I marvel at my daughter's recent metamorphosis, from mousy teenager to self-possessed amateur actress, and chase away the unnerving thought of what I would find in her journals if—heaven forbid—they were posthumously collected in a box.

In the end, I decide, we are all mysteries to one another. Which is, for the record, more or less what I believed years ago, before college and med school, before the psych degree and private practice and endless parade of what can go wrong with the human mind.

The sun chooses just then to make its first appearance of the morning, a thick buttery finger poking through the window, splashing across the opposite wall's exposed beams and pink fiberglass insulation.

I shove the boxes back into their orderly stacks. Maybe one day Anna will want to rifle through them. I won't. Opening them feels like a violation—or a disinterment rather. Whatever secrets the dead take with them, they should be allowed to keep. That's my new philosophy. Or put another way: the time to properly know someone is when he, or she, is still alive.

49. On Thanksgiving Day Russell drops by. This is okay: I've invited him. The restaurant is closed for the holiday, and winter has fallen hard and sudden. There's a dusting of snow on everything and the ground is frozen hard beneath it. Sounds are hushed, people walk with their eyes down, even the birds are tentative.

We sit in the living room for a time, sipping coffee, careful with each other, like teenagers. Bach organ concertos lend a certain appropriate weight to the atmosphere. Russell lounges on the couch and cranes his neck at the crows on silk overhead. "Still like it?"

"Love it."

"Me too." He sets down his empty cup. "So I've been thinking."

"Have you."

"I'd like to see more of you. Is that something we can agree on?"

I've seen this conversation coming for a while, but still can't quite believe it's happening. "Sure."

"It's something you want?" He fixes me with his sincere look. "Because I've wanted it for a while now."

"Of course." I hesitate. "But as you should know by now, I'm not the easiest person to get along with."

He grins. "You're not so bad, Gina."

"I'm serious. There are—I have—history."

He rubs the side of his nose. "Issues?"

"Oh yes, *issues*. Buckets of them." I'm not smiling and he catches on: The Grin vanishes, replaced by an earnestly furrowed brow. He says, "So let me in on them. And in the spirit of equal disclosure, I should mention that I have *issues* too."

I manage to snort out a laugh that sounds half-strangled, half-desperate. Not to one-up him or anything, but I suspect my *issues* are a tad more substantial than his. Not that I would ever say such a thing out loud, of course.

I tell him, "Okay. But I have to tell you, I may need to do this in fits and starts."

He grins again. "That's what we've been doing."

"Well, yes."

"I understand, Regina. Whatever you need, I understand."

I wonder if he does. These jumps can't take place in the course of a day or two: from student to mother, from student to wife; from wife to widow, from mother to grieving wreck. From grieving wreck to therapist to mother to wife? These things take time, and no doctor has ever found a shortcut for that.

I wonder also what Mom and Dad will say when I tell them, and Hugh. Hugh will probably buy me a drink, come to think of it. And Anna? Somehow I suspect Anna will take it just fine.

"Regina?"

He's watching me, brow creased. I smile at him, a real smile, small but sincere. "Right here," I tell him, and he chuckles. His restaurant is doing okay, he tells me. Not gangbusters, but okay. I'm glad for that. He asks if I've ever thought about getting a dog, and I say *Mmm*. It occurs to me to ask if he wants a glass of brandy, it's Thanksgiving after all. He laughs and says he's never had brandy in his life. I tell him that in that case, he has to try it. He says he thought it was only for rich people and I say *Oh please* and go into the kitchen to dig the bottle out of the cupboard. Half full and untouched for years but this stuff doesn't go bad, does it? Smells fine in any case. And then hunt around in the cabinet for the special glasses, the snifters. They were a wedding present from Hugh, handblown Italian glass. They haven't been used in ages and I need to rinse the dust off before I can serve the brandy in them.

BIOGRAPHICAL NOTE

In addition to *An Age of Madness*, David Maine is the author of four novels: *The Preservationist*, *Fallen*, *The Book of Samson*, and *Monster, 1959*. His novels have been praised in such outlets as *Time* magazine, *The New York Times*, *The Washington Post*, *The Christian Science Monitor*, *People* magazine, and *Entertainment Weekly*, and translated into Spanish, Italian, German, Dutch, Norwegian, Greek, Japanese, and Russian. *The Preservationist* was nominated for the First Book Award by British newspaper *The Guardian* and has been optioned for a film. July 2011 saw the release of his fantasy novel eBook, *The Gamble of the Godless*. From 1995 to 1998, Maine lived and worked in Rabat, Morocco, before moving to Lahore, Pakistan, where he lived until 2008. Upon returning to the United States, he relocated to Honolulu and taught at the University of Phoenix, Hawaii-Pacific University, and the University of Hawaii at Manoa. Currently he resides in Massachusetts.